Critical Acclaim for the Marvelous Romances of . . .

Jude Deveraux

LEGEND

"First-rate reading . . . Only Jude Deveraux could mix romance with tongue-in-cheek humor and have it all come out so perfectly right." —*Rendezvous*

"This dynamic author widen[s] the boundaries of the genre. . . ." —*Painted Rock Reviews*

"Another refreshingly optimistic love story . . . Any novel by Deveraux is just plain fun to read, and she keeps readers on the edge of their seats." —*The Advocate* (Baton Rouge, LA)

THE HEIRESS

"Deveraux's novels are always eagerly awaited by her fans, and *The Heiress* lives up to her usual standards." —*The Pilot* (Southern Pines, NC)

REMEMBRANCE

"Brilliant . . . unforgettable . . . as romantic as *A Knight in Shining Armor* . . . Ms. Deveraux brings this unusual romance to life, demonstrating that she is a superb craftsman and a mesmerizing storyteller. . . ." —Kathe Robin, *Romantic Times*

"One of the world's top romance novelists has outdone herself. . . . This is a book that Deveraux fans who loved *A Knight in Shining Armor* have anxiously awaited, and it certainly does not disappoint." —Cheryl Rosamond, *The Lake Worth Herald* (FL)

MOUNTAIN LAUREL

"Tenderness, humor, passion, poignancy and memorable romance . . . *Mountain Laurel* is a delight."

—*Romantic Times*

"Deveraux fans . . . will welcome yet another pair of feisty, independent souls whose conversation crackles with electricity."

—*Houston Chronicle*

THE TAMING

"Vintage Deveraux—a fast-moving, psychologically acute rendition of the battle of the sexes set in a richly textured historical landscape . . . Deveraux's mastery of every trick of narrative art creates depth and resonance. . . ."

—*Publishers Weekly*

"Delightful . . . *The Taming* is a winning combination . . . a very funny, engaging, fast-paced read that's sure to please."

—*Rave Reviews*

THE AWAKENING

"A tender, hilarious, intense love story . . . Everything Jude Deveraux readers expect from her passionate pen. . . . This is a keeper."

—*Romantic Times*

WISHES

"In *Wishes,* one of Jude Deveraux's most enchanting stories, she blends a pinch of magic, a dash of Cinderella fantasy, and spoonfuls of fun into a stunning romance."

—*Rave Reviews*

"Jude Deveraux always spins a gripping tale. . . . Plenty of passion—and the plot never slackens."

—*Booklist*

Books by Jude Deveraux

The Velvet Promise
Highland Velvet
Velvet Song
Velvet Angel
Sweetbriar
Counterfeit Lady
Lost Lady
River Lady
Twin of Fire
Twin of Ice
The Temptress
The Raider
The Princess
The Awakening
The Maiden
The Taming
The Conquest
A Knight in Shining Armor
Wishes
Mountain Laurel
The Duchess
Eternity
Sweet Liar
The Invitation
Remembrance
The Heiress
Legend

Published by POCKET BOOKS

Jude Deveraux

LEGEND

POCKET BOOKS
New York   London   Toronto   Sydney   Tokyo   Singapore

This book is a work of fiction. Names, characters, places and incidents are products of the author's imagination or are used fictitiously. Any resemblance to actual events or locales or persons, living or dead, is entirely coincidental.

POCKET BOOKS, a division of Simon & Schuster Inc.
1230 Avenue of the Americas, New York, NY 10020

ISBN: 0-671-00170-1

First Pocket Books paperback printing September 1997

10 9 8 7 6 5 4 3 2 1

POCKET and colophon are registered trademarks of Simon & Schuster Inc.

Cover art by Sue Rother

Printed in the U.S.A.

LEGEND

Chapter 1

"I LOOK LIKE A CHOCOLATE MERINGUE PIE," KADY SAID AS SHE grimaced at her reflection in the tall three-sided mirror. With her dark hair and ivory skin above the absolute white of the frothy wedding dress, she did indeed remind herself of chocolate and whipped egg whites. Cocking her head to one side, she reconsidered. "Or maybe a chicken dumpling. I can't decide which."

From behind her, Debbie, who had been at cooking school with Kady, laughed softly, but Jane did not.

"I don't want to hear another word like that," Jane said sternly. "You hear me, Kady Long? Not one more word! You are absolutely gorgeous and you full well know it."

"Gregory certainly knows it," Debbie said, her eyes wide as she surveyed Kady in the mirror. As one of Kady's two bridesmaids, she'd flown to Virginia from northern California the night before and had only met Kady's fiancé this morning. She was still reeling from the experience. Gregory Norman was one terrific-looking man: his face and body all hard angles and planes, with dark hair and eyes that looked at a woman as though to say he'd very much like to make love to her. When he'd raised Debbie's fingertips to his beautiful lips and kissed them, Debbie's upper lip had broken into a sweat.

"How can I walk down the aisle looking like this?" Kady asked, holding out what had to be fifty yards of heavy satin. "And look at these sleeves: they're bigger than I am. And the skirt!" With horror in her eyes, she looked down at the acres of white satin puddling about her, a pearl encrusted border sparkling on the seven or so inches of hem that bent into an overflow on the floor.

"Any of these dresses can be altered," said the tall, thin saleswoman, who with her stiff stance let Kady know that she didn't appreciate having her bridal salon's wares denigrated.

Kady hadn't meant to give offense. "It's not the dresses; it's *me*. Why can't the human body be like bread dough so we could shape it however we want? Add a little here, take a little off there."

"Kady," Jane warned. They had known each other all their lives, and she could not bear to hear Kady say anything derogatory about herself; she loved her too much to allow that.

But Debbie giggled. "Or as stretchy as pizza dough," she said, looking at Kady in the mirror. "Then we could elongate what was too short, and leave lumps where we wanted them."

When Kady laughed, Debbie was quite pleased with herself. They had gone to culinary school in New York together, but Debbie had always been in awe of Kady. While other students were trying to learn techniques and how to blend flavors, Kady just seemed to *know*. She could look at a recipe and tell how it was going to taste; she could eat a meal she hadn't cooked, then later re-create it exactly. While other students were juggling recipe cards and trying to remember the difference between scones and biscuits, Kady threw things into a bowl, dumped them onto a sheet pan, put them into an oven, and they came out divine.

Needless to say, at school Kady was the darling of all the teachers and the envy of every student. Debbie had been flattered beyond all reasoning when Kady had asked *her* if she'd like to go to a movie and thus started their friendship.

Now, five years later, both she and Kady were thirty years old. Debbie had married, had a couple of children, and her culinary talents were mostly directed toward peanut-butter sandwiches and barbecued steaks on weekends. But that's not the way Kady's life had gone. After school Kady had shocked—and horrified—all the other students and her teachers by accepting a job at a run-down steak house called Onions located in Alexandria, Virginia. Her teachers had tried to persuade her to accept one of the many job offers she received from fabulous restaurants in New York, Los Angeles, San Francisco, and even Paris. But she'd turned them down flat. And everyone had said what a shame it was for someone with Kady's talent to waste herself in that nothing little steak house.

But Kady had had the last laugh because she'd turned Onions into a three-star restaurant. People came from all over the world to eat at her tables. If a diplomat, jet-setter, or even an in-the-know tourist visited the eastern seaboard, he made sure he went to Kady's Place, as it was affectionately known.

And what made the food world especially envious was that Kady had done it *her* way. She'd been determined to bring people to her food, not to the restaurant itself. Today, Onions was still in need of refurbishing; it was tiny, seating only twenty-five people at once, and it accepted no reservations. Nor did it have a menu. People came and stood in line and waited until a table was empty, then they ate whatever Kady had decided to cook that night.

Debbie would never forget the video on the six o'clock news that seemed to amuse Peter Jennings so much. In it was President Clinton waiting in line outside Onions, talking to the king of some African country, both of them surrounded by hungry tourists and locals, while Secret Service men looked on in wild-eyed fear, anticipating danger.

Now, as Debbie looked at Kady in her wedding dress, she saw only her talented, pretty friend. Besides being an extraordinary cook, Kady had one of the most beautiful faces she'd ever seen. As far as Debbie knew, Kady had no idea how to apply mascara, but then why should she when she had lashes that thick and that black? And long, thick hair so dark and shiny you could almost apply your lipstick in its reflection. "Good diet," Kady always said, tongue in cheek, whenever anyone said she was pretty.

Although her face was exceptionally pretty, Kady had what the fashion magazines described as a "figure problem."

Kady was about five feet two inches tall, had a size twelve top and bottom and a size four waist. In school she'd always worn her chef's coat, a long, double-breasted jacket that went almost to her knees, completely concealing her waist, so she looked like a pretty face set atop a burrito. It wasn't until a school Halloween party, when Kady had shown up dressed as a streetwalker, that anyone had seen her little waist—and had seen her exaggerated hourglass figure. After that night several of the male students had made passes at Kady, but later, after she'd corrected their soufflés and crepes, they left her alone. "Gets them every time," Kady had whispered to Debbie, adding that she was waiting for a man she loved as much as she loved cooking.

And now she'd found him. Gregory Norman was the drop-dead gorgeous son of the widow who owned Onions, the woman who had so very wisely hired Kady. It was rumored that when Kady refused to allow the President of the United States into her restaurant ahead of a family of tourists from Iowa, Mrs. Norman had had to be revived with smelling salts. But later, after Mrs. Norman received a handwritten note from the President thanking Mrs. Norman and Kady for such a wonderful meal, Mrs. Norman had in turn thanked Kady by paying the extravagant bill for the white truffles Kady had ordered without one complaint, nor even a sarcastic remark. It was said that keeping her mouth shut had probably taken five years off Mrs. Norman's life.

"You can't wear *that* dress, that's for sure," Jane said in a no-nonsense way. "Actually, you can't be seen in any of these." As she spoke she glared at the saleswoman, daring her to comment. "Come on, get out of that thing, and let's go to lunch."

"I've heard of a new place about twenty miles—" Debbie began, but Jane halted her.

"Don't even try. Our Kady will eat nowhere except at an American deli. No one else can cook food good enough for her, isn't that right, Miss Picky?"

Kady laughed as she struggled out of the voluminous dress. "Delis have good, simple food. It is what it is."

"Ha! You just don't like anyone else's cooking, that's what. Come on, let's go."

Debbie was bewildered at the way Jane bossed Kady around, for to her, Kady was a bit of a celebrity, at least she was in the food world, since she was always being mentioned in those heavenly food magazines. "Food pornography," as Kady called them. "Sinfully rich and sinfully delicious to our weight-conscious society."

Twenty minutes later the three women were seated at tiny tables in a frantically busy deli, eating turkey breast sandwiches.

"So!" Jane said. "I feel a little guilty, having arrived days earlier, so why don't you tell Debbie all about your fiancé? In fact, I forgot all about the love part of all this."

At that Kady rolled her eyes. Jane was an accountant, and for the last two days the finances of the restaurant and Kady's bank account had been Jane's number one concern.

"Yes, do tell me," Debbie encouraged. "Tell me all about Gregory. Kady, he really is the most beautiful of men. Is he a model?"

"More important," Jane said with a secretive look, "how does he look with his face veiled?"

"What?" Debbie asked, leaning forward, looking puzzled.

"Since she was a child, Kady has . . ." Halting, Jane looked at her friend. "Stop sitting there looking like the cat that ate the canary and tell us *all*. Was it love at first sight?"

"More like 'love at first bite,'" Kady said, smiling, her eyes dreamy as they always were when she thought of the man she loved. "As you know, Gregory is Mrs. Norman's only child, but he lives in Los Angeles, where he's a high-powered real estate agent. He buys and sells those five-million-dollar houses for the movie stars, so he's pretty busy. He's only been back to Virginia once in the five years I've been here." After she said this, she glanced at Jane to make sure she'd heard. Financial solvency was what Jane considered a man's most important feature. "The one time he was here was the week I was in Ohio visiting my parents, so I missed meeting him."

Kady smiled in memory. "But six months ago, early one Sunday morning, I was at the restaurant with my knives and—"

At this Jane gave a snort of laughter, and Debbie tittered. Kady never, never allowed anyone to touch her precious knives. She kept them sharp enough to split an eyelash, lengthwise, and heaven help anyone who picked up one of her knives and used it to do something like, say, scrape a cutting board.

"Okay," Kady said, smiling, then turned to Debbie. "My dear friend here has for years been trying to make me believe that there is life outside a kitchen. But I have told her that, due to something called hunger, life comes *to* the kitchen." She looked back at Jane. "And it did. It came in the form of one Gregory Norman."

"Some great form," Debbie said under her breath, making Kady smile.

"Anyway, as I was saying, before I was so rudely

interrupted, I was in the kitchen at the restaurant, and in walked Gregory. Right away I knew who he was, since Mrs. Norman has shown me at least three point one million photos of him and has told me everything about him from the time he was born. But I don't think he knew who I was."

"Thought you were the scullery maid, did he?" Jane asked. "And what did you have on? Torn jeans and one of those shapeless coats of yours?"

"Of course. But Gregory didn't notice. He'd arrived from LA late the night before and he'd been out jogging, so he was sweaty and very hungry. He asked if I knew if there was any cereal or something he could eat for breakfast. So I told him to sit down and I'd make him something."

After that, Kady took a big bite of her sandwich and looked as though she were planning to say no more.

Debbie broke the silence. "Your pancakes?"

"Actually, crepes. With strawberries."

"Poor man," Jane said seriously. "He didn't have a chance." She leaned forward. "Kady, dear, I can fully understand that he fell in love with you, but are you in love with him? You aren't marrying him because he gushes over your food, are you?"

"I haven't agreed to marry the other men who have eaten my food, then asked me to marry them, now have I?"

Debbie laughed. "Have there been many?"

Jane answered. "According to Mrs. Norman, there's one a night, men from all over the world. What was it that sultan offered you?"

"Rubies. Mrs. Norman said she was glad he didn't offer me an herb farm or she feared I might go with him."

"What did Gregory offer you?"

"Just himself," Kady said. "Jane, please stop worrying. I love Gregory very much." For a moment, Kady closed her eyes. "The last six months have been the best of my life. Gregory has courted me like something out of a novel, with flowers and candy and attention. He listens to all my ideas about Onions, and he has told his mother that I'm to have carte blanche when it comes to buying ingredients. I didn't tell anyone, but in the months before Gregory returned, I was thinking about leaving Onions and opening my own restaurant."

"But now you're staying. So does that mean Gregory is going to leave LA and live here with you?" Jane asked.

"Yes. We're buying a town house in Alexandria, one of those beautiful three-story places with a garden, and Gregory is going to get into real estate here in Virginia. He won't make as much money as he did in LA, but . . ."

"It's love," Debbie said. "Any babies planned?"

"As soon as possible," Kady said softly, then blushed and looked down at her coleslaw, which had too much fennel in it.

"But how does he look in a face veil?" Jane asked again.

"You *must* tell me," Debbie said, when Kady didn't answer right away. "What is this about a face veil?"

"May I?" Jane asked, then when Kady nodded, she continued. "Kady's widowed mother worked a couple of jobs, so Kady stayed with us most of the day and she was like part of our family. She used to have—" She looked at Kady, one eyebrow raised. "Still does?" Kady nodded. "Anyway, all her life Kady has had a dream about an Arabian prince."

"I don't know who he is," Kady interrupted, looking at Debbie. "It's just a dream I have. It's nothing."

"Nothing, ha! You know what she did all the years she was growing up? She drew veils across the lower half of every man's photo she saw. My father used to threaten her within an inch of her life, because he'd open *Time* magazine or *Fortune* and, if Kady had seen it first, she'd have blacked out the bottom half of each man's face. She carried black markers with her wherever she went." Jane leaned toward Debbie. "When she grew up, she put the markers in the case with her *knives.*"

"She still does," Debbie said. "At school we all wondered what her black markers were for. Darryl once said—" She gave a look at Kady, then broke off.

"Go on," Kady said. "I can bear it. Ever since he heard me say that he couldn't even fry a chicken, Darryl has not exactly been my friend. What did he say about my markers?"

"That you used them to write letters to the devil because that's the only way you could cook the way you do."

Both Kady and Jane laughed.

"So tell me about the man with the veiled face," Debbie encouraged, and this time Jane nodded for Kady to tell her own story.

"It's nothing really. When I was growing up, I was obsessed with finding this man." She looked at Jane. "And now I think I have. Gregory looks very much like him."

"Him who?" Debbie said, frustrated. "Either tell me or I'll make you eat processed cheese!"

"I never knew you had such a streak of cruelty," Kady said dryly, then, "Okay, okay. I have a recurring dream, and it's always the same. I'm standing in a desert and there is a man sitting on a white horse, one of those beautiful Arabian horses. The man is wearing a robe of black wool. He's looking at me, but I can only see his eyes because the lower half of his face is covered with a black cloth."

For a moment, Kady's voice became soft as she thought of the dream man who had been such a compelling part of her life. "He has unusual, almond-shaped eyes. The outer lids dip down just slightly, so they give him a look of sadness, as though he has seen more pain than a person should have seen."

Abruptly, Kady came back to the present and smiled at Debbie. "He never says anything, but I can tell that he wants something from me and he's waiting for me to do something. Every time it frustrates me that I don't know what he wants. After a moment he holds out his hand to me. It's a beautiful, strong hand, with long fingers and tanned skin."

In spite of herself, Kady felt the power of the dream even as she told the story. If she'd had the dream only once or twice, she would have been able to forget about it, but there had never been a week since she was nine years old that she hadn't had the dream. It was always exactly the same, with not the tiniest variation.

Her voice grew so quiet that both Jane and Debbie had to lean forward to hear her. "Always, I try to take his hand. More than anything in the world I want to jump on that horse and ride away with him. I want to go wherever he is going, to be with him forever, but I can't. I can't reach his hand. I try to, but there is too much distance between us. After a while his eyes show infinite sadness, and he withdraws his hand, then rides away. He rides as though he is part of the horse. After a long moment he halts his horse, then turns back for just a second and looks at me as though he hopes I will change my mind and go with him. Each time I call out to him not to leave me, but he never seems to hear. He looks even sadder, then turns and rides away."

Kady leaned back in her chair. "And that's the end of the dream."

"Oh, Kady," Debbie said, "that gives me goose bumps. And you think Gregory is your Arabian prince in real life?"

"He is dark like him, and from the first moment, we were attracted to each other, and since he proposed marriage, I have been having the dream every other night. I think that's a sign, don't you?"

"I think it's a sign that it's time for you to leave your life of food and men on white stallions and join the real world," Jane said.

"I never looked," Kady answered.

"What?"

"I never looked under the horse to see if it was a stallion or not. Could be a mare. Or maybe a gelding. But then how do you tell if it has been gelded?"

"I'm sure that if people ate horse meat, then you would know," Jane said, making the other two women laugh.

Debbie gave a great sigh. "Kady, I think that may be the most romantic story I have ever heard. I definitely think you should marry your Arabian prince."

"What I want to know is what you are making poor Gregory wear to the wedding. A black robe?"

Kady and Debbie laughed; then Kady said, "My dear Gregory may wear as little or as much as he wants to the wedding. *He* isn't thirty pounds overweight."

"And neither are you," Jane snapped.

"Tell that to the woman selling wedding dresses."

Jane started to reply, but then a busboy began to clean their table, broadly hinting that it was needed and they should leave. In a few minutes, the three women were back out on the streets of Alexandria. Jane looked at her watch. "Debbie and I need to do some shopping at Tyson's Corner, so shall we meet you back at Onions at five?"

"Sure," Kady said hesitantly, then grimaced. "I have a whole list of things I'm supposed to buy for the town house. Things that don't go into the kitchen."

"You mean like sheets and towels, that sort of thing?"

"Yes," Kady said brightly, hoping Jane and Debbie would volunteer to help her with this incomprehensible task. But luck wasn't with her.

"Debbie and I have to pool our money and get you something nice for a wedding gift, and we can't do that with you around. Come on, don't look so glum. We'll help you look for sheets tomorrow."

"Isn't there a rather nice cookware shop in Alexandria?" Debbie asked, thinking she'd much prefer to go cookware shopping with Kady than gift purchasing with Jane.

"I believe there is," Kady said, laughing. "I never thought of that. Maybe I can find a way to occupy myself after all." It was obvious that she was joking and that she'd intended all along to visit the kitchenware shop.

"Come on," Jane said, taking Debbie's arm. "No doubt poor Gregory will be sleeping on cookie sheets and drying with waxed paper."

"Parchment paper," Debbie and Kady said in unison, a chef's inside joke that made Jane groan as she pulled Debbie away.

Smiling, Kady watched her two friends go, then breathed a sigh of relief. It had been years since she'd seen Jane, and she'd forgotten by half how bossy she was. And she'd also forgotten how worshipful Debbie was.

Looking about her at the beautiful fall sunshine, for a moment Kady didn't quite know what to do with herself. She had hours of freedom. And that freedom had been given to her by her dear, darling Gregory. For all that Gregory was heavenly, so kind and so considerate, his mother was a tartar. Mrs. Norman never took an afternoon off, so it never occurred to her that Kady should have time off either.

But then, truthfully, Kady didn't have many interests outside the kitchen. On Sundays and Mondays, when Onions was closed, Kady was in the kitchen experimenting and perfecting recipes for the cookbook she was writing. So, even though she'd lived in Alexandria for five years, she didn't know her way around very well. Of course she knew where the best cookware shop was and where to buy any produce imaginable and who was the best butcher, but, truthfully, where did one buy sheets? For that matter, where did one buy any of the things that Gregory said they'd need for their house? He'd said he'd leave all that up to her because he knew how important such things were to a woman. Kady had said, "Thank you," and had not told him she had no idea how to buy curtains and rugs.

She had, however, spent a bit of time redesigning the kitchen of the town house into a two-room masterpiece, with one area for baking and another for bone-burning, as the pastry cooks called the work of entrée chefs. The two rooms, one L shaped, the other U shaped, met on either side of a big granite-topped table, where Kady could beat the heck out of brioche dough and hurt nothing. There was open storage and closed storage and . . .

She trailed off, letting out a sigh. She had to stop thinking about cooking and kitchens and think about the problems at hand. What in the world was she going to wear to her own wedding? It was all well and good to be in love with a gorgeous man, but she didn't want to hear people say, "What's a hunk like him see in a dumpling like her?" Debbie and Jane had been so nice to fly to Virginia to try on bridesmaids' dresses and help Kady choose her dress, when they needed to return in six weeks for the wedding itself. But the three of them weren't making any headway. Seeing herself in that mirror this morning had made Kady want to skip the whole thing. Couldn't she just wear her chef's coat to the wedding? It was white.

While she was thinking, her legs carried her to a certain cookware shop that never failed to have something Kady could use. An hour later she exited with a French tart cutter in the shape of an apple. It wasn't a wedding veil, but it would last longer, she told herself, then started toward the parking lot and her car. It was early yet, but there were always things to do at the restaurant and, besides, Gregory might be there.

Smiling, she began to walk but stopped in front of an antique shop. In the window was an old copper mold in the shape of a rose. As though hypnotized, she opened the shop door, making the bell jangle. Reaching past an antique table and a cast-iron cat, she took the mold from the window, saw it was something she could afford, then looked around for a clerk to pay.

There was no one in the shop. *What if I were a thief?* she thought. Then she heard voices in the back and went through a curtain into a storage room. Through an open doorway leading into a yard, she heard a woman's voice raised in annoyance and frustration. "What am I supposed to do with all of this? You know very well that I don't have room for even half of these things."

"I thought you'd like them, that's all," said a man's voice. "I thought I was doing you a favor."

"You could have called me and asked."

"There wasn't time. I told you that. Ah, the hell with it," the man said, then came the sound of crunching gravel as he walked away.

Kady stood still in the storeroom, waiting to see if anyone would enter, but no one did, so she looked out the door. In the service yard was a pickup truck loaded high with dirty old trunks and boxes with tape around them. The tailgate was down, and on the ground were half a dozen more metal boxes and wooden crates. The whole mess looked as though it had been stored in a leaky barn for a couple of centuries.

"Excuse me," Kady said, "I wonder if I could make a purchase."

Turning, the woman looked at Kady, but she didn't answer her. "Men!" she said under her breath. "My husband was driving to a hardware store and saw a sign that said, 'Auction,' so he stopped and saw that lot number three-two-seven was 'Miscellaneous Unopened Trunks,' so he bought the whole lot. All of them. He didn't look or ask to find out how many there were, he just put up his hand and bought all of them for one hundred and twenty-three dollars. And now what am I going to do with all of these? And from the looks of them, most are trash. I don't even have room to store half of them out of the rain."

Kady didn't have an answer for her, and she did have to admit that the piles of crates and boxes didn't look very promising. Maybe "Unopened Trunks" was supposed to conjure the idea of hidden treasure, but she couldn't imagine any treasure inside these things. "Could I help you pull them inside?"

"Oh, no, he'll be back, and he'll stack them up for me."

With a sigh, the woman turned to Kady. "I'm sorry. You're a customer. You can see how upset I was, since it looks as though I left the front door unlocked. Could I help you with something?"

As the woman had been talking, Kady had been looking at all the boxes. Sitting on the bed of the pickup, under three cobweb-covered crates, was an old metal box that had once contained flour. It was rusty in places, and the writing was hardly visible, but it was still good looking in a craftsy way. She could envision the old box on top of the cabinets in her new kitchen.

"How much for that box?" Kady asked, pointing.

"The rusty one on the bottom?" the woman asked, obviously thinking Kady was an idiot.

"I have X-ray vision and I can see that that box is full of pirate's treasure."

"In that case, *you* have to carry it. Ten dollars."

"Done," Kady said, fishing thirty dollars out of her wallet, ten for the box and twenty for the rose-shaped mold.

As the woman stuffed the money in her pocket, Kady pulled the box off the truck, then shook it. "There really is something in here."

"*All* of them are full," the woman said in exasperation. "Whoever owned this stuff never threw away a piece of paper in his life. And the mice have been into most of them, as well as mildew and nasty crawly things. Go on, take the box. If there's something valuable inside there, it's yours. My guess is that it's still full of flour."

"In that case I shall make antique bread," Kady said, making the woman smile as she grabbed one side of the box and helped Kady pick it up.

"Can you carry that? I can get my husband to—"

"No thanks," Kady said, her forearms under the bottom of the box, which was bigger than she'd first thought; she could barely see over the top of it. "Maybe you wouldn't mind hooking that mold onto my handbag."

As the woman did so, she looked at Kady speculatively. "You know, I think I'll have a treasure sale on Saturday. I'll give these cases a good vacuum and sell them as 'Contents Unknown.' At ten bucks each, I might make a profit yet."

"If you do, your husband will take all the credit," Kady said, smiling from around the box.

"And he'll never pass another auction without buying everything in sight. I'm going to have to consider this one," she said, laughing as she led Kady around the shop into an alley. "Right through there is the street. Are you sure that isn't too heavy? It's nearly as big as you are. Maybe you should bring your car around."

"No, it's fine," Kady said honestly, for her arms were strong from years of lifting copper pots full of stock and kneading huge mounds of bread dough.

But as strong as she was, by the time she had walked the three blocks back to her car and put the tin box into the trunk, her arms were aching. Looking at the rusty old thing, she wondered what in the world had made her buy it. Gregory was moving some furniture from his house in Los Angeles to Alexandria, but he'd told her that he thought their town house needed Federal furniture, not the big, white sun-country sofas and chairs he owned, so he planned to sell most of what he had.

Closing the car trunk, she sighed. "Federal furniture," she said to no one. "Where's Dolley Madison when you need her?" As she got behind the wheel, she thought that for tomorrow night's dinner, she might do some experiments with rabbit in red wine, something eighteenth century.

Chapter 2

IT WAS ELEVEN P.M., AND KADY WAS EXCEPTIONALLY TIRED AS she entered her boring little furnished apartment. She'd chosen the place because it was close to Onions and because she wouldn't have to buy furniture.

For the life of her she couldn't figure out what had been wrong with her tonight. In theory everything had gone very well. Gregory had been at his most charming, and she appreciated the effort he'd made to entertain her friends. Even Jane had been impressed, telling Kady that her own husband felt no obligation to talk to her friends and, instead, often spent his days with his face behind a newspaper. As for Debbie she was so starry-eyed from eating Kady's cooking and having a man who looked like Gregory pay attention to her that she could hardly speak.

"You're tired," Gregory had said abruptly after Kady had suppressed her fifth yawn at the dinner table. "You've been on your feet all day. You should go home and rest."

"I don't think freedom agrees with me," Kady said, smiling sleepily. "I should have spent today in the kitchen."

17

Gregory turned dark eyes to the other two women. "Can either of you do anything with her? I have never seen anyone work as much as she does. She never takes time off, never does anything except work." As he spoke, he took Kady's hand and caressed it, then gave her a look guaranteed to melt her knickers.

But when Kady gave another yawn, he laughed. "Come on, baby, you're going to ruin my reputation as a lady-killer. What are Debbie and Jane going to think of me?"

Kady laughed, as Gregory always seemed able to make her do. Turning to her women friends, she smiled. "He really is the best man in the world. Very exciting and all that; it's just me. I don't know what's wrong with me tonight. I seem to be drained of all energy."

"Probably from thinking about having to choose furniture," Gregory said as he stood, then pulled Kady's nearly limp body up out of the chair. He was quite a bit taller than she was, and his face was as sharply chiseled as hers was soft planes.

Gregory turned to the other women, smiling. "I'll take her home then return for whatever Kady's made for dessert."

"Raspberries with kirsch and—"

She broke off when all three of them laughed, making her blush. "Okay, so I'm just tired, not dead."

Holding on to Gregory's strong arm, Kady left the town house, and he walked her home, saying nothing, just keeping his arm protectively around her. At her door, he put his arms around her, then kissed her good night, but he didn't ask to be allowed to spend the night. "I can see that you're exhausted, so I'll leave you." Drawing back, he looked down at her. "Still want to marry me?"

"Yes," she said, smiling, leaning her head against his hard chest. "Very much." She looked up at him. "Gregory, I really am hopeless at buying furniture. I don't have a clue about curtains and sheets and—"

She broke off as he kissed her. "We'll hire someone.

Don't spend another moment thinking about it. I have a deal going in LA, and as soon as it's closed, we'll be able to afford anything." He kissed the tip of her nose. "All the copper pots you want."

With her arms about his waist, she hugged him tightly. "I don't know what I've ever done to deserve a man like you. I feel so guilty that you're giving up your job in Los Angeles to live here with me." She looked up at him. "Are you sure you wouldn't want me to move there? I could open a restaurant there and—"

"My mother won't leave Onions, and you know that. It's the place she and Dad built together, so it's full of memories for her. And she's getting older. She may seem to have the energy of a teenager, but she hides a lot. It's easier for me to move here; then all three of us can be together." He paused. "Unless you're unhappy here and want to leave. Is that the case?"

Kady put her head back down on his chest. "No, I'm happy wherever you are. We'll stay here, run Onions; I'll write my cookbooks, and we'll produce a dozen babies."

Gregory laughed. "They'll certainly be well fed little crumb crunchers, that's for sure." Putting his hands on her shoulders, he set her away from him. "Now go to bed. Get some sleep. Tomorrow your friends are going to take you to a carpet store to look at rugs to buy for the house."

"Oh, no!" Kady said, clutching her stomach. "I can feel an attack of bubonic plague coming on. I think I must stay in the kitchen tomorrow and brew an herbal remedy."

Laughing, Gregory used his key to open her apartment door, then pushed her inside. "If you don't behave, I'll hire a bridal consultant to 'organize' you. You'll find yourself being asked to register for trash cans and monogrammed toilet-seat covers."

He laughed harder when Kady turned white at the very thought of such horror. Still laughing, he closed her apartment door, leaving her to get some sleep.

So now Kady stood with her back to the door and looked

about the pretty but bland apartment. She really was grateful that Gregory understood her total lack of talent in choosing furnishings. It wasn't that she didn't want a nice place to live; it was just that she had no idea—and, okay, no interest—in choosing chairs and such.

"I am the luckiest woman on earth," she said aloud, as she had twice a day since she'd met Gregory.

But oddly enough, as she stepped away from the door, her energy seemed to revive. As she felt the tiredness draining from her, she thought she might make herself some cocoa and read a book or see if there was a late-night movie on.

But even as she thought it, her eyes drifted to the big tin box sitting smack in the center of her living room. She could scarcely allow herself to admit this, but, truthfully, all evening this rusty old box had been in the back of her mind. As she'd been deglazing a roasting pan, she'd thought, *I wonder what is inside that box?*

She absolutely refused to think that her tiredness had been an excuse to get away from the others and get back to the box and its hidden treasure. "Probably a rat's nest inside," she said aloud as she went to her tiny kitchen to take a short, strong offset spatula and an ice pick from a drawer. It was going to take some work to get the lid off the rusty box.

Thirty minutes later, she had finally scraped away enough rust to pry the lid off enough to get her fingers under it. Her tugging made her fingertips hurt, and she was thoroughly disgusted with herself for her frantic pulling and scraping. After all, just as the woman at the antique shop had said, the only treasure inside was probably flour, complete with the dead carcasses of weevils.

With her fingertips jammed under one edge of the lid, Kady gave such a great pull that she went tumbling back across the room, the lid clattering to the floor. Pulling herself upright, she leaned over the box and peered inside, and saw yellowed tissue paper.

On top was a tiny bouquet of dried, faded orange blossoms, obviously put there with loving hands and undisturbed for many years.

Immediately, Kady knew that what was under the paper was something very special. And something very private. Sitting back on her heels, she looked at the flowers, pinned to the paper, so they had not been dislodged in all her frantic attempts to pry the lid off.

For a long moment, Kady hesitated with indecision. Part of her cried out that she should replace the lid and never open the box again—put it on top of her kitchen cabinet and look at the outside, forget about the inside. Or better yet, get rid of the box and forget she ever saw it.

"You are being ridiculous, Kady Long," she said aloud. "Whoever put this in here has been dead a long, long time."

Slowly, disgusted to see that her hands were trembling slightly, Kady unpinned the flowers, set them aside, then peeled back the tissue paper. Instantly, she knew what she was looking at.

Folded carefully, untouched by light or air for many years, was a wedding dress: perfect white satin with a deep, square neck edged in a white satin ruffle. Rhinestone buttons twinkled up at her.

There was still a feeling in Kady that she should replace the lid on the box and close it forever. But having just today had such a dreadful experience in trying to find a wedding dress and now seeing that the old flour tin she'd bought on impulse contained a wedding gown, she thought it was too extraordinary to let pass. Almost lovingly, she put her hands under the shoulders of the dress and lifted it out.

It was heavy, since there seemed to be many yards of the beautiful white satin, all of it aged to the most perfect color of heavy cream. The bodice ended just below the waist, and below that was a skirt, smooth and straight in the front, then yards of fabric pulled to the back in a heavily ruched train that would extend three feet behind the wearer.

Hand-knotted silk fringe graced the skirt and the top of the train. Below that were little pleats and the dearest hand-made silk roses.

Holding the dress up to the light, Kady marveled at it. Today she must have tried on a dozen modern wedding dresses, but she'd seen nothing like this. Compared to this dress, the modern gowns were peasants' clothes, with no embellishment, no thought to the design: mass produced versus one of a kind.

Kady couldn't seem to take her eyes off the dress. The long sleeves ended in buttoned cuffs, tiny piping about the edges; then what had to be handmade lace spilled from the bottom edge.

Shifting the dress in her hands, Kady glanced down into the box and caught her breath. "A veil," she breathed; then, with reverence, she spread the gown across her sofa and knelt before the box.

If a whisper could be made into fabric, then that was what she was looking at. Reaching toward the gossamer lace, she drew back, almost afraid to touch something as lovely as this; then, taking a deep breath, she slid her hands under the lace. It was so light it seemed to have no weight, no substance, as though it were woven of light and air. Standing, she let the lace drape over her arms, feeling the divine softness on her skin. It didn't take a costume historian to recognize this lace as handmade, the flower-and-vine pattern worked by tiny needles, and if Kady didn't miss her guess, it had been made with love.

Very carefully, she spread the lace on her sofa, feeling that it was almost sacrilege to allow that fairy fabric to touch modern, plastic-based upholstery fabric.

Turning back to the box, she slowly and carefully began to empty it of the rest of its contents. It was as though she knew exactly what she was going to find inside it: shoes, gloves, corset, petticoats of fine cotton, hose with embroidered garters. A buttonhook. More dried flowers.

Reverently, she set each item aside as she returned to the

box to look at the rest of the treasures. In the very bottom of the box was a satin case, sewn with white ribbon that was tied into a bow. As Kady lifted the case, her heart was pounding because, by some instinct, she knew that what was inside this case was the key to why this beautiful dress had been stored away so long ago in such an ordinary old tin. As she lifted the case, she could tell that there was something heavy inside.

Leaning back against the couch, she put the case on her lap and slowly pulled one end of the ribbon to untie it; then even more slowly, she lifted the top flap of the case, put her hand inside, and withdrew an old photograph. It was a tintype of a man, a woman, and two children: a very handsome family, all of them fair-haired with sweet, happy-looking faces.

Kady couldn't help smiling at them. The man was very stern-looking, as though he was uncomfortable in the high, stiff collar he wore. Sitting to his left, his hand on her shoulder, was a small, pretty woman with an impish gleam in her eye, as though she found the whole idea of photography a great joke. Standing to her right, in front of the man, was a tall, handsome boy, about ten or eleven years old, with some of his father's sternness, as well as his mother's devilish gleam. On the woman's lap was a little girl of about seven who was a beauty-in-the-making. It was obvious that when she grew up, she was going to break some hearts.

Turning the photo over, she found on the back was written the single word *Jordan*. Carefully, Kady put the photo aside then fished inside the case and pulled out a man's heavy gold watch. The watch was so big it filled the palm of her hand. On the worn cover was the word *Jordan*, and along one edge, just above the hinge, was a deep crease, as though the watch had been dropped onto something very hard.

"Or shot," Kady said, then wondered why she'd said that. "Too many westerns on TV," she muttered, but as she ran her thumb along the crease, it did seem to have striations, as though it had been grazed by a bullet.

Because of the deep indentation, the watch was difficult to open, but with persistence, she managed to make the hinge work. Inside, the face of the watch was beautiful, with ornate Roman numerals and elaborate hands. On the left in the watchcase was another photo, this time of the woman alone. There was no mistaking her, with her sparkling eyes and happy expression. Even in the photo she looked like a woman in love and happy.

Closing the watch, Kady smiled. What in the world had made her nervous? she wondered. Obviously, this was the wedding dress of a woman who had been very happy. She'd had a husband who loved her and two beautiful children.

Smiling, Kady put the watch beside the photo, then looked to see if anything else was inside the case. She pulled out a pair of amethyst earrings, the purple stones glittering in the artificial electric light.

Carefully, she laid the earrings on the silk of the case, leaned back against the couch, and looked at everything. On impulse, or maybe out of habit, she picked up the photo and placed the edge of her hand over the lower half of the man's face. No, no man with blond hair was her Arabian prince.

Gregory was that, she thought, smiling at the clothes piled around her, then thought, *Whatever am I going to do with all this? Shouldn't these things be in a museum?*

One second she was asking herself what she was going to do with all this; then the next she could envision herself walking down the aisle of her own wedding wearing this heavenly gown. With renewed energy, she leaped to her feet and picked up the dress, holding it at arm's length.

This dress was different from modern dresses: it hadn't been made for a woman who was five foot eight inches tall and had miles of legs, no hips, no breasts and a boyish waist. At this thought Kady allowed herself a smile. There had been several men in her life who had made some extraordinarily pleasant comments about her hourglass figure.

"This would fit me," Kady said aloud, turning the dress to hold it against her and seeing that it was indeed the perfect length.

Right away she knew that the sensible thing to do would be to go to bed now; then tomorrow she'd talk about this dress with Debbie and Jane. It was great that they were here and could give their opinions on something as serious as wearing a hundred-year-old dress to a modern wedding. Kady had no idea about these things. Was it done? Would she be laughed out of the church?

Even as she was thinking these very sensible thoughts, she was on her way to the bathroom, where she got into the shower and washed her hair. While she was conditioning it, then blow-drying it, she told herself that she couldn't wear a dress with a bustle to her wedding. It was really too outrageous to consider.

As Kady stood in her robe before the mirror, she began to arrange her hair. At the restaurant she pulled it back off her face and into a bun so it wouldn't fall into the food. She had never been very adventurous with her hair, nor actually very vain about her looks, but now she wanted to look her best. Using a comb, a round hairbrush, and about three pounds of hairpins, she managed to sweep her thick wavy hair into a high pouf off her face, then allowed long dark curls to tumble down her back.

When she'd finished, she looked in the mirror and gave a little smile. "Not bad," she said as she touched up her eyes and lips with cosmetics.

When she'd done what she could with her head, she went into the living room and began to try to puzzle together the wedding outfit. There seemed to be an outrageous number of undergarments, and it was difficult to figure out in what order they went on.

She put on a pretty, but shapeless, cotton slip next to her

skin, along with a big, long pair of underpants. Bending, she pulled on the hose made of finely knit silk and fastened them just above the knee with garters embroidered with pink rosebuds. She thought she'd better get the shoes on now because she guessed that once the long corset was on, she wouldn't be able to bend.

Feeling like Cinderella, Kady slipped her feet into ankle-high, cream-colored kidskin shoes that fit exactly, then used the buttonhook to fasten the little pearl buttons up the front.

After she'd managed to buckle herself into the boned corset, which took a bit of breath holding, she caught sight of herself in the mirror by the front door. "My goodness," she gasped. The corset had managed to shove her breasts practically under her chin, and looking at herself, she had to admit that corsets did have their advantages.

There were a couple more cotton half-slips, then a little camisole that seemed to fit on over the corset.

By the time Kady got to the dress, she was wearing more clothes than she did when it snowed.

Once the dress was on, she carefully avoided looking in the mirror until she was completely dressed. After putting on the earrings, with reverential hands, she picked up the lace veil and pinned it in place on her head. The lace was as light as a soufflé, reaching almost to her knees, concealing the long dark hair down her back, but exposing it as well. Lace gloves went on last.

When she was fully dressed, she turned and took a few steps toward the full-length mirror. As she moved, she wondered why the dress and the many undergarments didn't feel strange. The weight of all the clothes she had on should have felt burdensome or at the very least constrictive, but, somehow, they didn't. Somehow, the dress felt right.

With her shoulders back, her head straight, and managing the train as though she'd been born wearing it, Kady walked to stand in front of the mirror.

For a moment she just looked at herself in silence, not smiling, not thinking really, just gazing. She was not the same person she usually saw. Nor was she a twentieth-century woman playing dress up in antique clothing. It was as though she looked the way she was meant to look.

"Yes," she whispered. "This is what I will wear to my wedding." She didn't need to ask anyone's permission, for she knew without a doubt in the world that this was the dress she was meant to wear to her own wedding.

Smiling slightly, she walked back to the couch and picked up the photo of the Jordan family. "Thank you," she said softly to the woman in the photo, for she knew that it had to have been her wedding dress, a dress she must have loved and stored carefully away so that another woman in another time could wear it.

With the photo in one hand, Kady picked up the watch and unfastened the lid so she could see the second photo of the woman. "Thank you very, very much," Kady said, smiling at the whole family. "Thank you, Mrs. Jordan."

As Kady held the two objects, and as she said the name Jordan, she suddenly felt dizzy. "Must be the corset," she said as she sat down heavily on the sofa, the photo and watch falling to her lap. "I should get out of this dress. I should . . ."

Trailing off, she felt her energy leave her, as though she were falling asleep, but at the same time her weakness felt different. She felt that this dizziness was something she didn't want to give herself up to. At all costs, she thought, she *must* fight this. She must open her eyes!

"I say, let's hang the bastard," she heard a man say.

"Yeah. Get rid of him once and for all."

"Hear that, Jordan? Make peace with your Maker, 'cause these are your last moments alive."

"No," Kady whispered weakly. "Don't hurt a Jordan. Such a nice dress. You shouldn't hurt one of them." For a moment she almost succeeded in opening her eyes and sitting up, but then she heard another voice, a man's voice.

"Help me, Kady. Help me."

Kady could see only blackness inside her closed eyelids, but she knew that if her Arabian prince, the man she had seen in her dreams a thousand times, had spoken, his voice would sound like this man's.

"Yes," she said and quit struggling to sit up. "Yes, I will help you."

In the next second Kady collapsed against the sofa, unaware of where she was or even who she was. Limply, her hand fell to her side as she gave herself up to the deep swirling sensation that overtook her.

Chapter 3

KADY OPENED HER EYES TO DAZZLING SUNLIGHT, THEN caught herself to keep from falling as a wave of dizziness overtook her.

"Ow!" she said, covering her eyes against the glare, then looked at her palm, scraped bloody from where she'd fallen against a rock covered with a thorny bush. Feeling dizzy and weak, she leaned back against what she thought was a couch only to meet more rock.

It was several minutes before she could stop her head and body from spinning and squint against the sunlight to try to see where she was. Moments before, it had been night and she had been in her apartment, but now she seemed to be standing in front of a pile of enormous boulders, with scruffy little oak trees trying to grow in the cracks, and it was the height of the day.

With the back of her hand to her forehead, Kady stepped back into the shade, then sat down on the smallest rock.

"If I close my eyes and count to ten, I will wake up," she said, then proceeded to count. But when she opened her eyes, the rocks were still there, as well as the sunlight, and she was still not in her apartment.

29

There were aspen trees around her, blocking her from a long view of her surroundings, but a rocky, narrow path led down what could possibly be a mountain. It didn't take a degree in botany to know that this was not the lush greenery of Virginia. This was high mountain desert. Her head came up when in the distance she heard the high-pitched cry of a bird as it flew overhead.

"I have been working too hard," Kady said, smoothing out the skirt of the wedding dress she was still wearing. "Working too much, and now I'm dreaming."

When she tried to stand, she was again dizzy and had to steady herself against a boulder. The rock certainly felt as though it was real!

"Very real," she said aloud. "Yes, indeed, this is the most vivid, most realistic dream anyone has ever had, and if I have any sense at all, I'll enjoy it. I'll . . ." She looked about her. "Yes, I'll observe everything, then I'll have a wonderful story to tell Gregory."

It wasn't easy to concentrate because the dizziness kept coming over her in waves, and it was difficult to take deep breaths while fastened in the corset. Kady thought of loosening her stays, but she feared that if she did, she'd never be able to stand upright. At the moment, whalebone was the only spine she seemed to have.

"I will *not* be frightened," she said to herself sternly. "This is a dream, and as such, I cannot be hurt. Not really, actually, truly hurt," she clarified.

As she looked at the rocks, she saw something under a sparse little vine hanging down one sandstone side, so she pulled the vine aside. "Petroglyphs," she said, running her lace-encased fingertip over the ancient symbols. Stick-figure men with bow and arrows hunted what looked to be elk. One man seemed to have fallen, while three others pursued more animals that were running away.

As Kady touched the figures, suddenly it was as though, smack in the middle of the rocks, a doorway appeared, and through that open doorway, she could see her apartment.

There was her couch, her jeans and chef's coat flung across it, and on the floor was the old tin flour box the wedding dress had been in.

Never in her life had Kady seen anything as enticing as the view of her own apartment. Without bothering to toss the train over her arm, she took the two steps toward the doorway.

But as she reached the threshold, her foot paused in the air; she heard what sounded like a shot, loud and clear in the crisp air. Turning, she looked back toward the trees but could see nothing, so she turned again toward the doorway leading into her apartment.

But this time *he* was there. Her Arabian man on the white horse, his face and body hidden in great swathes of black. Kady drew in her breath sharply. Since she'd repeatedly seen this man almost all her life, he should have been familiar to her, but each appearance was always a wonder. And the sight of him always made her yearn for something she couldn't describe or explain.

But this time seeing him was different, for this time he seemed clearer, more real, as though he were not a foggy dream but an actual man before her.

"Who are you?" she whispered. "What do you want of me?"

He looked at her over the dark scarf covering the lower half of his face, and his eyes seemed to be full of sadness. "I am waiting for you," he whispered.

It was the first time Kady had heard his voice, and it sent chills up her spine, made the hairs on her arms stand on end. "How?" she asked, leaning toward him, and her single word told it all. She was not hesitating about whether she would go to him or not, but asking only how she could find him.

Raising his arm, he pointed with one long finger toward Kady, then raised his arm higher to point above her head. Quickly, she turned her head and once again looked toward the trees, but she saw nothing.

When she looked back, he was still there, her empty apartment behind him, as though he were standing in front of a large photograph. It was in that moment that she knew he meant for her to go down that skinny little path and turn her back on all that her apartment represented. In that moment Gregory flashed before her eyes, and she thought of the way he smiled at her, of how she felt when he held her. She thought of Onions and her customers and Gregory's mother. And she thought of her wedding and Debbie and Jane.

"No," she said without hesitation. "No thanks," then took a step toward her apartment.

In that split instant, everything disappeared, the apartment, the Arabian man on the horse, all of it. Instead, there was just a rough-surfaced rock, and Kady was jammed against it as though she'd tried to walk straight through the stone.

"No, no, no, no!" she said as she turned her face away and leaned against the rock. This dream was too real, and if it *was* real, it was something that she did *not* want. "I want to go home," she said, her mouth set in a firm line of stubbornness. "I'm not leaving here!" Crossing her arms over her corseted chest, she decided she wasn't going to move, no matter what.

But even as she said the words, something inside her made her want to go down that path. Once again, dizziness nearly overpowered her until she feared she'd lose consciousness. Bracing against a rock to steady herself, she waited for the compulsion to pass, but it merely lightened, refusing to leave her.

Her head came up when the wind carried what seemed to be the sound of male voices. Kady tried to fight the feeling, but there seemed to be a force outside of her telling her that she *had* to go down that path, that she could not stay where she was. And she had to go *now*.

Still dizzy and seeming to grow dizzier by the second, Kady took a step toward the path, then halted as her foot encountered something. On the ground was the satin envelope, neatly retied, a lump showing that it contained the watch. When Kady bent to pick it up, she almost fainted and it took several moments before she could stand upright.

Another shot came, and this time it was as though her feet had a will of their own as she started to stumble down the path. Twice the path branched, and even though her mind was disoriented and hazy, her feet seemed to know which way to go. Clutching the envelope tightly, her train thrown over her arm, she hurried forward. Twice she seemed to black out, and each time she opened her eyes again, she found herself still half running down the mountainside. Once she left the path altogether and stumbled across rocks and fallen timber before she found another path that led down the mountainside.

Abruptly, she stumbled out of the shady woods and into brilliant sunlight. Swaying, she leaned against a boulder and tried to clear her vision. Several feet below her was a scene out of a movie. On a horse, his hands tied behind his back, his head listing to one side as though he were unconscious, was a man with a rope about his neck, and the rope was tied above to a large branch of a tree. The man was about ten seconds away from being hanged.

Near him were three men on horses, guns strapped to their hips and smirks of delight on their faces. Kady didn't know who was in the right, who were the good guys and who the bad, but she didn't like the look on those men's faces. Frantically, she looked about for some way to stop this awful event before the poor man on the horse was left dangling.

A thousand thoughts ran through her head, but none of them seemed to be worth acting upon. Somehow, she doubted that she could walk up to the men and ask them to please stop. Nor did she think promises of cakes and chocolate pudding would make them cut the unconscious man down.

She hesitated for a few seconds, then nearly jumped out of her corset when she heard a hateful little laugh below her to the left. Turning, she saw that a man was standing there, a rifle across his folded arms, and he was grinning in anticipation of the gory sight he was about to see.

Maybe it was the thousands of television shows Kady had seen or all the violent movies, but she didn't seem to think at all. It was pure instinct that made her creep up behind the man, pick up a big rock, and bring it down on his head.

Silently, the man crumpled to the ground, and Kady grabbed his rifle. *Now what?* she thought, looking at the thing. *How do I fire it? What should I—?*

She didn't have any more thoughts because the rifle seemed to go off by itself and the kick of it sent Kady slamming back into a deep crevice between two rocks, the man she'd hit on the head at her feet.

Still holding the rifle, her eyes wide in astonishment, she peered through the shrubs at the men on the horses several feet away. There was a tree between her and them, and because of the angle, she realized, the men couldn't see her, but by the noise and confusion, she knew she had distracted them. Holding the rifle against her corseted belly, Kady pulled the trigger again, only to find that nothing happened. *Cock it,* came a voice into her head, and she remembered seeing TV shows where men pulled down a lever on the bottom of the rifle, then fired. After a bit of fumbling, she managed to do this, then fired again. This time there was a yell of pain, and she knew, to her horror, that she had hit someone.

The sound of horses' hooves, plus three shots directed toward her location, made her leap behind the rocks and crawl into a tiny cave formed by fallen trees and little bushes. With her breath held in fear, Kady listened as the horses came thundering her way.

"What about him?" one of the men yelled when they were so near Kady she could feel the warmth of their horses. She could tell that "him" was the poor man they'd been about to hang.

"Shoot the horse out from under him, and let's get the hell out of here."

It was all Kady could do to keep from yelling "No!" but self-preservation made her stay where she was, trying to make herself as small as possible, holding the train of the wedding dress close to her body so they wouldn't see her. There was another shot; then, to her horror, she saw the satin envelope on the path and prayed the men wouldn't see it.

But they were gone as fast as they could pull the man she'd bashed onto a horse; then all was quiet. Part of her wanted to run from her hiding place, but another part of her wanted to stay there until someone came to rescue her.

But her concern for the man about to be hanged won over her own fear. After disentangling herself from the underbrush, she slung the train of her dress over her arm, grabbed the envelope, then took off running in his direction.

As soon as she was in the sunlight, she saw that the man was still on his horse, still had the noose about his neck. The shot had obviously scared the animal as it had moved forward until the poor man in the saddle was stretched as far as his body could be.

When Kady reached him, she knew that she could lose no time. Gently, she spoke to the horse, caressing its nose as she coaxed it to move backward a few steps and relieve some pressure on the man's neck. Once the animal was back, she put her hand on the man's leg and looked up at him. "Sir?" she said, but saw that he was unconscious, oblivious to everything.

So how did she get him down? she wondered. The man was big, at least six feet tall and a couple of hundred pounds. His hands were tied, and he was dead to the world, and if that thick rope lashing his neck to a tree wasn't removed, he'd be even more dead very soon.

"Mister," she called up, shaking him with her hand on his calf. There was no response from the man, but the horse turned its head and rolled its eyes at her, then moved one foot forward. If the horse became impatient and decided to walk away, he'd leave his passenger hanging, so Kady knew she had to act immediately.

As quickly as she could, she divested herself of the heavy, trained skirt, all the half-slips, the lovely veil and the lace gloves, until she was wearing the long drawers, hose, and the nifty little boots, which easily slipped into the stirrup beside the man's booted foot.

With a great push, she propelled herself onto the back of the saddle behind the unconscious man.

"Great," she said as soon as she was in place. The rope was still a foot above her head, and even if she'd had a knife, the rope was so thick it would have taken her an hour to cut it. What she needed was a pair of bolt cutters. "Or a saw-blade bread knife," she said, looking up at the rope.

"You couldn't wake up and help me with this, could you?" she said to the man, her head against his back, but she received no reply. Leaning around the broad back of him, she looked down at the horse. "Look, I'm going to have to climb up to stand in this saddle, so I want you to hold very, very still. Got that? I'm no circus performer, so I don't want you chasing rabbits. Or whatever it is horses chase. Understand me?"

The horse turned to look up at her in a way that made Kady quite nervous. Using the man's body as though it were a ladder, she carefully and slowly climbed up until she was standing in the saddle behind him, leaning most of her body weight against his as she steadied herself as she reached for the rope.

The horse shifted on its feet, and Kady would have fallen if she hadn't caught herself by throwing her arms around the man's neck. "Be still!" she hissed to the horse, and it had the good sense to obey her.

It was not easy to loosen the treacherous hangman's

noose from around the man's neck. The rope seemed to have embedded itself in the man's skin, and only by much tugging and pulling was she finally able to free him.

And the moment he was free, he collapsed back against Kady's legs, almost causing her to fall from the horse. Crouching, she clutched him tightly as he leaned into her and she bore what seemed to be half of his two hundred pounds on her own body. With great difficulty, somehow managing to keep herself as well as him from falling, she eased back down into the saddle so she was sitting behind him.

His head was leaning back beside her own, his eyes closed, his breathing not detectable. "Wake up," she said, then pulled one hand up to pat his cheek sharply. She didn't have the heart to slap him, but truthfully she didn't think any slap would revive him.

"How do I get you to a doctor?" she asked the unconscious man in her arms; then, instead of trying to revive him, she stroked his thick hair from out of his eyes. His hair was dark blond, his skin was lightly tanned, and for the first time, Kady noticed that he was one gorgeous hunk.

"Not in the same class as Gregory," she said aloud, "but a woman could do worse."

"Stop it," she reminded herself. "There are more important matters at hand than some guy who likes to spend his days playing cowboy."

With superhuman effort, Kady pushed the man forward until he was leaning over the horses's neck; then she fiddled with the rope that was binding his hands. It took longer than it should have, but she had no knife, so she had to undo the tight knot.

At last she had him untied; so, slowly, with her hands bracing him against falling, she got off the horse and onto the ground. But once she was down and looking up at him, he seemed as tall as a mountain and about the same breadth.

Now all she had to do was get the rifle in case those

horrible men returned, and the skirt of her dress, then get back onto the horse and ride to the nearest town and hospital. Simple.

But the minute she reached for the rifle, she heard a sound behind her, then looked and saw, to her horror, that the big man was falling straight toward her.

There wasn't much time, but she did what she could to prepare herself for the impact. Spreading her feet wide apart, she braced herself. But no bracing could prepare her for the impact of his heavy body tumbling down onto hers. He fell against her hard, sending her sprawling onto a bed of leaves and gravel that cut into her lightly clad legs.

For a moment Kady lay where she was, blinking up at the lacy underside of the cottonwood tree branches, but the need to breathe brought her back to the urgency of the situation. Every ounce of the man was draped across her like some great, warm blanket. A blanket so heavy that she could not draw a breath.

When pushing against his shoulders didn't budge him, she realized that she was not going to be able to move him. Using what strength she had left, she did her best to wiggle out from under him; when she had the upper half of herself free, she paused to take a few deep, delicious breaths, and then finally managed to get the bottom half of her out from under him.

"Now what do I do with you?" Kady asked aloud, looking down at him, sleeping with all the innocence of a child.

"Feed you," she said brightly, then hauled herself up and began to search his saddlebags for something to cook.

Chapter 4

AN HOUR LATER KADY KNEW THAT SHE HAD DONE WHATEVER she could to save the man. He seemed to breathing all right now, but he hadn't regained consciousness. Since there was no way she could get him back onto the horse to get him to a hospital, she set about making a camp for the night.

She had searched through the saddlebags for what could be cooked, but had found only beef jerky, a canteen of water, and a tin cup. After she'd covered the man with the single blanket, she built a fire, something she was quite good at since she'd done a great deal of outdoor grilling in her life.

Within minutes she'd boiled a concoction of the dried beef, wild mustard, and some very nice greens she'd found growing nearby. After cooling the broth so it wouldn't burn him, she put the man's head onto her lap and began to try to get the liquid down his sore throat.

He'd fought her until she'd spoken quite sharply to him and told him she was going to tie his hands again if he didn't drink his broth and behave himself. Her stern voice seemed to reach the little boy in him because he grimaced, but he drank. Afterward, Kady let him sleep while she sat on a boulder a few feet away and tried to think about what had happened to her in the last hours.

She was certain she was no longer in Virginia, but she didn't know where she was now and certainly not how she'd come to be there. Once again she opened the satin envelope and looked at the photograph, for her instinct told her that that picture had something to do with what had happened to her.

It didn't take much deducing to see that the injured man lying on the ground before her was the boy in the picture. Even with his eyes closed and years older, he was the same. He'd opened his eyes once while Kady was trying to get him to drink, and she'd seen that they were dark blue, like sapphires.

But, of course, it was impossible for this man to be the boy in the photo because that picture was over a hundred years old. If he were the boy in the photo, then that would mean that when she went through the rock, she'd done a bit of time manipulation. Which, of course, was impossible.

After a while she went to the man and began to search through the pockets of his trousers. She found a half dozen coins, no paper money, and the coins were all dated in the eighteen seventies. There was a letter in the saddlebag dated July 1873, saying that Cole Jordan owed twenty dollars for cattle. The initials on the saddle were C.J.

Impossible, she thought as she shoved the items back into the saddlebags. *Better to stop thinking of this.*

The sun was going down, and it was growing cold, making Kady shiver in her corset and drawers. As she went to stir up the fire, the man began to thrash about and mumble something. Or at least he tried to say something, but his throat was too damaged to make much noise.

As Kady leaned over him, she ran her hand over his

forehead. "It's all right," she said softly. "I'm here, and you're safe. No one is going to hurt you any more."

She couldn't imagine how she could reassure him when the truth was she was quite frightened herself. What if those men who had been trying to hang him returned? What if they were the good guys and this man was a murderer and that was the reason they had been about to hang him? Maybe he'd done something really truly horrible to cause men to try to lynch him without a trial.

But as she stroked the blond man's forehead, he began to shiver, and even though she tucked the blanket tighter around him, he still trembled. So she did the only other thing she knew to do: she lay down beside him.

Immediately, his strong arms encircled her, drawing her to him, as he threw one big leg over her much smaller ones. At first Kady started to protest, but then fatigue overtook her. She'd been awake for nearly twenty-four hours now. Even so, out of habit she started to push the man away because she didn't like to sleep close to anyone. On the rare occasions when Gregory spent the night, they each kept to opposite sides of the bed. Kady always said things like, "If I rolled onto you in the night, I'd crush you." But with this man there was no threat of crushing any part of him. In fact, Kady thought maybe he could even sleep comfortably under the horse.

At that thought she giggled, and the man, his face and warm breath near hers, smiled in his sleep. He said something, but she wasn't sure what the word was. However, it sounded like "Angel."

Whatever the word was, Kady rested her head against the muscle of his arm and went to sleep.

She awoke slowly to someone kissing her softly on the lips, and not yet fully awake, she smiled and kissed him back. His hand was running up her thigh, over her waist, and onto her breast. Sleepily, Kady moved her leg so his thigh was between hers; then she moved forward to get closer to him. His kisses were so very nice, not urgent or frantic as though he had to do this quickly so he could get to work, but as though he had all the time in the world.

His lips moved to her neck, and as she arched against him, he put his face into her breasts, which were pushed high above the corset. "Oh, yes," she murmured, trying to get closer to him.

It was a noise from the horse that made her open her eyes for a moment, then close them. In the next second she opened them with a jolt. This most certainly wasn't her bedroom, and those trees with the snow-covered mountains in the background certainly weren't part of the Virginia landscape.

And if this wasn't her bedroom and this wasn't Virginia, then it was quite likely that the man whose face was buried between her breasts was *not* Gregory.

Arching her back in an attempt to pull away from him, she pushed at his shoulders, but his face was glued to her breasts—which for some reason were nearly fully exposed and—

Memory came flooding back to her. "Get your hands off of me!" she half shouted to the top of the man's blond head.

Instantly, he stopped kissing, but he took his time before lifting his head to look at her. What Kady saw was a man with the most innocent eyes she'd ever seen. *He's a choirboy*, she thought. *A huge, gorgeous choirboy, as innocent as fresh asparagus tips. But, oh, so deadly,* she reminded herself as she remembered his lips on her skin.

"You are beautiful," he said, then winced at the pain in his throat.

Kady was glad that his wince kept him from seeing her look of shock, for his voice was the same rich, deep timbre she'd heard last night from her Arabian prince. No two men could look less alike, but they certainly did sound alike.

"Would you mind releasing me?" she said, pushing at his shoulders since his hands were still on her body.

"Yes," he gasped out. "My apologies. I thought you were . . ." He swallowed painfully. "I thought you were my every dream come true." At that he gave her a little one-sided smile that almost made her slide back into his arms.

But she controlled herself and rolled away from him, then stood, hands on hips and looked down at him. But his look made her glance down at herself and become very aware of her dishabille. If a man had grown up surrounded by women who wore only long granny dresses, then suddenly saw a woman wearing a bikini, he'd probably wear the same expression as this man. By late-twentieth-century standards Kady was fully dressed, except maybe for her breasts, which were overflowing the top of the corset. But even that wouldn't have been shocking to a modern man.

Now, why did I think that? she wondered. *Why did I think this is not a "modern" man?*

Quickly, she grabbed the petticoats and slipped them on, then the heavy satin bodice and the skirt, all while he watched her with unblinking eyes. To her chagrin, the beautiful skirt was dirty in places, and there was even a tear down one side from when she'd jumped between the boulders.

When she was fully covered, the man was still looking up at her with wonder in his eyes, and Kady knew she'd never seen a man as appealing as this one. And in that moment she knew she *had* to get home. Home to safety—and to Gregory.

Once she was dressed, she straightened her shoulders and looked down at him, trying to look as stern and businesslike as possible. "Now that I have seen that you are all right, I shall leave you," she said, then turned on her heel and started back toward the rocks.

All she had to do was find the rock with the petroglyphs and go back through them to her apartment. Now that she had done what she assumed she was supposed to do and saved this man's life, she was sure she could return.

She had walked only a few yards when the man caught her by the arm; she hadn't heard him come up behind her.

"I can't let you go," he said. "Who will take care of you?"

"I will take care of myself. Would you please release me?"

He put his hand to his throat, a frown on his brow as he tried to speak.

"You should have a doctor look at your throat," she said, starting to step around him.

"You can't leave," he rasped out. "Where do you live? I'll take you home."

"There," she said, pointing toward the rocks. "Just a short way from here."

The man looked at the rocks, then back to her, a look of *Are you crazy?* on his face. "There are only mountains that way. No ranches or farms, nothing but rocks and rattlesnakes." He took her arm again. "I'll take you wherever you live."

"I live *there*," she said emphatically. "Anyway, where I live or don't live is none of your business. Now please go away."

He blocked her path. "Are you saying that you risked your life to save me, stayed with me all night to reassure yourself of my safety, and now I'm just to ride away and leave *you* here alone in the mountains without another thought for *you*? Do I have that right?"

"You have it exactly right." Again she tried to step around him.

But he swept her into his arms and carried her back to the campfire, and all Kady's struggling didn't make him falter.

"Release me or I'll scream."

"And who do you think will hear you?"

He set her down on a boulder, the one where she'd sat the day before and tried to sort out what had happened to her. *Calm down,* she told herself. She had to get away from this man and get back to the doorway in the rock where she'd entered this foreign place.

There was part of Kady that knew she was alone with a man in the middle of who-knew-where and yesterday someone had been about to hang him. He could very well be a rapist-murderer-escaped-lunatic or whatever, and she should tread lightly.

But some instinct said that he would never harm her and, if need be, he would protect her with his life.

But whatever he was, whoever he was, didn't matter. Her only concern was that she needed to get away from him and get back to the opening. She looked about for something to distract him from standing there and glaring down at her. "I'm rather hungry. What about you? If you find us something to eat, I'll cook it."

Smiling at her in the way men do when they are sure they have won an argument, he said, "That's an excellent idea. I'll find us a couple of rabbits."

She smiled at him sweetly. "Very good." Since she'd searched his saddlebags and his trouser's pockets, she knew he had no gun. "There's a rifle over there."

To Kady's surprise, the man seemed to pale, and in a lightning motion, he grabbed the rifle from where it lay propped against a tree, and before Kady could take a breath, he'd slammed it against a rock and shattered it.

"What are you doing?" she half screamed. "What if those men who tried to kill you come back?"

When the rifle was in pieces on the ground, the man dropped the bit of barrel that remained in his hands as though it were something filthy. "I don't like guns," he whispered harshly.

"Obviously." As she looked up at him, he seemed to sway on his feet. "Are you all right?"

"Sure," he said, but when he closed his eyes for a moment, Kady stood and pushed him toward the shade of the cottonwood tree, where he reluctantly sat down on the ground.

In concern, she knelt beside him, her face close to his as she felt his forehead for fever but found none. She smiled at him. "I don't think hanging agrees with you, so I don't think you should try it again."

He looked at her, his dark blue eyes intense. "Who are you and why are you out here at the Hanging Tree, miles from town and wearing a wedding dress?"

"I, ah, I was . . . in my apartment and trying on the dress because I'm supposed to be married in a few weeks, and I heard something, and I, ah . . ." She looked at him.

"You're not very good at lying."

"Thankfully, I haven't had much reason to learn how." Looking up, she scanned the rocks at the foot of the mountain, the place where she'd come down the path. "You wouldn't know where there are any petroglyphs, would you?"

"And who is that? Your—" He hesitated, and there was a definite sneer on his rather perfect lips. "The man you're planning to marry?"

"Petroglyphs are pictures carved on rocks. These are little stick men chasing an elk. And the man I'm going to marry is named Gregory Norman," she said; then, to her horror, she burst into tears.

Instantly, strong arms were put around her and her head was drawn to a hard, broad chest. "I'm sorry," she said. "I don't usually—"

"Sssh, sweetheart, you cry all you want," he said soothingly, as he stroked her hair.

Kady did cry, but not for long; but when she stopped and tried to pull away from him, he still held her close. It didn't take much pressure to make her remain in his arms, for it seemed that now that the immediate danger was over, she was frightened at what had happened to her.

"You want to tell me what misfortune has befallen you? I'm a good listener."

"I don't know," she said, her head against his chest. "I really don't know what happened or where I am. And I don't know why those men were trying to hang you. Are you a good guy or a bad guy?" As she said this, she looked up at him in question.

"A what?" he asked, one eyebrow arched; then he smiled and pushed her head back down to his chest. "I'm a good guy. Deacon of the church. I even sing in the choir every Sunday. Look." He drew up his leg, pulled up his trouser leg, then reached into the top of his boot and withdrew what looked like a small hunting knife. Imbedded in the handle was a little medallion.

He handed the knife to Kady, and she looked at the medallion. "One year," she read, then saw that there was a Christian cross in the center. "One year for what?"

"One year at church service without missing once." He gave her that one-sided grin again. "I even went once when I had chicken pox and infected most of the kids in Sunday school."

She laughed as, out of habit, she ran her hand over the blade of the knife, wondering if he had sharpened it himself. It wasn't a perfect job, she could do better, but she'd felt worse. "So if you're a paragon of virtue, then why were the men trying to hang you?"

"Ever hear of greed?"

"I do believe I have," she said, smiling. "You have something they want?"

"A few head of cattle and a piece of land."

"Ah, one of those. Millions of cattle and millions of acres?"

He laughed. "Not quite. Last I heard the Colorado Rockies weren't the best grazing land."

Lifting her head, she looked around her. "Is that where I am? Colorado?"

When she looked back at him, his eyes were intense as

he spoke. "You want to tell me what's going on? Why are you here? Who's abandoned you? Did this Gregory—" He sneered the name. "Did he jilt you?"

"Of course not!" she said, starting to get up, but he pulled her back down.

"All right, I apologize. It's just that a man doesn't usually see a woman wandering about the mountains alone wearing a silk wedding dress." He lowered his eyes a bit, and a husky quality came into his voice. "Especially not one as beautiful as you."

Kady blushed. "I'm not beautiful. I'm thirty pounds overweight, and I never pay any attention to how I look. Usually I have on baggy trousers and a dirty smock. I own one pair of black dress shoes and half a dozen pair of sneakers. I—"

She stopped because the man was laughing at her. "Do you find my situation amusing?" she asked with some anger.

"What kind of men do you know that do not think you are the most beautiful of women? I have never seen a woman as pretty as you. Your face and your . . ." He looked down at her, and when he raised his eyes, there was wonder in them. "All of you is perfection. No man could be so blind as to not see you for the Aphrodite that you are."

For a moment she just stared at him with her eyes wide and her mouth in a little O. "I see," she finally managed to say. "Just so . . ." She moved away from him a bit. "I think I'd better go."

Instantly, he was on his feet, offering his hand down to help her stand. "You must tell me where you want to go, and I will take you."

As Kady looked up into those blue eyes, she felt herself sway toward him, but she forced herself to stand upright. *Get hold of yourself!* she commanded. *What is wrong with you anyway? You're engaged to one man, dream about another, and now, you seem to be thinking of ripping the clothes off a third.*

"Is there a bus around here? Or an airport?" How she

was going to pay for anything, since she hadn't a penny on her, couldn't concern her, but, somehow, the look of consternation on the man's face didn't surprise her.

"What is an airport?" he asked, and for some reason she couldn't define, his query made Kady dizzy again.

"No, don't touch me," she said when he made a move toward her. She had to take control of the situation. "Look, I appreciate all your old-world chivalry, and I thank you for your shoulder to cry on, but I must leave you now. I really do want to go home." *And not get involved here,* she thought. *Nor do I want to find out why you don't know what an airport is.*

With as much dignity as she could muster, she looped her train over her arm and started toward the rocks that she knew held the path that led to the doorway back to Virginia—and back to Gregory.

Chapter 5

HE DIDN'T FOLLOW HER, AND KADY WASN'T SURE WHETHER she was glad or terrified. What if she couldn't find the opening? What if the cowboy left her alone in these mountains and she could never find her way out?

Right now she wasn't going to allow herself to give in to her emotions. But the question, Why me? was going through her head. Why had what appeared to be a supernatural thing happened to her? She was a very ordinary person, and all she wanted was what she had: her cooking, marriage to Gregory, and maybe a baby or two.

Since the cowboy she'd saved was obviously the man in the photo, she knew that what had happened was meant to save him from hanging. But now that he was saved, why didn't she instantly return to Virginia and Gregory?

She climbed the path as it wound higher and higher up the mountain, but she knew within minutes that she had no idea where the petroglyphs were. When she'd come down the mountain she had been dazed and dizzy. Not that she was a whole lot better now, she thought, since she hadn't eaten in many hours.

"Roast potatoes," she said out loud to the rocks surrounding her. "Buttered corn and tiny squabs on toast. Rare roast beef; salmon from Scotland. Strawberry tart. Chocolate truffles."

Mentally preparing a menu only made her feel worse as she trudged up the trail that seemed to branch off in many different directions at once. Her beautiful gown kept snagging on the bushes, but she took her time disentangling the fabric, since she still hoped to wear the dress to her wedding to Gregory. Maybe it would be her act of defiance to wear this dress after the donning of it had forced her to go where she didn't want to go.

She had no idea how long she walked, but with each step she took, she lost hope. She was never going to find the doorway to go home. She'd starve to death or freeze or be eaten by the unidentified animal she'd just heard cry out. Or maybe those men who were trying to hang the cowboy would return and . . . and . . .

Kady sat down on a rock, feeling utterly and absolutely alone. Maybe this was her punishment for having lived such a wonderful, happy life. Thirty years of nothing much going wrong. No dysfunctional childhood, no one who'd ever tried to thwart her career, the love of a beautiful man who treated her like a princess.

With a burst of energy, she stood and beat her fists against the rocks in anger. "No, no, no, no!" she shouted. "I *won't* give it up. I won't! Do you hear me? I won't give it up!"

Of course there was no one to answer her or even to hear her, and after a moment she slumped back down on the rock, her head in her hands, and began to cry. Maybe she'd not appreciated her life in Virginia enough and that's why she'd lost it all.

After a few minutes her energy was spent, and she leaned back against the rocks and closed her eyes. Maybe if she concentrated, she'd wish herself back into her apartment, back into Gregory's arms. Maybe if— She fell asleep.

Kady awoke slowly, more aware of her stomach than the

rest of her body. Did she smell roasting meat? With her eyes still closed, she smiled. Chicken? No, of course not. That was the unmistakable fragrance of rabbit. Rabbit cooked in wine, or baked in a crust, or smothered in twice-whipped potatoes. Carrots. Tiny peas fresh from the pods. Thyme and a lot of pepper.

"Oh!" she said as she nearly fell off the rock, but a large hand kept her from falling. When she opened her eyes, she was at first disoriented, not knowing where she was, but then she looked into the dark blue eyes of the cowboy.

"Hungry?" he asked, holding out his hat. The inside was lined with oak leaves, and on top were the cut up pieces of rabbit.

Kady was so hungry she grabbed a leg and thigh piece and began eating, barely noticing that the meat was cooked incorrectly: too high a heat had been used, so the meat was dry outside and almost raw inside. It was minutes before she could look up from the bone that she'd eaten clean.

With a smile the man offered her another piece and his canteen full of water. "Find what you were looking for?" he asked when she was on her third piece of meat. He was sitting on a rock across from her, lazily leaning back, his long legs sprawled out between them, his boots nearly touching her skirt.

"No," she said, not wanting to meet his eyes. She didn't want to accept help from him, didn't want to be in his debt. Truthfully, she didn't want to get into trouble with him; he was *very* appealing.

"You left something behind," he said as he held up the satin pouch.

Kady didn't answer him but concentrated on the rabbit.

"You want to explain why you're carrying a photo of my family and my father's watch?"

"No," she said, not looking at him, but she could feel his eyes on her.

"Who are you and where do you live?" he asked softly. When she finished the third piece of rabbit, she looked up. "Elizabeth Kady Long," she said. "But people call me Kady." She was looking about for something to wipe her greasy hands on. The cowboy took a bandanna from his pocket, wet it with the canteen, then bent toward her, took one of her hands, and began to wash it. Kady tried to pull away, but he wouldn't release her.

"I can do that myself," she said, but he ignored her. Either she needed some assertiveness training or this man needed a course in believing women were autonomous.

When her hands were clean, he leaned back, so Kady started to get up.

"You might as well stay there since there is no place to go. There's just mountains on three sides; Legend is that way, and Denver is a two days' ride past it."

"Then I'd better start walking," she said, rising, but his leg blocked her path.

"Get out of my way!" she demanded.

"Not until you give me some answers. Now listen, Miss Long, you saved my life, and I feel that I owe you. It's my responsibility to take care of you and see that you're safe."

"How can I be safe with a man who is about to be hanged? Maybe those men will return and hang *both* of us."

"That's a possibility, and it's one of the reasons I would very much like to leave this place and get back to town. But I'm not going to leave without you. If you would tell me who takes care of you, I'd gladly take you to them, but I'm not going to ride off and leave you here alone. You can't even feed yourself."

At that Kady's eyes widened. Not able to feed herself was the very last thing she thought she'd ever hear anyone say of her. The accusation was so absurd that it caused her to smile, then give a bit of a laugh.

"That's better," the man said. "Now, why don't you sit back down and tell me what misfortune has left you wandering about the Rockies in a wedding dress."

Kady was tempted. Very tempted. But she knew better

than to turn her troubles over to this man. Some sixth sense made her refuse to tell him anything because she didn't want her life involved with his. She just wanted to go home and never see this man again.

"You're the boy in the photo?" she asked, trying to divert his attention. Maybe if she could get some answers from him, she'd find out why she was here.

"Yes," he said, his jaw stiff, as though he didn't want to speak of that.

His attitude made Kady curious. "Is this your mother's wedding dress?" she asked softly.

"I don't know, I wasn't at her wedding."

In spite of her dilemma, Kady laughed, and the man smiled back. "I bet your sister grew into a real beauty."

The man didn't say anything for a while, then slowly withdrew the photo from the envelope. "No one will ever know. She was killed when she was seven years old."

Kady drew in her breath sharply. "I'm sorry. I . . . ." She looked down at the dress and remembered how she'd thought that the woman in the photo looked so happy. "Your mother—"

"Dead too," the man said coldly, then looked up at Kady, his eyes hard, still full of misery after all these years. "This photo was the last one taken. Just days later there was a robbery at a bank in Legend, and as the thieves rode out of town all the good citizens of Legend opened fire."

As Kady watched, his lips curled into a sneer. "When the smoke cleared, my sister and my best friend were dead. My father and grandfather rode out after the robbers, and two days later they too were dead. My mother died the next year of grief."

For a moment Kady could only look at him in stunned silence. "I am so sorry," she managed to whisper. "That's why you hate guns, isn't it?" she said, and the man nodded curtly.

Kady knew that this tragedy had something to do with why she was here. But that thought made her even more determined to return to her apartment, to go back through the rock and get out of whatever entanglement there was here. Standing, she walked to the edge of the path, then looked back at him.

"I need to find the petroglyphs," she said softly. "Do you know where they are?"

"There are lots of Indian carvings in these mountains," he answered. "You could hunt the rest of your life and not find them all."

"But I *must* find them!" she said passionately. "You don't understand. You understand nothing."

"I am willing to try to understand if you'll just tell me what is so important about a bunch of Indian carvings."

Kady's hands were in fists at her side. She was *not* going to start crying again. "I was born in nineteen sixty-six," she said fiercely.

"But that would make you only seven years old," he said, puzzled.

"Not *eighteen* sixty-six. *Nineteen* sixty-six."

As she looked at him, several emotions played across his handsome face, a face tanned by the sun and years spent out-of-doors. "I see," he said at last.

"*I* see that you don't believe me," Kady said, her mouth tight. "Not that I expect you to believe me." She glared at him. "What are you thinking? That I escaped from an insane asylum? Are you thinking of locking me up so I can't harm anyone? Are you—"

"You're not very good at reading thoughts, are you? I was thinking that no matter when you were born, right now you need someone to take care of you. You need food and shelter and something else to wear. I think you should marry me, and I'll—"

At that Kady began to laugh. "Men are always the same, aren't they? Their solution for everything is to go to bed with them. A night of fabulous sex will make all the woman's problems go away."

The man was frowning, his eyes almost angry. "If sex

was all I was after, I could have taken that from you before now. There's no one here strong enough to stop me."

That statement wiped the smile off Kady's face. She turned away from him and took a step down the path. But she hadn't gone far when his voice stopped her.

"I'll take you into town," he said, and she could tell by his tone that she had hurt his feelings. Her mother had told her to *never* laugh at a man's proposal of marriage, no matter how ludicrous she found it.

She turned back. He was still sprawled on the rock, his eyes on his father's watch, winding it, acting as though nothing had happened, but she could tell that she had offended him.

"I apologize," she said, moving to stand near him. "You have been nothing but kind to me, and I owe you. It's just that—"

Abruptly, he stood, and the size of him made her stop talking. He towered over her five feet two inches, and, besides, something about a corseted dress made a woman feel ultrafeminine.

"No, Miss Long, it is I who owes you." He did not look at her while he spoke. "I cannot in good conscience leave you here in the mountains alone, so I will take you into Legend. There I'm sure you can find employment and a place to live, and you can come back here to search for your Indian pictures whenever possible. Is that acceptable to you?"

"Yes," she said hesitantly. It was perfect, but somehow, his suggestion made her feel as though she'd lost something. A friend, perhaps?

"Would you care to follow me, Miss Long?" he asked coolly, making Kady wince.

She very much wanted to make amends for having been so nasty about his marriage proposal, even if it had been made out of a sense of duty. "Mr. Jordan—" she began but broke off when he looked at her sharply, making her realize that she had not asked him his name. "The name Cole

Jordan is written on . . . I mean . . ." She didn't want him to know that she'd been snooping through his belongings.

The look he was giving her made her face flush, and she felt about two inches high.

"You have the advantage of me as you seem to know a great deal about me, while all I know of you is your name." His mouth curled into a tiny smile. "And your birth date, of course."

That smug little smile erased Kady's guilt. "Since I did save your life, I guess the least you can do is give me a ride into town." She took a deep breath and looked up at him. "Look, Mr. Jordan, I think we should make things clear between us. Whether you believe that I'm from another time or another town makes no difference. The truth is that I am engaged to marry a man I care for very much, and I'm not going to marry someone else just to get a roof over my head. Where I come from, women take care of themselves, and as it happens, I happen to be a cook, so I can get a job just about anywhere. Any year. So, please, forgive me; I did not mean to offend you, and I would like to keep you as my friend. But nothing more."

As she made this speech, he'd stood there watching her, his face unreadable, but then he gave a slow smile that made her think she should get as far away from him as possible. She was engaged, but she was also human.

"All right, Miss Long, we'll be friends," he said, holding out his hand for her to shake.

In an instant he seemed to change from being overly concerned to being just what she wanted, a friend. In silence, she followed him down the mountain and back to camp, thus giving Kady time to think.

It's best not to dwell on the horror of this situation and to look at it as an adventure, she told herself. Since she didn't seem able to return to her home right away, she should do what this man suggested and get a job, a place to live, and as Cole, er, ah, Mr. Jordan said, spend her weekends searching for the petroglyphs that would show her the opening in the rock.

And while she was looking, she'd get involved with no one because without a doubt there was a reason why she had been sent here. It was just that she didn't care what that reason was and had no intention of getting involved with it.

By the time they reached the camp, she was feeling much better. She was *not* going to allow this thing to defeat her!

"Perhaps you'd like to get yourself onto the horse," Cole said politely. "I would not like to interfere with your independence."

When he turned around, Kady made a little face at his back, then turned to look at the horse. She'd already climbed onto its back when she saved that ungrateful, unappreciative, overbearing, etc., man's life. However, the first time she'd climbed onto the horse, she'd been wearing many fewer pounds of clothing. Mounting a horse while wearing ten pounds of satin, complete with a train, was for an expert, which Kady was not.

As she heaved herself up repeatedly, then repeatedly fell back to the ground, Cole busied himself in destroying evidence of the camp. When he was finished, he leaned against the cottonwood tree, produced a knife, and began to trim his nails.

"All right," she said, not looking at him. "Maybe I would like some help."

"I wouldn't want to interfere. There's no hurry."

Turning, she looked at him, her eyes narrowed. "Exactly why *were* those men trying to hang you?"

She saw him try to hide a smile; then, slowly, as though he had all the time in the world, he resheathed his knife in his belt and moseyed over to her. For moments he stood looking down at her in puzzlement. "I don't want to presume on our friendship, but am I allowed to touch you?"

Kady glared at him, then raised her arms for him to lift her. He did so, setting her down in the saddle with a teeth-jarring thump. Kady grabbed the pommel to steady herself while he mounted behind her. She was in the awkward sidesaddle position and felt that she might fall off any second. If the voluminous skirt hadn't been trapping her legs, she would have slung one of them over the horse's neck.

After he'd mounted behind her, Cole's arms encircled her as he took the reins, but he kept his arms at a respectful distance. However, his big, strong body was pressed close to hers, and she had an urge to lean back against him. To distract herself, she decided to talk.

"What's this town of Legend like?"

"Like most any mining town."

"I've never seen a mining town in my life."

"Oh, yes, I forgot for a moment. You've only seen— Exactly what is it that you *have* seen in . . . What year would it be now in your world?"

"Nineteen ninety-six," she said tightly. "And I'd appreciate it if you didn't laugh at me. A choirboy like you couldn't survive in my world."

"Choirboy?" he asked, and she could feel his amusement. "Tell me, has the future invented new crimes besides murder and war?"

"No, people have just refined them. In my time we have illegal drugs and atomic bombs and food critics. We have automobiles that travel at fantastic speeds and crash into each other, and serial killers and air pollution. And we have men who—" She cut off because she didn't want to think of the things that she heard daily on the news. "Mine is a very fast world."

"And you want to go back to it? Except for a few horse thieves, my world's a pretty boring place."

"Right. You just have lynching parties. And smallpox and typhoid fever and cholera. And outdoor plumbing."

"You seem to know a lot about us."

"I've watched a lot of television."

"And what is television?"

As they'd been riding, Kady had leaned back against him and now was feeling rather comfortable. As she looked about her, at the incredible, breathtaking Colorado mountains, she couldn't seem to remember exactly what television was. She'd never seen the Rockies before, and she'd had no idea they were so beautiful. Maybe she and Gregory could open a restaurant here. Maybe they could persuade his mother to leave Onions and come here.

"Pretty, isn't it?" he said softly, reading her mind.

"Beautiful," she answered. "I grew up in Ohio, went to school in New York, and have worked in Virginia. I've never seen this."

He didn't answer, but she could feel that he was pleased that she liked the countryside.

"Truthfully, why were those men trying to hang you?" The motion of the horse and the strength of the man supporting her were making her feel so safe that she was becoming sleepy.

"They tried to take some of my cattle, and I protested."

"Do you have many cows?"

He hesitated before answering. "Very few. I told you, the Rockies aren't the best grazing land."

"Then do you work in a mine?"

"No."

One of those silent cowboys, she thought with a sigh, and missed Gregory. He was always willing to talk about his business or listen to Kady's stories of what had happened in the restaurant.

"What's this Grover like?" Cole said, and there was a definite sneer in his voice.

Kady was sure that wanting a man to be jealous was not psychologically correct, but it did feel good. She'd always been too busy learning to cook to spend much time with men. Before Gregory, she'd had surprisingly few dates.

"I don't know anyone named Grover," she said with exaggerated innocence. "I can't imagine who you mean."

"The one you're planning to marry."

"*Oooooh,* Gregory. Well, he's absolutely gorgeous, very black hair, dark eyes, honey-colored skin, and—"

"Any brains?" Cole asked tightly.

"A degree from the University of Virginia— in business, which he is very good at. Buys and sells land in California. He's almost rich, actually, and he's bought me a three-story town house in Alexandria. Oh!" she said when the horse stepped into a hole and Kady nearly went tumbling. But Cole's arms caught her—and kept holding her.

"And what about you?" she asked sweetly. "No wife or fiancée? What about a girlfriend?"

"None," he said. "Just me and Manuel, my old cook."

"And is he a very good cook?"

"If you like beans and chili so hot it can blister your tongue. You wouldn't like to work for me, would you? I could pay you—" He cut himself off. "Naw, you want to be independent, have your own job. Tell me, are all women a hundred years from now like you?"

It was obvious that he was laughing at her and had no belief that she had ever seen the twentieth century. "Most of them. We have careers and earn as much money as the men. Women can do anything, you know."

At that he snorted. "So who takes care of the kids?"

Kady opened her mouth to answer, but she thought a discussion of day care and nannies might not make the point she wanted to. "Having children is a choice, and the children are taken care of." Unfortunately, some rather horrible images of child abuse that she'd seen on the six o'clock news flashed before her eyes.

"But if the women work all day, who—"

"Is that the town of Legend?" she asked, changing the subject.

"No, it's a rock formation."

"Isn't that amazing, that it looks just like—"

"If you are from another time, not that you are, why are you here? And where did you get the picture of my family and my father's watch? We thought they were lost."

"Who is we?"

"My grandmother and me. She's the only relative I have left." He shifted his arms around her, making them just a bit tighter. "You do have an amazing ability to change the subject. What were you doing with my family's photo?"

"I bought an old flour tin, and when I opened it, this dress was in it, and on the bottom of the tin was the packet containing the photo and the watch."

When she said no more, he said, "Then what happened?"

"I don't know," Kady said quietly, not wanting to think of those horrible minutes when she wavered between two worlds. She still expected to wake up any minute and be back in her apartment. No matter what time it was, she'd call Gregory and tell him she loved him and—.

"Come on," Cole said softly, "don't turn coward on me now. You're Little Miss Independent, remember? You can do everything all by yourself. Are you *afraid* to tell me what happened?"

His tone said he was making fun of her. "I can take care of myself, if that's what you mean!" she said angrily.

He was chuckling. "There, that's better."

For a few moments they were silent. "Why did you ask me to marry you?" Kady asked.

He didn't answer right away. "To protect you. Because I owe you. I wouldn't be alive right now if it weren't for you. You know, I think ol' Harwood thought you were a ghost, coming out of the mountains in that white dress."

"I thought you were unconscious! How did you see anything?"

"I was saving my strength."

Twisting around in the saddle, she glared up at him. "If you were awake, then you could have helped me save you!"

"*Mmmm,*" was all he'd say, and Kady could see the smile he was trying to suppress.

She turned back around. "You could have crushed me when you fell off that horse."

Instead of answering, he smoothed a curl back from her face and tucked it behind her ear.

Somehow, the simple touch of putting her hair behind her ears was more intimate than anything else he had done, and Kady frowned at it. Yes, it was definitely better to get away from this man.

Chapter 6

THE TOWN OF LEGEND WAS NOT WHAT SHE'D EXPECTED.
Maybe it was her innate cynicism, but she'd expected filth
and saloons. As a kid she'd believed the beautiful movie
sets that showed pretty little houses with white picket
fences, but as an adult she'd realized that the women in
those cowboy shows had spent three hours having their
hair and makeup done. And the streets were swept daily by
the crew.

But as she rode into town on the horse in front of Cole,
she had to change her mind, for Legend looked like
something Walt Disney had created. It was clean and neat,
and the people were all nicely dressed and bustling about
with smiles on their faces.

They rode down one street that Cole told her was named
Eternity Road, then took a left down a well-maintained,
wide road named Kendal Avenue. They passed clean, tidy
shops, a hotel, a freight depot, livery stable, and a huge ice
cream parlor that looked like something from a Judy
Garland movie. She saw only one saloon, and it looked like
a place you could take the kids on Saturday night. Between

the buildings were vacant lots, some of them rather prettily landscaped.

What further astonished her was that she didn't see a gun anywhere. Not a single man was carrying a firearm. In fact, for the most part, everyone looked clean and prosperous and absolutely peaceful. Maybe it had been Cole's story about the deaths of his family, but she'd expected Legend to be a little more, well, dangerous.

"So much for the Wild West," she muttered, and remembered hearing that that had been a myth. If so, then Legend was proof of that myth.

"Where would you like me to drop you?" Cole asked.

"Anywhere they need a cook," she answered. As she and Cole had passed by, all the townspeople had stopped what they were doing and looked at them. Was it the sight of her in the blindingly white dress, or were they shocked at seeing a man and woman so close together in public? she wondered. From the looks of the picture-perfect town, the only sin in this place was staying up past nine P.M.

"How about the Palace Hotel?" he asked.

Much to her chagrin, Cole's words made a feeling of panic run through Kady. She was going to be *alone*. Alone in a strange town, in even a strange time period, for that matter. She knew nothing, really nothing, so how was she going to cope? For a second she almost threw her arms around Cole's neck and begged him not to leave her alone.

Be strong, Kady, she told herself.

"This will be fine," she said, taking a deep breath to keep her voice from shaking. He'd stopped before a plain board, two-story hotel, probably the largest building in town. And like the other buildings, it was clean and tidy with lace curtains at the windows.

After Cole dismounted, he put up his arms to help Kady down, then stood for a while looking down at her. "Are you sure you don't want to change your mind? I could take care of you."

For just a second Kady swayed toward him, but she was too self-reliant to give in to her impulses. She'd always taken care of herself, so she couldn't very well start now, at thirty, depending on some man to take care of her.

"I'm sure." She straightened her spine, then held out her hand to him. "Thank you, Mr. Jordan, for all that you have done for me, and I appreciate your concern."

Cole took the hand she offered and solemnly clasped it. His face was grim. "I've never done anything like this. You are a woman under my care, and I can't just leave you without any protection. What if you don't get a job?"

Kady's smile was smug. She had every confidence that all she had to do was cook for someone and she'd be hired. "Didn't you say that this was a mining town? It must be full of single men, and surely some of them will want a cook. Now, please go," she said, feeling her confidence returning. How could she not find a job?

"All right," he said reluctantly, "but I want a favor from you."

Warily, she said, "What?"

"Tomorrow at two o'clock I will meet you in front of the church. It's that way, near the end of this road, you can't miss it. I want you to show up there tomorrow and tell me that everything is all right with you so I can rest easy. Agreed?"

Kady smiled up at him. "All right, it's a deal. I'll be there at two on the dot and tell you about my wonderful new job, and maybe I'll even have found someone who knows where the petroglyphs are."

"That's a good idea," Cole said with a smile. "There are some old prospectors around here who know the mountains backwards and forwards. Maybe they'll remember the place." Still holding her hand, he gave it a squeeze. "Now, you behave yourself, and I wish you all the luck in the world."

With a little tug on the brim of his hat, he turned and walked down the cleanly swept boardwalk.

It would be hard to describe the depth of the emptiness Kady felt when she saw the back of Cole Jordan. She'd known him only a day, but he was the *only* person she knew in this town. "The only person I know in this century," she said as she watched him pause near a group of boys. They were playing marbles in the dirt, and Cole interrupted to hand them something he pulled from inside his pocket. Since she knew what his pockets contained, she knew he wasn't giving them candy. What was he giving them then?

Money, she thought as the kids looked into their palms, then took off running in the direction of the ice cream parlor that she knew was just around a bend in the road.

"Choirboy," she said to herself, then tossed her train over her arm and went inside the hotel. Maybe she should have asked Cole to buy her a new dress, she thought. But no, a clean break from him was better.

Inside, the hotel was just as she'd imagined, quietly busy, filled with well-dressed men and women walking sedately arm in arm. Through a doorway she could see an area filled with horsehair-covered furniture, a huge Persian rug on the floor. To her left stood a high counter, with pigeonhole mailboxes behind it and a nice-looking young man writing in an enormous ledger.

Smiling, she went to the clerk. "Could I see the manager? Or the person in charge of hiring people?" she asked politely.

The man looked down at her white silk gown, then raised one eyebrow. Did he think she'd been stood up at her wedding? Kady wondered, feeling embarrassed. Number one on her agenda was to get a new dress. Maybe she could get an advance on her salary.

One o'clock, Kady thought, looking up at the clock on the tower on top of the firehouse. One more hour to go before she was to meet Cole and she could see the church from here.

What was she going to tell him? she wondered. Would she have to go onto her knees to beg him to buy her a meal? At the mere thought of food, her stomach growled. Due to how little she had eaten since coming through the rock, she could pull her corset in another couple of inches.

Turning from the firehouse, she started walking toward the church but had to stop. Not too fast, she told herself, save your energy. Trying to keep her shoulders back and her pride intact, she walked slowly down the dusty road, doing her best to ignore the townspeople who passed her.

Kady was sure that by now they knew all about her, how she'd arrogantly told the hotel manager that she was a better cook than anyone he'd ever had at his hotel. Just as arrogantly, he told her he didn't want any women in his kitchen, inciting the men to who knew what acts. He hadn't even considered giving Kady a job.

So much for equal rights, she had told herself as she left the hotel. So the first place she'd tried had turned her down. So what? There was an entire town full of employment opportunities; she'd find something somewhere.

But as night drew near and Kady still had no place to sleep, she began to give up hope that anyone would give her a job, and her despondency began to grow. When the cold Colorado night began to descend, she remembered with great fondness how Cole's warm body had held her during the night before.

By nightfall she'd tried nearly every shop in town. She'd even made her way out to the Tarik Mine and begged a job there. To her great humiliation, when the mine manager told her that a woman who looked like her would cause riots among the men, she had burst into tears. For a moment the he'd looked as though he was going to relent, but he'd glanced at another man who'd shaken his head no, so the manager did not give in. He did, however, say she could ride back to town on one of the wagons full of ore.

As Kady walked to the wagon with the two men, she saw

an open tent set up under the trees, with trestle tables inside, and the tables were covered with food. From the smell of it, everything was fried in the same grease that had been used to lubricate the wagon wheels, but at the moment the smell of any food made Kady's mouth water.

She forgot her pride. "Could I have something to eat?" she asked, and she could see by the manager's eyes that he was going to say yes. But the other man, his lieutenant, his evil wizard, as Kady saw him, firmly took her arm and told her that a mining camp was no place for a lady. Before Kady could think of an appropriately nasty reply, he half lifted her onto a hard board wagon seat and told the driver to go.

Within minutes she was back in town, and the driver let her out at the depot, where the silver ore would be weighed before being hauled down the mountain. Across from her was the laundry, so Kady went in and asked if they needed any help. She wasn't in the least surprised when they told her no.

Across the street, behind the ice cream parlor, was a large park, with big cottonwood trees and grassy lawns. At one end was what looked like a sports field with bleachers set up.

By the time she reached the sports field, night had fallen, and she was shivering. In the moonlight she could see what looked to be a perfect little schoolhouse, with a bell tower on top of the building and a little porch on the front. Half staggering, both from hunger and exhaustion, Kady made her way to the building, and when she found the front door unlocked, she offered a prayer of thanks, then went inside. By comparison with the outside, the schoolhouse was a haven of warmth. In the little cloakroom she found a couple of forgotten coats and what smelled like a horse blanket, put them on the floor, lay down on them, rolled them around her, and went to sleep.

When she awoke the next morning, the sun was up, and it took her moments to remember where she was. When she did, she refused to allow herself to feel any self-pity. Her mother had told her that self-pity was a bottomless well and once a person fell into it, you kept falling forever.

Since there were no children clamoring to be let in the next morning, Kady assumed it was Saturday, or maybe Sunday. She could barely keep up with the year, much less the day of the week.

She spent some time searching the schoolhouse for something she could wear. Maybe her dress, so unforgivably white in the brilliant mountain sun, was the reason she could not get a job. Or wasn't even given a chance to prove that she could do the job, she thought with some bitterness.

As she was about to leave the schoolhouse, she saw a mirror on the far wall and went to look at herself, then nearly screamed in horror. *This* was the woman who the mine manager said would cause trouble among the men?

Her hair, once clean and neatly pinned, was now dirty and as tangled as a cold dish of angel hair pasta. Her face had a black streak across one cheek. "Wonder how long that's been there?" she said aloud as she rubbed at the dirt.

As for her dress, it hardly resembled the beautiful creation she'd pulled out of the flour tin. One shoulder was torn at the seam, from when she'd caught it as she beat a hasty retreat from the sawmill. There was a black smudge covering one whole side of the skirt where she'd brushed it against a sooty stove in the newspaper office. A young man, with a pencil behind his ear, had aggressively asked her questions about her reasons for being in town and her relationship with Cole Jordan and where did she live and did she know anything about the recent robberies and why was she asking questions around town and was she one of the members of the gang and who had stood her up at her wedding and did her fiancé find out about her involvement with the robbers and where did they bury the loot and what—?

Kady had run from the office so fast she'd nearly

knocked the stove over. Thank heaven it hadn't been lit or she might have set herself on fire. "At least I would have been able to cook *something*," she muttered, as she trudged down the street.

After the cold night in the schoolhouse, she'd had no more luck the morning of the second day. She'd started knocking on the doors of houses. Once she'd looked into the kind eyes of a gray-haired woman and asked her for something to eat. The woman's face had dissolved into pity, and Kady felt the woman had been about to speak when her husband appeared by her side, glared at Kady, and said, "We don't take kindly to beggars in this town," then shut the door in Kady's face.

So now Kady was walking toward the church to meet Cole. What attitude should she take? That everything was fine and she needed no help? Should she keep her pride at all costs?

Odd how pride fled when one's belly was involved. When she got back to the twentieth century, maybe she'd write a book titled *Time Travel: The New Weight-Loss Plan.*

Dignity, she told herself as she walked along the road, she must keep her dignity. There was a long hill just behind the firehouse, crosswise of the road, with a short hedge running atop the ridge. As Kady walked up and over this hill, past the hedge, the town seemed to change. The part of Legend that she'd seen was pretty, but on the other side of the hedge, the town seemed to blossom into heaven. The road forked right and left and the church stood to the left. On the right was a perfect little building with a big porch and round-topped windows. A sign across the front said Legend Library. To the right of the library was a long dirt drive that led up a slight hill, and Kady had to blink twice at what she saw at the end of the drive. Unless she missed her guess, the beautiful white building, with the distinctive dome top, was a mosque.

She'd certainly never heard of a mosque in the Old West! she thought as the turned toward the church. Flowers grew beside the perfectly kept road, and the churchyard was a blanket of tiny blue blossoms amid the luxurious grass. Obviously, Legend's mines were prospering if they could afford to keep public buildings in this state.

As she neared the church, she could hear singing, and it made her smile. Perhaps the church people would have more pity on her situation. Perhaps she could talk to the pastor and he could help her find employment. Why hadn't she thought of that before?

Slowly, Kady climbed the steps of the church and sat down heavily in the shade of the porch overhang to wait for Cole. He would, of course, buy her a meal, she thought, then smiled at the prospect.

She didn't have to wait long, for he rode up on his horse just minutes later, and the sight of him made Kady feel relief. He was her friend; he'd help her.

"Am I late?" he asked anxiously. "I thought I was to meet you at two."

"No," she said, smiling, wishing with all her heart that her hair were clean and she had on something other than a filthy, torn wedding dress. "I'm early."

He took his time dismounting, slowly came up the stairs, then hesitated as though deciding what to do. "I'm to rehearse my solo for the service tomorrow. The pastor is leaving town for a couple of weeks, so we need music to fill up the time. After a couple of songs from me, they'll be begging for his return." He was grinning at her, not a care in the world, as though he didn't see what a mess she was.

He took a step toward the door, then turned back and sat down on the step beside her. "Are you all right?"

Part of Kady wanted to say that yes, everything was grand, but her stomach growled, so she couldn't lie. "No, nothing is all right."

He took her dirty hand in his big, warm, clean one. "Want to tell me about it? How's your new job?"

"I have no job!" she said passionately, but when he glanced at the half-open church door, she quietened. "No one would hire me. No one anywhere, not in a public kitchen or private. I even applied at the laundry, and they turned me down too."

"Family owned," he said, making her look at him in question. "The laundry is Mr. Simmons's, and he has six daughters, so he'd not want to pay an outsider."

Kady looked at him hard. Was he missing the point? "I couldn't find any job anywhere," she said evenly. "No one would hire me."

"Did you try the mines?"

She blinked, then said in a steady, slow voice as though explaining to an idiot, "I tried the Tarik Mine, but I didn't go to the others because they were too far away. I'm on foot. And in this dress it's a bit difficult to get around."

"Ah, yes. Bet you the manager was nice, but his foreman sent you away."

"Yes," she said, looking at him in wonder, since he still didn't seem to be understanding what her problem was.

"Last month the foreman's girlfriend in Denver married someone else, and he's, well, a bit off women at the moment. Doesn't want to see any of them." Cole put her hand back in her lap. "Rotten luck that you tried the Tarik first. I'm sure the Lily or the Amaryllis needs a cook. And what about the jail? It's a couple of miles out of town, on the way to Denver, but maybe they need someone." He glanced at the church door. "I have to go now. Thanks for coming, and I'm very glad to see that you're all right."

For a moment Kady sat there in stunned silence. He couldn't be going to leave her just like that, could he? "Cole!" she hissed at him, making him turn back, his body half inside the church.

"Yes, Miss Long?" he whispered so he wouldn't disturb the people singing in the church.

"I am *not* all right," she said. "I'm not all right at all." Then, to her disgust, she began to cry. Turning her face away so he wouldn't see her, she looked back when he handed her a clean handkerchief. He had seated himself beside her and was waiting with a small frown on his face. No doubt he was annoyed that she was keeping him from choir practice. She was in danger of starving to death, and he was worried he'd be late for choir practice!

"I don't mean to keep you here, but I . . . I need help," she said, the words foreign to her. Even in the kitchen she refused to ask the men to lift the huge copper stockpots; she liked to do things by herself.

"What can I do to help you?" he asked softly.

"I can't find a job," she repeated. "No one needs a cook; no one will even give me a chance to prove that I *can* cook."

He was silent.

Kady blew her nose. "Aren't you going to say anything?"

"I don't know what to say. You've made it clear that you don't want me to protect you, so there is nothing I can do. I can't very well force someone to give you a job, now can I? It's not as though I own the town." He chuckled at this thought.

"But couldn't you put in a good word—"

"If I did that, later you would hate me. You'd think I'd interfered in something that was none of my business and you'd hate me. Miss Long, I value your friendship too much to do anything to jeopardize it."

He patted her hand, glanced toward the church door, and looked as though he was going to leave again.

Kady grabbed his arm. "I wouldn't hate you no matter what. You've lived in this town all your life and—"

"Actually, I came here when I was four."

"That doesn't matter!" she gasped, then took a breath to calm herself. "All I'm asking is that you talk to some people."

He looked at her in sympathy. "The problem is that there are ten people for every job. When we needed a new schoolteacher, every man's wife and half the daughters in this town wanted the job. The town council had a devil of a time choosing just one person. It's the silver, you see. Legend is fairly rich in silver, and everyone wants to be here in hopes of striking it rich." His face lit up. "I could take you to Denver. Maybe there you'd find—"

"No! I can't leave here because I must find the rocks where I came through. If I'm ever to get back, that's the way."

Turning away, he looked out toward the lovely lawn in front of the church. "Ah, yes, Gilford."

"Gregory," Kady said. "The name of the man I love is *Gregory*."

Cole kept his face turned away, but she could see a tiny smile playing at the corner of his lips, as though what she'd said were a great joke.

But none of this was a joke to Kady, she thought as, once again, she buried her face in her hands. "You have to help me. I'm hungry. I haven't had anything to eat in—"

She broke off because Cole let out a rather loud belch.

"I do beg your pardon," he said, his hand to his mouth. "Beans. It's the only thing Manuel knows how to cook. It's beans for breakfast, beans for lunch, beans for supper. Beans and—"

"I can cook something besides beans," Kady said brightly, looking up at him with pleading eyes. "I can cook *anything*."

Cole looked at her with the eyes of a man explaining the very simplest concepts of life. "You are an independent, self-supporting woman, and I respect that. I know you take a great deal of pride in being able to care for yourself with the help of no one else on earth, so how could I—"

"Cut it out," she snapped. "You don't need to make me grovel. So you were right. At least you were right in this time and this place."

"Is that an apology? A full apology or half of one?"

"It's all you're going to get, so be thankful for it."

Cole gave her a little grin.

"Stop gloating and take me out and buy me the biggest meal this town has to offer. It'll be my final meal before I become your food slave."

He arched an eyebrow. "As opposed to what other kind of slave?"

"Just feed me and let's go."

But Cole didn't move, and his face lost its teasing look. "Kady, I can't give you a job."

"Because I said—"

Taking both her hands in his, he looked into her eyes. "You may have noticed that Legend isn't like other mining towns. No, that's right, you said you'd never been to a mining town, so you'll just have to trust me that it is different. Other towns have a lawlessness about them that we don't allow here in Legend."

She didn't understand. "It's illegal for me to cook for you?"

"No, of course not. It's just where I live."

At that she looked at him. He was clean, and the blue cotton shirt he had on had been ironed within an inch of its life. Somehow, she couldn't imagine Cole Jordan living in a shack.

"I live in a place out of town, that way," he said, nodding toward the east. "There are no other houses near me, and, well, Miss Long, it just wouldn't look right for you and me to live there alone with just old Manuel and a few ranch hands for chaperons." His eyes showed sadness. "After choir practice I can take you out for a meal, but I really don't know what else I can do. I can't force anyone to hire a cook they don't need. I'd give you all the money I have, but the whole town would know in a minute, and, well, your reputation would suffer." His voice lowered. "This is a town full of men, and if you were taking money from me, they might think you were a different kind of woman than what you really are."

Kady had a vision of drunken cowboys, liquored up after a trail drive, tearing down the door to her cheap hotel room and . . . She shook her head to clear it. "Too many movies, Elizabeth Kady," she heard her mother's voice saying in her head.

Cole pressed her hands in his. "I really don't know how to help you." He glanced at the door to the church. "I must go now. After choir practice, we can talk more. Maybe I can persuade someone to take you in. Some people in town owe me favors, so maybe—"

Kady's grimace made him cut off. "Charity," she said under her breath and imagined how uncomfortable it would be to live as an unwanted guest in a stranger's house.

It was at that moment that Kady changed her attitude. Extraordinary problems called for extraordinary solutions. As Gregory's handsome face flashed before her eyes, she thought how his mysterious dark looks were such a contrast to Cole's blue-eyed blondness, Cole's open and guileless face.

She loved Gregory, loved him very much, but he wasn't here. He wasn't even born yet, and she wouldn't be doing him any favor if she kept her pride and starved to death before she could get back to him.

After taking a deep breath to give herself courage, she straightened her shoulders and looked into Cole's candid blue eyes. "Is your marriage proposal still open?" she asked, and instantly she could see the shock on his face.

"You're engaged to marry someone else."

"Desperate times call for desperate measures."

Cole gave her a look that said, *Thanks a lot.*

"You know what I mean."

He looked down at her hands, still resting in his. "I offered marriage in the heat of the moment. I felt grateful to you for saving me, but now I wonder what people would say. I'm afraid they'll—"

"Why, you low-down, lying bastard!" she said, snatching her hands from his. "Here I am starving, *starving!* mind you, and all you can think of is what this overly manicured little town will say. Let me tell you, Mr. Jordan, that this town isn't worth thinking about. They'd let a lone woman starve to death before they'd sully their pristine reputations.''

She was so angry she forgot about her hunger and exhaustion and stood, which allowed her to look down at him. "Right now I wish I hadn't saved that overly muscled neck of yours. And when I'm found dead in some alley, my death is going to be on *your* head!"

With that utterly magnificent riposte, she grabbed her train, slung it over her arm and started down the stairs. Unfortunately for her self-esteem, she tripped over Cole's big feet and went tumbling forward. But he caught her in his arms and pulled her back to sit on his lap.

Kady was so angry she wouldn't look at him, but held herself as rigid as possible.

"I guess I do owe you a favor."

"No one has to marry *me* as a *favor*," she said through clenched teeth. "And put me down before one of your 'Legendary' saints sees us together."

Her play on the town's name made him smile. "Too late," he said, his smile widening.

Kady rolled her head back to look up at the entire choir of Legend, Colorado, as they jammed themselves together in the doorway to stare in open fascination at her and Cole.

"I'm afraid that now I have no other choice except to marry you," he said. "Now that I have—"

"So help me, if you say that you've ruined my reputation, I'll throw up on you."

For a moment Cole looked at her half in amusement, half in shock, then he glanced up at the choir, still staring as though they were natives seeing their first peep show. "If you will excuse us, Miss Long and I need to discuss a few matters in private."

When the spectators were gone, Cole looked back at Kady, opened his mouth to speak, but instead, looked down at her. The way she was positioned in his arms made the tops of her breasts push up out of the dress until they were nearly popping out of the neckline. And the tight dress showed off every curve of Kady's lush figure. She might be thought to have a "weight problem" in the late twentieth century, but she'd already been in this century long enough to know that here a woman was supposed to look like a woman.

"Touch me and you die," she hissed, her nose a quarter inch from his.

For a moment he just looked at her; then with a sigh of reluctance, he slowly set her back on the porch step beside him. "You are right," he said after a while. "I do owe you. I owe you my life, and I did offer to marry you, so I must—"

He stopped when he saw Kady's tight-lipped glare.

"I would be honored to marry you," he said solemnly. "Honored and pleased. And I want you to know that I respect your unusual circumstances, so you are under no obligation to perform your wifely duties. Unless you want to, that is," he added.

Kady hadn't really thought that far ahead. Right now she wanted a meal, a bath, and a bed, in that order. Her anger at this man was taking the last of her energy.

Kady drew a deep breath, but no matter how much she tried to calm herself, her voice still came out with a nervous tremor. "Yes," she said in a tiny voice.

"Pardon? I couldn't hear you."

She glared at him. "I can't quite put my finger on it, but there is something about you that I truly dislike. Only starvation would make me marry you."

He gave her a smug little smile. "Maybe I could find another man to take care of you. I'm sure someone somewhere would be willing to marry you."

She ignored his snide remark, refusing to think of what might befall her if she found herself married to a man who didn't own a badge for continuous church attendance. "I want to remind you that you owe me," she said levelly. "I saved your life and as for my wifely duties, if you try to force me to do anything I don't want to, I'll—"

The voice that cut her off was angry. "I do not force women or harm them in any way," he said, his jaw clenched. "I am marrying you as a necessary way of protecting you. It is as you say, I owe you. Now, if you are through disparaging my character, would you like to go into the church and get married or not?" he asked. "You are free to leave if don't want to marry me."

Kady knew she'd been put in her place. Maybe she was making more of this than there was. He had told her he thought she was beautiful, but that had obviously not sent him into uncontrollable lust. As he'd said, he could have forced her when they were alone near the Hanging Tree, but he hadn't.

A wave of guilt overtook Kady. "Marriage is very serious, and you must know that I will go back to my home the very second I can," she said. "Aren't you involved with some girl you'd rather marry? Maybe some woman is going to be furious when she finds out that a man she thought was hers has—"

"Pretty much all the women in this town are in love with me," he said solemnly. "Even the married ones want to widow themselves so they can marry me. Women follow me down the street like so many baby ducks. I have to change my sleeping place every night to foil their attempts to find me because they seduce me all—"

Kady grabbed his arm. "Shut up, and let's get this over with. The sooner this is done, the sooner I can get something to eat."

"After you," Cole said, smiling at her and pushing the door to the church open wider. "Mrs. Jordan," he said under his breath.

Chapter 7

KADY AWOKE BECAUSE HER SCALP WAS ITCHING FURIOUSLY, and there was something constricting her breathing. When she opened her eyes, it took her a moment to focus on the ceiling, which was constructed of closely set posts. Idly, she wondered when her landlord had redecorated and why he'd decided to give the rustic look to an apartment in Alexandria, Virginia.

Turning her head, she looked about the place as she rubbed her eyes and tried to clear what seemed to be pounds of crusty sleep from them. A cabin, she thought, a mountain cabin. One room, very clean, all homemade furniture, blue calico curtains on the windows.

Abruptly, Kady sat up as memory came flooding back to her. She was no longer in Virginia but in the mountains of Colorado, and the year was 1873.

For a moment she buried her face in her hands and remembered all that had happened in the last few days, especially what had happened yesterday. Cole Jordan, a man she hardly knew, had escorted her into a church that was nearly crushed under the weight of the flowers that adorned it. Kady's eyes had widened as she looked at the

81

lilies and roses and great swags of wildflowers that hung from every conceivable surface.

"There's a wedding later today," Cole had said, smiling down at her dirty face. "Or maybe the flowers are for us."

"Then they should all be dead," she said quietly, not meaning for him to hear, but he did, and she felt bad for the hurt on his face. It really was nice of him to help her in this way; it was just that this was not what she'd hoped for her marriage. She'd wanted her friends there, Jane and Debbie, and she'd wanted to look beautiful, not as though she'd spent the night in a coal bin.

As she walked down the aisle, she glanced up at Cole, saw the way the sunlight glanced off his blond hair, and she nearly ran out the back of the church. She'd wanted to walk down the aisle with Gregory, with the man she loved and not this stranger.

A minister was standing at the head of the church under a lovely arch of greenery and tiny white flowers. Had this been someone else's wedding, Kady would have marveled at how beautiful everything was. The choir was singing, but she could hardly hear them. At her wedding to Gregory, she had planned to have a soprano from the New York Opera Company sing.

She hadn't been aware when the minister had started the service, so she wasn't aware when he stopped it. She was only aware when she felt the eyes of everyone in the church on her.

Still holding her arm tightly as though if he let go, she'd flee, Cole handed Kady his handkerchief. She had no idea when she started crying. Not the great wrenching, noisy sobs that she could feel inside her body, just hot tears slowly running down her cheeks in a steady stream.

"Don't mind me, I always cry at weddings," she said to the minister, then, after a confirming look at Cole, he continued.

Somewhere during the short ceremony, Kady said what she was supposed to, so eventually she heard the words that declared she was now married to this man. Bracing herself, she expected him to kiss her. He had that right now, didn't he?

But Cole didn't kiss her. Instead, he accepted the congratulations of the choir members, never letting go of Kady's arm, and after a while, he led her out of the church onto the porch. There they were pelted with rice as the people wished Cole and his bride the best of luck and happiness forever. They also hoped the two of them would have a hundred children.

Amid all the laughter of friends, no one seemed to notice that Kady didn't say a word.

Cole helped her onto his horse, then, still fending off pelting rice, he led them past the church, then took a left and followed a deep creek until they came to a cluster of log buildings. To their right was a large opening in the side of a mountain that could only be one of Legend's silver mines.

"The Lily Mine," Cole said, the first words he'd said to her since their "marriage"—if that loveless ceremony could be called that. Cole dismounted, talked to a couple of men for a moment, then turned to help Kady down.

He led her to a small white tent, and inside was a little table covered with a white cloth, a broken and mended ceramic vase of wildflowers in the center.

"We'll bring you some food in a minute," one of the men who'd followed them in said. "You just tell us anything you need, Mrs. Jordan, and we'll do our best to get it for you."

It was the name that nearly did Kady in. She'd so looked forward to being called Mrs. Norman, but instead she had been given this stranger's name. "Thank you," she said, but the tears running down her cheeks increased in volume.

"Well, ah, yes, well, I'll leave you two alone," the man said, backing out of the tent nervously.

As Cole held a chair for her, Kady nearly fell down onto it. She'd sold herself for a plate of mush, she thought, her head on her hands.

Reaching across the table, Cole took one of her hands. "I'm not as bad you seem to think," he said softly. "Honest."

She forced a little smile. "I know. I am being horribly ungrateful, and I apologize. If you'd appeared in my time, I don't think I would have taken your predicament to heart the way you have mine. I wouldn't have made the personal sacrifice that you have. I do thank you."

"Good," he said, smiling. "Now, what do you want for a wedding gift?"

"Soap," she said without hesitation. "And a hot bath."

"Wise choice," he answered seriously, making Kady give a tiny bit of a smile.

She started to say more, but the tent flap was pulled back and in came the food, great quantities of it, all of it set on the table until it nearly collapsed under the weight.

Kady lost no time digging in, reaching into each dish with her fork, not bothering with putting it on the chipped plate that had been set before her. Cole also ate, but he was more interested in watching Kady.

"You like our Colorado cooking?" he asked.

"I would like to see the man's skillet," she said, mouth full.

"His skillet?"

"I figure the cook has a skillet big enough to fry a whole sheep, head, hooves, and all, and he half filled the skillet with lard, then cooked all of this food in the grease."

Cole blinked at her. "How else do you cook?"

So much information filled Kady's head that she could form no words. She just kept eating, one vegetable, one meat indistinguishable from another. Even the baking-powder biscuits had been fried in the grease. But now she was so hungry she'd have to worry about her arteries later.

After Kady had eaten all she could hold, she was

overcome with sleepiness. Yawning, she said, "How far away is your house?"

"Not far," he said in a way that, had she been less tired, would have annoyed Kady. He said it as though the location of his house was secret, something mysterious.

Kady didn't meet his eyes because she didn't want him to see what she'd already figured out. Cole was embarrassed that he was a poor cowboy, probably with only a horse and half a dozen cows to his name. His clean clothes to the contrary, she wondered if the place he lived in was any better than a shack.

"It's all right," she said softly. "It doesn't matter where I live. I won't be here long anyway."

He'd smiled at her, then tucked a curl of her hair behind her ear. "Where *we* live," he said, then withdrew his hand when Kady pulled away from him, a look of fear on her face.

Cole turned away but not before she'd seen the look of hurt on his face. He didn't think this was going to be a *real* marriage, did he? she thought. He couldn't. Not after all the things she'd said. Not after—

"Ready to leave?" he asked, pulling back her chair.

At least his manners are nice, she thought as she followed him out to the horse. Outside, the stars were overhead, and the night was quite cool, and when she was mounted in front of him, the position felt almost familiar. It seemed quite natural to lean back against his solid form, and feeling his strong arms around her, she fell asleep.

That was the last she remembered until she awoke this morning in the bed, looking up at the cabin ceiling. As her memory came back to her, she peeled the pile of blankets and quilts back to see that she was in her underwear, what she'd stripped down to when she'd first seen Cole. It didn't take a great detective to see that the space next to her, the side between her and the door, was indented from a larger, heavier form having slept there.

Rolling out of bed, Kady knew that she had to stop

looking at the past, what could have been, and start looking toward the future. She had to do whatever she could to get back home.

Flung over the back of a pine chair was the wedding dress that had caused all her problems, and for a moment she grabbed the torn, dirty garment, then raised her hand to fling it into the stone fireplace where a nice little fire burned cheerfully. But something held her back. Maybe it was her belief that it had been Cole's mother's dress that stopped her. Neither his mother nor he deserved to have such disrespect paid to a dress that had been meant for happiness.

There was a wooden chest against one wall, so Kady went to it, lifted the lid, meaning to put the dirty dress in there out of sight. But as she put the gown in one end of the chest, she saw what looked like boy's clothes: shirts, worn trousers, underwear, even boots and socks. Kady was sure that nothing in the world had ever pleased her as much as the sight of those clean, soft clothes. Now, if she could only find a bar of soap and a stream, she'd be clean for the first time in days.

But search as she might, she could find no soap. She did find an interesting heap of food supplies that she wanted to explore later, but what she wanted most, soap, was nowhere to be had. "So much for wedding gifts," she said as she went toward the cabin door, still wearing the underwear, the boy's clothes over her arm.

For just a second, her hand on the door latch, she thought that maybe the door would be locked. When the latch lifted easily, she told herself her fears were ridiculous. Cole Jordan was a very nice man who sang in the church choir. He was not a monster who imprisoned women.

The outhouse was in back of the house, up a little hill, or more correctly, further up the mountainside. Inside, Kady was intrigued to see a rope attached to one wall, a big blue calico bow tied to it. The rope went out through a knothole in the back of the sturdy little building.

When she left the outhouse, she walked around to the back and saw that the rope led into the trees. There were blue bows tied every few feet along the rope.

Curious, Kady followed the line, wondering where it would lead. Had Cole planned an ambush? A sexual tryst in the woods, maybe? With every step she took, she became a bit more cautious, hesitating now and then, looking about her in case he should pounce from behind a tree. They were married now, so he would think he had every right to do what he wanted to her, wouldn't he?

When Kady came to the end of the rope, she stood and stared, not believing what she was seeing. She'd always heard that Colorado had hot springs, and this divine little pool before her was obviously one of them. Steam rose from the warm water. Around the stone sides of the little pool were bunches of wildflowers and what had to be—oh, deliciousness!—at least six bars of soap. And there were three blue towels stacked on a rock just outside the pool.

Tears came to Kady's eyes. Cole Jordan really was the very nicest man! she thought as her hands tore at the fastenings of the clothing she wore. It flashed through her mind that he might be spying on her, but at the moment she didn't care. When she unhooked the corset and it fell to her feet, Kady breathed a great sigh of relief, then took so many deep breaths of the thin mountain air that she felt dizzy.

The other clothes quickly followed, and when she was naked, she cautiously stuck one toe into the pool. The water temperature was perfect!

Never in her life had Kady enjoyed a bath as much as this one. The water was fed by an underground spring, so it was replenished constantly. She lathered her body and her hair, sliding down under the water to rinse.

She probably spent at least an hour in the pool, until her skin was shriveled and her hair was squeaky clean. Reluctantly, she emerged and grabbed a towel to wrap around her naked body. When a comb fell from the first towel, she wasn't in the least surprised, as Cole seemed to have thought of everything.

By the time she got back to the cabin, she was a new woman. The boy's clothes fit her quite well, if she belted them tightly so the pants wouldn't fall down and rolled up the cuffs so they didn't drag the ground. She was a bit large busted to go without a bra, but she wasn't about to put that corset back on.

She half expected to see Cole in the cabin, but there was no sign of him, so Kady set about organizing the food supplies. There wasn't much variety: flour, beans, bacon, potatoes, dried fruit, dried peas. "How do I make bread with no yeast?" she asked aloud, then gave a cry of delight when she pulled the plug of a small keg and found it was full of beer. *"Biga!"* she said, giving the Italian name to the yeasty mixture that could be used to make bread. She could have used the potatoes to make the yeast, but beer would be quicker. Under the bags of flour was a crock full of butter and a basket of eggs.

Within minutes, Kady had food started. She mixed the beer with the flour to make a mixture that would form yeast, scoured the enamel coffeepot with sand, and used it for clarifying the butter so it would keep longer. After drawing water from a huge barrel in the corner of the room, she put the beans in an iron pot to soak. She had to make her own baking powder from soda and cream of tartar before mixing a batch of biscuits. Climbing on the bed, she pulled an Indian pot from a shelf high on the wall and was glad to see that the inside of it was glazed. She set the dried fruits to soaking in the pot.

Only when these things were done did she make herself an omelet. She hadn't done much cooking in an open fireplace, but she always loved to try new equipment and new foods, so she enjoyed the heat on her face. There was an iron spider, a sort of Dutch oven on legs, rusting at the side of the hearth, and after cleaning it and smearing it with butterfat, Kady set the biscuits to bake in the coals.

When they were done, she removed them, then made a cobbler from the dried peaches.

By now hours had passed, and Cole still had not returned. Kady had no watch, but she could tell from the sun coming through the windows that it was late afternoon. He hadn't put her in this cabin then gone off and left her, had he? she wondered, then told herself that could not be possible.

When another half hour or so went by and still there was no sign of Cole, she removed the eggs from the basket and filled it with what she'd cooked so far. She'd found a bottle of vinegar, so now if she could just find something to pickle, she thought, she'd make condiments to go with whatever game she could find.

With the basket over her arm, a blanket about her shoulders, and feeling a bit like Little Red Riding Hood, she set off into the forest to look for the Big Bad Wolf. At this thought she gave a little laugh, then told herself that this was definitely the wrong attitude. She had to remember that her one goal in life was to get out of this place. She didn't have time to make bread and pickles. Didn't have time to wander about the woods smelling clean, pure air that had never known the fumes of the diesel engine.

Cole wasn't difficult to find. Just a few feet from the cabin, down a sharp incline was a wide, deep stream. He was standing in it, naked from the waist up, a fishing rod in his hand, and concentrating on what he was doing. The sight of him nearly took Kady's breath away. He was one beautiful man! His upper body was sculpted with muscle over broad shoulders and a deep chest, all of it tapering to a waist that couldn't be more than thirty-two inches.

"Ever done any fishing?" he asked softly, not turning, but showing Kady that he'd known all along that she was there.

"I'm more familiar with what to do with them after they're caught," she said, trying to sound as though she wasn't affected by the sight of him. With her eyes averted, she went down the hill to stand on a flat, grassy spot by the stream, then spread the blanket and put the basket down.

When she looked back up at Cole, she could not control her involuntary gasp. What she had not seen from up the hill was that there were at least half a dozen ugly round scars on his torso that had to have been made by bullets.

As though he didn't know what could have caused Kady's gasp, he looked down at his chest, then back up at her. "Hand me my shirt and I'll put it on," he said, looking at her in question.

"No, that's all right. I didn't mean to stare," she said, turning away, but she couldn't contain herself and turned back abruptly. "Who did that to you? Those men who tried to hang you?"

Cole was looking at the water, pulling on his fishing line, but she could see by his little smile that he was pleased by her concern.

"No, it happened when I was a kid. When my sister and friend were shot, so was I." He hesitated. "I made it, they didn't," he said softly.

Looking at the scars, Kady didn't want to think of the pain he must have gone through to recover from wounds like those.

"I've been told that kisses heal all wounds," he said and when she looked at his face, she saw that he was teasing her, his eyes sparkling.

"Doesn't look like they've done any good so far," she said, turning away from him.

"I figure the kisses were never from the right woman." He'd left the water and walked up behind her. "What's in the basket?"

He was standing too close, so she stepped away. "Just bacon and biscuits and——" Her voice lowered. "A peach cobbler."

"Oh?" He stepped close to her again. "Washed your hair, didn't you? Like the soap I got for you?"

"Very nice." She turned on him, glaring. "Get on *that* side of the blanket and don't come near me."

For some reason, this declaration made him laugh as he walked to the stream and pulled out a long string of trout.

I shall smoke them, Kady thought, then corrected herself. She was going home and wouldn't have time to smoke fish. "Build a fire; I'll go get a skillet and some wild onions I saw, and we'll have lunch."

"Yes, ma'am," she heard him say as she raced up the hill, grabbing the onions as she went. What a cooking challenge, she thought as she ran. Here she didn't have every ingredient known in the world at her fingertips, as she did in Virginia. No lemongrass, no star anise, not even any olive oil. *Wonder if I could make—* she thought, then made herself stop. She wasn't going to be here long enough to make anything.

Be firm, Kady, she told herself. *You must demand that Cole take you to the rocks tomorrow. And if he refuses, you must go by yourself.* Even as she thought this, she realized that she didn't know the way back to town, much less the way to a bunch of carved rocks.

By the time she got back with the skillet, Cole had the fire going and was lounging on the blanket, eating what looked to be his third buttered biscuit. Right away she noticed that he hadn't bothered to clean the fish, but that was all right as Kady had her own way of cleaning and deboning trout.

"What do you need?" he asked when, minutes later, she had the fish in her hands and had glanced back up the hill toward the cabin as though dreading the necessary climb.

"A knife."

"What blade?"

She smiled at his question. Considering the lazy way he was lounging, it was very nice of him to offer to return to the cabin and get a knife for her, not that she'd seen anything there except a rusty old paring knife. "An eight-inch boning knife, long, thin blade," she said, smiling smugly. Let him try to find that!

A second later, a knife with a long, thin blade twanged as it stuck in the ground inches from her hand. Startled, she looked up at him, silently questioning where it had come from.

Cole looked away, his smile telling her that he expected her to ask.

But Kady would have died before she pleaded for information. "Thanks," she said, then set about boning the fish and slicing the potatoes.

Working in a restaurant for so many years had taught her to be fast and efficient. Within minutes she set a skillet before him that was filled with sautéed potatoes flavored with wild onions and perfectly cooked trout, touched with a splash of vinegar and raisins on top.

The look Cole gave her when he bit into the fish was all the praise Kady needed. Sitting down on the blanket, as far from him as she could get, she pulled her knees up to her chest and hugged them. It was one thing to cook for the President, a man who was used to excellent food, but it was another to cook for a man who was used to a monotonous, bland diet. Cole had looked at her food as though it were ambrosia, fit only for gods.

She sat in silence, watching the clear, unpolluted water, while Cole gave the ultimate tribute to a cook by cleaning his plate.

When the skillet was empty, he set it down and stared at her profile. "I never tasted anything like that," he said, awe in his voice.

Kady just smiled, then nudged the basket toward him. "Have room for peach cobbler?"

Cole took his time on the cobbler, and when he was finished, he leaned back on his elbows and stared at the creek. "If I hadn't already married you, I'd ask for your hand now," he said, his seriousness making Kady laugh.

As she busied herself with cleaning the skillet and handing Cole a jar full of the crystal-clear creek water, she said, "What time do we leave in the morning to go find the rock where I came through?"

When Cole didn't answer, Kady tightened her lips, then went to sit on the blanket by him, preparing herself for a fight. She knew without words being spoken that he didn't want her to go.

"Kady," he began. "I like you. I've never met a woman whose company I enjoy as much as yours. You have a wonderful sense of humor, you're smart, you're beautiful. And . . . and this . . ." He waved his hand at the basket, as though her cooking were indescribable. "I've never met anyone like you. Please stay here with me for just a few days. Then I'll help you get back. I swear that I'll do whatever I can to help you go anywhere you want. I'll move heaven and earth to get you back. Just give me these few days. Three days. That's all I ask."

Kady knew she couldn't do that. The temptation of a man who says he likes your sense of humor *and* thinks you're smart would be too much for any woman to resist. She loved Gregory, but with each passing hour he seemed to be further away. She didn't want to stay here in this time of no medical facilities, of no bathrooms, of no . . . Of no Gregory.

"I can't," she said softly. "Gregory might be looking for me."

"You don't know that he is. Maybe you could stay here six months or ten years, a lifetime even, then step through that rock and you'd be standing in your house wearing that white dress and not a moment will have passed."

It struck Kady odd that he had not asked her many questions about her statement that she was from another time period. He had never asked for verification, and she had no idea whether he still disbelieved her story or not. But he did seem to believe that if she could find the rocks, she would disappear. "But I don't know that, do I? For all I know Gregory will be frantic with worry now. There could be police looking for me."

"Then when you return he'll be doubly glad to see you."

"Ha!" Kady said. "Three hundred women will have taken my place by then. You haven't seen what Gregory looks like. Even my bridesmaid, Debbie, who is married and has three children, has a crush on him. She just sits there and stares at him."

"And what about you?"

"I don't sit and stare at him, if that's what you mean."

"*Mmmm.* Sounds a bit as though you do. Are you afraid of him?"

"Afraid of Gregory?" she snapped. "That's absurd. Gregory wouldn't hurt a fly. He's gentle and kind and . . . and sexy." She looked at Cole. He'd draped his shirt about his shoulders, but his washboard stomach was exposed and he was very appealing. "Yes," she said fiercely. "Gregory is very, very sexy, and I'm mad about him." She forced herself to calm. "I don't *want* to spend three days alone with you or any other man, I *want* to go home to Gregory."

Cole took a moment to answer. "All right, I'll take you back in the morning," he said slowly as he leaned toward her to remove a leaf that had fallen on the back of her hair.

But as he neared her, Kady jumped as though he were going to hit her.

"I can't figure out what I've done to make you feel that you can't trust me," he snapped.

"The only way I'd trust you is if you were a eunuch," Kady muttered, brushing the leaf from her hair.

For a moment Cole made no reaction to her remark, then, to her utter astonishment, she saw his eyes widen as his face turned pale. "How did you find out? Who told you?"

Kady was confused. "Who told me what? I don't know what you're talking about."

Cole didn't say anything as he began to hastily, almost angrily, gather up the cooking gear, and Kady couldn't figure out what was wrong.

"I'm sorry," she said, watching him. "I don't know what I said that's upset you so much. What is it that I'm supposed to have been told?"

Cole sat back on the blanket. "It's not you, it's me," he said. "I just can't bear it when women find out. I know you will think this is horrible of me, but I like it when a beautiful woman like you pulls away from me in fear of what I might be seeking from her. I hate the way the girls in town feel so safe with me. They treat me like another girlfriend."

Kady's eyes couldn't have widened any more. "I don't know what you're talking about. How could a woman feel safe with a man who looks like you?"

"Ironic, isn't it?" he said, turning his head a bit toward her and raising one eyebrow. "God's little joke. He made me grow to man size, but he took away my manhood."

"Your—? Your . . . ?" She tried to stop herself, but she couldn't help glancing down at the fork of his legs.

Cole looked away from her. "The bullets . . . These," he said, pointing to the five deep, ugly wounds that marred the upper half of his body. "They hit the lower half of my body too," he said softly.

Kady sat back on the blanket hard. "You mean you can't—"

Cole turned away so she couldn't see his face. "Can't make children? No, I cannot. This is why I'm thirty-three and not married. The women who know won't have me, and the women who don't, well, it wouldn't be fair to them, would it? Women want babies," he said softly.

"Not all of the women in my world want babies."

Turning, he glared at her. "Well, all of them in *this* world do."

Kady hesitated. She had, of course, read articles about

what to do if a man is impotent. Be understanding, kind, and gentle seemed to head the list. "Are you just infertile or are you, ah, impotent as well?"

A quick look of confusion crossed his face, then he said, "Everything," and took a deep breath. "Kady, I know that when I brought you to this cabin, I did a wicked thing, and I am sure I will be punished in heaven, but I couldn't help myself. I was hoping that I could talk you into spending three days with me. Alone. Just the two of us. Maybe it will make you hate me, but I thought of many arguments to try to persuade you. Even if you were three days late in getting back, would it be so bad to make the man who loves you frantic with worry? Wouldn't the homecoming be sweeter if you made him wait? You see, you are my only chance to have a honeymoon. I could find a woman who would marry me, but she'd hate me as soon as she found out the truth. But with you, because of your circumstances, I thought maybe you and I could, well, pretend that we were in love for a few days. A pretend honeymoon, so to speak. You wouldn't be angry with me because your future and whether you have children or not wouldn't depend on me. At the end of our honeymoon, you could return to the man you love, and no one would be hurt."

Kady looked at him, seeing the sadness in his eyes. Was this why she'd been sent back, to give this lonely man three days of love? To give him something that he would not otherwise have? Who would her staying hurt? he'd asked. If she returned to Gregory, Cole would have been dead for over a hundred years. Besides, if she went back to Virginia and said she'd had an affair with an impotent cowboy, who would believe her?

She didn't know if what Cole had said—that she could go back through the rocks ten years from now and no time would have passed—was true or not, but in the back of her mind she thought it might do Gregory a bit of good if he didn't know where she was for three whole days. Once he'd laughingly told some people at a dinner party that he always knew where Kady was: in the kitchen at Onions. So what if she did spend three days alone with this harmless man? They could talk about their worlds. Maybe there was something he knew or she knew that could help each other's worlds. There had to be a reason why she'd been sent back in time, so shouldn't she at least make some effort to find out what it was before she returned?

She took a deep breath. "Three days," she said. "Three days, then the morning of the fourth you take me back and help me find those rocks."

It seemed that a thousand expressions crossed Cole's handsome face, and every one of them was a form of ecstasy. "Oh, Kady," he whispered, "you have made me the happiest man in the world."

Before she could think, he'd put his arms around her and pulled her to his bare chest as he rained kisses on the top of her head.

The feeling that ran through Kady was so strong that she pushed away from him with much more force than was needed.

"I'm sorry. I didn't mean to do that," he said, releasing her.

Kady could feel her heart beating in her throat. Part of her said that she shouldn't kiss him, but part of her remembered that in real life she was only engaged, not married. The rest of America seemed to be jumping into bed with three different men a night, so couldn't she kiss another man before she got married? Besides, it was only for three days, and Cole's condition made it impossible for her to be unfaithful to Gregory, didn't it?

With determination, Kady put her hand behind Cole's head and pressed her lips to his. It wasn't much of a kiss, because, in spite of being a modern woman and being engaged, she really wasn't too experienced in kissing. "We're on our honeymoon, remember?"

With a beautifully tender smile on his face, Cole tucked a curl behind her ear. "You know, Mrs. Jordan, I think I may be falling in love with you."

Kady put a finger to his lips. "Don't say that. Don't say or do anything to make me feel guilty about leaving you. If I think that my leaving will hurt you, I'll have to go now."

"No," he said, pulling her close. "Three days, that's all I ask."

Chapter 8

COLE ROSE EARLY, QUIETLY BUILT UP THE FIRE IN THE FIRE-
place, then pulled out a chair so he could settle down and
watch Kady sleep. It truly astonished him how much he
loved her. In fact, he couldn't seem to remember what his
life had been like before he met her, and when he looked
back at his life, he seemed to think of it all as waiting-for-
Kady. Whatever he'd done, whomever he'd met, had been
in preparation for that day when she leaped from between
the boulders and hit one of Harwood's men on the head
with a rock.

At that moment, Cole had been strung to a tree, his neck
stretched almost to the breaking point, but he was conscious enough that he could see her. Looking like an angel
in a cloud of white silk, she'd leaped, brought the rock
down on the man's head, then stood there for interminable
seconds trying to figure out how to fire a rifle. When she'd
hit the trigger by accident, the bullet had whizzed so close
to Cole's ear that he'd felt its heat. Cole had been very
thankful that his horse had remembered what he'd been
taught and stood absolutely still. If the animal had moved
by an inch, Cole would have died.

The woman's shots sent Harwood and his men into turmoil as they tried to figure out who was shooting at them. Since the kick of the first shot had sent her hurtling back into the rocks, none of the murderers could see her. But Cole knew where to look. Barely able to stay conscious and opening his eyes only to slits, Cole watched as the woman tried to fire the rifle again. Cock it, cock it, cock it, he'd repeated in his mind several dozen times.

To his happiness, she pulled the lever down and fired again. This time she winged Harwood himself, and in an instant all the men were firing in the general direction of the rocks. Closing his eyes, Cole prayed that the woman wouldn't be found or hit by a stray bullet. He'd rather they finished the job of hanging him than find her.

But Harwood and his men had no idea how many people were spying on them, so they shot in the general direction of Cole's horse, then rode away. Again, much to Cole's happiness, his horse stayed where it was, never flinching, even when a bullet grazed its neck. Extra oats for you tonight, old boy, he thought.

For the next several minutes Cole moved in and out of consciousness, and each time he came back to the real world, he saw unbelievable sights. The first time he saw that the woman was undressing, taking off her white wedding gown. The next time he came to, she was on the horse behind him, her breasts pressed into his back. It was then that he was sure he actually had died and he was in heaven with this angel.

The next time he woke, he was on the ground and she was under him. Smiling in perfect happiness, he allowed himself to fade back into unconsciousness.

When next he awoke, he was sleeping with the woman in his arms. "You're an angel," he tried to say, but his throat hurt so much that not much of the words came out.

Sunlight woke him again, and he found that she wasn't a dream but a reality, and he quite naturally started kissing her. Within minutes, she had pulled away and started telling him some outlandish story about being from the future and how she was going to marry some other man and all sorts of bizarre information.

All he could see for sure was that she didn't know where she lived and some man had been stupid enough to let her out of his sight for five minutes. As far as Cole was concerned, finders keepers.

Had it been up to him, right then he would have swept her away to marry her and keep her forever, but little Elizabeth Kady Long had other ideas. First, she seemed to believe she was in love with another man. Cole had enough sense to know that when a woman believed she was in love with a man, no one could change her mind. At least not without a lot of time and effort—both of which he planned to dedicate to this project.

Maybe he'd been in an awkward position when he'd first seen her, what with a rope stretching his neck until he couldn't breathe, but he knew what he felt from that first moment. Kady was brave and good; she had risked her life to save a man she didn't know. As she'd said to Cole, she hadn't known if he was a bad guy or a good one, but she'd saved him and taken care of him just the same.

Smiling, he thought of the way she spoke, with her odd phrasing and strange words and even stranger concepts. It was enough to make him believe she was from the future as she said. Almost enough, anyway.

Wherever she came from, it wasn't from anywhere he knew about, as he was sure there wasn't another woman like Kady in the state of Colorado. One minute she was fierce and strong, the next she was soft and innocent.

But whatever she was, she kept herself locked inside a protective shell. It was as though she lived all by herself in the world because she was always making sure that no one paid her way or took care of her. She seemed to think she needed to exist all by herself in the world.

And she didn't allow Cole to get near her no matter how hard he tried. He knew she must be frightened, after all, she was alone in a strange place, but she refused to ask for help or even to let him see how afraid she was.

And she kept talking about this . . . this man named Gregory. Even when thinking of the name, Cole sneered. Kady didn't love this man. Maybe Cole wasn't an expert on love, since he'd only recently discovered it, but he knew enough to know that when Kady said the name, her voice didn't resonate with the feeling that he, Cole, had for Kady. Actually, she sounded more as though she were talking about a business partner than a man she planned to marry.

Or maybe that was how Cole wanted to see the situation. Now, sitting in the cabin in the early morning half light, he looked at Kady and knew that he'd never be able to hear love in her voice for any man except himself.

She was his. His for all time. Minutes before he was to die, she had been sent to save him. Save him from death, save him from loneliness. Save him from a life that had increasingly held little meaning for him. Since he was nine years old, since that day-in-hell when the bank had been robbed and the townspeople of Legend had opened fire, Cole had wondered why he had been spared. Just him, and no one else. In two days he'd lost his sister, his friend, his father, and his grandfather. The year after that his mother had died. His grandmother had said she couldn't bear the sight of Legend, so she'd moved to Denver. Cole had begged his grandmother, his only living relative, to be allowed to stay in the mountain town; he couldn't abide the city. His grandmother Ruth had a soft heart, so she'd allowed her grandson to stay with people she trusted in his beloved Legend.

For all that the people he'd stayed with had been good to him, the emptiness he'd felt at losing his family had never been filled.

Smiling, he looked at Kady, sleeping like the angel she

was, half buried under the pile of covers on the hard bed. She was so innocent, as innocent as she seemed to think he was. And as far as he could tell, she believed everything he told her. It was difficult to comprehend, but she had even believed his story about being a eunuch.

His lie had been spur-of-the-moment, the word triggering childhood memories for days after he'd been shot no one knew whether he was going to live or die, Cole had taken advantage of the worry he saw in everyone's eyes to get answers to all the grown-up secrets he and Tarik had tried to figure out on their own. One of his questions was, What was a eunuch? His grandmother had said it was a man who couldn't make babies and no women wanted to marry such a man. So now, years later, when Kady mentioned the word in jest, Cole had seized on it to concoct a rather marvelous lie.

And Kady had believed him! She'd believed him and agreed to stay with him. In amazement, Cole had watched her eyes soften, and he could feel her heart melting.

Maybe Cole should feel guilty for telling such a great, whopping lie, but he'd do *anything* to gain time with Kady. He'd even thought about throwing himself over a cliff, hoping to break a bone or two so she'd stay and nurse him. Maybe if he was wounded and she thought he was helpless, she wouldn't jump every time he got near her.

So now what was he to do with this time? he wondered. By lies and trickery, more lies than she could possibly know, he had made her agree to spend three days alone with him. He'd also managed to get her married to him. That thought made him smile. Planning the strategy that led to that marriage had taken some work on his part. But it had been worth it! Kady was now his, even if she didn't yet know it.

All he had to do now was erase from her mind all thoughts of this man she thought she loved and show her that she actually loved Cole and no one else.

He just had to figure out how to do that. Cole had once heard a man say that all you had to do was whisper a few sweet words to a woman, then kiss her on the neck in just the right spot, and she was yours. But Kady had that shell around her that kept him outside, and he didn't think all the neck kisses in the world were going to make her love him.

Now, looking at her, he wondered what this Gregory had done to get past her shell. Then, abruptly, understanding lit Cole's face. What if this Gregory *hadn't* penetrated Kady's shell? What if that's what she liked so much about him? Maybe this Gregory asked nothing of her except that she cook a few meals, maybe smile at his friends, and probably, he also wanted her to leave him alone. Cole didn't know for sure, but he guessed Kady wouldn't be the kind of wife who asked too many questions about where a man had been last night.

If all this was true, what did ol' Gregory want from Kady besides her accommodating nature? If all the man wanted was to not be questioned, why had he asked Kady to marry him? Cole had no idea what the answer was, but he thought he'd do his best in these next few days to find out.

And he'd do whatever he had to do to get close to her. He'd lie all that he needed to. He'd continue telling her that he had no idea where those petroglyphs were; he'd tell her he didn't even remember the tree where the men were trying to hang him if he needed to. He'd tell her anything that was necessary in order to keep her with him until she told him that she didn't want to leave.

Quietly, Cole went to the bed and knelt beside it, stroking her hair gently until she began to awaken. He'd stayed outside last night while she was getting ready for bed, even giving her time to fall asleep. When he'd returned, in the darkness, he'd stripped down to his underwear and crawled in beside her. She had snuggled next to him like a warm puppy, and he'd pulled her close to him, a smile on his face.

"I love you, Kady," he'd whispered just before he fell asleep. "I love you, and I have waited for you forever."

Kady awoke slowly, smiling from some unremembered dream, and when she saw Cole's handsome face, with those beautiful lips of his, she smiled even more broadly. He was sitting on the floor beside the bed, and maybe she should have felt nervous at his nearness, but instead, she just felt comfortable. "Good morning," she whispered, closing her eyes again. She wasn't sure where she was, but it smelled as good as freshly baked bread. And the blankets were so warm they seemed to be tempting her to stay forever.

Just as she felt herself drifting back into sleep, she heard the man say, "Did you ever ride a spotted pony when you were a kid?"

Turning to look at him, she smiled again; then she spent so much time thinking that he had such lovely long eyelashes, that it was a while before she responded to his earnest-sounding question. "My mother and I didn't have the time or the money to do such frivolous . . ." she began, then stopped. "Actually, I *did* ride a spotted pony. When I was five, one of the children who lived near me had a birthday party with a hired pony. All the children rode the pony, and we had our pictures taken on it."

"You were wearing a red dress," Cole said softly, playing with the curls of her hair, twisting them about his long fingers.

"Yes," Kady answered. "How in the world did you guess?"

"I didn't guess, I knew." Raising his eyes, he looked at her, and when he spoke, his breath was warm on her cheek. "When I was a boy, up until I was nine, I used to have a dream about a little girl wearing a red dress and riding a black-and-white-spotted pony. She never said anything, but she was always laughing, and I felt that she was my friend."

"Wh-what happened to her?" Kady asked, now fully awake, her mind full of her own recurring dream.

"Nothing. She disappeared right after the shooting when I was a kid. Or at least it seemed that way to me. I remember being delirious with fever and telling my mother that the little girl had gone away. But now I think the ending of the dream had to do with all the people who died that day."

When Kady looked very sad, he smiled and kissed her nose. "That was all a very long time ago. Twenty-four years to be precise, but I still remember that little girl who used to smile at me. You remind me of her, and since you did ride a spotted pony, I'm sure you actually were that little girl."

Kady had to bite her tongue to keep from telling him about her own lifelong recurring dream. She'd like to tell him that Gregory was the man whom she'd seen in her dreams so many times, but she had an idea Cole would see the lie in her eyes. But at least Gregory was closer to being the man of her dreams than this blond-haired, blue-eyed man was.

Standing, Cole took her hand from under the covers and tugged on it. "Come on, get up, lazybones," he said. "We have things to do."

Kady allowed herself a final, luxurious closing of her eyes, then tentatively stuck a toe out from under the blanket. "Tell me if I get close to the floor," she said.

"Come on and I'll fry you up some flapjacks."

"Using lard?" she asked innocently.

"Using bear grease."

"Oh? And what did you do with the rest of the bear?"

Cole had been looking down at her, quietly and calmly, but in the next second his voice lowered and he growled, "I ate his spirit and became him." Making his big hands into claws, Cole leaped on Kady and attempted to devour her neck with his teeth.

Kady was squealing with laughter, fighting him, telling him to get off, while his bear-claw hands clutched at her, easily holding her, then releasing her.

"Ah, now, here is a tasty bit of flesh," he growled, his hand taking firm hold of her breast.

"Cole!" she yelped, pushing at him, but not exactly with any strength. But when he opened his mouth and pointed his head downward, she saw where he was going. Kady was fairly strong from all those years of dealing with twenty-five-pound roasts and copper pots big enough to boil a hogshead of soup. Thrusting her hips upward, she caught him by surprise and sent him rolling until he landed against the wall with a thud.

The look of surprise on his face was worth everything as Kady tossed the blanket over him and made a leap for freedom. But he caught her arm and pulled her back into the bed, where he threw a leg and an arm over her to pin her into place, then lowered his face as though to kiss her.

With another great upward thrust and a twist, Kady wiggled out from under him, falling to the floor at the head of the bed. Another roll and she was on her feet, running to stand in front of the fireplace, where she grabbed a poker and waved it like a sword. "Touch me again, Sir Bear, and I'll take your hide and use it for a floor mat."

Sitting up, Cole's face feigned anguish as he clasped both hands over his heart and fell back onto the bed. "I am killed. You have murdered me. I am no more."

Kady replaced the poker into the holder by the side of the fireplace. "Oh, well," she said loudly. "If my bear is dead, I shall have more pancakes for myself." Cole didn't move. "Made with butter." He still didn't move. "With apples and cinnamon on them."

Cole opened one eye. "I think my heart has begun to beat again. To survive such a slaying, I must be immortal." He raised himself onto his elbow and looked at her.

"Immortals don't eat," she said.

"Then I am definitely of this earth," he answered, getting out of bed and heading toward Kady, but she sidestepped him.

"Go out and get firewood so I can cook," she said as sternly as she could manage, for he had removed his shirt in order to put on woolen underwear. Only after he'd left the cabin could she let out her pent-up breath.

Odd, she thought, remembering the mock battle with Cole. For all that he said he *couldn't* make love, it didn't feel as though he was a man who had been emasculated. Not that she knew what such a man would be like. Instead, it was almost as though Cole needed . . . The thought made her laugh out loud. A teacher, she thought. It was almost as though Cole needed a teacher.

You're getting fanciful, Kady, she told herself, then put her thoughts into the familiar routine of cooking; then, checking on her *biga,* seeing that it was bubbling nicely, she started planning what she would do that day. She'd wander about the mountainside and refresh her knowledge of edible wild plants. Then she'd—

"What are you doing?" she asked Cole, who'd come back to the cabin with a load of wood and was now filling a canvas bag with things like matches and a canvas tarpaulin.

"I thought we might go see some Indian ruins a few miles from here," he said. "It'll take a day there and a day back."

"We're going camping?"

That seemed to strike him as amusing. "Yes, camping. Under the stars, just you and me. Anything special you want to take?"

"A chaperon?"

Cole gave her a one-sided grin that made her turn back toward the fireplace to hide her nervousness.

He's harmless, she told herself, trying to remember the awful story he'd told her yesterday. And besides, in three days she'd be back to Gregory and true safety.

It seemed that everything was ready for the trip within minutes. Since there were no nylon tents to pack, no propane stoves, no bags of dehydrated trail mix, everything seemed to fit easily into one heavy canvas bag that Cole hefted onto his strong back. To Kady's amazement, he already had a bow and a quiver of arrows slung across one shoulder.

"Knives," Kady said as they stepped onto the porch, a small pack on her back, with a basket tied to it.

"You don't need those rusty things from the cabin," he said, echoing her own sentiments about the knives. "I have knives with me. Ready?"

As Kady pulled the cabin door shut, for a moment she searched for a way to lock it, then turned and smiled at him. "No lock."

"No, no locks," he said in amusement at the very idea of locking the door to a cabin in the mountains.

Cole led them up a winding trail that he said had been made by elk. After an hour, he paused, told her to be still, then pulled his bow from his back, fitted it with an arrow, and prepared to shoot a beautiful deer. After a second's disbelief, with a great leap, Kady fell against him, sending the arrow soaring into the trees.

"Why the hell did you do that?" Cole demanded. "You made me miss him. We could have eaten for weeks off that one deer."

A flood of words came from Kady as she told him that in her time there wasn't much game left because hunters had killed so many animals over the centuries.

Cole listened in silence, then reshouldered his pack and bow. "I don't think I would like your time very much," Kady heard him say as he began walking again.

A few hours later he stopped and asked her permission to shoot a rabbit. "You haven't killed all of them off, have you?"

Kady didn't like his insinuation that she personally had rid the world of game, but she told him rabbits were all right. Within seconds he had shot two arrows and brought down two rabbits. As he retrieved his arrows, Kady asked him to give her a knife; then she field-dressed the rabbits in the blink of an eye. When Cole insisted that *he* was going to cook them, Kady headed toward a little stream, saying she'd find them a salad.

Minutes later, she returned with a basket filled with watercress, wild sorrel, prickly lettuce, and a couple of violets. Without oil, the best she could do for a dressing was to chop a few ground cherries on top. When she presented Cole with this lovely salad with its different colors of green, various-sized leaves, topped with the tiny purple violets and red cherries, she was quite proud of herself.

But Cole wouldn't touch it. He acted as though eating anything but meat would destroy his internal organs. After a few comments about his immature taste buds, Kady happily ate all the salad by herself.

Cole wouldn't allow her to help him with the cooking. "Don't you know that a man is supposed to wait on his wife on their honeymoon?" he asked as he handed her a delicious quarter of roast rabbit.

"I'm not used to being waited on at all," Kady answered. "By anyone."

"What about Garvin? Doesn't he bring you gifts, shower you with every bauble a woman could want?"

"Of course he does," Kady snapped. "*Gregory* has bought me a house in Alexandria, plus all the furniture in it. He's rich and he's generous."

"He must have a few vices. How is he at the gaming tables?"

She smiled sweetly. "Gregory does not gamble, drink, or do drugs. He's a hardworking, clean-living man, and he loves me very much."

"How could any man not love you? I just want to make sure that my wife is going to be taken care of, that's all. So, tell me, how did this man make all his money?"

"I'm not your wife. Not really anyway. Gregory makes his money from buying and selling land. And from the restaurant," she said. "People like my cooking and they pay for it."

"Is he planning to retire and live off you?" he asked with eyes full of false innocence.

"Certainly not. He's thinking of running for mayor of Alexandria and eventually becoming governor, then, who knows? Maybe president." Cole opened his mouth to speak again, but Kady interrupted him. "Why don't we talk about *you*? How did you make *your* fortune? Why is there a mosque in Legend? And are you sure those men were trying to hang you because of some cows? Maybe you said something so awful to those nice men that you deserved to be hanged."

Cole turned away, but Kady could see his mouth curve into a bit of a smile, and she couldn't help smiling herself.

"You ready to go?" he asked, standing, kicking dirt over the fire he'd built.

As he helped her on with her small pack, he kissed her cheek. "I am a bit jealous of this Guwain."

"Oh? I hadn't noticed."

His eyes were twinkling as he said, "I never want you to leave me, Kady. Never."

With a frown, Kady turned away from him. She shouldn't have agreed to these days, she thought. Maybe her body was safe with him, but her heart wasn't. There was something so old-fashioned and protective about this man that he appealed to something she'd never known was inside her. He was like a grown-up boy, someone who hadn't yet been beaten down by the world.

Stop it, Kady, she told herself. Her mother had told her, "If you allow a man into your life, choose him carefully." Gregory was a carefully chosen man, perfect in every way.

And Cole Jordan was about as imperfect as a man could be, and she hadn't chosen him. Fate had.

Chapter 9

MAYBE IT WAS BECAUSE KADY WAS CONTEMPLATING HER LIFE so intensely that she didn't pay attention to her feet. She had paused on the trail to take a deep drink of water from a canteen and to tell herself that she had to keep her eyes off various parts of Cole's extraordinary anatomy as he walked in front of her. When she started walking again she slipped a bit and the next moment she was sliding down the mountainside on her back, rocks flying all around her as she raised her arms to protect her face.

When she hit the bottom, she stayed where she was, trying to assess if anything was hurt. But she seemed to be all in one piece, just bruised a bit. Lifting her head, she looked back up the mountain and was shocked to see how far she had slid. Far above she could see Cole's form, looking tiny, the late afternoon sun behind him. She raised her arm to wave to signal that she was all right, but she dropped her arm again when a sharp twinge went up her elbow.

With a sigh, she looked up the hill. Now she was going to have to climb all the way back up that very steep slope.

In the next second Kady twisted about as she heard Cole

coming down the mountainside. She'd never seen anyone move as he did. He was completely heedless of his own safety as he ran straight downward, staying on his feet even as rocks and sharp bushes tore at him. Kady wanted to yell that if he slid down as she had, he'd have an easier time of it, but she could tell that he'd never hear her.

He seemed to reach her within seconds, grabbing her in his arms with the fierceness of the bear he had imitated. Kady could tell by the whiteness of his face that he was frightened; she could feel his body shaking.

"I'm fine," she said. "I didn't hurt anything. I—"

He ran his hands over all of her body in a detached way as he checked for broken bones and looked for blood. Except for a raw place on her elbow and a couple of tender places on her right thigh, she was unhurt. She must have slid down on her pack, and the distance between her body and the gravel had protected her.

But nothing had protected Cole. There was a bloody scratch on his cheek, a cut on his arm, his trousers were torn.

"Lie still," he said, his voice low and full of fear. "I'll carry you back up. Then I'll run with you to the doctor and—"

"Cole!" she said loudly. "I'm all right. I'm not hurt." She could tell by his face that he hadn't heard a word she'd said, so she pushed away from him and stood. When he still didn't stop looking worried, she jumped up and down a few times. That caused some pain to her bruised leg, but she'd have died before she let him see it.

Cole didn't say a word as he stood, tossed her over his left shoulder, pack and all, then started the long climb back up to the top.

After the first few minutes of his carrying her, Kady didn't bother trying to get Cole to listen to her assertion that she was unharmed. And when he reached the top and she saw how pale his face was, she didn't say anything except to suggest that they make camp and spend the night right where they were. Cole made no protest.

Nor did he protest when she filled a canteen with water, then told him to remove his shirt so she could wash his wounds.

Maybe it was because the sight of his broad, muscular back made her hands tremble, but she started talking about her world. As she washed, carefully removing tiny rocks from the cuts in Cole's arms and back, she told him about Onions, and about the President coming to eat. She also talked about Gregory and his mother. While she had Cole remove his trousers so she could tend to a bloody place on his thigh, she told him of the wonders of the twentieth century. Maybe if she remembered every miraculous invention that the twentieth century took for granted, she'd remember why she so desperately wanted to return.

"There," she said at last as she wrung out Cole's red bandanna that she'd used as a washcloth. "You don't seem to be hurt fatally, but you'll be sore tomorrow. Coming down that hill like that was a really stupid thing to do. I waved at you and told you I was fine. Why didn't you—?"

She broke off as Cole put his head in his hands as though he was crying.

Without a thought, she went to him, and put her arms around him. He was naked from the waist up and wore only the torn long johns from the waist down. Abruptly, he went tumbling backward onto a grassy area, taking Kady with him, holding her very close to his nearly bare body.

"I have lost so many people," he said raggedly. "I am afraid to love anyone because whoever gets close to me dies. It's as though I'm a jinx on the people I love."

"*Ssssh*," she coaxed, stroking his hair, trying to calm him.

"Only my grandmother survived, and that's because she went to Denver to live. Legend is cursed for the Jordans."

His big hands buried themselves in her hair as he pulled her to him, holding her as close as he could without breaking her. "I'm afraid that if I love you, something horrible will happen to you too."

She tried to pull away from him, but he held her too tightly for her to move. "Nothing will happen to me because I'm not from here," she said, which, even to her, sounded dumb. "Cole, you don't love me. And I don't love you. I'm going to marry someone else, remember? I'm not even going to stay here. You *are* going to help me return, aren't you?"

It was as though she hadn't spoken, since he continued holding her in a way that felt safe and familiar. Maybe it was the unaccustomed exercise of the day, but Kady suddenly felt very sleepy. She should, of course, get up and build a fire and make some broth from the rabbit bones she'd saved, and she should put down some blankets between them and the cold, hard ground. But as she felt Cole's body next to hers, none of those things seemed very important. She knew she should remember Gregory and her pledges to him, but at the moment all she could think of was Cole's warmth and how good it felt to be in his arms.

With her mind drifting, she realized that one of the things she liked best about being near Cole was that when she was with him, she didn't feel fat. When she was in the twentieth century, she seemed to be aware of what society termed "excess fat" every minute of the day. Maybe she felt small because Cole was so large, not like so many modern men who had so little flesh on them their cheekbones looked like razor blades. Or maybe it was because people in the nineteenth century didn't seem to want women to have bodies shaped like pipe-cleaner dolls. Whatever the reason, Cole made her feel beautiful and voluptuous and so very, very desirable. She almost wished he would . . .

"Talk to me," she whispered, her lips on the warm skin of his neck. If she didn't have something to distract her, she would start kissing him.

He didn't seem to notice the cold ground as he caressed

her hair and her back, then moved one of his big legs over hers. "Three years after my friend Tarik's death, his father struck it rich with a silver mine. He used the money to build the mosque in honor of his son. The place hasn't had much use since Tarik's father's death, but I take care of it. I have a key and when we get back to Legend, if you want to, I'll take you inside. It is a beautiful place. Serene and full of prayers."

The last words trailed off as Cole fell asleep, his arms clasped about Kady. She started to pull away, but his arms were locked about her. She was hungry and there were things she needed to do, but the warmth of him and the quiet night quickly lulled her to sleep.

Kady awoke to the smell of frying fish. Smiling, her eyes still closed, she yawned and stretched and thought she must be in heaven. When Cole kissed her softly, it seemed perfectly normal when her arms went about his neck and she kissed him back in a sweet, closed-lip kiss.

"Good morning, Mrs. Jordan," he said softly against her lips. "I loved sleeping with you in my arms. I have never enjoyed a night more."

Kady just kept smiling, still not opening her eyes, her hands clasped about his neck. When his hand touched her hip, then moved upward, she let out a little sigh against his lips.

It was Cole who pulled away, frowning down at her.

"Oh!" Kady said, looking up at him. No doubt she had reminded him of what he could not do. Reminded him of—

"Breakfast is ready," he said, turning away, his frown gone, and his good humor seeming to be restored.

It took Kady a few moments to recover herself, and Cole laughed at her when she found she was stiff from sleeping on the ground. He offered to comb the tangles out of her hair, but Kady refused to let him touch her.

"You look like a woman who is enjoying her honeymoon," he said as he handed her two beautifully fried trout.

Kady almost said that she was enjoying it, but that statement might have been traitorous to Gregory.

Since they hadn't really made camp, it was a quick matter to pack before they started walking toward the ruins that Cole had yet to tell her about. They hadn't walked more than a couple of hours before the skies opened up and a freezing mountain rain came pouring down on them.

Though they took only minutes to get the tarpaulin up, Cole shouting orders over the noise of the rain, when they crawled under it, they were drenched. Wet and cold, they huddled under the tarp, a blanket draped around them.

"I'm hungry," Cole said.

As though those words were a clarion call to Kady— which they were—she tossed back the blanket and prepared to go out into the rain to gather greens. With no fire, she couldn't bake biscuits or roast anything.

Cole caught her arm, frowning. "You don't expect much from men, do you?" he said with anger in his voice. "*I* am the provider. *I* will get the food."

With that he grabbed his bow and arrows and slipped out into the rain. "And where are we going to build a fire?" Kady muttered as she watched the rain pour down around her.

Within minutes Cole returned with a couple of rabbits and set about building a fire under the tarp. Kady pointed out that the smoke from the fire would blow back on them and suffocate them, but Cole, with great patience, told her that if a man was a good woodsman, he knew how to position the fire so the smoke would blow into the rain.

His theory worked perfectly for about fifteen minutes; then the wind changed and the smoke blew back on them. To escape it, they tossed the blanket over their heads and hid under it. When Kady started telling him, "I told you so," he began kissing her until they tumbled backward, their bodies entwined.

Kady, trying to remember where she was and who she was with, made attempts to push him away while keeping her body stiff.

When Cole's kisses did not make her relax, he threw the blanket back, then rolled away from her, his hands clenched at his sides. "What can I do that would make you forget that man? Kady, do you love him so very, very much that you can see no other man? What did he *do* to earn every morsel of your love?"

Kady opened her mouth to speak, but then closed it. It wasn't right to compare Cole to Gregory, but, truthfully, there had never seemed to be time enough with Gregory. Phones were always ringing, people always knocking on the door. And she was always so tired from standing on her feet all day that most of the time she didn't care about romance. If Gregory gave her a kiss on the back of the neck while she was cooking, that was enough for her.

"All right," he said, "don't answer me." She could see that he was still angry as he sat up and began to tend to the fire. The wind had shifted again, so the smoke was blowing away from them. In spite of herself, Kady thought with regret, *No more huddling under a blanket.*

As she looked at Cole's broad back, bent over the fire, preparing food for them, Kady felt bad for the way she was treating him. He had been so good to her, taking care of her, even marrying her when she could find no way to support herself. If it hadn't been for him, she'd have starved to death in that ungenerous town. Her mind raced over all the nice things he had done for her: arranging a bath at the hot springs, always protecting her, risking his life when he thought she was hurt. And, as he'd said, this was the only honeymoon he was going to have.

"I like you too much," she said softly to his back. "I have never had a man pay as much attention to me as you have. You spoil me, and I'm afraid that I like it."

For a moment she didn't think he'd heard her, but when he turned, a piece of rabbit in his hand, he was smiling at her as though she'd just given him the greatest compliment of his life. Feeling embarrassed, Kady looked down at her lap and not at him. Did he have to be so very good-looking?

When Cole had his own food, he stretched out under the tarp, propped himself up on one arm, his long legs seeming to curl around Kady; then he looked up at her with a bit of a smile. "I want you to tell me everything there is to know about you."

At this statement Kady laughed, but when she saw Cole's face, she knew he was serious. "I have led a very boring life, and it would probably put you to sleep."

"I can't imagine that anything you have to say would bore me. I want to know everything about you, and I want to listen."

Maybe it was his sincerity or maybe it was that she wanted to sort out her thoughts and try to understand why what had happened to her had, but she started to talk and tell him about her life. She told him how she always knew she wanted to cook, that she had studied food instead of the other subjects at school. She didn't know who the kings and queens or presidents were, but she knew the food from each time period, and who the famous chefs were. She went to college to study food, then on to New York on scholarship to study at Peter Kump's Cooking School.

She told Cole how her goal was to open a small restaurant so she could experiment with food, and she wanted to travel and write cookbooks. When she was twenty-five, Gregory's mother came to her at school and told Kady of her family's steak house in Alexandria, Virginia. Mrs. Norman told how the restaurant was a dinosaur in the food world and she needed someone to turn it around. This appealed to Kady, so she set herself the goal to work at Onions for three years, even signing a three-year contract.

"And it worked," she told Cole. "It took a while, but eventually people began coming to Onions for *my* food."

"And was it pleasant working for Mrs. Norman?" Cole asked softly.

Kady hesitated before answering. "Truthfully, it was very difficult," she said, then began to explain. Despite Gregory's mother's claim that she wanted to modernize the restaurant, she didn't really want any changes and resisted all that Kady tried to do. And she was a true skinflint, refusing to purchase new equipment, so Kady had been stuck with a broiler that didn't work half the time and a stove that had been bought used in 1962.

"Kady," Cole said, "you were the whole restaurant. Why didn't you threaten to leave if she didn't buy you new equipment?"

Kady sighed, then looked skyward. "Why is it that everyone thinks I am helpless? And stupid?"

"I don't think—"

"Yes you do, and so did everyone at school when I accepted Mrs. Norman's offer, but I knew exactly what I was doing. I was offered jobs everywhere, but I knew that if I worked for someone like Jean-Louis, for the rest of my life people would point out that I had studied under a master and they would compare me to him. I took the job at Onions out of vanity. Pure, old-fashioned vanity. I knew that if I could take a horrible old restaurant like that, and turn it around, then I alone would get credit. And afterward I could get a job anywhere as *head* chef, not as an assistant, or I could obtain financing to open my own restaurant."

Cole smiled at her in a way to acknowledge her intelligence and planning. "So what happened?" he asked.

"Nothing happened. I did what I set out to do." She smiled. "And I got the boss's son in the bargain."

"Didn't you say you'd been there five years? Did you get a new stove after the three-year contract was up?"

Kady laughed. "Not yet, but I'm working on it. I don't think Mrs. Norman can deny her daughter-in-law a broiler, do you?"

She'd meant the words as lighthearted, but Cole didn't smile. "Kady, who owns this restaurant that you work at?"

"Don't give me that look, because I know very well where you're heading. After I marry Gregory, as his wife, I will own half of all he owns."

"Did he ask you to marry him before or after your contract was up?"

Kady almost smiled at Cole's refusal to say Gregory's name. "After. But don't start trying to make it seem that Gregory wants to marry me just to keep me cooking for him."

Kady took a deep breath because Cole's insinuations were beginning to anger her. "You don't understand about Gregory and me. We are a team. Gregory gives me the freedom to concentrate on the food. Since we met, he's worked hard for Onions. He writes to food critics and courts newspapers and magazines to get write-ups. He gives free meals to people of influence so they'll spread the word."

"I guess if all my income depended on one woman, I'd do everything I could to keep her, too."

"Well, his income doesn't just depend on me! He's in real estate. Plus he and his mother could replace me in a minute."

"Oh? And how many cooks did his mother try to hire before you agreed to take the job?"

Part of Kady knew she shouldn't answer him, but why should she hide? He could say whatever he wanted to and it still wouldn't change what she knew to be true. "Seventeen."

"What? I can't hear you."

"Seventeen! Is that what you wanted to hear? Mrs. Norman went to three cooking schools and interviewed seventeen graduates, but not one of them wanted the challenge of that restaurant. But that's because they had no vision. They all wanted to work for Wolfgang Puck or some other famous person."

"Maybe they just saw that Gregory and his dear mother would try to do to them what they have done to you."

"No one has done anything to me! I'm very happy and Gregory and I are getting married because we love each other. You don't know how wonderful he is. He has courted me like something out of a novel, with roses and champagne, concerts and plays and—"

"But he hasn't shelled out for a new stove, has he? And what kind of a buggy does he drive?"

"Not that *you* will know anything about it, but he drives a new red Porsche that he bought last year."

"And what is your buggy like?"

"A ten-year-old Ford Escort. Stop it! I didn't get into cooking to make money. And are you saying that *no man* could possibly love me for myself, that if he loves me it must be for some reason other than love?"

"I'm just saying that this man you think you love is making money off of you and that if you marry him, you'll be stuck behind that broken stove for the rest of your life. He'll be the big shot in the restaurant, wearing the nice clothes, glad-handing everyone, and you'll be in the back doing the work. And you've already told me he has political ambitions. I'll bet he could meet some pretty important people through your talent."

"Stop it," Kady whispered. "I don't want to hear this."

But Cole wouldn't stop. "Tell me, does your wedding contract include that you own half the business?"

She glared at him. "My wedding contract will say that we promise to love each other always."

Cole acted as though he hadn't heard her. "It seems to me that he has very cleverly fixed it so that if you leave, no one will know your name. You've not made a name for yourself but a name for *his* restaurant. And you've made the place so great in these five years that it's my guess if you left he'd be able to get another chef to carry on where you left off. If he buys a new stove, that is. And you would be left with no money to open your own place, and all you could do would be get a job working for another cook, and that's hard to do once you've been your own boss.''

"You're wrong! Gregory and I are getting married. I'll be half owner of everything.''

"Oh? I think any sane man would do what I did and get that ring on your finger in seconds. Or is he holding on to his freedom because he has everything he could possibly want right now? For the price of an engagement ring he can keep you hanging on. And you don't even demand a new stove!!''

"Stop it! Stop it!'' Kady shouted. Maybe the anger that raced through her was out of proportion to his questions, but he had hit too close to home, and she couldn't forget the words of her friend Jane. Just because Jane was an accountant, she thought she had the right to ask about everyone's finances. She was hardly off the plane before she'd asked Kady what the profits of the restaurant were and how much Kady's share was. Jane had been appalled to find that Kady received what Jane considered an inadequate salary, was not a partner, was not sharing financially in the success that her cooking was bringing to Onions, and actually had no idea how well Onions was doing. Kady had dismissed Jane's words with a laugh, saying she'd get it all if she married the boss's son. "Kady, I don't mean to be a cynic,'' Jane had said, "but if you two divorced, you could be left with nothing. You would have put years of work into that restaurant, yet your home, including the contents, would be in his name because everything was purchased before you were married. If there was a divorce, you'd be left with absolutely nothing. You'd receive what you brought into the marriage, which is exactly nothing.''

Kady had dismissed her friend's words, but Jane had planted a seed of doubt in Kady's head.

"Stop it!'' Kady said again to Cole, this time in a whisper as she buried her face in her hands. "I don't want to hear any more from *anyone* about how I should put a price on my love for Gregory.''

With a contrite look, Cole moved to put his arm around her. "You're my wife, and I want to take care of you, to protect you. Don't husbands do that in your time?"

Kady pushed his arm off her shoulders. "You are *not* my husband!"

"Yes I am," Cole said calmly and pulled her into his arms again, this time not allowing her to pull away. "I may not be when you go back to that man; I'll be dead then, but I most certainly am your husband *now*."

He clasped her to him tightly. "Kady, can't I make you see that I love you? Can't I make you see that I hate this man you say you love? I'll say anything, do anything to discredit him. I'm sure you're right, that he does love you with all his heart, how could he not? But can't I at least please try to make you dislike him? Please?"

For a few moments Kady's head whirled with her thoughts and emotions. She'd never been one of those girls who had men trying to impress her, falling all over themselves to invite her out. She'd always been plump and shy, and she'd had very little contact with men outside a kitchen.

"He does love me," she said softly, her head pressed against Cole's strong chest. "And he'd buy a new stove if I insisted, but we're spending a lot of money on the new house and—"

"Whose name is the house in?"

Kady couldn't prevent a laugh. "You are a wicked, horrible man," she said.

He tipped her face up to look at him. "No, I'm a man who is in love with a woman who loves another." Gently, sweetly, he kissed her. "You should be glad your Gaylard isn't here or I'm afraid I'd waylay him some dark night and put him out of his misery."

"Then they would hang you," she said, looking up at him, feeling his soft breath on her lips. At this precise moment she couldn't seem to remember who Gregory was.

And it was that thought that made her push herself out of

his arms. "My goodness," she said brightly. "It's stopped raining, so we'll have to leave. And just when I was enjoying myself so much."

As Cole laughed, he made a lunge to grab Kady's arm, but she eluded him and crawled out from under the tarp.

"Could we go now, please?" she asked as she stared down at him, hands on hips.

"Yes, of course," Cole answered innocently as he began to repack. "I live only to grant your every desire."

Minutes later they were packed and ready to start walking, but as Cole bent to shoulder his pack, Kady was almost sure she heard the word "coward." She thought about defending herself, but instead, she put her nose into the air and looked at the scenery as though Cole Jordan weren't anywhere on the planet.

Chapter 10

As they walked, Kady behind Cole, she kept delaying him as she paused frequently to pick plants, examining each one, searching her memory to recall all that she'd learned in school about plants that grew wild. While training to be a chef during the day, she'd often taken courses in botany at a local university during the night. The origin of foods and eating "off the land" had always fascinated her. She also had a deep belief that for every illness on earth, there was also a cure; someone just had to find the source of that cure.

Suddenly, she stopped walking and stared at some plants by the side of the trail: tall, some nearly six feet, with pretty, slender leaves. "Holy smokes!" she said under her breath, blinking, then shaking her head a couple of times to clear it.

"What are you staring at?" Cole asked, coming to stand behind her and seeing nothing but everyday weeds.

"About twenty years in a Turkish prison," she said, eyes wide. When Cole looked at her in question, she turned to him. "Hemp," she said. "Cannabis." She smiled. "Ever hear of marijuana?"

126

"Can't say as I have. Is it another of your weeds that you plan to try to feed me?"

"No, I think I'll pass on this one."

Cole started walking again, with Kady following him. "Why don't you tell me about this cannabis of yours?" he said over his shoulder. "And exactly what is it good for?"

Laughing, Kady talked as they walked down a trail flanked by the tall plants, telling Cole more than he wanted to know about the problems of the twentieth century.

A little after sundown, when Kady could hardly see the trail in front of her, Cole put up his hand in warning. Instantly she halted and listened, but heard nothing.

Bending, Cole whispered to her. "The ruins are just ahead, but there are people there. I want you to remain here and wait for me while I see who it is."

Without hesitation, Kady did as he said, slipping into the shadows behind some boulders, both packs at her feet.

Cole adjusted the quiver of arrows on his back, holding the bow in his left hand. "Stay here and don't come out until I return," he said.

"But what if it's the men who want to hang you?"

"If I'm stupid enough to get caught a second time, they *should* hang me." When Kady gave him a look that told what she thought of that idea, he grinned wide enough for her to see his white teeth in the darkness. "Kiss me good-bye for love?" he asked.

"Only with my fingers crossed," she said sweetly, returning his grin.

Cole chuckled, then slipped his arm around her waist and pulled her to him. When he kissed her, his lips soft and just barely parted, Kady could feel herself melting against him. "Who cares who the men are?" he murmured against her lips, then pulled her closer, and kissed her cheek. "Will you miss me?"

"I shall enjoy the peace."

She could hear his laugh as he slipped into the darkness. The minute Cole was gone, Kady looked about her, hearing the strange night sounds, and realized that when Cole was gone, she was afraid. What if something happened to him? What if those men came back? What if—

Slipping from the boulders as silently as she could, she tiptoed down the trail, stumbling now and then over rocks and holes. Within minutes she saw light coming from around a bend, and when she was near enough, she stared in wonder at what she saw.

Across a small ravine was a sheer mountain of rock rising high up into the dark sky. At the bottom of the rock, level with Kady, was a deep cut, and inside the natural hollow were the remains of ancient mud dwellings. In front of the old buildings, a fire glowed and three men sat around it, tin coffee cups in their hands.

Crouching down, Kady looked across the darkness at the men and was thinking that they didn't look very dangerous when she saw something that truly horrified her. Hanging from a wall behind them was the carcass of an eagle. When she moved from behind a tree so she could see better, she saw there were half a dozen eagle carcasses sprawled out, their huge wings lifeless.

Kady didn't think about what she was doing. Standing, she put her hands on her hips. "Eagles!" she said aloud, making the men look up from the fire and stare into the darkness toward her.

Instantly, a hand clamped around Kady's mouth and she was pulled back into deeper darkness. There was no doubt in her mind that the man holding her was Cole.

"Why didn't you obey me and stay where I told you to?" he growled into her ear. "No, on second thought, don't bother to answer that. Come on, let's go. They're just hunters, no harm to anyone."

Kady didn't move. "No harm to anyone?" she hissed up at him. "What about the eagles?" She said the last word with great feeling.

Even in the darkness she could see Cole's blank look. "You're right, they're hunters and men alone are not to be trusted. If I didn't have you with me, I'd probably join them, but I don't trust any man around you."

Ignoring the compliment, Kady glared up at him. "Are you going to just walk away from this slaughter?"

In the dim light she could see emotions cross Cole's face as he attempted to understand. Finally, enlightenment, then disbelief seemed to register. "Don't tell me you have something against killing a bunch of carrion eaters like those birds?"

Kady took a deep breath. "The eagle is the symbol of the United States. That bird—"

"What?" Cole gasped, bending so low his nose was close to hers. "An *eagle* stands for our great country? Are you out of your mind? Those birds eat rotting meat. They are little better than vultures. And they are a great menace to the ranchers. They *should* be shot."

With an abrupt turn on her heel, Kady started walking down the path. There had to be a way across the ravine so she could get to the ruins. She had no idea what she was going to do or say to the men when she got there, but she'd think of something to stop the slaughter.

Cole grabbed her by the waist, pulling her to him.

"Release me or I'll scream," she hissed, struggling futilely against his strong arm.

"If you calm down, I'll let you go." When she went limp, he released her, then turned her to look at him. "All right, so you don't approve of shooting eagles so—"

"Why did they do that? What good does it do those men to kill those magnificent birds? Even *I* can't cook an eagle."

"Glad to hear that," Cole said, then when Kady started to turn away, he caught her arm. "All right, it's done now. No one can bring the birds back. The men will sell the feathers and make some money; it's over."

"Oh? What about tomorrow? Will they get up tomorrow morning and kill more eagles?" She took a deep breath. "Cole, you just don't know what has happened to the birds and animals in my time. People have built houses on most of the open land, so there are no more nesting places; they use automatic weapons on the poor creatures; they—"

"I get the picture, but what can *I* do? Would you like me to pay a high price for the feathers so the men would have no more reason to hunt?"

"The higher the price, the more birds they'll kill. I know you can't stop all hunters everywhere from killing them, but can't you stop those men from their butchering? Just those three men?"

As Cole looked down into Kady's big, pleading eyes, he knew that he might not be able to stop the men, but he'd die trying. His mind raced with ideas of how to stop them. Put a few arrows into them? Threaten them that if they ever again killed one of those damned birds, he, Cole Jordan, would personally find each man and kill him? Even as he had the idea, he knew it would take more than one man to put a lifelong fear into those hunters. Money had a way of making men dare anything.

As another idea came to Cole, he began to smile, smile in a way that made Kady know that he meant to do something that wasn't exactly fair and square. Maybe wasn't even legal.

"You're not going to hurt anyone, are you?" she whispered. "You wouldn't use those arrows of yours to—"

"I want you to swear to me that you will sit right here, be quiet, and watch. Nothing more. You won't get involved. Promise?"

"I can't make a promise like that. What if those men try to shoot you?"

He tucked a curl behind her ear. "Would you care?"

"Of course. If you were dead, who would help me find the petroglyphs so I can get back to the man I love?" Kady knew she was reminding herself of her great love because right now she couldn't seem to remember any world except this one. And maybe she couldn't remember any man except this one.

A little frown crossed Cole's face as he took her hands

and squeezed them. "Remember that you need me. Please remember that if you make any noise or sudden moves, the men will shoot me. If I were gone, then who would be here to protect you?"

"Oh," Kady said, eyes wide; then from the look on Cole's face, she thought he might be teasing her. Or maybe she was afraid because she'd watched too many westerns where everyone was shooting everyone else. "What are you going to do?"

"Something groovy," he said, eyes sparkling.

For a moment Kady looked at him in consternation before she remembered her overly long lecture on the origins of illegal drugs in America. Maybe she had become a bit sidetracked in talking about slang and white go-go boots and crack and rap. Before she could make a reply, he kissed her mouth quickly and sweetly, then slipped silently into the darkness.

Settling herself as though she were in the audience at an amphitheater, she watched the men across the ravine prepare themselves for the night. Yawning, Kady couldn't help but envy them and wished she could cuddle up with Cole and— No! she told herself. She wanted to go back to her own bed in Virginia, and tomorrow she'd see Gregory. She did *not* want to snuggle in a sleeping bag with her husband—with Cole, she corrected herself. She wanted Gregory, not Cole.

A movement across the ravine caught Kady's attention, making her sit upright. But what she saw caused her to rub her eyes. A nearly naked man with skin the exact color of the mud buildings behind him silently moved in front of the now sleeping men and tossed a bundle of grass on the fire. Then, removing a pair of eagle wings from where they hung on the walls, he began to fan the flames, making the smoke envelop the sleeping men.

With eyes wide, Kady watched, knowing that the weeds on the fire were stalks of wild marijuana. *He certainly does catch on quickly,* she thought with no little disgust.

As tendrils of the smoke wafted across the ravine, Kady stretched out on her stomach and watched as Cole moved about in the light. He wore nothing but what looked to be a loincloth, his big, muscular torso almost totally naked, only the mud drying on his skin covering him.

Whether she liked him or not, whether she wanted to be with him or not, she had to admire the beauty of him. *He's my husband!* she suddenly thought, then told herself to get that idea out of her head. Husband of convenience only. Gregory was her *real* husband—or at least soon would be.

"Whatever is he doing now?" Kady whispered aloud as she watched Cole take down the wings and bodies of the poor, murdered eagles, then disappear behind the old walls. It seemed hours that he was gone, and for a while she watched the men, sleeping in their cloud of drugged smoke, but then Kady also started to drift into sleep. Maybe the smoke was reaching her as well as the men.

She awoke to an unearthly screech, coming awake so quickly that she bumped her head on a low tree branch as she looked across into the light. An apparition had leaped from the old ruins, and for a moment, Kady's heart beat so wildly that she didn't realize that the creature was Cole.

A phantom, vaguely shaped like a man, but as dark as a shadow, vaulted toward the men, its body covered with parts of the eagles until it looked like a two-hundred-pound bird ready to attack.

Cole had tied wings onto his arms; more wings encased his strong legs. His face had become the beak of the bird of prey, the distinctive white feathers of the bird covering his head and neck. He looked like a spirit set on avenging the deaths of his murdered brothers.

If his appearance weren't enough, there was his screech, the piercing call of an eagle, but louder, more maniacal, that cut the air like one of Cole's knives.

The three hunters, in a marijuana stupor, sat up slowly, looked at the gigantic eagle looming over them, then seemed to take an eternity before they could gather their wits enough to be afraid.

Cole, who seemed to be enjoying his role of terrorizing the men, spread his winged arms and flapped them over the head of one man until Kady almost felt sorry for the hunter. The other two men didn't need such close persuasion, as they leaped up, bumping into walls as they fought disorientation as well as terror. When they tried to grab their rifles and handguns, Cole's screeches became almost demented, as though the eagle was going to tear them to pieces.

Within minutes, the men, their boots under their arms, left everything else and began the mad scramble down the mountain path. And Cole was right behind them, his long arms outstretched as though the eagle he'd become would engulf and devour the men.

After the men had fled, Kady sat absolutely still for a long time, staring into the light in front of the ruins, looking at the empty campsite.

She was sure she should get up, go find Cole, and tell him his performance was great. She should thank him for terrifying the hunters because she was sure that those men would never again shoot an eagle. But instead, she just sat where she was. There was something so chilling about Cole's performance that, truthfully, he had frightened her. It was as though he actually were the spirit of those dead eagles. It was as though he'd cast a spell and the eagles' souls had entered his body and told him how to move. Even his screech had been as much like an eagle's as one could be.

Kady expected Cole to come across the ravine to get her, but he didn't. It seemed that every atom of her body was listening for him on the path behind her, but he didn't come.

When what seemed like hours had passed, Kady stood and listened, but she could hear no sound of the three hunters or of Cole. As quietly as she could, she started walking toward the end of the ravine and found the little bridge of earth that led to the ruins.

She was at the edge of the ruins, looking at the smoldering fire and realizing that the smoke was drifting her way, when out of the dark trees, Cole came screeching down upon her. He had a knife in his teeth and what skin that wasn't covered with feathers was caked with cracked mud. He was a formidable sight and involuntarily, Kady stepped back from him. He wasn't a choirboy now. Now he looked like something from the worst nightmare anyone had ever had.

Taking another step back, Kady almost fell into the smoky fire. *I don't know this man at all,* she thought, and when he came closer, she put up her arm as though to protect herself.

But Cole, grinning, grabbed her in his strong arms, lifted her off the ground and swung her around. When she struggled against him, he buried his face in her neck, feathers, beak and all, and said, "Trust me, my little wife. Give me your life and trust me."

Kady was still stiff in his arms, repulsed by the feathers and what they represented, but maybe the smoke affected her, because when he began to twirl her about, going round and round, holding her close, she started to relax.

"Let go, Kady, my love," he whispered. "Let someone else take care of you. Give yourself to me."

"I can't," she answered, but she could feel her body becoming more pliant in his arms. "My life is elsewhere, in another time." She'd meant to say the words with conviction, but instead, she began to hug him back, began to feel the way her face fit so perfectly into the curve of his neck. It was beginning to feel right that this man was clad in these gorgeous feathers, for she almost felt that he could fly away with her.

"You don't have to be the best little girl in the world," he said. "You don't have to be perfect. You don't have to do anything to make sure people love you. I love you just as you are."

"Just as I am," she said, feeling as though burdens in her life were lifting. It was all too much to think of—that she didn't have to be the best cook, the best daughter, the best at everything in the whole world. Maybe it might be . . . What was that word she'd heard but understood so little? Fun. Yes, that was it; it might be fun to—

Leaning back, Kady looked at Cole for a moment, with the eagle head over his own, the brown feathers of the poor creature's body tied under his chin so only the lower half of his face showed. The dark man in her dreams always had the lower half of his face covered, but Kady was sure that if she had seen the man's mouth, he would have lips just like Cole's.

It seemed the most natural thing in the world to bring her mouth down on his and kiss him.

She was dizzy with the sensations that ran through her body. Maybe it was the smoke, maybe it was the thin mountain air, or maybe it was this beautiful man with his big muscular body that made Kady react with such feelings of sensuality. It seemed quite natural when he put his hands under her seat and lifted her so her legs could slip about his waist.

"Kady, I love you, I love you," he whispered again and again as she leaned her head back and allowed him free access to her neck.

And Kady knew that at that moment she had never wanted any man as much as she wanted Cole Jordan. Maybe she wasn't in love with him, and maybe the great clouds of marijuana smoke were making her react in a way that was not normal for her. All she knew was that she desperately wanted him to make love to her.

"It's not true, is it?" she whispered as she buried her face in his neck. "You aren't a eunuch, are you?"

"Do you believe *everything* you're told?" he asked as he hugged her to him.

"Pretty much," she said, laughing, then brought her mouth to his to kiss him again.

They'd kissed several times since they'd met but each time it had been chaste, closed-mouth kisses, and they had suited Kady, as she'd wanted nothing more. But now she opened her mouth over his, wanting more than chasity.

But Cole did not respond. He did not kiss her back. Instead, he set her down on the ground and said, "Wanta put on some eagle feathers?"

Kady's head was too full of smoke—and maybe lust too—to respond to his words. "I . . . I, no, I don't want to wear the eagle feathers." She started to say more, but Cole put his hand to his forehead and seemed to sway on his feet and instantly, Kady went to him, concerned.

"I don't think I like your marijuana smoke," he said as he sat on the ground, his back against the wall of ruins.

Smiling, Kady kicked dirt over the fire to bury the last of the embers, and when she returned, Cole had slid to the ground and was sleeping with all the innocence of a child. Without any hesitation, she lay down beside him, and he snuggled her to him as though she were a teddy bear. Smiling, she fell asleep.

Chapter 11

KADY AWOKE TO THE SMELL OF FRYING, AND SHE FELT SO emotionally exhausted from the last several days that she didn't even try to guess what it was that Cole was attempting to cook. Wordlessly he handed her a thick white square that was a cross between a biscuit and a cracker and about half a pound of bacon. She ate some but not much. He'd obviously been up for a while because he'd washed off the mud and was wearing clothes. There wasn't an eagle feather anywhere to be seen.

After a while, Cole doused the fire, rolled up the goods the men had left behind and carefully stored them inside one of the ruined houses; then he bundled his and Kady's belongings and slung the pack over his back. "Ready?" was all he said, and Kady nodded, then got up to follow him.

She didn't have to ask Cole why he was so quiet for she knew he was thinking what she was: it was time to go home.

"Cole . . ." she began, but he wouldn't look at her.

"I'm a man of my word," he said, "and the three days are up." For a moment his eyes blazed into hers. "Unless

137

you want to stay," he said, but Kady shook her head no. She wanted to go home.

"I did something to displease you last night," he said softly.

"No, nothing," she lied.

"I didn't mean to fall asleep, but the smoke—"

"No. It was better that you did," she said as she looked away from his eyes, but she could see his frown and feel his puzzlement.

But what could she have said? That she was disappointed that he hadn't made love to her when actually she didn't want him to and when maybe he physically couldn't make love to her? *Kady, your brain is getting too little oxygen in these mountains,* she told herself.

On the way down the mountain there was no banter, no attempts by Cole to make her believe Gregory was after something other than just Kady. Cole walked in front of her, and even though she could see that his shoulders drooped, he walked with a step that said he was a man with a purpose.

They reached the cabin so quickly that she realized that he had led her up the mountain by a circuitous route that took much longer than necessary. After giving her only thirty minutes or so at the cabin to collect herself, he lifted her into the saddle of his horse, mounted behind her, and they started moving.

Once she was in Cole's arms again, leaning back against his strong chest, she began to think of never seeing him again.

"It's not that I don't like you and wouldn't want to be your wife," she said. "Especially after getting to know you over these last days. And it's not that going to bed with a man means you have to be in love with him. In my world there are women who think that going on a date with a man means going to bed with him. It's just that I'm different and I happen to believe in fidelity. Had you and I met under different circumstances, I'm sure I would now be madly in love with you. But I'm engaged to marry another man, so it can't be that way. I just don't want you to feel bad about anything that I may have said—"

"Kady, shut up."

Nodding at his words, she closed her mouth, then did her best to try to concentrate on Gregory. But the safety of Cole's arms and the gentle gait of the horse soon lulled her to sleep.

"We're here," Cole said softly into her ear.

Slowly, Kady opened her eyes to see a sheer rise of rocks before her that were familiar looking. The light of the day was fading, and she was having trouble seeing clearly, but there, almost hidden under some vines, were the petroglyphs.

Cole helped her dismount, then moved to stand beside her. "Is this what you wanted?" he asked softly.

Kady refused to hear the pain in his voice. He couldn't possibly be actually in love with her, she told herself. It was just that she was exotic and men loved the unusual. At the thought of being exotic, Kady almost giggled.

Tentatively, she walked toward the rocks, stopping once to glance over her shoulder at Cole, but he was looking at something over her head. Turning, she saw that the rock seemed to be fading away, turning into a ghost image. She had seen so many hours of TV and movies that maybe what she was seeing wasn't as terrifying to her as it was to a man who'd never seen an airplane. But even with her experience, she had to steel herself as the rock faded and in its place was . . . was . . .

"It's my apartment," she said aloud, turning back toward Cole, happiness on her face. "That's it! I can go back. I can—"

Breaking off, she saw such a bleak look on Cole's face that her heart went out to him. She didn't love him, she told herself, because she was in love with another man, therefore it couldn't matter what expression Cole wore. It didn't matter that—

Without conscious thought, she ran back and flung her arms around Cole's neck and planted her lips on his as she kissed him. "I will always . . . care about you," she whispered. "All my life. You have been very good to me, and I will always remember you. I wish . . ."

"What?" he demanded, holding on to her tight enough to crack her ribs. "What do you wish?"

"That there were two of me," she said. "I wish I could stay here and go back, too. I wish I could live both lives."

"Don't g—" he started, but Kady stopped him with another quick kiss; then, with a firm shove, she disentangled herself from his arms. When her feet touched the ground, she started running the few steps toward the entrance through the rock, because she feared that if she didn't go this very instant, she would never go.

Before her was the rented apartment with its cheap furniture. She could see the flour tin that the wedding dress had been in on the floor, plus her cook's jacket draped across her couch. The light was on on her message machine, so maybe Gregory had called. For all she knew, it was several days since she had disappeared and the police were searching for her.

With her hand outstretched, she lifted her foot to take the last step toward her apartment.

But, suddenly, the dark man on the white horse was there, and unbidden, the thought *This is the man I love* came into her head. It wasn't blond Cole or look-alike Gregory she loved but this man who had been with her most of her life.

As always, the lower half of the man's face was covered. In her dreams his eyes were so expressive that she understood him without words having to be spoken. But now Kady did not understand what he was trying to communicate to her. He was in front of her, seemingly close enough to touch, but when she instinctively reached out her hand to touch him, the distance between them increased until he was out of reach.

His eyes looked sad, as though he was afraid of seeing the end of something, as though he even feared losing her. There was no hesitation in Kady as she took a step toward him, as always, wanting to go with him, to be with him. But again the distance between them increased.

"How can I reach you?" she whispered, then saw the man lift his hand in invitation. "Will we ever be together?" she asked, holding out her hand, trying to reach him. "Will there be a time for us?"

The dark man did not answer, but his eyes smiled, and there was such love in them that Kady drew in her breath and when she tried to smile back at him, her breath caught in her throat. More than anything, she wanted to jump onto the horse with him and ride away to wherever he was going.

But Cole stopped her. With one great stride, he caught her in his arms and swept her away from the opening.

And as quickly as he moved, so did the opening in the rock disappear. One second there was a doorway back to her own time, and the next there was only solid rock.

At first Kady could not believe what had happened. "No," she whispered, trying to pull away from Cole, but he held her tightly.

"No, no, no!" she screamed, then began to beat him on the chest with her fists. "I don't *want* to stay here. I want to go back to my own time. You—" she screamed, then proceeded to call him a few names that he had never before heard a woman say. In fact, from the look on his face, he didn't know some of the words she used.

He released his grip on her arms. "Kady, I'm sorry; I didn't mean—"

Shoving away from him, she went to the rock to run her

hands over the hard, impenetrable surface. Was it open only at certain times of the day? Or only on certain days? What was the key to reopening the rock?

"Look, Kady," Cole said, eyes downcast, his demeanor that of a man who was truly sorry for what he'd done. "I am sorry. It's just that I couldn't bear to see you go." Tilting his head, he looked at her through thick lashes. "You can't blame a man because he's in love with you, can you?"

"If you loved me, you'd have helped me do what I want to do. You, Cole Jordan, are a very selfish person."

"If by that you mean that I want you to stay with me and that I will do everything in my power to keep my *wife* by my side, then yes, indeedy, I am selfish. When it comes to you, Miss Long, I might be the most selfish man alive."

"Do you think *that* is the key?"

"What key?" he asked, confused.

"You being alive. Do you think if I rammed one of those knives of yours into your selfish little heart that maybe the rock would open up again and I could go home? To the man I *love*?" She almost said "men."

"You could try," he said good-naturedly.

Kady threw up her hands in despair. "Now what am I going to do?" she said, mostly to herself.

"Live happily ever after with me?" Cole suggested.

Kady gave him a look.

"I see. Want to try again tomorrow?"

"You have left me no other choice." She took a step toward the horse, then turned back. "I want a solemn, sacred vow from you. You must swear to me that you will help me get home."

Cole's eyes lit up. "Oh, yes, certainly, I'll help you get home."

He had agreed much too readily. "What are you up to?"

"Kady, my lovely wife, it's late and you must be tired. How'd you like to take a bath in a copper tub and to sleep on a feather mattress with clean white sheets?"

Kady opened her mouth to tell him what he could do with his "clean white sheets," but every aching muscle in her body threatened to make her regret such words, so all that squeaked out was a helpless little, "With towels?"

"Warmed before a fire."

"I hate you," she whispered.

Cole chuckled. "I can see that you do." With that, he swept her into his arms, then tossed her into the saddle, mounted behind her, and started down a path Kady had never seen before.

And although she was furious with him, it was on the path down that she said, "Did you see him?" When he didn't answer, she elaborated. "At the doorway, did you see the man on the horse?"

But his look was enough for her to know that Cole had seen no one.

With a sigh, Kady turned back toward the road.

Chapter 12

KADY RELUCTANTLY AWOKE TO THE SOUND OF VOICES, SPECIFI-
cally, the angry voices of women. For a moment she
thought she might still be asleep, because she seemed to be
buried in a cocoon of warmth.

"Señora Jordan," she heard a man's voice saying.
"Señora Jordan, they have come to see you."

As Kady fought her way out of the cocoon, she realized
she was surrounded by an incredibly deep feather mattress,
and it was enveloping her as though it meant to swallow
her. After tossing two pillows from over her head and
noting that they were so light they made no sound when
they hit the floor, she did her best to sit up. But that wasn't
easy when every movement made her sink farther into the
cloudlike softness.

"I'm on my way," she called up to whoever was
summoning her, then grabbed the side of the heavily
carved mahogany headboard and pulled herself up. But
even when she was sitting up, what with being barely over
five feet tall, she could hardly see over the down comforter,
which had to be at least three feet thick. "An entire species

of geese must have given their lives for this bed," she mumbled, then looked around to see who was speaking.

An old man stood there, his face lined with years and weather, and he was watching Kady with eyes twinkling with amusement.

"Yes?" she said. "What is it?" Between the two sentences, she'd had to use her fist to beat the comforter down, as the thing was rising like bread in a hot oven.

The old man chuckled as he watched her fight the demon feathers. "The ladies of the town have come to tell you all about the boy."

"The—?" The effort of speech had made Kady slide down into the mattress, so she had to right herself, then try to regain her dignity. Truthfully, she didn't remember much about last night. Cole had promised her a bath and bed, and she vaguely remembered warm water, then falling into this soft mattress. "The boy?" she asked.

"Cole Jordan," the man said. "You *are* Señora Jordan?"

"Yes, I guess I am," she said, smiling at the way this man called Cole "the boy." "And I take it that you are Manuel?" Kady gave the growing comforter a couple of hard licks with her fists, then looked around her at the bedroom. This was *not* the house of a poor man. This one room was as big as her whole apartment, and the heavy mahogany furniture must have cost a bundle. The walls were covered with pale blue damask that, unless Kady missed her guess, was silk, and over the dresser was a framed mirror that looked like something from the Paris Opera House.

Just as Kady opened her mouth to try to reply to Manuel, the open door behind him filled with chattering women who all pushed and shoved to be the first into the room.

They were talking, but for a moment Kady couldn't hear them, for she was looking at their clothes. Having come from a time period when women seemed to wear nothing but black and their only embellishment was a small, tasteful necklace and earrings, these women were dazzling. They had fringe on their dresses, sparkling trims, rhinestone buttons, hats with feathers curling around their faces. There were plaids and prints and solids of the most outrageous colors. Blinking, Kady could do nothing but stare at all five of them.

"And we thought you should know what kind of man you have married," one of the women was concluding.

Kady knew she'd missed the entire lecture and was sorry for it, for she would have liked to hear what kind of man Cole Jordan was. "I seem to be a bit disoriented," she said. "Maybe you could start again and tell me everything in detail."

The women, all of them young and attractive, a couple of them beautiful, smiled at Kady, then lifted their long, heavy skirts and pretty much climbed into bed with her. This had the effect of lifting her somewhat higher, but the feathers seemed to absorb the extra bodies, and soon the mattress and coverlet were creeping over the brightly colored skirts.

"Perhaps we should introduce ourselves. I'm Martha," the prettiest one said, then held out a kidskin-clad hand for Kady to shake by the fingertips.

Kady tried not to think about the oddity of receiving guests while still in bed, but these young women seemed to think nothing of it. The other women introduced themselves as Mable, Margaret, Myrtle, and Mavis. Kady was lost by the third *M*.

"We think it is our Christian duty to tell you about the man you have married," Martha said, making Kady smile. Were they going to tell her that Cole Jordan was a liar and a manipulator? She already knew that. She also knew how charming he could be and how sweet and—

"You are never going to believe what he made the whole town do to you," M-Three said and got Kady's attention.

It took nearly an hour to get the entire story straight, what with all five Ms talking at once, then Manuel interrupting to bring coffee and some divine sopapillas dripping honey. Kady sat in bed, eating and listening, and becoming more angry and disgusted by the moment.

It seemed that Legend, Colorado, wasn't actually a mining town; it was a town that belonged to one man, and that man was Cole Jordan. He owned every mine, every house, every shop, every inch of land in the town. And every person in the town worked for Cole, or, according to the Ms, was his "bounden slave."

"Everyone does just what he says. We have to or he sends us away."

"My father has operated Reeve's Mercantile for ten years, but he doesn't own a penny of it," M-Two said. "Cole owns everything. All of it. So you can see why we had to do what we did to you."

What they had done, based on Cole's orders, was to refuse to give Kady a job or even a meal on those two horrible days when she'd been searching for both. Thinking back, she remembered that Cole had given something to some boys playing by the side of the road. It seems that he'd paid them nickels to run all over town and tell everyone that anyone who fed Kady or helped her in any way was going to be thrown out of town.

"And he did this while he was arranging his—your—wedding. He had the whole church decorated and made all the choir show up to sing for his wedding. Betty's mother was ill that day, but she knew better than to cross Cole, since every bite her family eats depends on him."

"He *trapped* you into marrying him, that's what he did," M-One said, her handkerchief to her eyes. "And we hate to see someone of our own sex so mistreated by a man like Cole Jordan."

"Do you know what the man you have married is *really* like?" Martha said, the only one of the Ms Kady could fit with a proper name.

"I don't think I know nearly enough," Kady answered. "Perhaps you should tell me more. Maybe you can tell me why someone was trying to hang him."

"Oh, that," M-Four said. "Half the country wants to

murder Cole. He won't sell anything to anybody. Once he decides something belongs to him, he keeps it, no matter what he has to do, and that includes keeping money. Why, even with the thirty million he now has— Are you all right?" she asked when Kady nearly choked on a mouthful of sopapilla.

"Thirty million what?" Kady asked when she had recovered.

"Dollars, of course. Most of it in gold and silver. Haven't you been listening? He owns three very lucrative silver mines, plus every business in town, so of course people are always trying to take that money away from him. They get so frustrated when he won't sell anything to them that they just decide to kill him instead."

"I can understand their reasoning," Kady said. "So why doesn't he hire bodyguards, men with guns who can protect him?" At that statement all the women drew back as though she'd said something shocking. "Did I say something wrong?"

In the next second Kady realized they had drawn back merely to fill their lungs with oxygen so they could let loose a string of descriptive phrases.

"Protect Cole Jordan?!" they gasped, then proceeded to tell Kady what she'd already seen. Cole carried so many knives on his person, concealed in every piece of clothing he wore, that once when he walked past some boys playing with magnets, the magnets had flown out of the boys' hands and stuck to Cole.

"Have you seen the whip he carries down his back?" M-Two asked. "He may have nothing to do with guns, but he makes up for it in other weapons."

"And to think I thought he was a choirboy," Kady muttered, which made the women laugh. But the way they laughed made her look at them speculatively. Why had they come to tell her this? If it was true that whatever they owned was actually owned by Cole, why risk his wrath?

She looked each of them straight in the eye. "How many of you tried to marry him?"

M-Three didn't hesitate. "Why all of us, of course. What young woman wouldn't try to win a handsome man worth thirty million dollars?"

The five of them sat there on the bed and looked at Kady as though they expected her to answer this question, but she could think of no reply.

Martha smiled prettily. "I can see that we've startled you. Two years ago the five of us were pursuing Cole with such vigor that we hated each other. And Cole—the skunk!—was playing us one against the other. He'd tell each of us what the other had done to try to win him so we'd try to outdo the other. We were dressing for Cole, cooking for him, studying ways to entertain him. Our lives were hell!"

"Martha!" M-Three said, shocked at the language, but the others nodded solemnly.

"It was my mother," M-Four said, "who tricked the five of us into getting together—because, you see, by then we were sworn enemies—and letting us see what fools we were making of ourselves over one dreadful man. Cole had no intention of marrying any of us."

"Yes, he was much too happy to marry one of us, because that would stop all of us from courting him. You can never change a happy man."

"I . . . I guess not," Kady said, never having thought of this before.

M-Two leaned forward, very serious. "What did you do to make him go to such effort to marry you?"

Kady wasn't really sure. "He asked me to marry him, but I told him no. I said I was going to marry another man."

"Ahhhhh," the women said in unison and looked at Kady as though she were a brilliant strategist.

"No, you don't understand. I *don't* want to marry him.

Didn't anyway, and I *do* love another man." *Or maybe two other men,* she thought, but didn't say so.

"If it's someone here in town, Cole will discharge him and send him away."

"No, the man I love lives in Virginia." *And in my dreams.*

At this the women looked at each other, then back at Kady, as though to say, *Then what are you doing in Colorado?*

"Look," Kady said, "I can solve all of this. Do you know someone who knows where there are rocks with carvings on them? Something like this," she said, then used a bit of bread to draw an elk in the honey on her plate.

When the women said nothing, she looked up at them and saw they hadn't even looked at her plate. "What's wrong?" she said in a small voice.

Martha looked at the others before she spoke. "You might as well know, Mrs. Jordan—"

"Kady, please."

"Kady . . ." Martha took a deep breath. "Cole left early this morning, and he's to be gone for days—heaven only knows where, as he can be quite mysterious at times—and he left word that you are not to leave town."

Kady could feel her heart start to pound. "I don't want to leave town; I just want to go for a walk, that's all. I saw these rocks yesterday and thought it would be a nice place for a picnic. We could all go."

M-Three shook her head. "Cole has said no. You're not to leave the ranch. He's set guards all around the perimeter of the ranch so you can't leave."

"And he's taken all the horses, too."

"You can have anyone from town come to see you, but you can't even go into Legend."

"He's afraid you'll steal a horse and ride down the mountain to Denver."

Kady could not comprehend what she was hearing. "Are you trying to tell me that I am a prisoner?"

"Exactly."

"Couldn't be more of a prisoner if you were behind bars."

Kady sat there blinking for several moments. "Wait a minute, this is still America, isn't it? I'm not a criminal, and he doesn't have the right to hold me prisoner. I'm a free person, and I—"

"Are you a suffragette?" M-Three asked.

"I'm a human being, with all the rights and privileges that encompasses."

"Maybe in Virginia but not here in Legend. Here you're a subject, just like the rest of us."

"Oh?" Kady said, one eyebrow raised. "We shall see about that. I think Cole Jordan has been dealing with women who don't know the tricks I do. Will you five help me?"

The women looked from one to the other, then back at Kady. "No," Martha said. "We're very sorry, but we have too much to lose. Our fathers would kill us if they lost their jobs."

"But we're sisters," Kady said, and even to herself that sounded stupid. She didn't know these women, so why should they risk anything for her?

"Then I shall do it myself," she said with all the strength she could muster. "I'll get out of here, you'll see."

The five women just sat on the end of the bed and looked at her in pity. Their faces said that Kady would soon find out what they already knew.

Two days, Kady thought, her fists clenched at her side. Two days of doing absolutely nothing. Another day like this and she was sure she would go mad.

After the five Ms left yesterday morning, Kady was so full of righteous indignation that she had been determined to find the petroglyphs and get out of this time period forever. All she wanted in the world was to get back to Virginia and Gregory.

But after a day and a half of trying to escape, she had failed as badly as when she'd tried to get a job in Legend. She certainly had to give it to Cole that when he gave an order, it was obeyed.

After the Ms had left, she'd found a note Cole had left for her on the dresser saying he was very sorry but he'd *had* to leave and he'd see her again in about ten days. There was no mention of her incarceration during that time period, nor had he even had the courtesy to explain where he'd gone and why.

For the entire first day, Kady had tried to escape, but, truthfully, where was she going? Anyone she asked looked blank when she mentioned the rock carvings, so even if she had managed to steal a horse and ride, she had no idea where to go.

She had become so frustrated that last night she'd even written a letter to Cole's grandmother, begging her to come to Legend and help her escape.

So now, the afternoon of the second day, Kady sat at the desk in what had to be Cole's office and asked, Why me? Why had *she* been chosen for this outrageous time mix-up? First of all, she wasn't heroine material. She was just a simple girl from Ohio who wanted to cook. There was no great tragedy in her life, or in Cole's for that matter, that needed to be righted. So why was she here?

Somewhere around one o'clock that day, she'd given up fighting. She had talked, begged, pleaded with every person she saw on the ranch to help her, but they looked at her as though she were crazy. How could she be complaining when she was the mistress of so much? And Kady had to admit that Cole was the owner of a great deal. His house stood on the most beautiful piece of land she had ever seen, and the house itself was breathtaking. There had to be twenty rooms, and each of them was furnished luxuriously in a cozy, comfortable style. It was the house Kady had always dreamed of and had never known how to achieve.

Her favorite room, the kitchen, was a dream, with a huge

wood-fired iron stove, giant oak worktable, four ovens built into brick walls, and a pantry big enough to hold a 7-Eleven store. Unfortunately, the cooking utensils consisted of four stupendously greasy cast-iron pieces and a few wooden spoons.

"If things were different," Kady muttered now as she sat in the library-office, doodling on a piece of paper with a fat pencil. Thinking back, she remembered the yeast starter she'd made at the cabin and how she'd thought of making pickles and jams.

"Kady is such a helpful child." The words echoed in her head, the words she'd heard Jane's mother say a thousand times. When Kady was a child her mother had had to work two jobs. When Jane's parents had offered to look after her daughter, she'd accepted the favor without hesitation. She never knew that Jane's family treated Kady as little more than an unpaid servant.

What was it Cole had said? "You don't have to be the best little girl in the world. You don't have to be perfect. You don't have to do anything to make sure people love you. I love you just as you are."

"Just as you are," she said aloud. To be accepted as you are, isn't that a sort of freedom? And in her heart, she knew that Cole had been telling the truth. She could sit here in his beautiful house for the next eight days, or eighty years, for that matter, and do absolutely nothing if she wanted and he'd be perfectly pleased.

She wasn't sure how she knew this, but she knew that with Cole she didn't have to earn his love. She didn't have to clean the bathrooms as she'd done for Jane's mother, didn't have to cook economically as Mrs. Norman demanded. She didn't even have to keep her mouth shut and not complain as she'd had to do with her mother.

"I can do anything I want," she said, lifting her eyes and staring straight ahead at the bookshelves filled with leather bound volumes in front of her. Abruptly, she pushed the chair back and stood. "Maybe I can't leave this place, but I *can* bring anything that 1873 Colorado has to offer here to me.'' As she stood in front of the window to stare out at the view of mountains and valleys, she whispered, ''So what do I want to do more than anything else in the world?''

As she looked out the window, she thought of her favorite movie, *Babette's Feast*. The heroine was a great chef who, for some political reasons, had to hide in a remote village with two poor sisters. When Babette inherited some money, enough to allow her to quit her job, instead of being ''sensible,'' she'd spent every penny of it on the ingredients to prepare a feast such as no one had ever eaten before.

Kady owned the video of that movie and had played it hundreds of times. At each viewing her imagination went wild as she thought of what she would cook if she had no constraints of money and ''pleasing the public.''

I would first have to make an inventory, she thought. I'd have to see what was here and what I could buy. Maybe I can't go to Denver, but others could go for me. Then I'd have to dig pits, make outdoor ovens, and start pickling vegetables. I'd need help in picking mushrooms and salad greens and herbs. And I'd need—

By the time she got to the last thought, she was at the desk and making notes. ''I'll invite the whole town,'' she said aloud. ''For three days they will eat at Cole Jordan's expense.'' She bit the end of the pencil. ''If you'll eat it, I'll cook it,'' she wrote, then marked that out. ''I won't cook anything cute or endangered,'' she wrote. ''No turtles, raccoons, mountain lions. And no bugs!''

Grabbing the notepad, she left the library and headed for the kitchen. But as her mind raced, so did her feet, and she entered the kitchen in a rush. Manuel and his wife, Dolores, were slowly chopping vegetables for the evening's enchiladas. ''Do you two know where I can hire people who know these mountains and can gather mushrooms for me? And people who can help with butchering and fish cleaning?''

Manuel and his wife looked at each other; then Manuel spoke. "In our town of Socorro there are such people."

"How many people live there?"

"Thirty-six."

Kady smiled. "Can I hire them all?"

Manuel seemed to have been rendered speechless, but Dolores spoke up. "For what? No one will kill Señor Jordan for you."

"Perhaps Juan would," Manuel said matter-of-factly.

"Is this what you want?" Dolores asked, looking at Kady hard.

Kady blinked for a moment, considering this possibility, then shook her head. "No, I don't want to kill Cole, even though he deserves it. I want to put on a feast. A feast such as no one has ever before dreamed of. I want to experiment; I want to create new recipes and eventually write a cookbook. I want to try every dish I've ever contemplated and see what it tastes like. I want to wrap fish in paper, salt, clay, and in wet leaves. I want to marinate meat in herbs that no one has ever tried before. I want to make mistakes and have some triumphs. I want . . . I want . . ." She smiled as she looked at the two old people, their faces unreadable. "I want freedom."

At that she could see Manuel did not understand and that he was about to tell her she could not leave the ranch. "I want to spend Cole Jordan's money. Lots of it. Will you two help me?"

"Gladly," Manuel said, grinning.

"All right, then, come with me and let's start planning this thing. Oh, and send someone to fetch all the inhabitants of Socorro. Tell them I'm paying everyone ten dollars an hour."

At that Manuel had to catch his wife to keep her from swooning. Kady wasn't sure, but she figured the average wage in 1873 was a dollar or so a week, so ten dollars an hour was more than they could comprehend.

"And the babies?" Dolores gasped, her husband's arms around her.

"Bring them and I'll pay them as taste testers. I'd love to write a baby-food cookbook. Come on, time is wasting."

In a state of bewilderment, Manuel and his wife followed Kady into the library.

Chapter 13

As Cole Jordan rode into Legend, Colorado, he was sure that in the ten days he had been away, it had become a ghost town. His first thought was that Harwood's men had returned and slaughtered everyone, but if that had happened, there would be evidence of such murder. As he looked into the windows of the hotel and saw no one, he thought maybe everyone had gone through the rock with Kady. But that couldn't have happened because he'd given orders he knew no one would dare disobey.

If not violence, then maybe smallpox had wiped them out. Or maybe . . .

He couldn't think of any more things that could have happened to everyone, but the eerie feeling of the empty town was making him nervous. Something horrible had happened; it must have. But he could see no signs of disaster, no burned-out buildings, no one walking about with tragic faces.

There was just a deserted town and no clues as to what had happened to everyone.

"Is anyone here?" he shouted, but his voice echoed off the empty buildings and came back to him. Dismounting, he tied his horse up, then went into the mercantile, where he was further shocked. Two-thirds of the shelves were empty. Clothes still hung on the racks, and there were boots for sale, just as always, but the grocery part of the store was picked clean; not so much as a can was left. Even the "mystery" cans that had fallen into a river and had their labels washed off were gone. No barrels of crackers or pickles stood before the counter.

Cole went back outside and started walking. The laundry was empty; the barber's chairs had no customers; the freight depot had a wagon in front of it, loaded with ore, but there were no horses attached to it, no driver in the seat.

The more he saw, the more anxious he became, and he started running. The livery stable had no horses; the boarding house was empty. No one was at the newspaper office or the telegraph office. The ice cream parlor had no people in it, nor did it have anything to eat. The icehouse out back had no milk or cream; in fact, even the ice was gone.

He ran past the Jordan Line up to Paradise Lane, but he could see that the church and library were as empty as the rest of the town.

"Kady," he whispered, fear running through his body. Whatever had happened to the people of this town had also happened to Kady. Turning abruptly, he began to run down the street to get to his horse. He *must* save Kady!

He was in such a blind panic that he ran into Ned Wallace without seeing him, sending them both flying, and the little beer barrel on Ned's shoulder went crashing, its contents spilling on the boardwalk.

"Now look what you've done!" Ned yelled. "Kady *needed* that, and now what am I gonna to tell her? Damnation! but I don't think there are any more full barrels."

Cole had fallen hard against the horse rail, and what with various injuries he had sustained over the last few days, it took him a moment to regain his awareness. By the time Cole's head cleared, Ned had reentered the saloon.

Cole threw open the swinging doors, but Ned was nowhere in sight. "What the hell is going on?" he bellowed. He received no answer, but he did hear noises in the back.

There was a room on the back of the saloon that was usually packed full of bottles and barrels, but now every shelf was empty. A trapdoor he didn't know existed was thrown up, and at the bottom Cole could see a light. He lost no time climbing down the ladder, where he saw Ned tossing about empty wooden crates, becoming more frustrated by the second.

"That *was* the last one," Ned said angrily. "Now what will Kady do? Today is pasta day, and she wanted to make a sauce with beer and cream. So how the hell is she gonna do that now?" Ned stopped ranting long enough to glare at Cole as though he'd committed some unforgivable sin.

"I guess it will be up to me to tell her," Ned said in disgust, then stepped past Cole to go up the ladder.

Cole, too bewildered to move, stared at the ladder. "What the hell is 'pasta'?" he said under his breath, then grabbed the lantern Ned had left behind and went up the ladder.

He caught Ned just as he was leaving the back door of the saloon. "So help me, Wallace, if you don't tell me what's going on, I'll—"

"You'll what?" Ned said fiercely. "Make me miss pasta day? And the mesquite is ready today, and I'm in charge of candyin' the violets, and Juan says the second risin' of the brioche is my job, and—"

He stopped because Cole had pinned him against a wall and was holding a knife to his throat. "You aren't going anywhere. You're going to sit down and tell me everything. Do you understand me? If you ever want to see this man Pasta again, you'll do what I say."

Ned gave Cole a look of disgust, then muttered something about pasta not being a person and Cole probably couldn't tell puff pastry from strudel dough, but he went back into the empty saloon and sat down. Taking out his big pocket watch, he propped it open on the table. "Ten minutes; that's all I can spare."

"You can spare all the time that's needed. I want to know everything that's going on, and to start, you can tell me where everyone is."

Ned started to rise. "Why don't we just go out to Kady's Place and you can see for yourself? That way we won't waste any more of my time."

Cole had to count to ten before replying to that one. "And just where is 'Kady's Place'?"

"The Jordan Ranch, you know, it's—" Ned broke off as he seemed to realize for the first time to whom he was talking. Sitting back down, he drew a deep breath. "A few things have happened in the days you were away."

"You know, I figured that out about two minutes after I entered town. So now, why don't you tell me just exactly what it is that has happened?" Cole thought that if Kady was in any danger, he wanted to know its exact nature so he could plan how to save her. In the time since he'd arrived in town, he'd prepared himself for anything, whether it was natural disasters, illness, massacres, or even the return of the plagues of Egypt. What he was not prepared for was the story that Ned Wallace began to tell him, reluctantly at first, but with increasing gusto as he watched Cole's face, the eyes widening and the jaw dropping down further with every word Ned spoke.

Ned wasn't a very good storyteller, as he tended to start in the middle of a story, go in one direction, then backtrack and go in another. Rather like he was trying to draw a spider, Cole thought as he tried to piece together what Ned was telling him.

It seemed that Kady had decided to occupy herself during her husband's absence by cooking for the whole town. When Cole first heard this, he'd smiled indulgently, but as the story expanded, he heard things that he didn't like.

"She kissed who?" Cole asked.

"Hog's Breath Howie," Ned said, by now having lit a pipe and drawing deeply on the stem.

Cole was aghast. "But he offered two hundred dollars to any of Les's girls who'd kiss him, and none of them would do it. That man's breath has been known to fell horses."

"It didn't seem to bother Kady, not when he pulled the tarp off that wagon and she saw them pots and pans."

It seemed that three days after Cole left town, Kady had hired five drivers with wagons to go to Denver to buy cooking things for her. "Things nobody had ever heard of," Ned said, sounding as though Kady was buying ingredients for a witch's brew. "But of course we all know what they are now," he said smugly. He paused long enough to make sure he had Cole's attention. "She wanted things like semolina and olive oil and star anise."

Cole leaned closer to Ned, his eyes narrowed. "You want to tell me why *my wife* was kissing Hog's Breath Howie?"

"I'm gettin' to it; don't rush me." Ned took another long draw on his pipe. Having the owner of the town at his mercy was a dream come true. "Kady gave instructions to the drivers that they were to bring back all kinds of food that they had never heard of. If they saw an Italian family or Chinese or any other color or religion, whatever, the driver was to pay *very* high prices for—"

"Why *high* prices?" Cole interrupted.

"Kady said that the national economy would be helped if you shared your wealth with other people rather than hoarding it," Ned said, eyes twinkling.

"Go on," Cole said solemnly.

"Kady told the drivers they were to buy any food that

sounded strange, anything they'd never heard of. She also gave each man a list of things that she wanted in quantity, like olive oil and great barrels of flour. Did you know that brown flour with the bran still on it is better for you than white flour?"

Cole glared at him.

"All right, just be patient, will you? Kady gave the job of findin' some decent cookware to Hog's Breath, and you shoulda seen him! A couple of us tried to warn Kady that ol' Hoggie wasn't to be trusted, but she wouldn't listen. She put a bag of gold in his hand and told him she was dependin' on him. We all thought Hoggie was gonna melt, and we were sure we'd never see him again."

Ned took another deep draw. "But he fooled all of us. The next day he came back with an incredible story. Seems some man in Denver decided he wanted to open a French restaurant, so he hired three French chefs straight from Paris, France, and they arrived with crates full of copper pots." Ned gave Cole a serious look. "Copper conducts heat quicker and more evenly than any other metal except silver. Did you know that?"

"Get on with it," Cole said with no humor in his voice.

"The chefs arrived with all their equipment—Kady calls it a *batterie de cuisine*—but two days later them cooks deserted to go prospectin', leavin' all the pots and pans behind. Hog's Breath bought the lot of 'em, and when he showed up at the ranch with a wagonload of saucepans and molds and au gratin dishes, Kady was so overwhelmed, she kissed him. On the mouth."

At this Ned waited for Cole's reaction to what he thought was a wonderful story, but Cole didn't give any indication that he'd heard. "Who is Juan?" is all Cole asked.

"Barela," Ned said in a tone of false innocence. "You musta heard of him."

For a moment all Cole could do was blink; then he rose, making motions to check all the knives on his body as he moved. Juan Barela was a killer, would kill a man as soon as look at him. No one knew for sure exactly how much violence he was responsible for, but then no one was stupid enough to ride up to Socorro and investigate, in spite of the huge reward on the man's head.

Ned grabbed Cole's arm and motioned for him to sit back down. "You don't have to worry. Kady has him eatin' out of her hand. And I mean that for gospel truth. Juan's running the whole show, keepin' order over all the workers and the people comin' to eat. And he's doin' a great job, 'cause he's only had to shoot a couple of people."

"Shoot—" Cole said then started to rise again.

"It was only ol' Lindstrum," Ned explained, making Cole sit back down. There wasn't a man who'd ever met Lindstrum who didn't want to shoot him. If a heavenly angel came to Lindstrum, he'd find something to complain about.

"Lindstrum wouldn't eat his field-green salad, said it was no more than a bunch of weeds, so Juan shot him. Just a little bit along the top of his arm; then Dolores wrapped a bandanna around it, and Lindstrum ate his greens."

"I see," Cole said. "And what did my wife say to having a man shot for not eating his salad?"

"Kady told Juan not to shoot anyone else, but then she said from the looks of the man's teeth maybe someone should have made him eat his greens a long time ago. She and Juan are the best of friends."

When he spoke, Cole's voice was very quiet. "My wife is friends with the most notorious killer in the country? A man who strikes fear in the hearts of everyone who hears his name?"

"Kady says that Juan is just trying to support the whole town of Socorro and all his children. His methods are bad, but his motives are good." At this Ned paused and smiled dreamily. "Kady sure is a wonder. On that first day Juan came down from the mountain with the others from Socorro. None of us ever thought we'd see *him*, but he said even he was willin' to hunt mushrooms if it paid ten dollars an hour so he——"

"What!?" Cole gasped. "Ten dollars for *one hour?*"

"That's what Kady is payin' everyone who helps her," Ned said, trying but not succeeding to suppress his smile. He'd been trying to buy the saloon from Cole for six years, but Cole wouldn't consider selling or even going into a partnership. "You wanta hear about Juan or not?"

"Yeah, tell me," Cole growled. "But, wait a minute, are you sure there's no whiskey in this place? I truly do need a drink."

"Not a drop," Ned said cheerfully. "Kady needs everything. Anyway, about Juan. He showed up——first time anyone on the right side of the law had seen him in ten years——and we all kept lookin' at him cause it was like lookin' at a legend. I must say he is one fine-lookin' man. Kady calls him a 'hunk.'"

"Go on!" Cole snapped.

"That first day the whole town of Socorro came down out of the mountains, and in the back of a wagon there was this little boy that was the spittin' image of Juan, so Kady congratulated Juan on havin' such a beautiful son. Then some old man with a nose like a potato started sputterin' and said the boy was *his.* Kady apologized, but after she helped the fifth child out of the wagon that looked just like Juan, she started laughin' and looked at Juan, and he started laughin' too."

Cole leaned across the table. "Why don't you just tell me the facts? Is Kady all right?"

"More than all right, I'd say. Oh, lordy, but that woman can make people work! She's had us diggin' pits and constructin' spits. She's got the blacksmith rollin' puff pastry and Les's girls have been pullin' strudel dough. You know, don't you, that that stuff has to be stretched until you can read a newspaper through it?" Ned stopped long enough to chuckle. "You know, there ain't nothin' that girl can't cook. She give a couple of hunters a list of things they couldn't bring back, like mountain lions and such, so ol' Ernie got the bright idea of bringin' her back a bag full of rattlers. He thought it would be a great joke."

"You allowed someone to give my wife rattlesnakes?" Cole said through clenched teeth.

"Don't worry; Juan shot their heads off, then Kady cleaned 'em in a flash, marinated the meat in milk for half a day, then fried 'em. They was right good eatin', if I do say so myself."

"You ate rattlesnake?"

Ned leaned forward, his face *very* serious. "Hell, I've eaten snails." When he'd given Cole time to absorb this, he said, "Kady mixes 'em with garlic and wild parsley, and they ain't half bad."

"Snails?" Cole whispered.

"It was either eat them or get shot by Juan," Ned said in defense. "And, besides, we've all come to trust Kady. You should taste what she can do with a dove. She stuffs them with rice, then cooks 'em over charcoal—Garson made the charcoal. Anyway, them doves are crisp on the outside and the meat is so tender Toothless Dan can eat it."

For a long moment, Cole sat at the table in silence, looking down at his hands clasped tightly in front of him. "What else?" he asked softly; then when Ned didn't answer, he looked at him. "What else?" he asked louder.

"Well, everyone in town knows how you tricked Kady into marryin' you. They feel *real* bad about turnin' her away when she was hungry, so they . . . Well, they . . ."

"Out with it!"

"All the men have been offerin' to marry her. You know that she's the most beautiful gal to ever come to this town, and if she wanted to open a restaurant, people'd come from miles just to eat her cookin', so she don't need your money. So, anyway, all the men have asked her to marry 'em."

"Including you?" Cole asked nastily.

"I was one of the first," Ned said with his jaw set, preparing to be told he was fired from his job and to get out of town. But Cole didn't say anything. Instead, he turned away and looked out the window.

"I don't blame any of you," Cole said after a while. "She is beautiful, and there's something about her that makes a man feel good. You know, don't you, that she has no idea what a prize she is—which is, of course, half of her charm."

"Yeah, we all know," Ned chuckled. "Kady thinks she's *fat.*"

At that the two men looked at each other, their eyes alive with laughter. "Fat," Cole said, then chuckled as he began to think of all Kady had done. Maybe he should take offense at her action of feeding the entire town at his expense, but he couldn't suppress his humor. "Hog's Breath?" he said, making Ned laugh harder.

"Thought he was gonna drop dead on the spot. And you should see Juan! Kady says he has the lightest hand with pastry she's ever seen. She's tryin' to get him to open a French bakery and make somethin' called cwoisannts. More butter than bread, but they sure are good."

For a moment Cole stared into space. What did money matter to him? Ever since the murders when he was a kid, he'd been afraid to spend anything. It was as though his whole family had died trying to protect that money, so it was his duty to keep it safe. But Kady had used the money to help people who needed it and to give joy. He had no doubt that the entire town of Socorro could live for the next two years off what she had paid them over these few days.

"You ready to go back?" Cole asked Ned. "I seem to have worked up a powerful hunger."

"Then Kady's the one to fix that."

"I think Kady just might be able to fix everything that's wrong with me."

"And maybe the whole town," Ned said under his

breath so Cole couldn't hear him. Cole may have owned the town, but in the last days Kady had given her opinion of what she called Cole's "obsessive monopoly." She said she believed in "free enterprise." And, as they had seen, Kady put into action what she believed in.

"I'm ready," Ned said as he followed Cole out the door.

Chapter 14

WHAT COLE SAW WHEN HE RODE INTO HIS OWN RANCH WAS controlled chaos. At first he thought it was more chaos than control until he heard the shouts and a couple of shots fired into the air. It looked as though his ban on guns within the city limits had been forgotten.

"I told you to get back in line," came a man's voice; then Cole had the reins grabbed from his horse as he felt a man's hand on his leg.

"You want to let go?" Cole said calmly, looking down at the man with his hand on Cole's calf.

"Oh, sorry, Señor Cole," the man said. "But Juan ordered—"

"I know what you've been told," Cole answered as he dismounted and tossed the reins to a boy standing nearby.

Cole had to practically shove his way through the people there to get into his own house. As far as he could tell, Kady was feeding a certain number of people at a time, and the people who weren't eating stood around outside and waited for the next serving time assigned them. To prevent them from fainting from hunger between meals, they were served trays full of something that seemed to be called whorederves.

For a moment Cole thought he was going to have to kill someone to be allowed in the front door, because Juan had decreed that no one was to enter. But after some words were exchanged, Manuel was called to verify Cole's identity.

"What the hell have you done to my house?" Cole asked once inside, his back to the door and looking about.

In each of the downstairs rooms, all the furniture and rugs had been pushed to the side and covered with sheets so each could be turned into a makeshift kitchen. People and flour seemed to be everywhere.

"They prepare the food in here, then bake what they can in here and take the rest outside to bake," Manuel said. "Kady says—"

Cole lifted one eyebrow. "I'm sure it's either Kady or Juan," he said with great sarcasm. "Where is she?"

Manuel gave him a look that said, *Need you ask?*

With great strides, Cole went to the kitchen, then stood in the doorway and watched until he was pushed aside as people ran from one room to another. Any general of an army would have been pleased to have the authority that Kady did as she managed what looked to be fifty or more people moving quickly about the kitchen and entering and leaving through three doors. Cole was amazed to see the space so full, but no one was trying to murder anyone else. This was especially astonishing when he recognized three men whose faces he'd seen on wanted posters.

Juan Barela came in through the outside door, three empty trays in his hands. He stopped abruptly, then turned and saw Cole standing to one side of the doorway.

Nothing wrong with his instincts, Cole thought, and looking into Juan's dark eyes, Cole knew Juan was questioning whether Cole was going to cause any trouble. Was he going to turn him over to the sheriff?

Frowning, Cole nodded toward a pile of crescent-shaped rolls in a basket on a table by the wall.

With a bit of a smile, Juan grabbed one and tossed it to Cole, then went to the ovens, where, as Cole watched with interest, the "hardened killer" pulled out three huge metal sheets covered with cookies.

One by one, people in the kitchen began to see Cole as he stood to one side of the doorway, and each face asked what he was going to do. Would he stop feeding the whole town for free? Would he be so angry that he'd do something horrible, like kick everyone out of the town he owned?

But Cole's eyes were on one person, and that was Kady, with her dark hair tumbling down her back and one of his shirts covering most of her lovely body. The heat of the stove made her skin glow, and he'd never seen her look so meltingly beautiful.

"You'll burn those!" she said as she grabbed a copper saucepan that was nearly as big as she was, then slid it to the cool side racks of the stove. "Look at—" She broke off as she caught sight of the person in charge of that saucepan and saw he wasn't looking at the stove.

When Kady turned and saw Cole standing there, his heart leaped because he saw in her eyes that she was glad to see him. Maybe it wasn't the love that he wanted to see, but she wasn't angry with him, and she certainly didn't hate him.

It took her several seconds before she got her emotions under control so she could look at him the way she thought she *should* look at him, which made Cole smile. His little Kady of the Shoulds, he thought, always doing what she thought she should do.

"Won't you join us?" she asked sweetly. "We're having a bite to eat. I do hope you have time to share a meal with us."

There were several snickers at that. Over the last days it had been agreed upon by the entire town that Cole was an idiot for leaving Kady alone for even seconds. The general opinion was that any man in his right mind would have all the time in the world for a woman like Kady.

Cole, not really versed in the ways of women, was pleased by Kady's tone. Maybe things were going to be all right now. Now that she'd seen that Legend wasn't such a bad place, and since she'd seen the advantages of being his wife instead of returning to that Garvin, he was sure she'd come around.

Still smiling at Cole, she said a few words to Juan; then he left the room. "We have a special table just for you," Kady said, "and I am going to prepare your meal with my own hands. No one else will be allowed to touch it."

With two strides, Cole crossed the room to his wife. He meant to pull her into his arms, but she stepped back, so his kiss touched only her cheek. "You have to go now, or I'll never get anything ready," she said with a flutter of her lashes.

Cole wanted to take her upstairs to bed, but there had to be at least a hundred pairs of eyes watching him, so he just nodded, then went outside. There'd be time for privacy later.

Under the cottonwood trees at the back of the house were about twenty-five tables of different sizes set up, and each table was loaded with delicious-looking food. Cole started toward the biggest table, but one of Juan's cousins held out a chair at a solitary table set deep in the shade of the biggest tree.

When Cole was seated, he was aware that he was alone at the table, alone under the tree, and that he was the focal point of all eyes. Martha and Mavis were serving food, and now and then they would look at him, but when he glanced at them, they turned away. On the ride to the ranch Ned had made Cole laugh by telling him that Kady called the women the five *M*s.

Kady, he thought. In a mere ten days she had changed the town's interest from silver to food—and to Kady herself. His hair still bristled when he thought of Ned's telling him of all the marriage proposals made to Kady. What did they think she was going to do about the husband she already had?

After about thirty minutes, Kady came outside, a plate covered with a big napkin in her hand, and a hush fell over the crowd. By now all the people from the front of the house had moved to the back so they could watch what was happening. What was Kady going to serve her husband?

With feelings of pride, Cole looked at the plate Kady set before him, then took her hand and kissed it as she started to pull the napkin away.

At first Cole could do little more than gape as the napkin revealed what was under it. On his plate were potatoes, carrots, slices of buttered bread—and a rat. A great big black rat that she had rolled in bread crumbs and fried, but leaving the head and tail intact, so there was no mistaking what it was.

As Cole stared in disbelief at the monstrosity on his plate, the people around him began to laugh. And laugh. And laugh. It was as though they had been waiting years to play such a joke on him, and now their pent-up laughter could escape.

Slowly, Cole turned to look up at Kady and saw that she was smiling as though he were what she'd just served: a rat for a rat, so to speak.

It was at that moment that Cole changed. Why was he trying to force a woman to love him? Force her to stay here against her will? What did he hope to accomplish with a woman who didn't want to be his wife?

In one motion, he was out of his chair and had thrown Kady over his shoulder and started walking toward the stables. For a split second Juan stepped in his path, but the look Cole gave the man made him step aside. No matter how fierce an outlaw, he didn't want to get between a man and his wife.

As Cole strode through the people, they parted for him,

and they were still laughing, but now the tone of their laughter had changed. Now they weren't so much as laughing at him as with him.

"Put me down," Kady hissed, and when Cole ignored her, she pinched his side. For this Cole slapped her smartly on her fanny that was pressed so enticingly against his right ear.

For once Cole was glad to see that no one had paid any attention to his tired horse and the poor creature was grazing, unattended, on the flowers at the front of the house. Cole threw Kady into the saddle, then mounted behind her.

"I thought you could take a joke," she said when he was behind her and had led the horse away from the house. "That's all it was, a joke. Don't you have a sense of humor?"

Cole didn't answer, and after a while Kady stopped trying to talk to him. If he wanted to sulk, let him, she thought, then folded her arms over her chest and decided that two could play at this silence game as well as one.

They had traveled for only minutes before Kady realized where they were going. He was taking her back to the petroglyphs. He was going to send her back to her own time!

As soon as she realized where he was going, it was as though her mind started a war with itself. Of course she wanted to return to Gregory and Onions and to all the people she knew and loved there. Well, truthfully, there weren't many people outside of Gregory and his mother that she knew very well. And, truthfully, it had been difficult to find women who could be bridesmaids at her wedding. But it was where she belonged!

But then, here in Legend she had made new friends. Many, many friends. In the last days she'd come to know people. For one whole day she'd sat with women and peeled and chopped vegetables. There wasn't a child or adult from Socorro she didn't know by name, and they appreciated what she had taught them about how to cook foods that grew for free on the mountainsides.

And there was Legend itself, a town she planned to help, just as soon as she got it out from under Cole's rule.

"There," Cole said coldly as he dismounted, then pulled Kady down to stand beside him. As usual, Cole had taken a shortcut, and they were already at the petroglyphs. When she didn't move around the horse so she could see the rock, he grabbed her hand and pulled her.

Before her was the opening, that odd fading of the rock, and beyond it she could see her dim, gray apartment, just as she'd left it, the rusty flour box on the floor. How different it looked, away from the Colorado sunshine that brightened everything here.

"Go on," he said, giving her a little push. "It's what you wanted, isn't it?"

"Yes," she said tentatively, but she didn't move. She looked back up at him. "I left some puddings steaming on the back burner, and I didn't take the bread out of the oven. I think I better go back and—"

Cole put his hands on her shoulders, making her turn back to the scene before them. "*That* is where you belong. Not here."

"You're angry because of the money I spent, aren't you? And the rat. Look, I'm sorry. I'll cook you a dinner that will bring tears to your eyes. You'll see."

Again, Cole turned her back toward the opening, slowly but steadily pushing her toward it.

When Kady's foot stepped through the opening, she could see that her leg was already in the apartment. Cole's hands were pressing down on her shoulders, refusing to allow her to back up. *Maybe the dark man on the horse will show up,* she thought, looking about her. But there was no sign of him, and Cole kept pushing.

At last she was standing in her apartment, Cole's hands no longer on her shoulders and she turned back to look at him. For a moment her breath caught in her throat, as she feared that she'd see only the wall, but he was still there, looking at her, the sun shining on his blond hair.

As she watched, the opening through time was growing smaller and Cole seemed to be getting farther away. Suddenly it seemed that a thousand images went through her head as she remembered him dressed as an eagle. She thought of the ribbon he'd tied to the outhouse and how he'd prepared a bath for her at the hot springs. He'd raced down the side of a cliff when he thought she was injured.

Now, with the opening growing smaller, she looked into his eyes, but she could not read them. Why wasn't he holding out his hand to her? Why wasn't he telling her that he loved her? Why wasn't he telling her that he needed her and wanted her as no one else in the world had ever told her?

As she looked at him, she saw a stain on his shirt on the left shoulder. It was a stain that was growing darker and larger as she watched, and all of a sudden she understood. Those ten days he'd been gone, he'd been trying to keep her safe. He had ordered her not to leave the ranch not because he was a monster but because he wanted to protect her in case there was any trouble. Maybe protect her in case he didn't return.

Kady didn't think about what she was doing, she just leaped. Like a dog jumping through a burning hoop, she dove through the circle that was left in the wall and leaped into Cole's arms.

"Kady," was all Cole could manage to say as he held her so tightly her ribs nearly cracked. "Are you sure? Are you sure?"

"I don't know," she said honestly. "I don't seem to know the answers to anything anymore." She was kissing his face. "You're hurt and bleeding and—"

He pulled away to look at her. "You came back to be my *nurse?*"

She looked into his eyes. "I really don't know why I came back. I still love—"

175

To keep her from saying the name, he kissed her. "Maybe you'll change your mind later, but I'll take what time we have now. Shall we tell it to go away?"

Turning in his arms, Kady looked back at the rock and saw that the hole had widened. There was her apartment, her clothes still tossed over the couch, the light on her message machine still on.

"You can still go," Cole said softly. "I won't force you to stay here."

Tightening her grip on him, she put her head against his neck. "No, I think I'll stay," she said. "At least until I get bored with you."

At that he laughed. "As long as I have money, I think you can occupy yourself."

"Is that what you think? That I only like your money?"

"Of course," he said. "Isn't that what all the women like about me?"

"Well, not *this* woman! I like the way you take care of people and the way you put others' needs before your own. And I like the way . . ." She trailed off because she could feel him chuckling against her.

"You *are* a rat," she said as she kissed his neck.

"Come on, let's go home; I'm hungry."

"Oh? And who do you think is going to feed you?"

"Martha, Mavis, Myrtle, and—" He didn't say any more because Kady was kissing him and pulling him down to the ground.

Behind them, the opening in the rock closed.

Chapter 15

"*Mmmm*," KADY MURMURED OVER HER COFFEE CUP. SHE AND Cole were alone in the kitchen, and they'd just finished breakfast. In the three days since she'd decided to remain in Legend, at least until the supernatural force that had brought her here took her away again, they had had a delightful time. They had ridden together and talked, and Cole had taken her all over Legend and the surrounding countryside. She had never had such an old-fashioned good time with anyone else.

So what if he never tried to make love to her? So what if when they kissed it never went beyond the closed-mouth stage. That's what she wanted, wasn't it? After all, she was still engaged to marry Gregory, even if she was married to Cole. Or something like that.

"It seems rather sinful just to sit here," she said, looking out the window at the beautiful Colorado mountains.

Raising his head from his own coffee cup, Cole looked at her. "What else should we be doing?"

"I can't seem to think of a thing," she said with delight and thought how the modern world was controlled by the clock and the calendar. She didn't know what time it was or even what day of the week.

"Sure?" he asked, teasing. "We could go for a ride."

"No," she said as she got up to refill their cups.

"You could cook something and we could go on a picnic."

At that Kady laughed. "I think the town hates you."

"Yes, I'm sure they do," he answered, sipping his coffee and watching Kady with adoring eyes. Three days ago, after Kady had chosen to stay with him, they had returned to the Jordan Ranch and Cole had dismissed everyone from his property. At that moment he'd been the most hated man in the country. That is until Juan had stepped in and threatened to shoot anyone who complained because Cole wanted to keep Kady in private. "What man does not envy him?" Juan had asked, making Cole roll his eyes, glad Kady had not heard that comment.

Juan finished cooking what had been started, and Manuel took charge of the cleanup, and everyone had gone home with as much food as he could carry so, in the end, the townspeople were happy enough.

"We could . . ." Cole said, looking up, his eyes teasing. "We could go look for the Lost Maiden Mine. Millions of dollars in gold, and it's very near here."

"Already found it," she murmured, looking out the window.

"What?" Cole asked, looking at her sharply. "You found the Lost Maiden Mine?"

"Not me," she said. "They."

Cole stared at her. "What do you mean 'they' found the Lost Maiden Mine?"

"It was found in nineteen eighty-two, and it was in all the newspapers and magazines. For a while the whole country was possessed by Maiden Fever, as it was called."

When she didn't say any more, Cole grabbed her hand and held it tightly, while locking eyes with hers. "Okay, okay," she said. "I don't remember much about it, really.

Some hikers found the gold in a little cave near a rock that looks like the face of an old man. And don't you dare ask me where that is, because I have no idea. I thought the mine was found in Arizona."

Cole gave a snort of disgust. "The old prospector who said he'd found the mine used to come into the saloon in Legend when I was a kid."

"What were you doing in a saloon if you were a kid?"

"Getting drunk and doing naughty things with the girls. Now tell me more about this treasure."

"I don't know much, except—" She turned to look at him and was tempted to ask about the "naughty things." "Did the prospector have a glass eye?"

"A great big ugly one, why?"

"People thought he must have had, but no one was alive who had seen him, so they weren't sure it was him they found in the cave."

When Kady said no more, Cole, in one easy motion, pulled her from the chair and put her on his lap. With her head on his shoulder and his big arms around her, Kady sighed dreamily. "The whole thing was wonderfully romantic. There was the legend that this old man had found a mine that was guarded by the spirit of a beautiful Indian maiden, but no one believed him."

When she looked at Cole in question, he guffawed. "He was a drunk and a cheat at cards, as well as a thief and a liar. Of course no one believed him. The newspaper printed the story because they needed to fill up the space."

"Obviously, he wasn't always a liar, and you should work on believing in people more."

"You believe everything anyone tells you, so you're gullible enough for both of us. Now tell me what was romantic about this mine and how much was in it?"

"Leave it to you to think about the money. Anyway, a couple of hikers saw a bat fly into some rocks and started investigating and found a small cave. Inside were two skeletons, one of a young woman wearing the remnants of a beaded dress and the other of an old man wearing a leather coat. He had a glass eye and—'' She looked up at Cole. ''Even though carbon dating showed the woman's skeleton to be about a hundred years older than the man's, they were holding hands when they were found.''

''And that's romantic to you? Two dead people? Skeletons are romantic? *Life* is romantic.''

''You are a man, that's all that's wrong with you.''

''And since when did you start complaining about that?''

When Kady smiled, Cole gently kissed her, but she had already learned not to introduce true passion into their kisses. Passion made him pull away. ''Let's go find it. The mine. Let's go find the mine.''

''But it's—'' She started to say that the mine had already been found, but that wasn't true, not when now was 1873. ''What do you want the money for? Don't you have enough?''

''It's not the money; I want the excitement. Finding treasure. That would be wonderful! Oh, wait. What did the people who found it in 1982 do with the money? Some of your good deeds?''

Kady grimaced. ''Fought over it. The man and woman who found it were engaged to be married, but after they found the treasure, they spent ten years in courtrooms fighting over who saw inside the cave first and therefore owned the lion's share of the loot. In the end the lawyers got nearly all of it. I think the hikers ended up with about twenty grand each, out of a total of about thirteen million. And of course their lives were a shambles.''

Raising her head, she looked at him. ''And what would you do with more millions than you already have?''

He took a moment before speaking, and when he did, his voice was soft. ''I'd bury it under the mosque. No one goes there except me, so it would be safe; then, Kady, if you do go back to your own time, you can come back here and know where to find it. You'd be smarter than to let the lawyers have it.''

For a moment Kady was speechless because she knew that he meant every word of what he was saying.

"Do you love me, Kady?" he whispered, kissing the top of her head.

She hesitated before she spoke, as Gregory's face flashed before her eyes. Then she seemed to also see the man in her dreams, the man with the veiled face, who had haunted her most of her life. "I—" she began, but he put a finger to her lips, then lifted her chin so he was looking into her eyes.

"Someday I want to see love in your eyes when you look at me," he said.

Kady started to protest that statement, but Cole wouldn't let her speak.

"I may not be an expert in love, but I know that when you love someone, you *know* it. You don't hesitate or have to think about it. Nor does anyone else come to your mind when you think of love."

He kissed her softly. "When I look into your eyes, I'll always know what is in your heart."

His words were so true that they brought tears to Kady's eyes, and she buried her head in his chest to keep him from seeing.

"Are those tears you're shedding for me?" Cole asked cheerfully as he pulled her head up to look at him. "I don't think any girl's ever cried over me before."

That made Kady laugh. "As far as I can tell, you've made every woman in this town cry."

"Me?" he asked innocently. "I've never—"

"Señora Jordan," came Manuel's voice from outside the door.

"Go away!" Cole shouted. "We don't want to see anyone."

"We haven't seen anyone for three days now," she reminded him. "What if the house is on fire?"

"Then call the fire brigade," Cole answered, as he planted a kiss on Kady's neck.

"What is it, Manuel?" Kady called.

"The Señora Ruth Jordan wants to meet with you in one hour at the Hanging Tree."

It took Kady a few moments to digest this information. First of all, who was Ruth Jordan? Why did she want to meet with Kady? When she looked at Cole, she saw he was smiling at her as though he could read her mind.

"Tell him you won't go," he urged.

Ignoring him, she tried to solve the riddle. "Your grandmother!" she said, her face showing pride that she had remembered without any help from him. "I forgot that I sent her a letter pleading for help. Oh, heavens, but that will take some explaining. And the Hanging Tree is where I first met you, isn't it?"

"Right on all counts," he said, still smiling at her, but his eyes were eating her up, as though he were trying to memorize every curl of her hair, every curve of her face.

"I'll be right there," she called to Manuel, then heard the old man go down the hall.

"Kady," Cole said, and she knew he was going to try to persuade her to stay with him.

"Why doesn't your grandmother come here to the ranch? Why does she want me to meet her so far out of town?"

"She refuses to set foot in Legend. She hates the place."

Cole said the words without any hint of anger, but Kady knew he must be hurt that his only living relative refused to have anything to do with the town that belonged to Cole. A town that Kady knew very well that Cole loved. She kissed the underside of his chin. "I shall try to persuade her to come home for supper."

"Home," Cole whispered, as he set Kady off of his lap and moved to stand before the window, his back to her as he stared sightlessly outside. "She doesn't consider this her home, so she leaves it to be haunted by the spirits of people long dead."

In spite of the warmth of the room, Kady shivered at his words. "You have to go with me," she said. "I can't very well meet your grandmother by myself. How long has it been since you two have seen each other?"

For a moment Cole turned toward her, a look of deep melancholy on his face; then his expression changed and he smiled. "Why don't you go see her alone, then bring her back here? You can make something wonderful for supper. She'll like having a granddaughter-in-law who can cook."

His sadness seemed to have left him as he moved across the kitchen to stand before her, and he smiled warmly as he tucked a curl behind her ear. "She'll love you, Kady. And she'll be very happy that her wayward grandson has at last found a woman he can love for all eternity."

Again, Kady had the feeling that something was wrong. "I don't think I will go," she said as she took one of his big hands in both of hers. "I'll send Manuel to tell her that she must come here and visit both of us."

Chuckling, Cole pulled away as he bent to look at her. "You're the woman who faced down Juan Barela, and now you're afraid of meeting my sweet little grandmother all by yourself?"

"But—"

"But nothing. She wants to see you first because she wants to tell you about all my bad habits. She'll want to make sure you know what you're in for with a spoiled brat like me. And she'll want to talk to you about money."

"Money?"

"Oh, yes, my grandmother believes a woman should have money of her own, so she'll want to settle funds on you. And, besides, if I know my grandmother, she will show up with a ladies' picnic." At that he curled his lip in disgust. "Little teacups that break if you try to hold just four of them in one hand."

"Know that from experience, do you?" she asked, laughing.

"All too well. She said I could break china by looking at it. And she won't have any food worth eating, just little sandwiches and tiny cakes. You can put the whole meal in your mouth at one time.''

"And do you know that for a fact, too?" Her eyes were dancing with delight, as Cole's memories were those of a child.

"Yep, sure do. Tarik and I tried it and did it."

Kady laughed as she thought of a ladies' elegant tea being decimated by a couple of greedy boys seeing if they could stuff all the food into their mouths at once. "I think I will go. I'll tell her all about the five *Ms* and how you played them one against the other and how I served you a rat for dinner."

Suddenly, he grabbed her and pulled her up into his arms. "And what else are you going to tell her? What *good* things are you going to report about my character?"

Looking up at him, she caressed his whisker-stubbled cheek. "I shall tell her about how you saved the eagles and how you have done everything you can to make me welcome." When he didn't move, she knew he wanted more. "And I shall tell her that you love me."

Smiling, he kissed her, but when she put her arms around his neck and started to want more, he pulled back. "My grandmother is very punctual. You'd better get out of here."

Kady's eyes widened. "I could wear the new dress you bought me," she said, looking down at her long skirt that was dusty with age and food stained, as all her clothing was.

"Kady, my dear, you could go naked and still be the best-dressed woman in the world."

Kady smiled at him in pure delight, for she knew that what he was saying was from his heart. Whenever she'd been to bed with Gregory, she had been careful to keep her modesty, always covering herself up, always thinking how unattractive her plump body was. It was amazing how in twentieth-century America one's weight became the over-ruling factor of one's life. But with Cole she felt beautiful.

In fact, the whole town of Legend made her feel beautiful and desirable and as though she were worth everything.

With the smile of a temptress, Kady took Cole's hand in hers and led him up the stairs. Maybe he was waiting for something from Kady, such as for her to tell him that she loved him, before he made an attempt at seduction. But maybe he was waiting for a signal from her.

"Why don't you have a seat?" she said in her Mae West-imitation voice as she went to the big wardrobe and withdrew the many garments that a nineteenth-century woman was supposed to wear.

With wide eyes, and as though he were watching a striptease, Cole stretched out on the bed, shoved pillows behind his head, and watched Kady get dressed. For her part, for the first time in her life, Kady took an extraordinarily long time dressing in the clothes Cole had bought for her. She even propped each leg, one at a time, on a chair and very slowly pulled on the stockings that left the upper part of her thighs bare.

When she was dressed, she walked over to Cole, who was now staring at her oddly. And when he grabbed her head to pull her down to kiss her deeply—for the first time—she knew what his expression was. Smiling in satisfaction, Kady had to use all her strength to pull away from him.

"Hold that thought," she said, breathless from the passion she'd just felt from him. "I, ah, I'll be back as soon as possible."

Cole was looking at her with such hot eyes that she wasn't sure she could escape him. It took some strength to back toward the door and fumble with the latch behind her.

"Kady," he said as she opened the door. "Remember that I love you." The way he said it made her heart start to pound. "And you won't forget me?"

That made her smile. "I don't think so," she said, smiling in return. "You aren't a man a woman forgets."

As she stepped through the door, he called out to her, "Remember that the truth is in a person's eyes."

"Yes," she said, then quickly closed the door to the bedroom. Another minute and she'd never be able to leave. She'd jump into bed with him and never get out.

Outside the house, Manuel had a nice, docile horse saddled for her, and to Kady's surprise, she found she was to go to the Hanging Tree by herself, without so much as an escort. After many days of not being given any freedom, this seemed odd, but Manuel just pointed her down the main street of Legend, then told her to take a left on Eternity Road. The Hanging Tree was at the end of it.

With that the old man turned away and mounted the steps onto the porch, and when Kady looked back, he and Dolores were standing there, their faces filled with sadness. When she was mounted, Kady smiled at them, for she guessed that they were worried that she'd never return. But Kady knew how to get back to her own time, and she knew that she was not going to take that route. Not when Cole was waiting for her.

She hadn't had much experience with horses, but the animal seemed to know where she was to go, so she just held on to the reins. As she rode away, she turned back and waved at Manuel and Dolores on the porch, and at Cole in the upstairs window. Some of the ranch hands had come in from the stables, and they, too, were watching her ride away.

As Kady turned the corner and was out of their vision, she looked at the road ahead. "Sure a bunch of gloomy Guses," she said, then thought how nice it was to finally have freedom. She rode past the library and glanced up the short road toward the beautiful mosque, thinking of Cole's saying he'd bury the treasure from the Lost Maiden Mine there.

It was a short ride down Paradise Lane, then a left onto the main road of Kendal Avenue, then another left onto Eternity Road. She passed the firehouse, the telegraph office, and one of the many tent cities, temporarily housing mine workers. She passed the Amaryllis Mine, then continued on the road, away from all human habitation and toward the mountains.

All along the way, people stopped what they were doing and waved at her, making Kady smile and wave back. "I guess I'm famous," she said, laughing. "I guess I'm the woman who fed the town." As she rode she wondered if someday she'd be written about in one of those tourist brochures that you purchase in ghost towns.

But she didn't like to think of Legend as a ghost town, so she put that thought out of her head and concentrated on the scenery.

Once the town was behind her, in the distance she saw a carriage, a lovely thing with a roof on it and a man unhitching the horses. On the ground, sitting on a white tablecloth, was an elegant-looking woman surrounded by all the accoutrements of an old-fashioned afternoon tea. There was a silver teapot and cups so thin that even this far away, she could see the sun shining through them.

She dismounted some distance from the picnic, tied the horse in the shade near a grassy spot, and went forward to meet her grandmother-in-law.

Chapter 16

WHAT APPREHENSION KADY FELT ABOUT MEETING THE ONLY living relative of a man she was coming to care a great deal about was soon gone when Ruth Jordan put out her hand in warm friendship. She was a tall, thin woman, wearing an exquisite white dress with big sleeves and a slim, sleek skirt, showing Kady just how out-of-date the big-skirted fashions of Legend were. As the older woman smiled, Kady saw that her eyes resembled Cole's. What else she could see in those eyes was pain, and Kady remembered too well the horrible tragedy that had befallen Cole's family. In a very short time this lovely woman had lost everything, and from the look of her, she still hadn't recovered from her losses.

"Here, my dear, you must sit down and tell me everything there is to tell about you and my grandson. I want to know everything," she said graciously, motioning toward the cloth on the ground.

As Kady took her place and Ruth poured the tea, for a moment or two there was an awkward silence between them. Then, as Kady picked up a teacup, she smiled.

"Does my choice of china amuse you?" Ruth asked stiffly.

"No, of course not," Kady answered quickly. "I was thinking of the story Cole told me about Tarik and him stuffing all the sandwiches and cakes into their mouths at once. Was he really such a horrid little boy?"

As Kady watched Ruth—for some reason she could not think of her as Mrs. Jordan—the older woman's face turned pale, as though she were on the verge of fainting.

Quickly, Kady put down her cup and reached out her hand, but Ruth pulled away. "Are you all right?"

"Yes," Ruth said softly, looking at Kady in an intense way that was exactly like Cole. "My grandson must love you very much if he mentioned his friend to you. He does not usually speak of . . . of Tarik."

"Cole and I talk a great deal, really. He has a lot to say about everything."

Ruth put her hand on Kady's. "I am an old woman, and I have not seen my grandson in many years, so please, tell me everything. From the beginning."

At that Kady laughed. "You would not believe me if I told you."

The woman's eyes were as intense as those of the eagles Cole had saved. "Yes I would," she said. "You must trust me that nothing you tell me will shock me or make me disbelieve you. I must know *everything*."

It was on the tip of Kady's tongue to say that if she wanted to know more about her grandson, then she should swallow her pride and visit him. Or, better yet, live with him. With *us,* she corrected herself.

But as Kady looked into the woman's eyes, she couldn't bring herself to give advice. Besides, who was she to judge a woman who had been through what this one had?

Kady took a deep breath. "I was born in nineteen sixty-six." As she said this she watched the woman to see if she was going to scoff, but when she did not so much as blink, it was as though a dam were released inside Kady. She had no idea how much she'd wanted to talk to someone about what had happened to her.

Once Kady started, she couldn't seem to stop, and she must have talked for hours. Ruth was the best listener in the world, graciously refilling Kady's plate every time it was emptied and never once losing a look of interest so strong that it seemed to consume her. Once in a while she'd ask a polite question, such as, "Mavis Benson?" then smile at the answer. She had to suppress laughter when Kady told her of Juan Barela, as though she knew something Kady did not.

It was late afternoon by the time Kady finally wound down, and when she looked at the empty dishes, she was embarrassed. "I seem to have eaten everything, and I've taken all your time when you must be anxious to see Cole." She said this as though she didn't know that Ruth Jordan had vowed never again to set foot in Legend.

Ruth did not move but instead sat on the white damask cloth with her hands folded on her lap, her head down, her eyes hidden from Kady's view. When she did look up at Kady, her eyes were so full of anguish that Kady instinctively pulled back.

"I believe you," Ruth said after a moment.

At that Kady smiled. "I don't see how you could. Time travel is not something that actually happens to a person. Except that this time, it did."

Ruth waved her hand in dismissal, rings flashing in the sun. "Your traveling through time is the easy part to believe. What is difficult to accept is believing that you met my grandson."

"But why is that difficult to understand? Oh, I see. It is difficult to believe that out of all the people throughout history I could have met, I came back to your grandson." She leaned toward Ruth. "I have puzzled over that, too. Why Cole? I have never met anyone who needed me less than he does. He is rich and gorgeous, and he has women dying to love him. He is, after all, very easy to love."

"And did you love him?"

Kady looked down at her hands. "Is it possible to love two men?" Her voice lowered. "Maybe even three of them?" When Ruth did not answer, Kady looked up to see that the woman was smiling.

"Oh, yes, I can guarantee you that," Ruth said, eyes twinkling. "I am living proof that a woman can love more than one man."

For a long moment, Ruth looked deep into Kady's eyes. "You are so young, my dear. So very young and so very innocent. When I look into your eyes, I see no pain. Nothing or no one has hurt you so deeply that your soul has been damaged."

Frowning, Kady said, "I have lost both my parents and—"

Ruth cut her off. "Natural deaths. No one has ever been taken from you who should not have been."

"If this is a competition, I hope I lose," Kady answered, still frowning.

Ruth didn't say anything for a moment, then she turned and said loudly, "Joseph!" From out of the shadows of nearby trees stepped a tall man, gray hair at the temples, wearing a silver gray uniform. "The brandy, please, Joseph."

Within seconds a silver flask and two tiny silver cups were handed to Ruth, and she filled one, then handed it to Kady.

"No thank you," Kady said. "Drinking in the afternoon either puts me to sleep or gives me a headache."

"I want you to drink this because you are going to need it."

Instantly Kady was alert. "Has something happened to Cole? No, of course it hasn't. I just left him, and no one has come to tell us anything."

"I want you to drink this," Ruth said more forcefully.

Kady leaned away from her. "What is going on? I've told you everything about me, so I think you owe me the courtesy of telling me whatever it is that makes you think I'll need a shot of brandy to be able to stand the news."

As though for courage, Ruth took a few deep breaths before she spoke. "The year now is eighteen ninety-seven. My grandson died when he was nine years old. In eighteen seventy-three." She looked hard at Kady. "My grandson has been dead for twenty-four years."

At first Kady was puzzled; then she smiled; then she began to laugh. "That's very funny. I think that whoever told you your grandson died told you a great whopping lie. I left your grandson about three hours ago, and I can assure you that he was *very* much alive."

For a moment Ruth sat there, the tumbler of brandy in her hand; then she downed it in one gulp. "All right, my dear, shall we go?"

"Go where?" Kady asked.

"Why, to visit my grandson of course. The invitation to dinner is still open, is it not?"

Kady hesitated, not at all sure that she wanted to go anywhere.

Standing, Ruth held out her hand for Kady. "Come, my dear, we're going to visit my grandson."

Kady stood, but she stepped away from Ruth Jordan. Maybe the tragedies years ago had left the woman insane. Quite suddenly, the only thing that seemed important to Kady was to return to Cole. To Cole the *man,* not a nine-year-old boy.

Turning, Kady ran past the Hanging Tree to the grassy area where she'd tied her horse. But the horse was not there.

"Would you like the brandy now?" Ruth Jordan asked Kady softly; when Kady didn't respond, she held it to her lips, forcing Kady to drink.

"No," Kady said, turning away, gasping for breath and trying her best not to look at the ruins of what had once been the thriving town of Legend, Colorado.

Ruth, in her carriage, had caught up with Kady as she was running toward the town and defiantly, Kady had climbed into the carriage behind the driver. And as they rode into the town, the horror had begun. Only a few hours earlier Kady had ridden out of a pretty little town full of people who had waved to her, called her by name. But now there was only a ghost town full of rickety buildings that had never been solid to begin with.

The first place they passed was the Amaryllis Mine, but now the collapsed, boarded-up old mine had a broken sign that said The 9 Mine. "But that's the Amaryllis!" Kady exclaimed.

"Amaryllis was the name of Cole's little sister, who was killed on the same day he was," Ruth said softly.

Quietly, Ruth had her driver go down one lane after another, and Kady saw that everything in the town was different. Every street, every house, every building had changed. There were more crumbling saloons than anything else in the town, and over them were what had unmistakably been brothels. The school wasn't the pretty building Kady had seen but a ramshackle shed. There was no sports field, no ice cream parlor. The lovely Palace Hotel was a thin-board shanty that she doubted had ever had glass in the windows. There were no boardwalks and no vacant lots, as every inch along the streets was covered with what looked to be one house of iniquity after another. To guess from what she could read from the faded signs, gambling was the major industry of Legend.

Too stunned to speak, Kady just sat in the carriage and looked, her mind too full to comprehend what she had been told and what she was seeing.

At the end of the town, on a road that she had known as Paradise Lane but now with a sign declaring it as Damnation Avenue, was a disintegrating stone wall that seemed to separate this section of the town from the other she had just been through. A nice hedge had been growing there a few hours before.

"The Jordan Line," Ruth said softly, then tapped Joseph on the shoulder and told him they would walk from here. Ruth seemed to sense that Kady was too shocked to speak, but also that she needed comfort, for when they were on the ground, Ruth took Kady's arm tightly in hers.

"Legend was a horrible place," Ruth said. "Worse than you can imagine. In 1867 my husband and my only child, Cole's father, found silver here. They were good men and were determined not to allow to happen to this place what had happened to other silver towns in Colorado. They didn't want a cesspit of brothels and saloons; they wanted families and churches and schools."

"Idealists," Kady whispered, holding on to Ruth's arm as though she might fall without it. In front of her should have been a library, a church to her left, but instead there were a couple of makeshift buildings and open land.

"They were very much idealists, and since they were going to be very rich men, they thought they could carry out their schemes. All they had to do was refuse to sell the land or the mines, then they'd have control." For a moment Ruth paused, sighing as she looked about the empty, decaying town. "We should have known that nothing was going to work when the mine workers renamed the town Legend. My husband called the town Acropolis, but some wag said it ought to be called Sink Hole, Colorado, then someone else said the glory of the place was a legend in Adam Jordan's mind and nowhere else. The name Legend stuck."

"It never happened," Kady said softly, trying to comprehend what she was seeing and hearing. Somehow, she could accept that she had gone back through time, but now she was to understand that she had gone back to a dream, to a place that never existed. She had met a man who had never grown to manhood.

Ruth was looking at her sharply. "I think you'd better sit down. I've had years to deal with this, but you, my dear, haven't had time to recover or even to comprehend."

Leaning heavily on Ruth's strong arm, Kady allowed herself to be led up a path that had once led to the mosque. But Kady didn't have to ask to know that no mosque had been built in memory of Cole's dead friend. In its place was an old house that was surely the most substantially built structure in town. It had once been a nice house with a big porch and windows and . . .

"You lived here, didn't you?" she asked Ruth.

"Yes, all my family lived here together. The wall of the Jordan Line separated that part of town from this end, and Lily and I did our best to keep the children separated from that part of town. We had our own church and school, and that tiny building there we liked to call the library. Cole and I spent hours dreaming of what we'd do with Legend someday. We were going to make it a center of learning, a place people would come to from miles around to read and rest and enjoy the hot springs. He was a child who had great plans for the future."

"And he wanted a big house with a deep porch and furniture from San Francisco," Kady said.

Ruth took a deep breath. "And did he get that house?"

Kady looked down the road to her left, the end of which she could not see. "He built a beautiful house right down there."

Ruth didn't say anything for a moment, then took Kady's arm. "Shall we go see the site?"

Minutes later, when she and Ruth stepped around a curve in the grassy road, Kady was not surprised to see that the site of Cole's house was a cemetery. The Legend she had known with Cole did not have a cemetery. When Ruth started to pull Kady forward into the midst of the gravestones, she dug her heels in and wouldn't move.

"I don't want to see where he is buried," Kady said. "I don't want to think that he never lived to be thirty-three years old and that he never . . . he never . . ."

Ruth didn't press her. "Let's go back to the house and talk. Kady, there is a reason for what has happened to you, and to me, and we must put our heads together and figure out what that reason is."

Kady could only nod as they walked back to the house that Ruth Jordan had once shared with her family. As they mounted the steps, Kady said, "Why did you laugh when I mentioned Juan Barela?"

Ruth smiled. "He was no more an outlaw than you or I. He was a pretty little dark-haired boy whose father worked for us in the stables, but I think he and Cole had a disagreement, so Cole swore Juan was an outlaw-in-the-making. Truthfully, I think some girl chose Juan over Cole."

For the first time since hearing what Ruth had to tell her, Kady smiled. "And the five Ms?"

"All of them worked in the, ah, saloons, very pretty girls, so young and innocent, and they all teased Cole and Tarik mercilessly. Poor Cole used to blush furiously whenever he saw one of them."

On the porch of the old house, Joseph had set up lanterns and chairs, with lap robes ready to protect the women from the cold mountain air. As they settled themselves, it was Ruth's turn to speak and tell Kady all that she had pieced together from hearing Kady's story.

Within minutes, Ruth was telling Kady of Cole's childhood friends that when Kady met them were adult yet were still seen through the eyes of a child. The owner of the laundry who Cole said had six daughters actually was an alcoholic who spent every penny he pulled from the mines on prostitutes and slept in the door of the laundry because it was warmer there. Hog's Breath was a wagon driver named John Howard who loved raw onions. Ned's father ran one of the saloons, and Cole envied him because he was allowed to drink beer.

Ruth talked on and on, her voice light and entertaining, her stories sometimes making Kady smile, but as the sun set Kady became aware that there was an undercurrent to

Ruth's voice. Either she was leaving something out or she was building up to something dreadful.

Just after sundown, silent, almost-invisible Joseph served them cold chicken and salad, and Kady said softly, "What is it you're hiding from me?"

"I have no idea . . ." Ruth began, then stopped herself when she saw Kady's face. "I guess I don't have time to pretend that everything is all right, do I?"

"No, I would say not. I think it's too late to try to hide anything from me. For whatever reason I was chosen, I now seem to be involved up to my neck."

When Ruth spoke again, her voice had changed. No more was she trying to be entertaining. She told of her anger and hurt when she first received Kady's letter, for she thought it was yet another attempt to extort money from her. "But your letter was different. You spoke of Cole as though you might like to wring his neck."

Kady smiled. "Yes, often. He has a way about him that causes that reaction. He tells one what to do rather than asks." Her breath caught in her throat. "Or he did tell people."

Ruth continued. "There have been reports for years that Legend is haunted. The spirits of the people who once lived here seem to still be alive. Or at least alive in some way."

"What happened to the people of Legend after Cole and his family died?"

When Ruth did not answer right away, Kady turned to stare at her and saw that she was so distressed that she appeared to have aged about ten years in just a few minutes. Unless Kady missed her guess, Ruth Jordan was hiding some big secrets, and when Ruth didn't answer the question directly, Kady was sure she was right.

"I didn't know that Cole knew his family had died," Ruth said softly. "On that horrible day we tried to keep the truth from him. His sister and his friend Tarik were killed outright, but Cole lingered for three days. We told him that they were fine but couldn't visit him because they had to go to school. It was a lame excuse, but in the midst of everything it seemed perfectly feasible, and Lily and I thought Cole accepted it. During those three days I stayed with Cole every minute. His mother tended to her daughter's body, then later to . . ."

Hesitating, she looked at Kady. "Lily took care of her daughter, and later she laid out the bodies of her husband and mine when they were brought in, killed by the men who had robbed the bank." Ruth's handsome face suddenly turned bitter, her mouth twisting. "It wasn't the outlaws who killed the children but the 'good' "—she sneered the word—"people of Legend who murdered them."

For a while Ruth kept her face from Kady's as she stared into the dark night. When she looked back, she had recovered herself enough to smile at Kady. "I lost everyone that night. Three days after the shooting the only person left alive was Lily, Cole's mother, and I could see in her eyes that she was retreating. She couldn't face what had happened to all the people she loved."

Again Ruth was silent, but Kady could tell there was more to the story, maybe a lot more, but it was obviously difficult for her to get the words out. Kady sat in silence and waited, the only sound around them the wind in the trees and a coyote in the distance.

"I can't describe those days of horror," Ruth began slowly and so softly Kady could barely hear her. "Now I hardly seem able to remember them. My husband, my only child, both grandchildren, all of them were dead. After Cole's death, Lily became catatonic. She just sat there in a rocking chair, refusing to eat or even to cry. She stared out the window in a way that made me know she might as well have died, too."

Ruth took a breath. "The only person left alive was young Tarik's father, who worked for us," she said, then her face softened. "Oh! but he was a good-looking man. As dark as my family was blond. It was rumored he'd seduced half the women of Legend, but if he had, he was very discreet about it. He was a silent man, devoted to my husband, and always polite, always courteous.

"But that week-in-hell, after everyone was dead, Gamal—that was his name—was still alive. When the first shots were fired, he'd made a leap to put himself in front of the children, but he received half a dozen bullets in his left leg that halted him. Days later the leg was removed, and for a while we thought he'd live, but then his eyes started burning with fever, and I knew that he, too, was going to die."

Ruth looked at Kady, her eyes as hot as though she, too, had a fever. "He was my last link with my family. All I had to do was look at Lily to know that it was only a matter of time before she would will herself to die."

Ruth was looking at Kady as though she were pleading for understanding, but Kady still couldn't comprehend what she was trying to tell her. Reaching across the short distance that separated them, Kady clutched Ruth's hand.

When Ruth spoke, her voice was almost defiant. "When Gamal opened his arms to me, I went to him, and we spent the night making love. The next morning he was burning up with fever, and he never regained lucidity. Two days later he was dead."

Ruth kept her profile to Kady as though she was waiting for some censorship, but Kady only squeezed her hand tighter, encouraging her to continue.

"We made a child that night."

Ruth kept very still, as though waiting for Kady to pronounce judgment on her, but a twentieth-century woman looked at things differently than a nineteenth-century female did.

"A boy or girl?" Kady asked.

Only the tiniest of smiles showed that Ruth was grateful for Kady's not passing judgment, and there was a loosening of tension in her shoulders, as though she had been relieved of a heavy burden. "At the time I never thought of pregnancy. I was forty-eight years old and had already skipped a monthly or two. After the funerals I moved Lily to Denver to see if I could find a doctor who could help bring her back to life. But part of me envied her; I, too, wanted to retreat from the world. How could I think of life after all the death I'd seen?

"As for the symptoms of pregnancy, I felt so bad they seemed normal. And since it had been thirty-two years since my last pregnancy, I didn't remember the symptoms very well. And as I was nursing Lily all day, I rarely got out of my wrapper."

Finally, Ruth turned to look at Kady, who was staring at her with wide eyes, fascinated by the story. Where was she leading?

When Ruth saw Kady's face, she relaxed more. "I finally went to the doctor when I felt the baby kick."

Dreamily, Ruth looked off into the distance. "That was the strangest day of my life. I went to the doctor, knowing something was wrong inside my belly, and I know it is a sin, but I was praying that whatever it was was terminal, as I so wanted to join my family in heaven."

She turned back to Kady. "But I left the doctor's office with thoughts of life. I had forgotten that God gives as well as takes."

Kady still didn't speak because she could tell that this was not the end of the story. If Ruth had given birth to a baby and everyone had lived happily ever after, Kady would not have been pulled through time smack into the midst of this situation.

"I have made many mistakes in my life," Ruth said softly, "but none I regret as much as what I did when I learned that I was going to have a baby."

She grabbed Kady's hand so hard that Kady nearly cried out in pain. "After my family was murdered, I was numb. I didn't care if I lived or died. There was nothing inside me, not hatred, not love, and certainly not thoughts of revenge."

Abruptly releasing Kady's hand, Ruth looked back into the night. The moon was rising, and it was growing late, but Kady had never felt less sleepy in her life.

Ruth continued. "When I found out that I had a life growing inside me, all I could think of was protecting that child. No matter what it cost in money, blood, or tears, I was going to protect *this* child from all harm."

Ruth's lips tightened. "First of all I made my house in Denver into a fortress. No prison was ever as secure as my house and garden. Armed guards with dogs patrolled the grounds night and day. Not even delivery men were allowed onto my property, and servants entering and leaving were searched thoroughly."

For a moment Ruth paused as she thought back over the past, and when she spoke, her voice was quiet, deep with emotion. "It is many years later now, so it's difficult to describe why my hatred took the direction it did. Maybe I should have hated the outlaws who robbed the bank, but I didn't hate them. They never fired a shot in the town. No, it was the overzealous citizens of Legend who did the shooting. All of them owned firearms, half of them had never used them, but that day they saw their silver riding away, so they opened fire. They killed three children that day. And three adults in the days that followed. All in an attempt to keep their bloody silver."

When Ruth turned to Kady, her eyes were burning hotly. "Can you understand the hatred I felt? I was carrying a child, and there was no doubt in the world that this child would be the only family I'd have for the rest of my life. I *had* to protect him from those people in Legend."

"But you were in Denver," Kady said softly.

"Yes, I was." Turning away, Ruth looked into the night. "Don't try to make sense of it, because there is none to be made. I was a crazed woman, not in my right mind."

Kady hoped she never learned this from experience, but it was easy to guess that profound grief could make a person do irrational things. "What did you do?"

"I shut down Legend. I owned the whole town, as my husband and son had held on to every inch of land in the hopes of creating a Utopia. I had the mines blown up, so they couldn't be worked, then I hired guards and dogs to patrol the empty town. I didn't allow so much as a vagrant to live there."

It took Kady a moment to digest this information. "And what happened to the people who lived in Legend?"

For a while Ruth looked at the moon, taking her time before answering. "They left, of course, and they came to hate me as much as I hated them. Oh, not the saloon owners and the girls or even the miners, they could get a job anywhere; but my husband and son had worked hard at bringing decent families into Legend, and there were several of them living there then. They had planted gardens and repaired houses; they had made homes for themselves and their families."

Kady sat in the still darkness for a while, trying to imagine the rage that Ruth's evictions must have caused. Something like a smaller version of the Cherokee's Trail of Tears.

When Ruth spoke, her voice was very quiet. "There was a cholera epidemic that winter, and many of the former residents of Legend died, including some of Cole's young friends. The parents sent me photos of their dead children. They—"

Pausing, Ruth took a deep breath. "They cursed me. One old woman spit on me on the street and said she hoped my dead grandson haunted me forever. And she hoped my new baby would come to hate me."

As goose bumps rose on Kady's arms, she rubbed them. She wasn't Catholic, but she felt that she should cross herself against such an evil wish.

"It has all come true," Ruth said. "Cole haunts this

town, wanting desperately to grow up, to love, to have children of his own. And my living son—"

Kady listened while Ruth told of how she'd imprisoned her youngest son, how he was never allowed off the grounds. When he was three, Ruth had received a kidnap threat from a person who had once lived in Legend, so Ruth redoubled her attempts to keep him safe.

When Ruth paused and seemed as though she was going to say no more, Kady said, "What happened to your youngest son?" then tried to prepare herself to hear of yet another tragedy.

"When he was sixteen, he climbed over the fence and ran away." Ruth took her time before she spoke again. "He left behind a letter that said my hatred of Legend was stronger than my love for him. He said I had allowed my grief for the dead to override my love for the living."

Ruth looked at Kady. "I was furious at first, and as always, I blamed Legend for taking yet another loved one from me, but as the months, then the years passed, I came to realize that my son was right. I was the one who had lost my only remaining child. I could blame this tragedy on no one else."

"Have you heard from him?" Kady asked.

"Yes. I heard nothing for years, then six months ago he wrote me a letter. He's in New York trying to make a life for himself. He wants no help from me; actually, he wants no contact from me. He is . . ."

"Angry," Kady said, trying to imagine a child who had grown up imprisoned by a woman obsessed with hatred.

"Yes," Ruth said softly, "my son is very, very angry."

When Ruth turned to look at her, Kady instinctively knew what was going to be said. And more than anything in the world, Kady didn't want to hear it. Ruth Jordan was going to ask Kady for help. She was going to ask her to help with the people of Legend and to help with her angry young son.

But before Ruth could speak, Kady put up her hand. "I

think I should tell you about myself. I think there are things you should know about me. I didn't want to come here, I don't want to be here, and I plan to go back to my own world and to the man I love *immediately*."

There, she thought, that was out in the open. Tossing back the lap robe, she stood and began to walk about the porch. It was very late now, and it would be daylight before long. As Kady began to talk, she tried to conjure the image of Gregory and of Onions. She wanted to remember a world full of cars and jets and computers. Right now atomic warfare seemed safe compared to blood feuds involving curses and ghosts.

Through all of what had happened, Kady had never been able to understand why *she* had been chosen to go back in time, and now she knew she'd come to know a man who had never lived to be a man. Right now she did not want to think of Cole, for if she did she'd remember too many things about him that she'd come to love. No! No! she corrected herself, she had *not* come to love him. She was in love with nice, safe Gregory, a man who had lived all of his thirty-one years as a human, not as a ghost, a man whose mother had been cursed by no one (except maybe a few restaurant supply delivery men).

"Do you have lots of money?" Kady asked as she paused in pacing the porch.

"Masses."

"Then why don't you rebuild Legend? You could make it into the place that Cole dreamed of. Maybe that's why I was sent back to this place, to see what Cole wanted and to tell you about it."

Ruth arched an eyebrow. "Who would want to live high in the Colorado mountains?"

At that Kady smiled. "Maybe I should tell you about downhill skiing."

"I see, and you think that if I make the town of Legend into a pretty little resort, that will right all the wrongs?"

"I don't know if you *can* right the wrongs," Kady said

quickly, while silently begging Ruth not to ask her to stay. Right now the only thing in the world she wanted was to go back to her own time and place, and to be with people who were familiar to her.

While Kady had been pacing nervously, Ruth had been watching her. "Dear, do please sit down. Joseph can't sleep if you are moving about so restlessly."

Kady had not noticed the older man stretched out on a couple of blankets at the far end of the porch, now raised on one elbow and watching the two women sleepily. Kady sat back on the chair.

Ruth took her hand and squeezed it. "I'm not going to ask you to stay. What would be the use? What could you do now that you have not already done? You gave my grandson a chance to live for a while. You gave him the chance for revenge."

"Revenge?" Kady asked, startled.

"When your letter arrived telling me you were now my granddaughter-in-law and that my hardheaded grandson was holding you prisoner, I threw the missive in the trash. Over the years I have become used to such hateful pranks, and I always ignore them. But the next day Joseph brought me a newspaper clipping."

From inside a cleverly concealed pocket in the sleeve of her dress, Ruth pulled out a piece of newspaper and handed it to Kady, but when she held it nearer the lantern light to read, Ruth spoke.

"It says that an old wrong had been righted. The men who robbed the bank in Legend so many years ago were never caught. My son and husband were both killed while pursuing the three men, but the robbers seemed to vanish into the mountain. No trackers ever found a trace of them.

"Years later a man showed up in Denver with a great deal of silver—there was a *lot* taken from the bank in Legend— and it was rumored that he was one of the robbers and he'd murdered his partners. No one could prove anything and he had a talent for buying the silence of any investigators."

Ruth looked at Kady. "Three days ago the man was found dead in his study, a knife through his heart. The person who killed him never fired a shot. He silently slipped over a high wall, fought several guards, and entered the man's study. On the man's desk was a signed confession of his participation in the holdup in Legend so many years ago."

Ruth's eyes bored into Kady's. "The knife found in the man's heart had a medal in the top of it, a medal given for one year's attendance at Sunday school." She took a breath. "I asked the sheriff to show me the knife. It was Cole's medal, and I . . . I had made sure he had been buried with it."

Turning away from the sight of Ruth's pain, Kady remembered how Cole had looked when he'd returned from his ten days away from her: his shoulder bleeding from a deep cut and many bruises on his face and neck. Thinking of it now made her feel sick at the senselessness of revenge. Killing that man had brought no one back.

Ruth continued. "Along with the confession was a will, witnessed and legal, and it left the man's millions to build orphanages all over Colorado."

Suddenly, it was all too much for Kady, and she put her head in her hands and began to cry. Cole, she thought, had to be the best, most pure-hearted person she had ever met. Maybe killing out of revenge was wrong, but he'd been able to use the money that had cost so much blood for a good purpose.

Ruth sat in silence for a long while, letting Kady cry softly into her hands, leaving her alone, interrupting only to offer her a handkerchief. When Kady seemed to have herself under control again, Ruth spoke. "You will be wanting to go back to your own time now."

"Yes," Kady said softly. "I want to go home. I think I've done what I was supposed to do here. Cole had his chance at . . . at life." But not at love, she thought. She'd cheated him out of that. But how could she love him when her heart already belonged to Gregory?

Abruptly, Ruth said, "Who put the wedding dress in the old flour tin?"

"I beg your pardon?"

"I was thinking of your story that you found a wedding dress and my son's watch inside an old flour tin. Who put it there?"

"I have no idea. I assumed it was Cole's mother's dress, but . . ." Remembering, Kady gave a soft smile. "But Cole said he hadn't been at the wedding, so he didn't know what she'd worn." At the memory of Cole's joke Kady almost started crying again.

"Describe the dress to me."

Kady thought that now was not the time to have a fashion recounting, but this seemed to be important to Ruth, so she began to sketch the lovely gown with her hands.

Kady had not said three sentences when Ruth said, "Wrong skirt. The skirt is wrong. My daughter-in-law was married in eighteen sixty-three and the skirts were very full then, with hoops, but your dress had a bustle. *Your* wedding dress was the style of eighteen seventy-three."

"Then who was it made for, if not Cole's mother?"

Ruth gave Kady a raised eyebrow look.

"Oh, no, you can't believe that it was made for *me*. I know it fit me, but how could anyone know that I was . . . I mean who could guess that—"

"Me," Ruth said simply. "I could have the dress made and put into a tin box."

Several times Kady opened her mouth to speak, but each time she closed it. Finally, she fell back against the chair. "This really doesn't make sense. I think this is one of those chicken-or-the-egg things. I found the dress *before* I met you."

"Yes, but by your own admission, *now* is almost a

hundred years before you find the dress. What's to keep me from having the dress made and putting it in a box?"

"Does that mean that all this is going to happen again? That I'm going to find the box later and return to Legend and put on a feast and—" Kady cut herself off, as the memories were too fresh and too painful.

For a moment she tried to clear her head and think about what was going on. "What is it you want from me?" she asked Ruth cautiously. "What is it that you're leading up to?"

"I wish you could bring Cole back to life. I wish you could stop all the killings of my family and even—" She gulped. "I even wish Legend could have lived. But I don't see how that can be achieved. Kady," she said, smiling, "I am grateful to you for giving my grandson what you did. I wish I could have seen him as a man, but I know that, had he lived, he would have looked and acted just as you described."

Kady was waiting for the other shoe to drop because she could tell that Ruth Jordan was building up to something. "What do you want of me?" she asked again.

"When you get back to your own time, I want you to see if I have any descendants. I want you to meet them."

Kady smiled. "And what do I tell them? That I knew their great-great-grandmother back in 1897? Or that I had a great adventure with their great-grand . . . cousin, or whatever, as an adult, but in reality he died when he was only nine years old? And that everything happened over a hundred years ago?"

Ruth laughed. "Does sound a bit far-fetched, doesn't it?"

"And what about Gregory?" Kady asked. "No offense, but you Jordans have a knack for ignoring the man I love. The man I am going to *marry*. Somehow I don't think he's going to understand any of this."

"You're going to tell him about this?" Ruth asked incredulously.

"Tell him that I've spent the last days before my wedding with another man? Hardly."

"All right, I understand. I'm not going to ask for a promise from you. You've done more than enough for my family, for all of us, dead and alive. But promise me that if the opportunity comes up, you will visit my descendants. If I am so lucky as to have any, that is."

"All right, I promise," Kady said, then yawned. The sky was beginning to show pink, and right now all she wanted was to go to bed. She'd told Ruth about the petroglyphs, and Ruth had said that everyone in Legend knew where they were. Yet another of Cole's little jokes on her.

"Are you ready to go home, my dear?"

"Yes," Kady answered honestly. She'd had enough of time travel and witchcraft. Now all she wanted was to sleep for a few hours, then go see Gregory. From now on she just wanted her life to be normal. Normal and boring.

"Joseph!" Ruth said sharply, and instantly the man was beside her, helping her from the chair. To Kady's eyes, Ruth had looked much younger when she'd first seen her. Right now she didn't look as though she had much longer on earth.

They rode in the carriage past the Hanging Tree, and as the sun came up, Kady could dimly see the outlines of the deserted town. And everywhere she looked she seemed able to hear voices calling, "Hello, Kady," and "Thanks, Kady," and "Great grub, Kady."

When Ruth distracted her with questions, Kady was grateful. As they rode, Ruth wrote in a little notebook facts about Kady's twentieth-century life: where she was born, mother's name, father's, her address in Alexandria. Laughing, Kady supplied her social security number as well. "I wish I knew my passport number, too," she said.

Ruth didn't so much as smile. "What was the date when you came to Cole?" she asked, and when Kady told her, Ruth said, "I will give you six weeks from then. If you haven't contacted my son's descendants by that time, it will be clear that you're not going to."

"Fair enough," Kady answered as the carriage halted at the base of the rocks she had come to know rather well in the last weeks.

"Are you sure the way will be open?" Ruth asked, sounding as though she hoped that Kady would have to stay in the nineteenth century forever.

"I think it's like Dorothy's ruby slippers and I've always had the power to go home." At the puzzled look on Ruth's face, Kady smiled, then on impulse, grabbed the older woman and hugged her frail body.

"Thank you, Kady," Ruth whispered. "Thank you for what you did for my grandson." Pulling away, she looked at Kady, and just like her grandson, she smoothed a dark curl behind Kady's ear. "Thank you for what you've done for me. I am going to do what I can to repair the hurt I caused my younger son. And maybe, if I can, I'll be able to do something about Legend." Her voice lowered. "If I have time."

Kady didn't like to think what she meant by that. When Kady returned to Virginia, Ruth Jordan would have been dead for many years.

As Kady started to get out of the carriage, Ruth told Joseph to go with her, but Kady said that no, she wanted to go alone. She could tell by Ruth's eyes that she understood that Kady wanted to say good-bye to Cole, for every inch of the path up the mountain reminded her of her time with Cole.

After one more press of her hand, Kady turned and ran toward the path up the mountain, hurrying up it as fast as she could go. Her time in the past was over, and it was better to put it behind her. Now she should look to the future, to the future and to Gregory—the man she loved.

When she reached the petroglyphs, she was not surprised to see what was now almost a familiar sight: the opening in the rock through which she could see her apartment with the flour tin on the floor, her dirty chef's smock tossed across the couch. Refusing to allow herself a backward glance, she leaped through the opening, and instantly, the hole behind her closed.

For a moment Kady stood alone in her apartment and looked about it. It had been more than two weeks since she'd been here, and she had no idea how much time had passed in the twentieth-century world. Feeling disoriented, she picked up the remote control to the TV, and after a moment of looking at the instrument as though it were from another planet, she clicked the TV on, switched to Channel Two, and saw that it was about two A.M. on the day she'd left. No time at all had passed.

Again feeling awkward, she pushed the button on her answering machine only to hear a computer trying to sell her aluminum siding.

At her feet on the stained, cheap carpet of her apartment, was the empty flour tin. There was no wedding dress or Jordan watch, or a photograph of a once-happy family. All those things had been left behind in Legend. What she did have were the clothes she was wearing, a long prairie skirt, cotton blouse, and a wide leather belt. Nothing in the least remarkable about them; they weren't even very old looking. She had absolutely nothing to show that she had just returned from an extraordinary adventure.

For a moment, loneliness so overwhelmed Kady that she thought she might collapse on the floor and cry, but she wouldn't allow herself to do that. She was not going to allow herself to grieve for a man who had never lived to be the man she'd met. She was going to think of everything in the way Ruth did: that Kady had given Cole something he would not otherwise have had.

Smiling, she thought of Scarlett. "I'll think about it tomorrow. If I think about it today, I'll go crazy."

Still smiling, Kady went to her bedroom and fell across the bed. She was asleep instantly.

Chapter 17

KADY'S FIRST WAKING THOUGHT WAS, WHERE WAS COLE AND why was the house so quiet? It was a full minute before she realized that she was home in Virginia, home in her own time period. And, more important, home to Gregory.

Smiling, she eased herself out of the bed, feeling a bit stiff and sore from the exertion of the last days. "Better not think about that," she said aloud as she made her way to the bathroom, and for a while she just stood there, marveling at the luxury of a modern bathroom. Running water! Flushing toilet! *Hot* water!

She took a shower that threatened to wash away her skin, then spent half an hour massaging lotion onto her body. Usually, she was in too much of a hurry to get to work to take time to do something this hedonistic, but today . . .

With a panic she looked at the clock and saw it was ten A.M., but she calmed when she remembered that it was Sunday and Onions was closed. However, usually by this time on Sunday she was already slipping something into the oven. Gregory and his mother liked to sit down to a lavish dinner on Sunday at two, and Kady prided herself on the meal she served them.

"How about fried rattlesnake today?" she murmured, laughing as she went to her closet. It was a small walk-in closet, but that only made Kady's meager wardrobe look even more sparse. Frowning, she pushed aside the hangers and pondered her drab, oversized tops. She could hear Jane's complaint, "Don't you have anything smaller than a circus tent? Where do you find these clothes anyway?" Kady had never answered her friend, but had stood there tight-lipped, thinking it was all right for Jane to wear snug-fitting clothes since she was a size six, but Kady wanted to hide the bulk that was her body as best she could.

Today, as she sorted through her few clothes, Kady seemed to feel different. Maybe it was all the men in Colorado who'd asked her to marry them. Or maybe it was just Cole's incessant attention.

Leaving the closet, Kady went to the big chest of drawers in the bedroom and began to rummage. Last Christmas, Jane had given her a red blouse, and years before that she had given her some earrings. Now, if Kady could only find them.

An hour later Kady walked into Onions, and her first sight was of Gregory sitting at one of the tables, a newspaper before his face, a coffee cup by his hand. Turning a page, he glanced up at her for just a second before returning to his paper.

At his look, Kady's breath caught. It had been so very long since she had seen him, and since then she'd spent a great deal of time with another man. Would he know? Would he see the guilt on her face? Would he sense that something was different about her?

"Mom made the coffee," Gregory said without looking up. "I don't think I'm going to die from it, but I might."

Smiling, Kady started for the kitchen. "Coffee coming up." Nothing had changed, she thought with relief. To Gregory it was only hours since she had last seen him. He had no idea that she'd been away for days or that she'd—

As Kady passed him, she glanced at his profile and

thought for the millionth time how good-looking he was. Almost as beautiful as Cole, she thought, then, to rid herself of that thought, she pushed the paper out of his hands and plopped herself onto his lap. Taking Gregory's head in her hands, she put her lips on his and kissed him deeper and with more passion than she ever had before.

"Hey, what is this?" Gregory asked, his hands on her wrists and pulling his face away. His tone was disapproving. "Before breakfast?"

"I missed you," Kady said, sliding her arms about his neck and hugging him.

"Well, I missed you, too," he answered, but again pulling away, and this time there was a frown on his handsome face. "Kady," he said sternly, "I think there is a time and place for everything, and in the middle of Onions on a Sunday morning isn't quite the place or the time."

She was beginning to feel embarrassed, but she tried to make light of it. "How about going to my place then?" she said with what she hoped was a lascivious look.

Drawing back, Gregory studied her for a moment. "What in the world has come over you today? And what do you have on?"

"Like it?" Kady asked, looking down at herself. "It has lycra in it. Jane said that if she had . . . well, if she were endowed like me, she'd show herself off, so she gave me this." Looking up at Gregory, she fluttered her eyelashes. "Think it does?"

Gregory was frowning rather a lot now. "If you're asking me if I like to see you hanging out of the top of your clothes, the answer is no."

Kady brightened. "Jealous?"

"Not quite," he said as though this concept amused him. "But it's not very sanitary, and with the top half of you naked, you could be burned at the stove. And, Kady dear, as delightful as this position is, both of my legs have gone to sleep. You aren't exactly the light-as-a-feather type, now, are you?"

Abruptly, Kady got off his lap. "No, of course I'm not," she said hastily. "I'll make you some coffee and get started on Sunday lunch." Stiffly, she turned away, but Gregory caught her arm.

"Kady, honey, you look great. Really you do, but maybe I'd rather you showed yourself just to me and not to the entire world." He kissed the back of her hand, and Kady left the room smiling, feeling that she was glad to be home.

"Something has happened to you," Jane said softly, "and I mean to find out what it is." They were in a furniture store in Tyson's Corner Mall, and Kady was inspecting every piece in the big showroom.

"Is that why you're still here?" Kady asked as she looked at the price tag on a green velvet sofa. "How do you think this would look with the lacquer lamps I bought at auction? And with the new rug?"

"New rug, new sofa, new lamps! That's just what I'm talking about. What has happened to you?!"

"People are beginning to stare," Kady said calmly, referring to Jane's raised voice.

"They are going to stare more when I grab those overpriced curtain cords and tie you to that iron bed and keep you there until you talk to me."

"I had no idea you were so kinky," she said, but when Jane didn't smile, Kady sighed. "I've told you a hundred times, nothing is wrong with me. I'm just getting married, and I'm choosing things for my house. And I'm sending the bills to Gregory. Doesn't that please you?"

"Four days ago you were frightened of buying so much as a sheet, but now you walk into stores and say, 'I want this and I want that,' as though you were a born shopper. And the way you bargained with that poor rug merchant I almost felt sorry for him."

"Did you?" Kady asked, smiling.

"And that's another thing, Miss Kady Long, you keep flirting with men."

"I'm getting married, not going to my execution. What's wrong with flirting a bit?"

Too many words raced through Jane's mind for her to speak. The Kady she had known all her life ran away when a man looked at her. But three days ago Kady had spent an hour and a half drinking mint tea with a rug merchant and arguing over the price of the rug. Jane and Debbie thought they were going to pass out with boredom, but Kady had seemed to enjoy every minute of it. And when they'd left the store, she'd said, "He asked me to be his second wife. With my own apartment, though." All three women had laughed about the outrageous proposal as they drove Debbie to the airport so she could return home.

"Kady," Jane said seriously, "I must return home tomorrow. My husband is threatening to leave me if I don't return, not to mention what my boss is saying, so we have to talk *now*."

"All right," Kady said, knowing she could put off the inevitable no longer. Part of her liked that Jane saw that she was different, but another part of her wished her friend were more like Gregory and his mother and noticed nothing at all different.

Ten minutes later they were ensconced in the coffee shop of Nordstrom's, and since it was early, it was quiet in the restaurant. "What's going on with you?" Jane asked again.

For a moment Kady thought of lying yet again and saying that nothing had changed, but Jane was too perceptive for that. Kady wasn't in the least tempted to tell her about Cole and the people of Legend or about Ruth's unbelievable story. And if the truth were told, with each day that passed the story seemed to fade from Kady's mind until she sometimes wondered if it had really happened. The only clear memory she seemed to have was of when she'd cooked for people who needed to know what she could teach. That memory seemed to get stronger every day.

Kady toyed with the straw in her lemonade. "I think I want to *do* something with my life. Like building orphanages all over Colorado. Cooking fabulous meals for people who've eaten many fabulous meals suddenly seems a frivolous thing to do with one's life."

"Orphanages?" Jane asked, eyes wide. "What do orphanages have to do with cooking?"

"Cooking for people who don't have much is more rewarding. And it feels good to teach people how to combine bland ingredients in different ways."

"Kady, what in the world are you talking about?"

"Welfare mothers," she said, looking up at Jane's stunned face. "Did you know that Americans make casseroles with potato chips on top of them? No nutritional value at all. In other countries people are taught to cook, but kids in America grow up thinking McDonald's is a good meal."

"So what is it you want to do? Open a cooking school?"

"I don't know." Kady thought of the children in Legend and how she'd persuaded them to like vegetables. "I know that everyone thinks the world's evils are caused by drugs, but maybe kids wouldn't be so lethargic if their nutrition was better."

"What's your idea?" Jane asked, staring at her friend in wonder. As long as she'd known Kady, she'd never heard such ideas from her.

"Nothing really. It's just something that's forming in my head. Cooking classes for women on welfare."

"Cooking classes? Welfare?" Jane said, smiling in a smug way that made Kady angry.

"Yes! Cooking classes. Poor people need self-esteem just as much as rich people! Not all the people on welfare are bums who are too lazy to work. Think how much better they would feel if they knew how to cook a simple, nutritious meal for their children. And the women could learn a skill that might get them off welfare."

For a moment Jane could only stare at her friend. Never had she seen Kady show passion. Oh, everyone knew she loved cooking, and she treated those knives of hers as

217

though they were her children, but Kady had never been the type of person to fight for a cause. If there was a protest going on, Kady would probably say, "I'll make lunch," then disappear into the nearest kitchen.

"Something's happened to you," Jane said softly.

"No it hasn't," Kady snapped.

"It's Gregory, isn't it?"

"Gregory is just fine. Why does every woman assume that the cause of every other woman's problem is a man?"

"History?"

When Kady smiled, Jane clutched her hand. "I've known you all your life and you've never been a crusader. You've always been content to stand in the background and let others walk all over you."

Gasping, Kady snatched her hand away. "That's a horrible thing to say. I do not allow people to walk over me."

"Ha! That mother-in-law of yours—"

At that Kady straightened her back. "I think this has gone far enough. I think I'd like to leave now."

Jane leaned toward her friend. "I don't mean to offend you. I want to help you and—"

Kady's mouth tightened into a thin line. "I'd like to remind you that you are not my therapist nor are you my business manager. If you want to help me then keep your nose out of my business. Are you ready to go?"

"Yes, of course," Jane said just as stiffly. "I do indeed think it is time for me to go home."

Kady didn't answer that remark but made her way out of the restaurant, took a left, and went to the parking garage to her car, Jane behind her. They drove back to Onions in silence.

What is wrong with me? Kady wondered, not for the first time. Everything seemed to bother her. In the three and a half weeks since she'd returned from Legend, it was as though her whole life had changed. Mrs. Norman now got on her nerves so much she could hardly stand to see the woman walk into the room.

Kady tried not to think this way, but it was as though her time in Legend had ruined her life. Things that she had once liked, she no longer did. It seemed that instead of accepting what was, now she was asking how things could be different—and did she want them to be different? In just a few weeks she had gone from being content to wanting . . .

And that was the real problem. She didn't know what it was that she really wanted, and not knowing was making her crazy. She'd told Jane she wanted to start cooking classes, and maybe she did, but that wasn't all of it. There was something deeper that she wanted, and she had no idea what it was.

For one thing, her recurring dreams of the Arabian man were beginning to bother her. In the past the dreams had been a curiosity, but now there was an urgency to them that haunted her even in the daytime. His eyes were asking something of her; maybe even pleading with her.

It had been easy to figure out that the dark man had something to do with Legend; his appearance at the opening in the rock had shown her that. And while she had been in Legend she'd not had the dreams. Also, in her heart she knew her dream man bore a resemblance to Cole. That night with the eagles she'd realized how much alike the two of them were. He was connected with Cole and Ruth, and with all the people she wanted to put out of her mind, so she tried to tell the veiled man to get away from her. She wanted nothing further to do with going back in time and halfway falling in love with a man who never grew past age nine. Kady knew that all she really wanted was a home and a couple of kids, and at thirty years old she knew she couldn't wait much longer. She didn't have the time or inclination to dabble in time travel or whatever it would take to find out why some man kept appearing in her dreams.

But if she knew what she wanted in life, why did she feel so restless? Everything with Gregory was perfect. He was everything a woman could want in a man: kind, courteous, even-tempered. She had everything: a home, the restaurant, Virginia was lovely. Her life was perfect, but she knew that if she didn't behave herself and stop finding fault in every little thing that happened, she was going to lose it all.

In the long run, what did it matter that Gregory rarely made love to her? In the weeks since she'd returned from Legend, they'd had one very brief tryst in her bed in her apartment. And what did it matter that when Kady reached for him afterward, he'd rolled out of bed and pulled on his clothes? There was a great deal more to life than sex!

But Kady kept thinking that she'd never noticed Gregory's lack of sexual interest in her before because she'd had no one to compare him to. Maybe she hadn't actually gone to bed with Cole, but she kept remembering the way Cole looked at her. It had felt good to tease with him, to giggle and have him chase her about the room. Even without consummation, when he'd looked at her, he'd made her feel beautiful and, oh, so very desirable.

But Gregory made her feel secure. Secure was good, wasn't it? So what if he didn't tease her or nibble her neck and try to make her forget cooking and go to bed with him? Gregory loved her so much that he'd asked her to marry him. What better proof of his love did she need than that? Besides, what else did she have that he could want? It wasn't as though she were a great heiress and he was after her money, so he had to have asked her to marry him out of love. Right?

But in spite of all of Kady's attempts at reason, yesterday she had turned on Gregory, almost in anger, and said, "Why do you want to marry me?"

Gregory had smiled. "Is this one of those trick questions where no matter what I say, I'll be wrong? I want to marry you because I love you."

This should have been enough for her, but Kady persisted. "Yes, but I need logical reasons. Reasons other than that I can cook."

"I think you will be easy to live with."

Kady had tried to hide her horror. What woman wanted to be "easy to live with"? "That's good," she said. "What else?"

"You are quiet and undemanding and . . . and, what can I say? You don't ask a lot from a man, and I like that."

"But what if I were to ask a great deal from you?"

"Such as?" He was in the restaurant office, looking at a stack of papers, and he wasn't really paying attention to her questions—which further annoyed Kady.

"I'd like to be half owner of Onions, and I'd like to have my name on the deed to the house you bought. I'd also like to have my own accountant go over the books to the restaurant and see how much it is making, and I'd like to share in the profits."

For a moment, Gregory looked up at her, his eyes wide, then he threw back his head and laughed. "Kady, my dear, for a moment there you sounded just like that dreadful friend of yours, Jane." Smiling, shaking his head, he looked back down at his papers. "If you want to buy anything, just let me or Mother know and we'll make sure you have the funds. I think running the kitchen is more than enough for you to handle. You don't need to start trying to become a bookkeeper as well." Still highly amused, he looked up at her. "Stick to frying eggs, and I'll handle the rest of it."

At that moment Kady knew that she had a choice, she could either start a blazing argument or let it die. If she started a fight, she knew she'd have to stick to her guns, and she wasn't sure she wanted to do that. Why did she want to be part owner in the restaurant anyway? Was it just because Jane and Cole had made her believe she *should* be a part owner? What happened to her own convictions that she would be half owner of the restaurant when she was married to Gregory?

Quietly, she had left Gregory's office and cooked dinner

that night just as always. But today, she had been restless to the point of being angry. She had thoroughly disliked Gregory's remark about her sticking to frying eggs. Is that what he thought of her cooking? That she was an egg fryer?

After dinner she dismissed the four young men who worked with her in the kitchen, and she cleaned up herself. There was nothing better to dissipate anger than a towering stack of dirty pots to scrub.

She was just finishing and wiping her wet hands when Gregory strode into the kitchen. "What are you doing here so late?" he asked.

"Since I'm only good for frying eggs, why shouldn't I do clean-up as well?" she said.

"Just because you had a fight with your friend is no reason to take it out on me," he said cooly.

Again, Kady knew she had a choice. She could tell him that Jane was not the cause of her bad mood, or she could accept this way out. All in all, it was better to have peace with the man you loved, wasn't it? "Sorry," she said. "Jane and I did have a falling out." When Gregory was silent, Kady thought, *Cole would have asked me what the argument was about.* "Don't you want to know what we argued about?" she snapped, then regretted her tone.

But Gregory just smiled. "If I don't, do I get labeled Insensitive Man?"

Kady smiled, too. "It gets branded on your forehead."

"In that case, tell me. But first, could I have one of those things?"

After handing him one of the bread puddings she'd made that night, she told him about her idea for teaching classes to welfare recipients. When she'd finished, Gregory was silent for a long while.

"And where do you get funding for this project?" he asked quietly as he handed her his dirty utensils.

"Funding? I'm not thinking of doing something on a national scale. At least not yet. I was just thinking of something on a personal level. Just me, one afternoon a week. Free cooking lessons, not to rich housewives who want to learn the latest technique for making focaccia, but something for women who'd like to learn inexpensive, healthful ways to feed their families."

"I see. And where would you hold these classes?"

"Here, at Onions. On Sunday or Mondays, when the restaurant is closed. There's plenty of room and lots of equipment."

"And what about ingredients? Who pays for them?"

Kady drew herself upright. "I would."

Smiling at her as though she were a little girl, Gregory put his arm around her shoulders. "I think that is the noblest idea I've ever heard. However, I don't think our insurance would allow strangers in here."

"Everyone who comes in through the front door is a stranger," she said, incredulous.

"I think we should talk about this later when you're not so upset."

Kady moved out from under his arm. "You don't mean strangers, you mean thieves, don't you? You think all poor people are thieves. You would have hated every person in Legend."

It was the first time Kady had said the name aloud in the twentieth century, and hearing it seemed to release something inside her. Collapsing onto a stool, she put her head in her hands and began to cry.

When Gregory put his arms around her and held her, she clung to him. "Of course you can use the restaurant for whatever you want," he said softly. "Kady, please, won't you tell me what's wrong with you? You've been acting strangely for a couple of weeks now."

"I don't know," she said honestly. "Suddenly my life seems to have no meaning or direction."

"What's caused you to say this? Has something happened that I don't know about?"

How could she tell him that sometimes when she looked at him, a blue-eyed face grinned back at her? How could she explain what she didn't understand herself?

When Kady said nothing, Gregory kissed her hair and said, "Why don't you go home? You work too hard. Go home, spend a couple of days in bed watching TV. Do nothing for a while. Rest. Come back Tuesday and you'll be a new person."

Rest, she thought, that's exactly what I need. "Yes," she said to Gregory, then stood as he kissed both her cheeks. "I think I will go home."

He helped her gather her things, then held the front door open for her, but he didn't offer to walk her to her apartment, and he didn't say he'd come by and check on her over the next couple of days. Kady thought, *I should be grateful he's not telling me I have to come back and cook Sunday dinner for him and his mother,* but she stamped that thought down. All she needed was a little rest. A few days' rest and she'd be fine.

Chapter 18

BUT KADY DIDN'T REST DURING THOSE TWO DAYS. WHEN SHE
got back to her apartment, she seemed to be wide awake.
Sometimes it felt as though being around Gregory and his
mother drained the energy out of her.

Even though it was one in the morning, she decided to
write recipes down. She'd write about the food she had
experimented with in Legend.

She took a shower, got into her nightgown, and snuggled
into bed, a clipboard on her knees, and began to write. But
instead of writing recipes, she began writing the story of
Legend, Colorado. She wrote down facts and dates, people's names; she drew maps. Maybe if she wrote it all
down, she could make sense of it.

But as the hours passed and the pages accumulated, she
could see that there was no sense to be made of any of it.
Had she been sent back just to give Cole a chance at an
adult life? Or maybe it was to give him a chance to revenge
the deaths of his family.

The sun came up, and she continued to write, but
toward midmorning she fell asleep, and as always since
she'd returned, she dreamed of the veiled man. It was

exactly the same dream, not so much as a gesture in it had changed. He held out his hand to her in invitation, and try as she might, she could not reach his hand.

When Kady awoke, she was sobbing, and for the first time since she'd returned, she allowed herself to think of how much she missed the people of Legend. Not just Cole, but everyone. "They made me feel important," she said aloud. "They made me feel useful and as though I was needed."

She tried hard not to compare her life then to what it was now, but she realized that Gregory made her feel as though he were doing her a favor by marrying her. With a jolt that was almost sickening, Kady realized that before she had been to Legend, she had agreed with that idea. Before Legend, a hundred times a day she had asked herself why a gorgeous man like Gregory wanted to marry a fat frump like her. Sure, Kady knew she had a pretty face, but that was a cliché: "Such a pretty face . . . Too bad she doesn't take more care with her figure."

She spent the weekend in her apartment, thinking about how she used to feel, how she felt now, and trying to come up with a solution to her dilemma. Had she been in love with Cole? Was she in love with Gregory now?

And, most important, what did she want to do with her life? At one point she had been crystal clear in her lifetime goals. But somewhere around her thirtieth birthday she seemed to have changed and she'd started wanting a home and children. She began to think that there should be more to life than a kitchen.

By Tuesday afternoon she had come to no decisions, had reached no conclusions. She trudged off to Onions as though nothing had changed, but somewhere inside herself, she knew that everything had changed. It was just that Kady didn't yet know how these internal changes were going to manifest themselves.

* * *

LEGEND

The first thing that happened at Onions involved Mrs. Norman's penny-pinching ways.

As usual, while Kady tried to prepare dinner, Mrs. Norman hovered at her elbow. "Do you have to use that expensive extra virgin olive oil? Why do you have to use vanilla *beans*? Isn't extract good enough for you? It's much cheaper, you know. No, no don't start wrapping fish in paper. If they wanted fish wrapped in paper, they'd go to a fish-and-chips shop."

It was an exceptionally busy night, and customers were lined up three deep outside the door, and Kady knew that tonight was not the time for any emotional hysterics, but she had reached her limit. "Out, out!" she yelled at Mrs. Norman. "Get out of my kitchen!"

For several moments Mrs. Norman looked at Kady in shock, started to say something, but when Kady's face didn't soften, she turned on her heel and left the kitchen in an enraged huff.

The silence that permeated the kitchen after the little woman's retreat was deafening. Then, one of Kady's assistants said, "Three cheers for Kady," and three times they all let out a loud "Hip hip hooray." Then someone started singing "The Battle Hymn of the Republic" (it was Virginia, after all), and two staff cooks grabbed each other's arms and started dancing, while another banged pot lids and beat a rhythm on the stainless countertops.

For a moment Kady was too stunned to move; then she started laughing, and someone grabbed her arm to do-si-do her around the kitchen. When a champagne cork popped and someone produced full glasses, it only added to the hilarity.

It was the first time Kady had really laughed since she'd left Legend.

"What the hell is going on in here?" Gregory bellowed above the noise as he entered the kitchen with a powerful swing at the door. Instantly all fun stopped, and everyone

227

except Kady skulked back to his workstation. She was left alone in the middle of the room, holding a full champagne flute. Gregory's dark eyebrows drew together into one black bar across his forehead. "My mother is in my office *crying*," he said, his voice low and almost menacing. "We have a full house and a line two blocks long of people waiting, and you, Kady, are in here drinking the customers' champagne and . . . and dancing."

Lifting her glass, Kady looked at the bubbles of the wine. "I tell you what, Gregory dear, if anyone complains, shoot him. Not much, just a little. Just enough to teach him to mind his manners."

At that Gregory was speechless, and the other cooks froze at their tasks. It was one thing to yell at dreadful little Mrs. Norman but quite another to defy the owner's son. The staff was well aware that Kady was an employee just like them, and from the look on Gregory's face, right now the couple's engagement didn't count for much.

Gregory's face did not lose its hardness. "Are you going to cook or drink?" he asked coldly. "I'd like to know so I can inform our guests." He made it sound as though Kady had a drinking problem and he was begging her to lay off the booze just for tonight.

Kady didn't flinch. After one had faced a hanging party, an angry fiancé didn't seem too dangerous. "Perhaps I shall do both," she said, her eyes never leaving Gregory's.

At that he backed down, his face softening as he took a step toward her, but Kady turned her back on him. "Perhaps you should join your mother in the office and leave my kitchen to me," she said over her shoulder.

For a moment Gregory looked as though he was going to go into a rage, but, with a glance at the employees, who were now openly staring, he gave a little shrug. "Sure, honey, whatever you say." Then he winked in conspiracy at a couple of the men, as though to say, *Women!* and left the kitchen.

* * *

For a few moments after Gregory left, Kady felt shaky and frightened. She had an almost overwhelming urge to run after him and apologize, but then the feeling began to be replaced with a sort of buoyancy she'd never felt before.

"Someone want to slice me three potatoes?" she said into the silence in the kitchen.

"Me!" one of the men said loudly.

"No! Me!" another yelled; then all four men, in an excellent imitation of the Three Stooges, ran smack into each other, and Kady laughed until she had tears in her eyes. After that the feeding of the customers went faster and more smoothly and certainly more pleasantly than she had ever before experienced at Onions. During the evening, one of her assistants kissed her cheek and whispered, "Thank you." He didn't have to say what he was thanking her for. The absence of Mrs. Norman's constant complaining was like hearing the music of heaven.

After the last meal was served, one of the waiters called out that "the boss" was waiting to see Kady.

"By 'the boss' do you mean Mr. Norman?" one of the cooks asked. "I think that the guard may have changed tonight. You are looking at 'the boss,' right here," he said, pointing both hands at Kady.

The waiter guffawed. "Yeah, right," he said, then went back to the dining room.

Does everyone see me as a wimp? Kady wondered. *Does no one think I can stand up to anyone?* No one had thought that of her in Legend.

"And I was the same woman then as I am now," she whispered to herself as she headed for Gregory's office.

One look at his face and she knew that he was not going to let her off with a few sentences. As she sat down on the chair he silently pointed to, she knew she was in for a Serious Lecture.

"Kady," he said in a voice heavy with disappointment and "duty." "I found your behavior tonight intolerable. I can bear the way you humiliated me in front of the help, but I cannot allow you to talk to my mother in the way you did. Right now she is upstairs lying down. I had to give her a sedative to calm her."

He was standing, his hands clasped behind his back, then he leaned over the desk toward Kady. "She was crying."

Kady knew this was her cue to say she was sorry, but for the life of her, her mouth would not open. She just sat there looking up at Gregory, waiting for him to continue.

"My mother and I have been good to you; we have given you free rein in this restaurant. My mother—who is not a strong woman—worked very hard to bring Onions back to its former glory, which was difficult for her to do without a husband. But somehow she did it, and she has included you in every aspect of the rebirth of this restaurant."

His statement was so absurd that Kady almost laughed aloud. She, Kady Long, was responsible for the rebirth of the run-down old steak house, and what she'd managed to do she had done in spite of Mrs. Norman's constant interference.

Gregory seemed to be waiting for Kady's apology, but she just continued to look at him, so he sighed heavily, then withdrew a thick file folder from an open desk drawer. "I wanted this to be a surprise." He glared at her in reproach. "A surprise for our wedding night, but your conduct tonight is forcing me to forgo that lovely surprise."

At this Kady did feel the tiniest bit of guilt. What was it? Jewelry? Keys to a new car? Maybe he had put her name on the deed to the house. Or given her a third share in the restaurant that *she* had made into a success.

With a gesture of disgust, he tossed the file folder onto Kady's lap, and she opened it, but, truthfully, the papers inside made no sense to her. It looked as though Gregory and his mother were buying into something along with a lot of other people. But look as she might, Kady didn't see her name anywhere on any of the papers.

"Kady," Gregory said in a heavy voice. "I have never told you this, but I have made great plans for us after we are married. Just recently you ridiculed me when I was hesitant about your welfare scheme. You assumed that I was a snob and a bigot, but you never asked me if the reason I was hesitant was because I had other plans for us."

Pausing for a moment, he pointed at the folder on her lap. "I am going to take some of your best recipes, especially the ones you've served the President, and mass produce them."

Kady blinked at him, having no idea what he meant. "Mass produce my recipes?"

"Yes. But you have now ruined the surprise," he said, not able to resist another dig. "I have been working with investors, all of whom have eaten here, and they are willing to put some big money into the Norman House Restaurants that will open all over the country. My surprise was to tell you on our wedding night that I was going to allow you to develop recipes that could be produced on a large scale and very cheaply."

It took Kady a moment to digest this information. "You were planning to franchise me?"

Gregory didn't seem to hear the horror in her voice. "Women all over America are complaining that men think of them only as someone to stay home and take care of the kids, but I have never thought of you that way, Kady," he said with pride. "To me you are . . ." His face brightened. "Big business. Yes, to me you are big business." The way he said it was as though it was the highest compliment he had ever given anyone.

"You never loved me, did you?" she said softly.

Gregory rolled his eyes as though to say that was unimportant, and his voice sounded bored with the whole concept. "Of course I did. I *do* love you. I love what we are going to do together, what we can achieve together."

"But what about passion? What about *sex?*"

"Kady, really! In case you haven't figured it out yet, I am

a very practical man. Oh, I know that my extraordinary good looks make women see me as a romantic figure, but I can assure you that I have a brain behind these eyes. And, let's get real here, Kady, if I wanted a wife for passion and sex, I would have chosen a woman who is less . . ." He looked her up and down.

"Fat? Is that the word you're looking for?" she asked.

"I don't think we need to go into this now or at any time in the future, for that matter. Marriages based on passion end in acrimonious and expensive divorce. Our marriage will have a foundation of concrete."

Suddenly, it was as though a great weight lifted from Kady. She knew she should be devastated by what Gregory was telling her. After all, she was hearing that the man she loved, the man she planned to marry, had never really loved her. He'd only wanted to get her under contract so he would have the power to bully her into helping him force yet more greasy, nonnutritional food down the throats of the American people. And he was going to call them Norman House Restaurants. *Wonder if he planned to give me even a slice of the action?* she thought.

But Kady wasn't devastated. Instead, she had never felt lighter—or happier—in her life. She didn't have to go through with her marriage with Gregory! Maybe she had known it wouldn't work since that first day when she'd walked into the restaurant so glad to see him, only to be told not to kiss him. Maybe she'd even known while she was in Legend that she didn't love Gregory. Maybe telling herself that she was in love with another man made her believe she couldn't love Cole.

From inside her pocket, she withdrew her key ring, then removed the two keys to the restaurant and put them on Gregory's desk. "Good-bye, Gregory," she said, then turned on her heel and started out the door.

He caught her arm before she reached the door. "Just what do you think you're doing?" he asked, but when he saw her face, he dropped her arm and his face softened.

"Kady, I love you. I asked you to marry me because I love you. Out of all the women I could have had, I—"

Kady's face reflected her amusement. "You chose me. You with your 'extraordinary good looks' chose fat, frumpy little Kady, the poor little mouse who was so grateful for attention from someone like you that she asked for nothing in return. You didn't have to send me flowers, or take me out to fairs or on picnics. You didn't have to buy me an engagement ring. You didn't even have to take me out to dinner."

"Kady, it wasn't like that. Look, I've just bought us two tickets to the ice show next Thursday night," he said as he pulled the tickets out of his coat pocket and thrust them into her hand.

"I work on Thursday nights, did you forget that?" she said as she looked down at the tickets, then saw that someone had written on one of them. "Can't wait to see you, Greggy. Bunches of love, Bambi." All the i's were dotted with little hearts.

Kady looked up at Gregory and laughed. "Tell Bambi hello for me," she said as she walked out the door, leaving Gregory sputtering behind her.

Chapter 19

"DONE!" KADY SAID WITH A SMILE AS SHE LOOKED AT THE PILE of neatly addressed and stamped envelopes. Thirty-one of them, all ready to go to restaurants and hotels all over America.

It had been three days now since she had walked out of Onions and left Gregory standing there with his tickets and his Bambi. That night she had felt free and ready to take on the world, but by morning, she was thinking, What in the world have I done? She had $6,212.32 in the bank, not much to live on until she found a job. And besides that, how did one find a job? Or at least one that Kady wanted. She had been her own boss for too long to try to work as an under chef for some bad-tempered head cook.

But maybe having been through what she'd experienced in Legend had given her courage, because Kady didn't waste time fretting over her unknown future. Instead, she made a few calls to former classmates, asked some questions, then tried to make a list of the places she thought she could work. It had taken her a while to prepare a résumé, get it copied, then find the addresses of the hotels and restaurants. But now she had everything ready, and with a confident smile, she dropped the letters into a small shopping bag to carry them to the mailbox.

As there were every day, flowers from Gregory were outside her door. She stepped out, picked them up, put them inside the door, took the card, and locked the door behind her. "Wonder what he has to say today?" she murmured, opening the card as she walked out of her building, smiling as she scanned the note. "Love you . . . miss you . . . come for a visit? . . . sending Mother to Florida . . ." Smiling even more broadly, Kady dropped the note into a trash receptacle as she passed. She wasn't tempted by Gregory's pleas or his talk of love and sending-Mother-to-Florida. Maybe if he sent the deed to Onions, she might be tempted, but, then again, she might not.

By the time she neared the mailbox, she was almost skipping, and it seemed part of her euphoria that the display inside the big window of a bookstore she was passing should be draped in gold lamé. *Is there a gold mine in your future?* was written on a banner above the several books displayed below.

Thinking of Legend, Kady drew nearer and began to read the descriptions on the covers of the books. "Find the mine of the Flying Dutchman," one read. "New information on the Triple Star Mine," said another. "The Lost Maiden Mine could be yours," said another.

"The Lost Maiden Mine?" Kady said aloud. "Boy! those books are out of date!"

Turning away from the window, she started down the street toward the mailbox but stopped when she reached the door of the bookstore. On impulse, she went inside. Near the door was a table spread with at least twenty different books, all on the same theme of lost treasure. There were books on mines, ghost towns, ships that had sunk, curses, hauntings; the variety seemed endless.

Idly, as though it meant nothing to her, Kady picked up a book about lost mines in the western U.S. and looked up the Lost Maiden Mine. Expecting to see a recounting of what had been found in the mine back in 1982, she was puzzled to see that every book on the table read as though the mine had yet to be found. Surely, they couldn't *all* be out-of-date, could they? she wondered.

She stopped a clerk and asked where she could find books on the Lost Maiden Mine by itself. Kady seemed to remember that when the mine had been found, the stands were covered with produced-in-a-minute books about every aspect imaginable about the mine. Impatiently, the clerk said, "What we have is on the table," and moved on, too busy to bother with something as unimportant as a customer.

Still puzzled, Kady walked back to her apartment. Maybe those books on the mine had a short life span and were only of interest for a few months, she thought, and that's why there were no more copies of them. Not noticing that she hadn't mailed her résumés, she dropped the bag on the floor by the door, put Gregory's flowers next to the other six arrangements on the dining table, then called Jane.

It was the first time Kady had called her friend since they had parted with so much coolness between them a few weeks before. Kady knew she should have called her friend earlier and told her of her breakup with Gregory, but Kady had postponed it because she knew what every woman knows when she breaks up with her boyfriend: she was going to have to hear how horrible he was.

Jane's tirade lasted a full fifteen minutes, but Kady thought she got off cheaply. "You should have seen how he came on to Debbie after you went to bed that night! He was really too handsome for his own good, and I never trusted him. And furthermore—"

"Jane," Kady said sharply, "what do you remember about the Lost Maiden Mine?"

"What's to remember? I've heard of it, I think, but I don't remember much. Kady, what are you going to do now? I know Gregory and that mother of his never paid you much, so you couldn't have much to live on, so—"

"Don't you remember when the Lost Maiden Mine was found and the whole country went wild about the romance and the court case and everything else?"

Jane's silent pause was Kady's answer. "I don't know what you're talking about," Jane said suspiciously, "but I'd like to be told what's going on."

At that Kady got off the phone fast. There was no one on earth more perceptive than Jane, and Kady wasn't about to start talking and maybe mention things she didn't want to tell anyone about.

With the phone still in her hand, Kady turned and looked at the flowers on the table. If the Lost Maiden Mine had never been found, then maybe Cole found it. And if Cole found it, it was because she had told him where it was. And if Kady had told him, that meant Cole had lived past nine years old.

Grabbing her keys, Kady ran out of the apartment and into the nearest library.

Leaning back against the ugly couch in her apartment, Kady rubbed her eyes. What time was it now? Three A.M.? Turning, she saw that the clock read five; it would soon be daylight.

It had been a week since she started out to the mailbox with those résumés, and now they still sat in the little shopping bag on the floor by the door. The flowers that had covered the dining room table were on the floor, dying, dried up, unnoticed. The dining table and every other surface in the apartment was covered with books, faxed sheets, photocopies, and pages covered in Kady's handwriting. For a week now she had been researching what had happened in Legend, Colorado.

The first thing she had done was research the Lost Maiden Mine. She had looked at three years of covers of back issues of *Time* magazine because she distinctly remembered seeing the mine on the cover of that magazine. But there was no mention of the finding of the mine in that magazine or in any other. Nor was it in any newspaper or in the memory of anyone Kady asked.

As far as she could tell, she was the only person on the face of the earth who remembered something that had swept across America like a tornado. The get-rich-quick idea always appealed to Americans, and the idea of finding millions in gold just lying there for the taking was an American fairy tale. There had been Maiden clothes, Maiden shoes, Maiden hair. And the TV was full of specials, one-, two-, and four-hour reenactments of the romantic story of a man who loved a ghost and had died holding her hand.

A year later, after the romance had faded, came another kind of show Americans love: exploding myths. It wasn't love that had caused the miner to stay with the woman's skeleton; both his legs had been crushed when gold fell on them and he had been trapped. As for holding the hand of the other skeleton, it was speculated that the dying miner had been reaching for the knife by her side. What was he going to do with the knife? Kill himself to put himself out of his misery? He had died of thirst within days, surrounded by millions in gold. As with every other such story, it was concluded that the gold was cursed, and this was proven by the bad luck of everyone who had touched the money. "Caused by their greed," Kady had said at the time and still believed.

After Kady had proven to herself that the Lost Maiden Mine had not been found, she started to look into what she could find out about Legend itself. This had been more difficult, and she'd had to take the Metro into DC to haunt the Library of Congress to plow through miles of microfilmed newspapers.

Everything she found showed that Ruth had told the truth. There was a short but poignant article about the tragedy in Legend that had left so many adults and children dead. However, there was no mention that the residents of Legend had been the killers, not the bank robbers.

Later, there was a tiny notice that Mrs. Jordan and her widowed daughter-in-law had moved to Denver, and eight and a half months after that was a notice that Mrs. Jordan had given birth to a nine-pound baby boy, who was named Cole Tarik Jordan.

Kady went through three years of curled-up microfilmed newspapers until she found a mention of a kidnap attempt on Mrs. Ruth Jordan's young son. The reporter, who was obviously on the side of the residents of Legend, almost brushed aside the nearly successful kidnaping as though it were justified after what Ruth had done to the people of Legend. Kady's stomach turned as the reporter went on and on about how Ruth had had the mines blown up and how she'd thrown people out of their house into the storms (it had been summer, but that didn't seem to matter to him). He went on to hint that Ruth had somehow brought on the attack of cholera that killed so many people who had once lived in Legend.

Days went by while Kady searched the archives, but she could find nothing else about the Jordan family. Then in 1897, she found the article that Ruth had shown her, the one that said that a Mr. Smith had been found murdered in his home in Denver and he'd willed his entire estate to be used to build orphanages. This was the man Ruth thought Cole had killed while Kady had cooked.

In the next year, 1898, Kady found Ruth Jordan's obituary. It said that she was survived by one son, C. T. Jordan of New York City, but unfortunately, urgent business had prevented Mr. Jordan from attending the funeral.

When she read that, Kady had to look away as tears came to her eyes. It didn't look as though Ruth had had enough time to reconcile with her son before she died.

Kady read on to find that the funeral had been "sparsely attended" and there had been some unpleasantness that had to do with something that had happened long ago.

After Ruth's obituary, Kady found only bits about the

Jordan family. The Jordan mansion was sold through lawyers, then torn down in 1926.

She searched the old New York directories but could find nothing on C. T. Jordan or Cole Jordan, leaving Kady to wonder what had happened to Ruth's son who had been so full of anger.

After the newspapers, Kady began to search the books, and there she found what she didn't want to see. A book on ghost towns had a chapter titled, "A Town Destroyed by Hatred," which was a highly dramatized account of Ruth's closing of Legend. When Kady turned the page, she gasped aloud as she saw a line drawing of an emaciated, wire-haired old shrew laughing in glee as the children of Legend died of cholera. "You took away my family, now I'll take yours" was the caption.

Never in her life had Kady wanted to destroy a book, but she wanted to destroy that one with its lies and poison. She closed the book with such a sharp thud that the man across from her frowned.

Now, sitting in her apartment, the sun about to rise, Kady felt at a loss as to what she should do next. As far as she could tell, her adventure in Legend was over. What she should do now is go to bed, sleep for a few hours; then tomorrow she would mail her nearly forgotten résumés and try to start a new life.

But Kady couldn't seem to work up the energy to walk into the bedroom, so instead, she pushed half a dozen pages of notes off the sofa and stretched out on it. She was asleep instantly.

And the minute she closed her eyes, she began to have the dream. At first everything was the same. The veiled man was holding out his hand to her, and Kady was trying to reach it, but this time something was different. This time she seemed to be moving away from him, and she could tell by the expression in his eyes that he was angry with her.

"Now," he said, and for the first time Kady heard his

voice. It was deep, with a strange quality to it, as though the bottom of it were filled with dried leaves.

"You must come now," he said. His voice seemed to be a command, but at the same time it was a plea. "If you do not come now, I cannot return."

With those words he disappeared in a flash, and Kady was left alone in a dry, sandy place that was eerily empty. "Where are you?" she called and began to turn around, looking for him, looking for some clue as to where to go. "How can I go to you if I don't know where you are?" She was shouting and frantically turning about, looking for anything that would tell her where she was.

She awoke with a start, and her face was lying in a wet place on the couch; she had been crying in her sleep. For a moment she didn't remember the dream, but then it came back to her with all its frustration. Where was she to go? How was she to go when she had so little money? She needed to get a job, needed to get on with real life.

On impulse she went to the wall that had once opened and made an entrance into Legend. Now it was just a wall. "Damn all of you!" she said, turning and leaning against it. "You want me to do something, but you give me no help."

It was at that moment that she heard Ruth Jordan's voice inside her head. "I will give you six weeks. If you haven't contacted my son's descendants by then, it will be clear that you're not going to."

Six weeks? Kady thought, then leaped toward the couch to find her date book and tore through the pages. Her heart was pounding so hard she could hardly think. How much time did she have left? Even if she had all the time in the world, how was she going to find Ruth's descendants? What were their names? Where did they live?

"Three days," she said aloud, looking at the calendar. "I have three days left." But where? she thought, her eyes roaming the room as though she might see something written on the wall.

Kady looked up at the ceiling. "Damn you, Ruth Jordan! Help me! *Where* do I look?"

The words were hardly out of her mouth when she again seemed to hear Ruth's voice and what she'd said that night on the porch. "He's in New York trying to make a life for himself. He wants no help from me, actually, he wants no contact from me."

"New York," Kady said, then ran to the bedroom to pack a bag. A train could have her in the city in three hours.

Twenty minutes later she opened the door to her apartment, overnight case in hand, and ran smack into Gregory.

"Oh, Kady, my darling," he said, trying his best to pull her into his arms. "You don't know how much I've missed you. I forgive you for everything, and I ask that you forgive me, and I hope we can—"

"Would you please move? I have a train to New York to catch."

"Train? You can't think of leaving me. If you do, I'll—"

She could tell she wasn't going to get away from him easily. "If I leave you, you'll have even fewer customers than you've had this last week," she said with satisfaction. Kady was disgusted by her own vanity, but each night she'd made sure she walked near enough to Onions to see that the street was no longer filled with customers. Hardly minutes after she walked out, some dear food critic had published the word that Kady's Place was now just a steak house. He'd even speculated on where Kady was going to be cooking next, which could only help her find a job.

"All right," Gregory said with disgust, pulling away from her but completely blocking her way to the stairs. "You win. What do you want? Ten percent of the action?"

"If you're asking me if I want ten percent of Norman House Restaurants, the answer is no. Now, would you please get out of my way so I can leave?"

"Fifteen percent, and that's my final offer."

"Good! I refuse, so now you can move." She tried pushing him aside, but he wouldn't budge.

"What is it that you want of me?" he asked, making it sound as though she were a demanding shrew.

Kady set her suitcase down and looked him in the eye. "I don't want anything from you. Nothing whatever. To tell you the truth, I never want to see you again."

"Just because we had a lovers' quarrel is no reason to—"

"Aaaargh," Kady growled, then gave him a good kick in the shins that made him move to one side of the stairs, and grabbing her case, she ran down them. She was on the Metro and heading toward Union Station before he could catch her.

Chapter 20

WHEN KADY GOT TO NEW YORK, SHE KNEW HER MEASLY SIX grand wasn't going to last very long. Between lack of time and lack of money, she would have to hurry to find Ruth Jordan's descendants. She took a room in a less-than-desirable hotel by Madison Square Garden and wasted a day at the library and on the telephone, calling people named Jordan. She soon found that people in New York City did not know who their great-grandmothers were and, for the most part, didn't want to be bothered.

By late afternoon Kady was ready to give up. She was sitting in a New York deli eating sliced turkey on a bagel, her notebook open before her, and wondering where she could look next, when she noticed the knife in the hand of the man at the table across from her. Looking down at her plate, she remembered how Cole had had knives concealed inside his clothes and how he was one of the few people she'd ever met who knew how to properly sharpen a knife.

Idly, she picked up her pen and began to doodle, and when she had finished, she saw that she'd drawn a sword, a

long-bladed, round-hilted sword that looked like something out of a pirate movie.

As she chewed and looked at the drawing, she wondered
if a love of something could be passed down through
generations. Cole had loved knives. Could a relative of his
also love knives and swords?

Grabbing her sandwich, Kady ate as she went back to her
hotel room and checked the Yellow Pages for antique
dealers, and when she had a few addresses, she hit the
streets again.

It wasn't until midmorning on the third day—the
last day—that she had any success. She'd been given the
address of a tiny shop downtown, one that reeked of
money because only a serious collector could find such a
place, and when she saw it, she knew that only a
connoisseur would have wanted to go inside. The windows hadn't been cleaned since the store was built many
years before, and there was nothing inside the filthy
display window except dead flies and layers of dirt. The
glass door had been painted black, and the only indication that she was in the right place was the name *Anderson*
in faded gold paint. Beside the door was a buzzer and a
speaker.

Without much hope that she'd meet with any success,
Kady pushed the buzzer, and after several minutes the
haughty voice of a man came out. "Yes?"

Kady took a deep breath. "Mr. Jordan sent me," she said
into the speaker. When there were no questions asked and
no hesitation before she was buzzed inside, Kady could
only stand there and stare in astonishment at the door for
precious seconds before pushing it open.

Inside the tiny shop the dirty walls were covered with
swords, the kind found only in museums: curved blades,
thin blades, rusty and pitted blades, some looking pristine
new, some as though they'd been buried for centuries.
Glass cases were filled with knives of every size, with

handles of every conceivable substance. Looking about in wonder, Kady could only gape.

"And what is Mr. Jordan looking for today?" said a man from behind her. Turning, Kady saw an older man, tall and thin, gray at the temples; he had a look on his face that let a person know that he was the best in his field. He was as perfectly groomed as the store was ungroomed.

"Actually, I was thinking of a gift."

At that the tiniest smile crossed the man's face as he looked down at Kady's very ordinary and very inexpensive clothes. She was aware that there were no price tags dangling from the swords. "I think you should look in Bloomingdale's, a nice tie perhaps." Pointedly, he glanced at the door.

Wildly, Kady searched her mind for something to prevent his throwing her out. "I was trying to get an idea of what Cole liked, and I——" Kady had no idea what she said, but something had certainly piqued the man's interest, because, for a flash of a second, his eyebrows nearly hit his hairline.

"I see," he said as he tried to get his face back under control, but before he could say anything, there was a commotion in the back of the store, and she heard a door opening and closing. "If you'll excuse me," the man said, then disappeared into the back, leaving Kady alone to wander about. But she was more interested in what was happening in the back of the store than in the swords, for there was a great deal of furious whispering going on.

Minutes later a handsome, young blond man came into the store from the back, his arms full of packages, looked at Kady for a moment, then whispered, "He'll do anything to find out what the *T* stands for," then disappeared again into the back.

For several stunned minutes, Kady didn't understand what the young man was talking about, but then she almost swooned with happiness. She had just found Ruth's descendant, Mr. C. T. Jordan. Now all she had to do was trade her information for the proprietor's, for she full well knew what the *T* stood for.

Fifteen minutes later she left the store with an address clutched in her hand and a smile on her face.

Chapter 21

"I HAVE TOLD YOU SEVERAL TIMES," THE RECEPTIONIST SAID sternly, "Mr. Jordan sees *no* one without an appointment."

"But you don't understand, I *must* see him *today*. This is the last day!" Twice now Kady had tried to explain why she had to see Mr. Jordan this day, but what could she say? That his great-great-grandmother who had been dead for ninety-eight years had told her she had only six weeks in which to contact a man who had yet to be born? Even when she said that this was the last day, it carried no weight because she couldn't answer the question, Last day of what?

When the woman only glared at Kady, she went back to her seat in the elegant waiting room, where she had been sitting for the last hour and a half.

During the past hours she had not only been unable to break through the receptionist's reserve, but she'd been unable to pry any information from her. The office of C. T. Jordan was the entire top floor of an expensive marble-clad building, and when she'd entered the ground floor and told the guard whom she wanted to see, he had laughed at her. Thinking as quickly as she could, she showed him the sword dealer's card. Thankfully, the guard made a call, and Kady had been allowed into the private elevator that took her to the top floor.

But here she'd met opposition in the form of a large, humorless woman who at first wanted to have Kady physically thrown out. But a telephone had rung, she'd picked it up, listened, put it down, then told Kady she could not see Mr. Jordan. It had taken Kady a moment to realize what was different in her tone: the woman was no longer saying Kady was going to be dragged from the room by guards. She could remain on the premises, but could *not* see C. T. Jordan.

"I'll stay here and wait," Kady said tentatively, but the woman had merely shrugged her shoulders in dismissal, then turned away.

As Kady sat there for the next ninety minutes, she was more confused than ever. Why was she being allowed to stay? Was someone checking with the sword dealer before having her pulled screaming from the room? And why wouldn't the receptionist answer any of Kady's questions, such as what Mr. Jordan was like, what his company did, did the man have a family? But the woman had told Kady that she had no intention of gossiping about her employer. Her attitude said she could not understand why such a poorly dressed young woman was being allowed to stay in this place.

On impulse, Kady took a piece of notepaper from an antique desk in a corner of the room and wrote a note.

Dear Mr. Jordan,
    You do not know me, but I would like to talk to you about your grandmother Ruth and what happened in Legend.

Below this she wrote her New York hotel address, then folded the note and, with pleading eyes, asked the receptionist to please see that Mr. Jordan received it. "He will be very angry if you don't," she said as ominously as she could manage. This seemed to do the trick, for the woman took the note and left the room.

When Kady turned back, she saw there was a man now sitting in the waiting room, a briefcase open on his lap, and when he looked up and saw Kady, she could tell he was interested in her. A few weeks ago Jane had said that Kady had become a shameless flirt, so maybe she could use a little bit of what she'd learned in Legend to her advantage.

Kady took a seat across from the man. "Applying for a job?" she asked in wide-eyed innocence.

He gave Kady one of those up and down looks, and what he saw seemed to please him, because he smiled a bit and nodded his head.

Kady gave a sigh that was meant to say she was glad to have a friend. "I'm applying for a job, too. Maybe if you get *your* job, I'll be your secretary," she said as she fluttered her lashes and leaned a bit toward him. "You must know what he's like. C. T. Jordan, I mean."

The man took the bait. He gave a very macho stretch, then put on his wise look. "Private. Jordan is a very private man. Rarely seen in public."

"The agency sent me over here, and I don't even know what this company does."

"Buys and sells. Owns things, you know, like states of the union, that sort of thing."

Kady's mouth made a round little O. "My goodness, is he rich?"

"You don't read *Forbes* magazine, do you?" the man said, chuckling.

"I'm more of a *Cook's Illustrated* type."

"Let's just say that the elusive Mr. Jordan is a very wealthy man."

"My goodness! You don't say! And how does one get in to meet him?"

"By invitation only. No one knows when he's here or

when he's not. He deals with only a few men who have worked for him for years—and his private secretary of course."

At that moment the receptionist returned, gave Kady yet another hostile glance, then told the man Mr. Caulden was ready to see him. After the man left the waiting room, the receptionist turned to Kady with a smug little smile. "Mr. Jordan has gone home for the day, so he won't be able to see you."

Kady's heart seemed to drop to her feet. "You gave him my message?"

"Yes, he says he knows no Ruth Jordan and has never heard of Legend, Colorado."

Well, that's that, Kady thought, then asked if she could use the rest room, and even at that the receptionist was reluctant. "Would you give me a break?" Kady snapped, making the woman look the tiniest bit guilty as she pointed the way down the hall.

Minutes later, Kady was washing her hands when she glanced up at the mirror and paused. She had put "Legend" on the note, not "Legend, *Colorado.*"

"He's here and he knows," she said aloud. She didn't know what Mr. C. T. Jordan knew, but it was enough that he'd allowed Kady to remain in the waiting room and enough that he'd refused to see her.

Grabbing a paper towel, she quickly dried her hands, then crumpled it angrily. Ruth had given her six weeks to contact her descendants, and Kady was going to do anything she had to to give that lovely lady peace.

Slipping out of the rest room, Kady did not turn left, toward the receptionist's desk, but instead went right, toward the offices. It was after five, and the offices she saw felt empty. In fact the whole place seemed deserted. Brass nameplates were on each door, and each name rang of Harvard and Yale; there were numbers like III after some of the names.

At the end of the long hall, before it turned and started back toward the receptionist's desk, were double doors with no name on them. The doors themselves were impressive, made of ancient teak and carved with dragons and horizontally branched trees. Without a doubt in her mind, Kady knew that this was C. T. Jordan's office.

She didn't think about what she was doing; she just grabbed the handles of both doors and threw them open.

A man was standing just inside the doors in the sumptuously furnished reception area of the office. He was dressed all in black, as though for a martial arts class, with voluminous black cotton trousers, a black T-shirt, and he was pulling a black sweatshirt over his head. When Kady threw open the doors, he halted in pulling the sweatshirt on over his head, leaving it half on, half off, so only his eyes were visible. The lower half of his face was covered — almost as though his face were veiled.

Kady stood utterly still, hardly able to breathe, and stared at him. She would know those eyes anywhere. He was her veiled man.

For what seemed to be a lifetime she stared at him, her head filling with the hundreds of times she had seen him all through her childhood. Whenever she had been upset or worried, he always came to her, always soothed her, always made her feel less alone.

Still with her breath held, she watched as he pulled the sweatshirt down, and for the first time, Kady saw his face.

It seemed to be all angles, with sharp cheekbones cutting down to a square-tipped chin that was slightly cleft. His nose was straight, lean, with nostrils that flared out to the side, an aristocratic nose. The only softness on his face was his full-lipped mouth that Kady couldn't help thinking was as soft as a child's.

But what else she saw deep within his eyes was pain, a pain so deep he probably had no idea where it had come from. But Kady knew.

She remembered how she'd once thought Gregory

looked like this man. No, she thought, Gregory did not look like this man. No one on earth looked like this man.

"I take it you are Miss Long," he said, and his voice was like in her dream, very deep, but at the bottom of it was a raspy quality, maybe even a growling quality.

Kady thought that she'd better sit down before she fell down. With her eyes never leaving his, she clutched the rolled arm of a big chair covered in burgundy velvet and almost fell back onto it.

"Now that you have forced your way in here, what is it that you want of me?"

For the life of her, Kady couldn't answer. All she could do was stare up at him, feeling exhilarated and frightened at the same time, for it was very strange seeing this man in the flesh.

Frowning, C. T. Jordan stared down at the woman, wishing she weren't so damned pretty. She had what looked to be several feet of silky dark hair pulled back into a braid as thick as his arm and it curled over the velvet of the sofa. Thick lashes surrounded beautiful dark eyes above a tiny nose, and her lips of dark pink were undisguised by cosmetics. As for her body! She had that concealed under yards of cheap fabric, but he could see the lush curves that, just looking at them, made his palms sweat. He had been accused of being a throwback to the past, for he liked women to look like women, not what seemed to be the current fashion, women with bodies like twelve-year-old boys topped by large, artificial breasts.

Lust, Jordan, he told himself. *You're too old to allow lust to rule your head.* He knew why she was here and what she wanted. After all, hadn't he known all his life that this day would come?

She *had* to stop looking into his eyes, Kady told herself. She had to get her mind back, had to think of her mission, had to remember who she was, where she was. Maybe if she made herself recite the recipe for brioche, she could concentrate.

Pulling her eyes away from his, she began to think . . .

But no recipe came to mind because behind him was a floor-to-ceiling lighted glass case, and inside, suspended from invisible wires, were swords of exquisite workmanship, from every part of the world, every historical period. They were the kind of swords one saw in slick auction magazines, then later read about having been sold to an "anonymous bidder" for a quarter of a million dollars.

Turning back to look at him, she saw that he had not moved so much as a muscle as he stared at her. She could tell that under his clothes he was whipcord lean, and she had an idea that he knew how to use every one of those swords in the case.

"I . . . I met your grandmother," she managed to say.

"My grandmother died when I was three, and I doubt that you were even born then."

"No, I . . . I met the one who died long before you were born." Even to herself she sounded stupid, like some New Age guru.

His patronizing smile said that he agreed with her. "Ah, I see. Am I right in assuming you mean the one my grandfather—when he was alive, that is—so affectionately called Ruthless Ruth?"

Kady winced. "Ruth Jordan was a very nice lady, and she was only trying to protect—" She stopped because he was smiling in such a patronizing way that she couldn't continue. For some reason, she could feel her anger rising, which made no sense, since she had invaded his office and so had no right to be angry at him. But his image had been an enormous part of her life. He—or his clone—had appeared to her hundreds of times. Shouldn't he recognize her? Or at least feel some jolt at seeing her?

But he was looking at her as though she were nothing more than a great nuisance and as though he were waiting for her to do something predictable. "I am beginning to see now," he said slowly. "You believe yourself to be a clairvoyant, and you have come here to give me—what is it?—a message from the past? So tell me, how much am I to pay you for this information? Hundreds? Or are you after thousands? Surely, I hope it's not more."

Kady's lips tightened and her brow knitted. "I don't want any money from you."

"Oh?"

With that he looked her up and down, and when he looked back at her eyes, Kady felt her entire body break into a fine coat of sweat. The fire and intensity behind his eyes made her feel as though she were going to be consumed by him.

Part of her wanted to run toward him, but another part of her was frightened and made her want to run out the door. Did he look at *all* women as he was looking at her?

Patiently, but with one eyebrow raised in disbelief, he was waiting for her to continue.

For Ruth! she reminded herself, then sat up straighter. "Ruth regretted what she had done to her son, and she wanted to make up for it, but she died too soon. He didn't attend her funeral." Even to herself she wasn't making any sense. She took a deep breath to try to calm her nervousness. "She asked me to find her descendants and . . . well, just to contact them, that's all. And I wanted to tell you that—"

His lips curled into a cynical smile. "Are you asking me to *believe* that you met my long-dead grandmother and she asked you to come see me? Just to say hello?"

Kady smiled ever so sweetly. "I not only met your grandmother, I also married Ruth's grandson who died when he was nine years old." *Let him figure that one out,* she thought.

All Kady had wanted to do was wipe that knowing look off his face. No doubt he was used to people who cowered before him and jumped at his every request, but she was unprepared when he looked at her with such anger on his face that she was almost frightened. But something else about his rage made her heart beat wildly. He's jealous, she thought, then told herself that was ridiculous.

With great, long strides, he went to a cabinet on the opposite wall, opened the doors to reveal a liquor cabinet, then poured a cut-glass tumbler half full of smoky single-malt whiskey and downed it one gulp. When he didn't flinch, Kady thought he must either be a budding alcoholic or something had greatly upset him. She was well aware that he had offered her nothing.

He turned back to her. "Miss Long, I don't have time for this. And I can assure you that I am not going to give you any money, no matter how outrageous your story."

Stunned, Kady just sat there. He was a hateful man, so in love with his money that he thought everyone else was, too, but still, something kept her there with him. He was a stranger, but at the same time it was as though she'd spent most nights of her life with this man.

He was glaring at her, brooding, as he watched her. With a pounding heart, she got up, and with her back to him, she walked to the wall behind her. Just as in the wall case, here, too, was a display of knives, these smaller and very much like those Cole had often produced from inside his clothing. Since she'd spent most of her life with a knife in her hand, it was an easy thing for Kady to surreptitiously pick up one of the knives, whirl about, and throw it.

With a gesture like lightning, he caught the knife by its handle in midair.

And it was at that moment that Kady saw Cole. For just a second the dark, scowling man in front of her disappeared and there stood Cole with his laughing blue eyes, sunlight on his golden hair. As fast as the image came, it faded, and she was left alone in the office with a man she'd seen hundreds of times, always holding out his hand to her, always urging her to ride away with him.

But this man just stared at her, with his hot eyes and his

look of disbelief. "If you're planning to faint, I must tell you that other women have tried that before, and I can assure you that fainting has no effect on me." He looked at the knife in his hand. "However, no woman before has tried throwing a blade at me."

"More's the pity," Kady said, looking back at him; then she slipped her bag over her shoulder. "I've given you my message, so I'll leave now."

"Are you sure? As you can see, I have other weapons you can throw at me."

She whirled to face him. "Mr. Jordan, your ancestors were the nicest, kindest people I've ever met. Cole Jordan was a man who knew how to love a woman, to love her so much that he created a whole world for her. And Ruth Jordan did what she did because she had loved too hard and been too hurt when she lost that love." She glared at him. "It is disgusting that those lovely people could have given birth to someone like you, someone who thinks only of money."

Pausing for a moment, she looked at him in contempt. "And to think that I spent all those years searching for you," she said softly before walking to the door.

He stopped her as her hand was on the latch, standing to one side, very close, but not touching her. "Who was Ruth's lover?" he asked softly.

She was angry, but when she turned and looked at him she was not prepared for the impact his nearness would have. She may have thought she had felt love, desire, lust, other emotions for other men, but nothing had ever prepared her for how it felt to be near this man. Every atom of her body seemed to vibrate as she looked into his dark eyes, and she had the feeling she was falling into a bottomless pool, down, down, down.

As though she were poison, he stepped away from her, and his action made Kady come back to her senses. She knew he was testing her. Ruth's youngest son was believed to have been fathered by her husband. "He was the father of Cole's friend, Tarik, an Egyptian man," she managed to say in a hoarse whisper. "That's why you have his name. And it's why you're dark when the rest of the Jordans were blonds." With a shaking hand, she managed to open the door and leave the office.

After Kady left the sumptuous offices of C. T. Jordan, she didn't return to her hotel room right away but wandered around the city streets. Shock threatened to overwhelm her. She had recognized him, but he had felt nothing for her except, maybe, well . . . Perhaps she'd also seen lust in his eyes. But that didn't matter. What was important was that she'd told him, and that was the end of it. She'd met him and she didn't like him.

But if she didn't like him, then why did the idea of never seeing him again hurt more than losing Cole or Gregory had? While she was with Cole, she'd always known it wasn't real, that what was between them wasn't going to last. And when she'd been with Gregory, she'd felt more gratitude than love, grateful that such a man would be interested in her.

But with her Arabian man, the man she'd always dreamed of, she had always believed that if she found him, she'd find True Love.

But life does not imitate fairy tales. She'd found him, and he'd felt nothing. There was certainly no love-at-first-sight.

So what now? she wondered. Now that her Legend adventure was officially over, what was she to do with her life? Get a job, try to save money to open her own restaurant or a cooking school or . . . Suddenly, she felt very alone. Her life now was just where it was after she'd graduated from cooking school, but then all the world had been before her. Now, years later, she was lower than the bottom. Now she was no longer the sought-after graduate, the—

No! she thought. She was *not* going to lose herself in self-pity. She'd done what she could to help Ruth and Cole and Legend, so now it was time to go begging for a job. Correction, it was time to start a new life, with new adventures, with . . .

Turning, she went back to her hotel, trying to lighten her spirits but not doing very well at it. When she opened the door to her room, the first thing she saw was the blinking message light on her telephone, and she wondered who had called her. For a millionth of a second she thought it might be Tarik Jordan, but when she checked, she was told that she had a package and could it be brought up now?

Minutes later Kady was handed a large express package from Virginia, and her heart sank. How in the world had Gregory found where she was staying? Tossing the package on the bed, she took a shower, washed her hair, turned on the TV, and only then did she notice that Jane's name was on the air bill.

Curious, she opened the package. Inside were two legal-size envelopes, one thick, the other thin, and two letters. The first letter was from one of the young men who had worked for her at Onions, and as Kady began to read, her heart did indeed begin to lighten. He said that since she had left, business had been so bad that all the cooks trained by her were applying for jobs elsewhere. He went on to say how much he had learned from Kady and thanked her for keeping horrid little Mrs. Norman off their backs.

Smiling, Kady called room service, ordered a bowl of onion soup and a fruit salad, then continued to read. The young man went on to say that since all of them would get a better job by putting Kady's name on their résumés, they all felt they owed her, and they had found a way to repay her in a small way.

At this Kady laughed out loud, for it seemed that snooping, spying, and amateur sleuthing were their ways of saying thanks. First they had haunted Gregory's office, never allowing anything to be taken out of the office that they didn't first inspect. "The fat envelope is the result of the first weeks," he wrote. "We grew bolder after that."

With eyes wide from curiosity, she opened the thicker envelope and dumped out at least a dozen letters. Most were on the letterhead of a famous restaurant or hotel, and each was begging Kady to come work for them. Some were from people who wanted to open restaurants and were pleading with Kady to run them.

For a moment, she couldn't believe what she was seeing. The words "Please," and "begging you," and offers of money and housing and "will give you a free hand," were in the letters. Two of the letters had been torn to shreds, but some dear person had painstakingly taped the pieces back together.

When Kady realized what she was seeing, she began to dance about the room; then she called room service and ordered a bottle of their best champagne.

"No job interviews," she said. "No begging for a job. No . . ." She couldn't think what else, but when the food and wine arrived, she tipped the man ten dollars, then opened the wine, poured a glass, and toasted herself.

Amazing how the world could change in so short a time, she thought, glancing back at the letters on the bed. One minute she had nowhere to go and the next she had choices from all over the world, as one of the letters was even from London and another was from Paris.

How did they find me? she suddenly wondered, then went back to the bed and looked at the second unopened letter. When she saw that it was from Jane, her heart nearly stopped. Was ever-sensible Jane going to lecture her about doing something as stupid as walking out of one job before she had another?

Kady finished the first glass of wine and filled the second before she opened Jane's letter. The first half page told in detail how much trouble Jane had gone to to find her, calling nearly every hotel in New York. She had found out that Kady was in New York by hinting to Gregory that she was going to try to get them back together. "That man certainly believes that every woman has the hots for him, doesn't he?" Jane wrote, making Kady smile.

"I envy you," Jane wrote. "You have inspired a great deal of love from the people who worked for you. They risked a lot by going through Gregory's trash, and when they called me, they knew that I'd do whatever it took to find you."

Kady ate some of her soup, then finished Jane's letter. "Kady, maybe I haven't made myself clear lately," her friend wrote. "I know I tend to be bossy, heaven knows many people have felt the compulsion to tell me, but I hope you know how much I care about you. The only thing Gregory had going for him was his good looks. He treated you like a lowly servant—just the way my own family tended to treat you. I had to become an adult to see that. I want to tell you that I think you are the kindest, most generous person I've ever met in my life, and I feel I owe you for past transgressions. So when I see you with a man who isn't worthy to eat at your table, forgive me if I say so. Whatever you do with your life, remember to take what is offered and don't give everything away. When you meet another man, make sure he gives you something in return. You deserve it!!"

Maybe it was the wine, but when Kady's eyes misted over, she brushed the tears away with the sleeve of her bathrobe. After rereading Jane's letter a couple of times, she slipped it into her pocket and dug into her food. What had been a rotten day was turning into something extraordinarily good.

It was only after she had finished eating and drunk another glass of wine that she remembered that she still hadn't opened the thin envelope. Wiping her hands first, she then rummaged under the lovely letters from the even more lovely people offering her jobs and pulled out the envelope. It was white, excellent quality paper, and had a return address of a law firm in New York. Madison Avenue in the sixties, no less.

"My goodness," she said aloud as she used a table knife to slit the top open. "I am indeed honored."

When Kady saw that the letter was addressed to Mrs. Cole Jordan, she nearly choked on her wine.

The letter itself was very short. Mr. W. Hartford Fowler IV requested that Mrs. Jordan call him as soon as possible on urgent business. There followed a long list of telephone numbers with descriptive phrases like, the *country house, the lodge, the mobile, ship-to-shore,* as well as four office numbers. "I cannot begin to tell you how urgent this is, Mrs. Jordan," he wrote. "You must contact me right away if you are to make the date set by Ruth Jordan. Call me at any time. Call collect. Wherever, whenever. Just do it quickly."

Kady read the letter three times before she noticed that it was dated a month earlier. Which meant that Gregory had received it before she walked out. And it also meant that someone had snooped inside his filing cabinets to find this. What was more, she saw that the envelope had been sent to her apartment, not the restaurant, which meant that Gregory had been monitoring her private mail. "Wonder what he paid my landlord to get his hands on my mail first?" she said, her mouth a tight line. For a moment she wondered how many other offers of employment she had received while she was at Onions but Gregory had intercepted. All in the name of Norman House Restaurants, of course.

No use wasting time on that, she thought, then picked up the telephone and began to dial some of the numbers on the letter from the lawyer. After she reached a machine at the office numbers and left a message, she turned the TV volume back on and tried to watch, but then she read the lawyer's letter again, turned the TV off, and called more numbers.

She got him on his mobile, and as soon as she introduced herself, she heard the screech of wheels as he skidded his car to a halt.

"Kady Jordan?" he asked in disbelief. "You're sure?"

She laughed as she had an idea this man didn't usually lose his composure as he was doing now.

"What is today?" he said almost frantically. "It's ten P.M., isn't it? If I send a helicopter, can you get to New York from Virginia in two hours? Can we still do it?"

"I'm already in New York. Could you tell me what this is about? What do you know about Ruth Jordan?"

"Less than you do, I'm sure," he said hastily. "Look, Mrs. Jordan—"

"I would appreciate it if you'd stop calling me that. I am Kady Long. Kady, please."

The man didn't seem to hear her. "Okay, you're in New York, I'm in Connecticut, and he's in . . . Where the hell is he?"

Kady was getting frustrated. "Where is *who?*" she said fiercely.

"Jordan. C. T. Jordan. You *must* see him before midnight tonight. If you don't, the will will be invalid."

"I don't know what will you're talking about, but I *have* seen Mr. Jordan today. I had to sneak into his office, but I—"

She stopped because the man was laughing. No, he was whooping. Actually, he was, as far as she could tell, jumping up and down and singing and yelling at the top of his lungs, the mobile telephone waving about in his hands.

"Mr. Fowler," she was shouting into the phone, but he didn't hear her.

With the hotel phone on her shoulder, Kady reached for her glass of wine and waited for this insane man to calm down and tell her what was going on.

She had a good long wait, and when the man did speak again, she thought maybe he was crying. Crying in that way men do when they win the Indianapolis 500.

"Kady," he said, trying to control his erratic breath, "did anyone see you at Jordan's office today? Anyone at all?"

"Several people. The receptionist, a man applying for a job, the guard downstairs, at least half a dozen other employees, and—So help me, Mr. Fowler, if you start whooping again, I'm going to hang up."

At that the man laughed and made an attempt at getting himself under control. "Could I see you tomorrow?" he asked politely. "We have some, ah, business to transact."

"Would it be too much to ask what business?"

The man took a moment before he answered. "Kady, do you have any dreams in life?"

"Of course I do," she snapped, glancing at the phone. Was this man crazy?

"What is the very wildest of your dreams?"

Not that it was any of his business, but she looked at the letters on the bed and smiled. "I'd like to own my own restaurant."

For some reason this seemed to spark the man off again into drunken hilarity, and again Kady had to wait. "You'll get your restaurant. You'll get anything you want, but you must come to see me tomorrow."

"What time?"

Again he started laughing. "You come any time you're ready, Kady. When you arrive, I'll be waiting for you. And a car will be waiting for you at your—May heaven help me, but I don't even know where you're staying."

Kady hesitated as she thought twice about telling this man anything about herself. "I don't need a car, and I'll come to your office tomorrow at ten A.M. Is that too early?"

"No," he said, amused. "Whatever time is convenient for you. We'll all be waiting for you."

"I'll see you then," she said and hung up. What a very

odd man, she thought, looking at the phone in wonder, then, dismissing him, she looked back at the job offers. *Which one shall I take?* she thought. *Living in Seattle might be nice.*

Thirty minutes later she fell asleep amid the letters and didn't wake until fifteen minutes till ten, which is why she was late for her appointment with Mr. Fowler. But, as he'd said, it didn't matter, for they were all waiting for her.

Chapter 22

THE OLD-WORLD ELEGANCE OF THE OFFICES OF FOWLER AND
Tate made Kady more aware than usual of her old, worn
clothing. This place is made for Chanel, she thought as
she walked across the marble lobby. Not that she had ever
seen Chanel outside a magazine ad, but she had an
imagination.

"I am Kady Lon—" she said to the receptionist, but the
woman didn't so much as allow her to finish her sentence
before she started gushing.

"Yes, please come this way, Mr. Fowler is expecting you.
Could I get you some coffee? Tea perhaps? Would you like
anything ordered in?"

Kady hardly had time to say no to all the offers before big
double doors with ornate brass fittings opened and out
stepped a tall, handsome, gray-haired man wearing a drop-
dead-gorgeous three-piece suit.

"Kady," he said, breathing out the word as though it
were what he'd been waiting all his life to say.

"You're Mr. Fowler?" she asked in disbelief, since she
couldn't reconcile this elegant man with the whooper on
the telephone last night. This man looked like he should

star in one of those sophisticated 1930s movies that usually featured Cary Grant.

"Bill," he said, his hand on the small of her back as he steered her into his office, a room that made Kady give an involuntary gasp. It was like a library in an English country house, all dark green and burgundy, with walls of carved wooden paneling. There was a picture on the wall that looked very much like an original Van Gogh.

"Can I get you anything? Anything at all?" he asked.

Kady felt so out of place that she tried to make a joke. "New shoes?" she said, smiling as she took a seat on a pretty little dark green sofa, and he smiled back at her warmly.

When she was seated, Kady looked up at the man. There was no way she was *ever* going to be able to call this man Bill. "Would you mind telling me what this is all about?"

For a moment he remained standing, towering over her; then he sat on a chair facing her and nodded toward a neat stack of papers on the antique coffee table. "I must admit that never has a client engendered as much curiosity in me as you have. I know nothing about your connection to a woman who has been dead nearly a hundred years. I only know that you were married to her grandson, but if that were actually true, you'd have to be nearly a hundred years old." At this he chuckled and gave her what she was sure was his best you-can-confide-in-me look.

Kady gave him a little smile in return, but she wasn't tempted in the slightest to tell him what she had been through.

"Yes, well, I won't pry." Again he chuckled. "No, I probably will pry a great deal, but I have a feeling it may get me nowhere. If you are half as secretive as the rest of the Jordans, I will find out nothing."

Kady started to tell him again that she wasn't a Jordan, but then refrained. The less she said, the sooner she'd get out of here and the sooner she could go back to her hotel room and start calling about those job offers. Some of them were three months old, meaning Gregory had received them some time ago, and she wondered if they were still open.

"I guess we should start with this," he said and handed her an envelope, yellowed with age, tied with ribbon, and sealed with red wax.

Before Kady touched it, she knew it was from Ruth, and she had to blink away quick tears. It was painful to think that the woman she had met just weeks ago had now been dead for so very long. Sometimes it seemed to Kady that she'd open a door and Ruth would be standing there. Sometimes she thought, I must tell Ruth about that, then she'd have the hurt of realizing that the woman she'd come to care about was no longer alive.

Kady put the envelope on her lap and looked up at the man across from her. "Don't you need some identification to make sure I'm who I say I am?"

Smiling at her, he pulled a sheaf of papers from a fat leather case on the floor beside the table and handed the papers to her. Kady saw that the yellowed sheets were covered with pen-and-ink sketches of her and Ruth, all scenes from the afternoon and night they had spent together. They were shown walking together, talking, laughing, sitting in the shade at the picnic, in chairs on the porch.

"The other woman is Ruth Jordan?" the lawyer asked softly, seeing the way Kady so tenderly touched the papers with her fingertips.

"Yes," Kady whispered as she saw the name Joseph written at the bottom, the name of Ruth's uncomplaining servant who had served them and waited while they talked. How much had he heard that night?

"She certainly looks different from the image in 'A Town Destroyed by Hatred,' doesn't she?"

"She was lovely, truly lovely," was all Kady could manage to say, and when Mr. Fowler leaned back in his chair with a self-satisfied look on his face, she knew she had said too much. It was easy to see that he had wanted to know if Kady had somehow actually met Ruth Jordan and now he did know.

"Excuse me," he said, rising. "I think you should read the letter from Ruth in private. When you have finished, just push that button on the table beside you and I'll return. I will be waiting for you." With that he left Kady alone in the room.

For a moment she hesitated before opening the yellowed envelope, for she knew that what was inside would once again involve her in the Jordan family and Legend, Colorado. Part of her wanted to throw the letter down and go back to her hotel room and start finding a new job. But the larger part of her was haunted by the eyes of C. T. Jordan.

Quickly, before she changed her mind, she used the silver letter opener Mr. Fowler had so thoughtfully provided and slit the envelope open.

My dearest Kady,

If you are reading this now, then I know you have tried and succeeded in finding my descendants. I gave you a time limit to persuade myself of your interest. If you had put off your search for longer than six weeks, then I would have known there was no hope that you'd have the love and passion that you were going to need to help us. I felt that six weeks was long enough for you to realize that you couldn't be in love with your Gregory. If you were, you wouldn't have been sent to us.

If you are reading this and you have contacted my family within the time limit, then you now have absolute control of all my family's wealth.

At this Kady drew in her breath. But no, what she was reading couldn't be correct. She looked back at the letter.

Perhaps I have left you nothing. For all I know, ninety-eight years from now my family is poor, but, if my descendants are anything like my son Cole Tarik, I somehow doubt it. It is my guess that at this moment you are a very rich young woman.

So why have I given you so much and trusted you so completely? Kady, you can solve this. You can right a horrible wrong, not only what happened to my family but to all the inhabitants of Legend. Because of what happened in that fateful week when my family was murdered, hundreds of people suffered for generations.

I don't know how you can do what I'm asking of you or even if it can be done, but I beg of you to try. The people you met in Legend never had a chance to live. They never had a chance to grow up, to have children of their own, to grow old.

We made the mistakes, Kady, not you. You have been a pawn in all this, but your kindness and generosity were so great that you were able to raise the dead. For a while you gave us hope; you gave us life.

And now I am asking that you figure out a way to do it again. I have done what I could to help you. I have given you the power that money gives to people; I have disinherited my own kin in favor of you, a woman I spent mere hours with. But I trust you because you were chosen to come back to us. You can use the money for whatever purposes you want; it is yours without any strings attached. Build yourself a mansion, buy a dozen carriages dripping gold, I have given you that right.

But I cannot see you doing such a thing. Please, I beg of you, please, Kady, help us. We need you. All of us need you so very much.

> *Yours with love and hope,*
> *Ruth Jordan*

When Kady put down the letter, she felt as though the breath had been knocked out of her. "For a while you gave us hope; you gave us life," she reread. "Your kindness and generosity." Those were almost the very words that Jane had used.

How? she thought. How could she accomplish what Ruth asked of her? Her head was reeling so fast that she could think of nothing, could formulate no plan. She pushed the button on the table, and instantly, Mr. Fowler reappeared.

When he was seated, Kady held up Ruth's letter. "Does C. T. Jordan know of this?" she asked.

"Know of what?" he asked, his eyes twinkling, but it was a lawyer's non-answer in an attempt to find out exactly how much she knew.

"Does he know that since he saw me yesterday, now everything is mine?"

Mr. Fowler smiled at her. "Yes, he knows."

No wonder he refused to see me, she thought. And that's why he'd refused to allow her to be thrown out of the office. After all, from the moment she walked in the front door, she was the owner of the building.

Her mind was tumbling over itself with a thousand thoughts. *What am I to do now?* was the one on top.

Tarik must help me, she thought, and immediately it struck her odd that she would call him that, as everyone else referred to him as C. T.—or, actually, as Mr. Jordan. Maybe it was because she'd heard the name so often from Cole or maybe it was because she'd spent a lifetime of seeing C. T. Jordan in Arabian dress that the Arabian-sounding name suited him.

Whatever his name, she knew he must help her. That was the only thing she knew for absolute sure, because somewhere under his dark exterior, he was Cole. The pain and hardness in his eyes were from what happened to Cole and from what had been done to Ruth's youngest child. Cole had managed to avoid the hatred by pretending it didn't happen. Or maybe he was just so happy to have been given a chance to live as an adult that he had filled his time on earth with love.

And revenge, she thought, remembering that during those ten days he'd been gone, he'd rid the world of the man who had caused his family to be killed. But she couldn't believe that revenge was the full reason Cole had been given a second chance at life, even so brief a second chance.

And now Ruth had done what she could to enable Kady to give Cole and all the inhabitants of Legend a real chance at life.

Tarik must help, went through her mind again; then she thought of him in the ways she had seen him: in her dreams, and, yesterday, in his office, with his sneering remarks. He was not going to help her just for the asking.

"What do I own?" she asked Mr. Fowler.

"Basically, everything. All assets that Ruth Jordan owned at the time of her death, which were several million, and everything made from those assets in the ensuing years were put into trust for you, to be administered by the descendants of her youngest son. There was a further stipulation that the eldest son of each generation be named Cole Tarik Jordan." Mr. Fowler's eyes twinkled, and Kady thought he'd probably never done anything he liked as much as telling someone that she owned everything that had once belonged to C. T. Jordan. "Of course over the years the name has become unfashionable, and it is a closely guarded secret what the initials stand for."

Kady nodded, as she'd already encountered that secret. "Do I own the clothes on his back, that sort of thing?" she asked earnestly.

At that Mr. Fowler frowned, and she could tell that he thought her greedy or vengeful or something else equally dreadful. Or maybe he was just concerned about lawsuits involving what he had or had not done.

She leaned forward on the sofa. "Mr. Fowler," she said, "you are obviously the attorney representing at least part of the wealth that once belonged to C. T. Jordan, and since that wealth now belongs to me, may I assume that you will now be *my* attorney? May I speak to you in confidence?"

"Yes, of course," he answered, and she could see that he was relieved as well as curious.

She held up the letter. "Ruth Jordan has asked me to do something for her. What that is, I can't reveal, but I believe I am going to have to enlist the help of Tarik, er, ah, C. T. Jordan. You know him, I've met him, and I think we are both safe in saying that he'll refuse to help me. Unless I can blackmail him in some way, that is. I want to know everything I own, especially anything personal, like those swords of his, that I can use to make him help me. And I want you to start drawing up a contract that states that if he helps me to my satisfaction, everything will be returned to him. Every penny. I want nothing."

Mr. Fowler smiled indulgently. "I think that's very noble of you, but I don't think you have any idea how much you're giving away. You could keep a few million and he wouldn't miss it."

At that Kady blinked, and her first thought was that she wanted enough to open a nice restaurant, in Seattle maybe, with classrooms attached and lifetime funding so she could teach free cooking classes. It was on the tip of her tongue to say just that, but she didn't. It wasn't her money, and she had no right to it. "I will take nothing over what is needed for the job."

"I don't think you realize—"

"No, Mr. Fowler, I don't think *you* realize what this is all about. If Ruth hadn't asked this of me, I would sign everything over to her descendants this minute, but I can't. As she says, I'll need power, and money will give me that power. Now, would you tell me what I need to know?"

He sat there for a moment, still smiling, and Kady could tell what he was thinking. She might believe she could give away all rights to that money, but when the time came, would she be able to? But what he didn't know was that

Kady had seen firsthand the great evil that money could cause. The shots fired by the people of Legend in an attempt to protect their wealth had caused a hundred years of misery. No, she didn't want any of Ruth's money.

"All right," he said when Kady said no more. "Shall we start going over the portfolios? It will take a while."

"I plan to dedicate every minute of my time to this until it is finished," she said, and for all the nobility of her words, she could have burst into tears. Would the jobs still be open a few months from now? A year? She might be a star in the cooking world today, but people had short memories. Six months from now it might be, "Kady who?"

She took a deep breath. "Shall we get started?"

Chapter 23

As she turned the wheel of the heavy, powerful Range Rover sharply, Kady concentrated on staying out of the center gully in the old dirt road that led straight up the side of the mountain.

It had been several days since her confrontation with Tarik Jordan in his office, and for all of those days she had cursed herself for ever thinking *he* would help her. What in the world had made her think he'd do anything to help anyone?

As the car hit the gulley, sending everything in the back flying upward, Kady swallowed hard. "I will not cry," she said, holding on to the steering wheel with all her might. "Will not, will not, will not." But keeping the tears back was almost impossible. With a glance skyward, she wondered if Ruth Jordan was looking down on her in disgust. She had every right to, since Kady had failed at every attempt to help correct the evil that had happened in the past.

It was amazing to think that during the past days since she had been told she owned all the Jordan money, one person could have made so very many errors, in such a short time. In fact, thinking back on it, had she even done one teeny, tiny thing *right?* No, now that she looked at it, everything she had tried to do she had screwed up. Not just a little bit but in a great big flashy way.

First there had been Mr. Fowler. What was it she had told herself early on that first day? It was something grand and noble about how *she* knew what evil money could do, so she'd not be tempted by the Jordan wealth, no matter how tempting it was.

How little we know ourselves! she thought with disgust as she turned the wheel hard.

That day in Fowler's office had been seductive, oh, so very seductive. Going from being Nobody to Somebody was so very pleasurable. All day she had been wined and dined and feted in a way that was guaranteed to make her forget all her noble thoughts.

She had to give it to Fowler: he missed nothing. The law firm's private chef had left his kitchen and come out to meet Kady, then humbly asked her to show him how to make her squab with currant sauce, which he been told of and had never been able to duplicate. While everyone watched and applauded, she had demonstrated that she knew her way around a kitchen, using her own knives, which she happened to have brought with her. As a result of limitless praise, she had done the unthinkable: she had usurped another cook's kitchen. But the chef must have been well coached (and well paid), because he never made a hint of protest, and Kady had come away walking on clouds, feeling that she was the greatest cook on earth.

All that day had been like that. She had been asked her advice, listened to, consulted. It seemed that everything she said was wise and worth noting.

As Mr. Fowler had shown her property that she now owned, he had slowly, and almost as though it were not important, told her about Tarik, or Mr. Jordan, as everyone called him. It seemed that only Kady thought of him as Tarik.

C. T. Jordan was a very private man. Even with a firm of attorneys that had dealt with his family for two generations, he had been exceptionally closemouthed. "He trusts no one," Mr. Fowler said in a way that let Kady know he thought the young man ought to get professional help. "Though I first met him when he was nine years old, I know very little about him."

Kady didn't want to ask about a man who had been so very rude to her, but she told herself that if she was going to try to enlist Tarik's help, she had to know what there was to know about him, didn't she?

Tarik Jordan had an apartment in New York that was now owned by Kady and a sprawling farm in Connecticut that was his private property.

"Married?" she asked, trying to sound as though the answer meant nothing to her.

"No . . ." Mr. Fowler said hesitantly.

"Ah," Kady said in a way that she hoped sounded worldly. "Women."

Mr. Fowler smiled. "Actually, no. At least not the way I think you mean. When he was younger, there were a few starlets, but since then it's been one-at-a-time."

When Kady didn't look back down at the papers, Mr. Fowler continued. "What else can I tell you about him? His only extravagance is those swords of his, and he's a master at all forms of martial arts. As a boy he won contests in nearly everything he entered." His voice lowered. "But he does seem to have an unhealthy love of sharp instruments."

Kady didn't comment on that, as a few people had accused her of feeling the same way, but she stopped pretending she wasn't interested. "What about his family life? What about his mother?"

"I only met her a few times. She is elegant, beautiful, and as glassily cold as his father. As far as I could tell, after the woman gave birth to a son, she was free to live her own life, as long as she created no scandal. She lives in Europe, and her husband lived in New York, when he wasn't on his private jet, that is. The child, C.T. the third, was brought up by servants in the house in Connecticut.''

For a moment, Kady's heart lurched, but she refused to allow the loneliness of this man's childhood to stand in her way. What was a lonely childhood compared to no childhood at all?

At one point during the day, Kady asked Mr. Fowler why he seemed to be so glad that she had been given the money.

He put his hand warmly over Kady's and smiled avuncularly. "Let's just say that I'd like to see a nice person like you given an opportunity to do some good with so much wealth.''

Kady smiled back at him, and she remembered how Cole had established orphanages with his money, and she wondered what *she* could do. If it were actually her money, that is, which it wasn't, so she had to erase that idea from her mind.

As the day wore on and Kady was shown file after file of papers showing even more of ''her'' assets, she began to ask Mr. Fowler for advice as to how to deal with Tarik. At first the lawyer was reluctant, but after repeated questioning, he relented and settled back in his chair and began to give her his true thoughts.

''I have no way of knowing what it is you want from him.'' Here he paused to allow Kady to explain, but she said nothing. ''However, I do know that you must be tough with him. He's used to dealing with the Big Boys, not a little cook from Virginia. Pardon my saying that, but I think you'd rather know the truth of how he'll probably look at you.''

Nodding, Kady told him she was grateful for his advice. He continued. ''You must state your demands and make them plain. I don't think baking him a chocolate cake will work," he said with an avuncular smile.

But Kady didn't return his smile. Maybe all this was a joke to Mr. Fowler, but it was very serious to her.

When she'd left his offices that night, she had been driven away in a long, black, stretch limo, and she'd never before encountered anything so luxurious. After what she'd seen that day, she wasn't at all surprised when the limo let her out at the Plaza Hotel and a young man was waiting to take her up to her suite. Nor was she especially surprised when she looked in the closet and saw that it was full of designer clothes in just her size. Looking back on the day, she remembered a man who had come into the office and looked Kady up and down as though he were measuring her for a coffin. No coffin, just Versace and Chanel, she thought now. Shoes to match were on a rack on the floor, handbags on the shelves. In the drawers were piles of silk underwear.

As Kady headed for the shower, she told herself she shouldn't accept any of this. For all that she legally owned the money, she had no moral rights to it. But her strength of will fell in front of a red silk nightgown. Never in her life had she slept in silk.

"If only I had listened to my higher self," she said now as she guided the car up the old, washed-out mountain road toward Legend. If she'd kept her higher morals, she wouldn't have faced that scene in Tarik's apartment, a scene that still made her nearly sick whenever she thought of it.

When she thought of her attitude when she'd entered the apartment building where she was told Tarik Jordan was probably staying, it still made her cringe. She had been prepared for battle; she had prepared herself to fight like the "Big Boys," not like a cook from Virginia. The way he sees me, she thought with disgust.

Mr. Fowler had called ahead so she had no trouble

getting past security, but when the elevator stopped at the penthouse, she started to push the doorbell. But why should I? she thought. It was her apartment, wasn't it? Besides, she doubted very much if he was actually there. For all that Mr. Fowler said otherwise, Kady figured that a man like Tarik had lots of women. Many, many, many women.

From the moment Kady unlocked the door, she hated the apartment. Even she could see that it was decorated in what some designer had obviously thought was "class." There were fake Oriental vases and Steuben glass and lots of chrome and black leather.

Was this what Tarik Jordan liked? she wondered.

She made her way around the apartment to the kitchen. She might not know much about decorating but she did know about kitchens, and this one struck her as worthless, just some designer's idea of what a kitchen should look like. Utterly useless, she thought, looking at the black glass surfaces that would look horrible after cooking one meal.

The bedroom was like the rest of the apartment, done in burgundy and black, and she had no doubt that if she pulled back the expensive spread, she'd find black silk sheets under it.

She pushed open the bathroom door to see acres of black marble, brass fittings, and mirrors everywhere.

She didn't know how long she had stood there, looking about, before she realized that standing by the glass-enclosed shower was Tarik Jordan, having paused in toweling himself off and staring at her in disbelief.

"Oh," she said, startled, but she couldn't stop herself from looking at him, for the towel covered only the lower half of his body. He was lean and tightly muscled, not round like Cole or thin like Gregory. No, this man had a body that made her eyes hurt just to look at him.

But what made Kady's skin seem to grow tighter than normal was the unmistakable look of desire in the man's eyes. The way men had looked at her in Legend had been a mild version of how this man was looking at her now. No one had ever made her feel like this.

"Care to join me?" he asked in that rough-smooth voice of his.

With a gasp, Kady turned and fled. Back in the living room, she had to fight to get her senses back under control. *Control,* she reminded herself. *That's what you must have now. As Mr. Fowler said, you're dealing the Big Boys now, and you must remember that you are a millionaire. A multimillionaire.*

When he returned to the room, he was dressed casually but expensively, all in black, and he looked so much like the man in her dreams that she felt weak-kneed. As he walked across the room to the liquor cabinet and made himself a drink, she had to hold on to the back of a chair to steady herself.

"Since you do not seem to have come here for illicit purposes, what do you want?" he asked when he turned back to her.

Kady took a deep breath; it was difficult to think when she was near this man. "I need your help."

"Oh? Now, why would a woman as rich as you need *my* help? You can buy anything you want. Didn't Fowler explain that to you?" He looked her up and down with one eyebrow raised. "Nice suit. You didn't waste any time spending the money my family has earned, did you?"

A little wave of guilt went through Kady, but she stamped it down. Drawing her shoulders up, she looked him in the eyes. "I didn't come here to be insulted."

"Then you'd better leave. But then, what am I saying? This is your apartment. Everything is yours, isn't it?"

Kady was going to do what she could to prevent getting into an argument with him. "I have a proposition to make you. A business deal, so to speak." She looked at the glass in his hand. "Would you mind if I also had something to drink?"

"Help yourself. It's your liquor."

"You really are the rudest man I have ever met," she said as she poured herself a gin and tonic.

"Why don't you just say what you came to say and be done with it? Or have you come to throw me into the street?"

"Stop it!" She took a deep breath. "I will give everything back to you if only you will do what I ask you to do."

For a long moment he stared at her. "That's a pretty big condition isn't it?" He refilled his glass with straight single-malt scotch. "When you know that no matter how much you work in your life, it's all going to be turned over to a stranger from Ohio, it makes you curious about her."

When Kady blinked at him without comprehension, he smiled in that smug way he had. "I've known of you all my life. My father knew of you and his father before him. After all, ol' Ruth's will has been in effect for nearly a hundred years. All the Jordan men knew that the money, the companies, all of it was theirs until one Miss Elizabeth Kady Long was born in a small hospital in Ohio in 1966." He seemed to be fully aware of her shock. "Now, what is it that you want of me? More than you've already taken, that is?"

Kady was having difficulty thinking, as too much information was clogging her brain. All her life the very wealthy and powerful Jordan family had known of her. Turning, she looked up at him. Had he seen photos of her? Was that why she had dreamed of him? Was there some psychic link between the two them because of Ruth's will? Long before she met Cole or Ruth, Ruth's will had been in effect. She just hadn't known about it.

"Now, tell me what you and Fowler have planned." He set down his empty glass. "As fascinating as this conversation is, I think you should tell me what you want of me."

She swallowed hard. "I want you to go to Colorado with me and try to find a way to go back to eighteen seventy-three Legend and—"

She stopped because he had begun to laugh, and it was in the same tone that Ricky had when he laughed at Lucy, as though she were quite cute but totally daffy.

"Time travel?" he asked. "Is that what you're hinting at? Is that what you think happened and that's why Ruthless Ruth left all her money to you?"

Kady didn't bother to answer, but just looked at him in silence as he took a few steps across the room to stand very near her, still laughing at her.

"You want me to return to some ghost town and try to go back through time and . . . and what? Change history? Is that where this is leading? You know, I've had a lot of women try different things to get into my bank account, but this is a new one."

Lowering his voice, he gave her a look of seduction. "Tell me, Miss Long, have you been reading too much H. G. Wells?"

Kady didn't know when she'd ever disliked anyone as intensely as she disliked this man. With one swift gesture, she tossed her drink in his face.

Stepping back from her, he wiped the drink away with one hand. "First a knife, now a drink. What next? One of your soufflés?"

Standing, Kady advanced on him. "Let me make myself clear, Mr. Jordan, I never wanted to do this. I never asked for any of this. Had you contacted me three months ago, I would have gladly signed all your money back to you because it's not mine and I don't want it."

"Ha!"

She ignored him. "But my life has changed in the last months, changed drastically, and it's all because of *your* family. Not mine. *Yours!* I made a promise to a very nice woman that I would try to find her descendants, and I did that. Then she sent me a letter from her grave begging me to help her. And since she has gone to so much trouble to give me the power to help her, I'm going to try. Here's the deal, Mr. Midas, you help me and you get the money back, every penny of it. You don't help me and I keep it. All of it. Take it or leave it.''

He stood there staring down at her for a while, and for a flash of a second Kady was frightened of him. But not because she feared he'd purposely harm her. No, she was frightened that the intensity of being so near those hot, dark eyes of his might consume her.

Kady's heart seemed to leap to her throat, and for a second she thought he was going to kiss her. But the moment passed, and he stepped back, then reached into his pocket, withdrew a set of keys, and put them on a glass-topped table. "It's yours," he said. "All of it is yours. I wish you the best, Miss Long.''

With that, he walked out the door, leaving Kady alone in the expensive, cold apartment.

After he left, it was as though all the energy left the room and her body. Collapsing onto the sofa, she sat there for a good half hour in stunned silence.

And while she was sitting there, she started to come to her senses. Tarik Jordan had been right to be angry with her. Utterly and absolutely right. It *was* his family's money, and she had no right to so much as a penny of it. Furthermore, she had no right to attempt to blackmail him. Ruth had asked Kady to help, no one else.

She gathered her things and left the apartment.

When she returned to her hotel, she called Mr. Fowler and told him she wanted to give everything back to C. T. Jordan, and she wanted to do it *immediately!* The only thing she wanted to keep was the ownership of the town of Legend, Colorado, and twenty-five thousand in cash to pay for her expenses. She had no idea what she was going to do when she got to Legend, but she'd try her best to help in some way.

When she told the man she wanted the papers by eight the next morning, all he'd said was, "Yes." Smiling as she hung up the phone, Kady knew there were some things she was going to miss about being rich.

As promised, the papers arrived by messenger at eight. Minutes later, as she was reading them, there was a knock on the door of her hotel room, and when she opened it, she was faced with a young man who told her he was a process server. He then handed her a thick stack of papers. It didn't take much reading to see that C. T. Jordan was suing her for everything he thought she had "stolen" from him.

Right away, she called Mr. Fowler, and he told her not to worry about anything, that it would all be taken care of. Of course, he was a lawyer and lawsuits were an everyday thing to him. But not to Kady, who thought that Tarik Jordan had wasted no time in attacking her, had he? She asked Mr. Fowler how she could present the papers to the man in person.

It seemed that Jordan owned more than one apartment in New York, and until Kady signed the papers returning ownership of everything to him, she owned both buildings.

By the time she was dressed, Mr. Fowler had sent an escort that would help her get past building security.

Now, days later, traveling in the Range Rover up the mountain to Legend, Kady frowned in memory. She'd gone to his apartment, yet another penthouse, put her finger on the doorbell and left it there. Several minutes later she was rewarded with his throwing open the door, his face drawn into a dark scowl.

"What the hell is—" he began until he saw her; then his look changed to one of astonishment. "And what do you want from me today?" he asked, amused. "Space travel? Or shall we try to find out what happened to the little princes in the tower?"

He had a remarkable ability for making Kady feel like an idiot. Looking at him, she saw that he was wearing only a bathrobe; he looked as though he hadn't shaved in a week, and Kady was pleased to see that she had obviously awakened him. Glancing behind him, she saw that in the marble floored foyer was an eighteenth-century table, and even Kady, with her limited knowledge of antiques, could see that it was real. This apartment was quite different from the other one, and, incongruously, she wondered which apartment was the real him.

"I wanted to return these to you," she said, frowning up at him, refusing to succumb to the surge of attraction she felt for him. Obviously, he thought she was a crackpot.

"And what papers are they?" he asked, but did not take them. "Come, Miss Long, you couldn't be suing me, could you?"

"Suing *you?*" she gasped. "*You* are the one—" She cut herself off because he was smiling again and that smile had the odd power of making her want to fling herself onto him and kick him, both at the same time.

With her mouth made into a tight line, she glared up at him. "Do you *ever* give anyone a chance to explain?"

"Not usually," he said, eyes twinkling. "One of my tricks of business. I like pictures. Flashy video presentations."

Now he really *was* making fun of her, and the words "little cook from Ohio' echoed in her ears. And no matter what he said or how he laughed at her, the truth was in her hands. He'd brought a lawsuit against her without so much as *asking* her to return the money.

Since he was blocking the doorway so she couldn't enter the apartment, Kady dropped the whole stack of papers regarding his lawsuit on the floor, but he didn't so much as look down at them.

She then held up the few sheets that Mr. Fowler and his assistants had spent the night drawing up. "If you had had the courtesy to call me, to talk to me, you would have been told that yesterday I decided to give everything back to you. No strings, no blackmail, and, especially, without asking for any help from you."

She held the papers aloft, but still he didn't take them.

He just stood there silently staring at her. And Kady had to give it to him, because he had a look of complete innocence on his face. She could almost believe he didn't know what a lawsuit was. She could also almost believe that he found her nearly irresistibly attractive. But it was one thing for lonely silver miners to lust after her, but a man like C. T. Jordan, who could have any woman on earth, who could—

"C.T., honey," came a purring voice from behind them, and Kady looked around the man's broad shoulders to see a woman standing there. She was tall and thin; only constant starvation could make a person that thin. She was also quite, quite beautiful in that blonde, elegant way that reeked of money. She was wearing an ivory silk bathrobe that Kady was willing to bet cost more than she made in a month. "Is everything all right?" the woman said in an educated voice that sounded as though it had been trained in boarding school.

"Fine," Jordan said in a tone that was almost a snap. But he still didn't move, just stood there looking at Kady.

The woman glided over to Tarik, her robe falling away to reveal long thin legs, and she took his arm in hers, holding it tightly to her.

"Darling," she purred. "Is this the little cook you told me about?"

At that Kady gasped. It wasn't any of her business what Tarik Jordan talked about with his mistress, but maybe it was because she'd seen him so many, many times in her life that his "betrayal" of her hurt.

"I am glad I gave you some amusement," she said softly, handed him the papers, then turned on her heel to push the elevator button.

"Kady," she thought she heard behind her, but the woman's tones drowned out anything she thought he might have said.

"Perhaps we can hire her," the woman said loudly. "As an under-chef to Jean-Pierre. I'm sure he'd like some help in the . . . kitchen." She said the last word as though it were a euphemism for "garbage scow." Whatever else was said, Kady didn't hear because the elevator arrived and she got into it, her back still to Tarik and his skinny lover.

Once in the elevator, once she was out of Tarik's mesmerizing presence, Kady worked to control her anger. Now what did she do? she wondered. How in the world was she going to be able to do what Ruth asked of her and to help Legend? Was she going to have to try to find a way to go back into time? If she didn't know how she did it in the first place, how could she repeat it and how was she going to do all of this *alone*?

When she returned to her hotel room, there was a package from Mr. Fowler waiting for her. She'd told him of her plan to go to Legend, so he'd sent her a first-class plane ticket, a prepaid hotel reservation, and a letter saying there would be a car and some camping gear waiting for her upon her arrival. He also wished her luck in whatever it was she wanted to accomplish.

The next day Kady had flown to Denver, where a sedan and driver were waiting to take her to her hotel. The hotel clerk had given her the keys to a brand-new Range Rover that was filled with beautiful state-of-the-art camping gear for her stay in the ghost town of Legend.

"I didn't put in any food though," Mr. Fowler wrote, and she could almost hear him laughing. "I somehow thought you might like to buy that for yourself. And I just want to say, Miss Long, that it has done my soul good to meet someone like you. You have renewed my faith in humanity."

At that Kady grimaced. She wished *her* faith in humanity had been renewed.

After a day in Denver, Kady had risen early and started the long trek up into the Rocky Mountains in search of what was left of Legend, Colorado. According to the brochures she could find and a book on ghost towns, it was derelict, falling down, and generally dangerous to even try to explore. Also, it was privately owned and trespassing was strictly forbidden, as all the signs around the place told any potential explorers. But since Kady now owned the town, she wasn't trespassing.

The road up the mountain was horrible, with ruts over a foot deep running down the middle, so Kady had to try to drive on the side, keeping the wheels on the ridges. It was difficult for her to do, especially since her experience with driving had been on city streets. And to think that she used to complain about potholes!

Now, according to her map, she was less than three miles from Legend, but she could see nothing, and the road, if possible, seemed to be getting worse. So far, she'd seen three signs warning trespassers to keep out, that this was private property, but she hadn't paid much attention to the warnings. After all, she now owned the place, didn't she?

And that thought made Kady smile in derision. Mr. Fowler had said, "Kady, you are giving up your rights to millions, and all you ask for is the deed to a worthless ghost town? You aren't thinking of trying to mine the silver, are you?"

Kady had smiled and shook her head. No, she wasn't going to try anything that sensible.

"Good," the attorney continued, "because that was tried about thirty years ago. There was a belief that Ruthless Ruth had sealed up mines that were producing millions, so C.T.'s father reopened them. Turned out that the truth was that the mines were nearly empty of silver. I've often wondered if maybe Ruth's husband and son knew that and that's why they wouldn't sell the land to homesteaders. They didn't want to cheat the people, because what would they do with the land if the silver was gone?"

"No," Kady had said softly, "I'm not after the silver," and she thought of all the hatred that had been caused over mines that were on the brink of being empty. If Ruth had allowed the men to continue instead of blasting the mine entrances shut, then the people of Legend wouldn't have hated her and maybe her youngest son . . .

Kady didn't want to think anymore on what could have been but wasn't. Instead, she tried to concentrate now on getting the car up the mountain and into Legend. Truthfully, she didn't want to think about what she was going to try to do once she got there.

Maybe it was because she was thinking so hard about the last few weeks and trying to keep her mind off Tarik Jordan's perfidy that she didn't see the great, deep, washed-out hole in front of her. In fact, it was almost as though it had been dug in an attempt to keep people out. One minute Kady was driving, anticipating arriving in Legend, and the next she was stuck.

"Damn, damn, damn," she said, pounding her fists against the steering wheel. She was about twelve miles past nowhere, and she was stuck!

For a moment she resisted an urge to put her head on the wheel and cry; then, reluctantly, she opened the door and got out. Maybe if she looked at the wheels, she could figure out what to do to get unstuck.

"Only if it involves a recipe for a soufflé," she muttered; then the thought of a soufflé reminded her of C. T. Jordan and his hateful remark, so when she got out, she kicked a rock. Which of course hurt her toe, which made her hop around; then in frustration, she kicked the tires of the car and hurt her foot even more.

Now what do I do? she thought, but didn't have time to think about it because as she leaned over to check if her toe was broken, a shot rang out over her head. On instinct, she straightened and looked about her, only to be shot at a second time.

For a moment she was sure that she'd already gone through the time warp and any minute she was going to see Cole, and she was going to run into his arms and he'd hold her and—but if she were back in time, she wouldn't be staring at an automobile.

The third shot came so close to her that it cut the sleeve of her heavy wool cardigan, and that's when she realized that someone was shooting directly at *her*. Kady leaped toward the back of the car, heading for the woods on the opposite side, but then a shot came from that direction, too, and fear made her freeze. Paralyzed, she stood where she was in the middle of the road, blinking and not knowing where to run, since she was being shot at from both directions.

It was at that moment that she heard horses' hooves coming toward her, and still in shock, Kady looked up to see a man on a white horse thundering toward her. He had on something black, a scarf over the bottom of his face, and he was as familiar to her as her own hand.

More shots rang out, but this time they were aimed at the man on the horse, but, ignoring them, he kept coming toward her, and when he got to Kady, he bent down, held out his hand and she took it. Due to the many times she'd ridden with Cole, she knew how to put her foot in the stirrup he had vacated and swing herself up behind him.

When she was on the horse, she put her arms around his waist and held on with all her might as he kicked the horse forward and went galloping down the mountain. She thought that a couple of times he jumped over some things like logs and deep ruts, but she buried her face into the back of him and didn't look.

After a while he slowed the horse and turned it, but instead of going down the mountain, they started going up again. Kady opened her eyes long enough to see that they had left the road and were on a mountain trail, but she closed them again and put her head against the man's back. Of course she knew who he was, and she did remember that she didn't like him at all, but right now it felt good to be taken care of, to be rescued, to be . . . She didn't want to think anymore, but just closed her eyes and held on.

Her peace didn't last long, for he soon halted the horse and dismounted. Then, with a scowling face, he held his arms up for her, and once she was on the ground, he turned on her.

"I have never seen a woman who could cause more trouble than you!" he began. "Do you have any sense at all? If I hadn't come along when I did, do you realize that you'd be dead by now? Dead! Ol' Hannibal would have shot you, and no one would have found the body. Who would have looked for you? Fowler? That boyfriend of yours who wants to open hamburger joints in your name? Or did you think—"

Why did he *always* have to make her feel incompetent? "Why did *you* come here? Were you angry that I took *any* of what Ruth left me? You wanted it all?"

Moving closer, he bent, towering over her. "I came to save your neck. I knew this was going to happen. Couldn't you see the No Trespassing signs? Or can you only read cookbooks?"

If he made one more derogatory remark about her cooking, she was going to throw a rock at his head. Or maybe she'd take his suggestion and throw a soufflé. Still in its thick porcelain pot. "Since I own the place, what do the signs matter to me? And who is Hannibal?"

Tarik gave her a little smile that made her think he could read her mind. "He happens to be the man who has a ninety-nine year lease on the place, that's who he is. Whether you own the town or not, you have no right to enter it, at least not for eighty-two more years, that is." His smile increased until a dimple appeared in his cheek. "But then, I forgot. You pop around time like a jackrabbit going from one hole to another. So what's eighty-some years to someone like you?"

With a tightened mouth and fists clenched at her side, Kady turned and started walking down the mountain.

He caught her after two steps. "Mind telling me where you're planning to go?"

"As far away from you as I can get. You are the most unpleasant, unreasonable, horrible man I have ever met, and I don't even want to be in the same state with you, much less on the same mountain."

With his hand still on her arm, she saw that he was quite startled at her words. No doubt, between his looks and his money, he'd never before had a woman say an unkind word to him. She wondered if any of his women called him anything except *Mr.* Jordan.

When he touched her, Kady tried to pull her arm away, but he wouldn't release her.

"You can't leave," he said, holding her tightly.

"You're hurting me," she said, and he dropped her arm, but when she started walking again, he put himself in front of her.

"Are you planning to hold me prisoner?"

"If I must. You can't wander about these mountains. I doubt if you know east from west."

"I managed to get myself up here, and I can get myself down."

"You," he said ominously, "got a Range Rover stuck. You can't even drive, much less walk, so I cannot allow you to—"

It was the word "allow" that did it. "I am a free citizen, and you have no right to keep me here," she shouted at him, then took a deep breath. "I have work to do, and I'm going to do it. And so help me, if you stand in my way, I'll fight you with every—"

"Fine," he said, stepping aside. "Go. Please don't let me stand in your way. Just tell me one thing."

"What?!" she snapped.

"Where's your will so I can make sure your heirs get whatever you leave behind."

The fact that he was obviously laughing at her made her even more determined to do what she had to do *alone*.

With her nose in the air, she did her best to sweep past him as she started down the path toward the road.

An hour later, she at last reached her car. She was tired, sweaty, and now that the sun was beginning to set, she was cold and hungry. When she looked at her brand-new, shiny red vehicle and saw that the tires had been taken and it was completely empty of all her new camping equipment, as well as the several bags of food she'd bought, she sat down at the side of the road and put her head in her hands.

"Ready to give up and return to civilization?" came a deep voice from over her shoulder, and she didn't have to look up to see who it was.

"I can't go back," she said tiredly, and she could hear the tears in her voice. But she'd be damned if she was going to let *him* see her cry! He'd probably laugh even harder at her tears.

But he didn't laugh. Instead, he sat down beside her, close but not touching, and for a moment he was silent.

"Did you love him that much?" he asked softly.

Kady's first impulse was to say, "Who?" but she suppressed it. For some reason she remembered the gorgeous blonde in his apartment. "Yes, I loved him very, very much." Truthfully, she wasn't sure if he meant Cole or Gregory. But did it matter?

"Look, I've set up a camp a few miles back down the mountain. Why don't we go there and see if we can work out something together?"

Turning, Kady looked up at him in the growing darkness. He was asking her to spend the night alone with him? Share a sleeping bag maybe?

"You don't have to look at me like that. Despite the bad opinion you have of me, I'm not a rapist. Besides, Leonie'd have my hide if I touched another woman."

"The blonde?" Kady asked. Of course, she had nothing against the woman except for a few unkind remarks she'd made about Kady's life work. But if that shapeless, bag of bones was what he liked, who was she to object?

"Yes, the blonde," he said with a little smile that made her feel as though he could see right through her.

When Kady didn't answer, his face changed. "Look, I'm not after your body, no matter how enticing it is. I have a business deal to work out with you."

"Such as?" Kady said, eyes narrowed in distrust.

"Look, it's growing dark and Uncle Hannibal's eyesight isn't great at best, so maybe he wouldn't recognize me and might start shooting again. So could we continue this at my camp?"

Kady knew she didn't really have any other choice. She couldn't very well climb down a mountain in the dark, and besides, she was very tired and very hungry. In spite of her discomfort, she hesitated. "What business?"

Tarik glanced over his shoulder into the darkening woods as though he expected someone to jump out at any moment. "Ol' Ruthless Ruth left a codicil to her will."

"Stop calling her that!" Kady said sharply. "She was a very nice person, and I want to help her."

"Oh, yes, I keep forgetting that you met her, that you're a hundred years old and—"

"What do you have to eat?" She was not going to be lectured by him again.

"Trout. I'll cook it myself."

Like Cole, was her inadvertent thought.

"Unless you would like to cook it. My reports are that you're a fair cook." He was laughing at her again!

"No, not me," she said, standing and starting to walk away. "I can only make soufflés, not real food like fried fish. And my soufflés are so heavy that if I threw one it would probably break bones." When she stopped walking and turned back toward him, his eyes were twinkling more than the stars above them.

His horse was not far away, and this time Kady mounted behind him with reluctance, and now that no one was shooting at her, she leaned away instead of clutching him to her. A short time later they were at his camp, which was complete with a tent, a Jeep, and a horse trailer. Before a fire that was nearly out was a table and chairs.

"You travel light, I see," she said with all the derision she could muster as she dismounted. "I almost expect to see a butler and a couple of maids."

"Even Jordans have to rough it sometimes."

Kady had to bite her tongue to keep from saying anything else, as he seemed to be amused by anything she said. Part of her said that she should be thanking him for saving her life, for coming to her rescue, but somehow the words would not cross her lips. Maybe it had to do with having seen this man so many times during her life. As she sat down on one of the chairs and watched him prepare the fish, she thought how even the movement of his hands was familiar to her.

He poured her a glass of wine—an excellent vintage, of course—and as she began to get warm as the wine seeped into her system, she was very aware of the growing darkness, and even more aware of his dark good looks.

"So what did the codicil say?" she asked, and even to her, her voice sounded nervous.

He dished up the trout, two to each of them, and some roast potatoes flecked with bits of charred wood, flavored with smoke, and took a seat across from her. "It didn't make any sense really. It said that if Cole Jordan, born in 1864, died when he was nine years old, then no Jordan could accept the return of the money from you for three years after nineteen ninety-six."

As he looked up at Kady, the firelight playing on his features, he seemed to be waiting for her to say something, but she concentrated on eating.

"I've done a bit of research into my family history, and there was a Cole Jordan, born in eighteen sixty-four, who did indeed die when he was nine years old."

Kady kept her head down. What had she hoped for? That he'd come to save her because he'd fallen madly in love with her? Couldn't stay away from her? That he'd say he'd been dreaming about her all his life?

"What do you know about this?" he asked impatiently when she remained silent.

"I'm sure that my stories wouldn't interest a business-man like you. What was it you said, that I pop through time like a rabbit in and out of holes, so how could an idiot like me say anything that would interest someone like you?"

"You're going to make me work for this, aren't you?"

Kady took another sip of wine and smiled at him. "Is there any reason I should be nice to you? Did it cost you a lot to bring a lawsuit against me? Did you have it all prepared for months before I showed up?"

He didn't get angry at her reply, but instead gave her a smile that she was sure had melted many hearts. "Every-thing was done before I met you. But if I'd known what a lovely, kind person you are, then——"

"If you have tracked me since birth, then you must have learned a lot about me, so could you please stop treating me as though I'm stupid? What do you want me to do to help you get your precious money back?"

As he leaned back in his chair, his smile disappeared. "All right, business it is. I haven't any idea what ol' Ruth was talking about in her letter, and furthermore, I couldn't care less. What happened a hundred years ago is of no interest to me."

"I know. You just want the money."

At that he raised an eyebrow at her. "Yes, of course, I've sold my soul to the devil and care only for money. You, however, are so noble that you can afford to be given millions and give it away. I am curious, though, on one point: What happens to the many thousands of people who are paid by Jordan money if there is no one to run the company for the coming three years? Do the banks suspend the employees' mortgages? Do their children stop eating for three years? Do——?"

"All right, you've made your point. You're a saint, and you want to do nothing but help other people."

"It doesn't matter what my personal interests are, does it? It just seems that the two of us both want the same thing, so I thought perhaps we could work together on this."

"I don't need any help," Kady said, her jaw set. Looking at him now in the moonlight, she thought that the less time she spent with him the better. He wasn't a sweet man like Cole, or even an ordinary man like Gregory. This man was . . . was different.

He refilled her wineglass. "I do wish you'd stop looking at me like that. Contrary to what you seem to think of me, I am not a monster."

Kady didn't pick up the glass. "What do you want of me?"

"You once asked me to help you, and now I'm saying that I'm willing to do so. Why don't you start by telling me everything that happened between you and my, *ah*, great-great-great-grandmother?"

Standing, Kady put her hands on the table and leaned toward him. "I'm not going to tell you anything," she said sweetly, with a little smile. "I don't like you, and I don't trust you, and I don't want to spend another minute in your company." With that, she started to walk away into the darkness, but she had no idea which was the way back to Denver.

As silent as the wind, he moved to stand in front of her. "Look, Miss Long . . ." His voice softened. "Miss Long, you and I got off on the wrong foot. I apologize, but you must know that since I was a boy your name has been something to be hated."

Kady gasped at that.

"Many years ago my father told me in private about the will and about you. I grew up hearing about you and . . ." He reached out his hand to her. "Couldn't we start over? Couldn't we help each other? You seem to have something you feel you must do in Legend, but you'll never be allowed into the place without my help. My uncle knows me, and if you go with me, he won't shoot you.''

Kady knew he was right, and it seemed only fair that a Jordan should help her with the impossible task Ruth had set for her. Cocking her head to one side, she said, ''You wouldn't happen to know where there are some petroglyphs, would you?''

''Out past the cemetery? Not far from the Hanging Tree? Those petroglyphs?''

Kady couldn't prevent a smile. ''Yes. Those petrogylphs.''

When he smiled back at her, Kady felt herself weakening, and she could tell by the way he smiled at her that he knew she was weakening.

''I got into some trouble when I was fifteen, and my father sent me to Uncle Hannibal in an attempt to . . . to jerk a knot into my tail, is, I believe, the way he put it.''

''Did it work?''

''Not in the least,'' he said, grinning; then he offered her his arm. ''I have some fresh peaches for dessert. Interested?''

''Yes,'' she said and allowed him to escort her back to the fire.

But it was an hour later, as she was feeling drowsy and as she watched him stirring the embers of the fire that she vowed that she was not, not, *not* going to allow herself to get close to him. His every movement was graceful, and she could well believe that he was a master at all forms of martial arts.

''Why did you give the money back?'' he asked, taking her out of her own thoughts.

''Why did you bring a lawsuit against me?'' she countered.

''It never entered my head that you'd peacefully give the money back,'' he said, smiling at her.

Kady didn't want to think how that smile was making

her feel so very warm. Had he brought two sleeping bags or one? "If your Leonie were in my situation, would she have given the money back?" The words came out with more force than she had meant them to.

But he didn't seem the least perturbed. "Leonie would have spent all of it in four days."

Kady had expected protestations of the perfections of the woman he probably loved. "On what?" she asked, wide-eyed. How did one spend so much so quickly?

"Jewels, a yacht, a jet or two, houses around the world," he said as he squatted by the fire and revived it.

"It's a good thing you stayed rich then, isn't it? Maybe she wouldn't be so anxious to marry you if you were poor." She knew she was fishing to find out if he was engaged. And she wanted to kick herself for wanting to know.

"If that's supposed to shock me or make me reconsider marriage to Leonie, it isn't working. She and I suit each other. I work all the time, and I'm gone a great deal, so I can't have a wife who is constantly nagging me because I'm never home."

"So why bother to marry at all?"

"Children. I'd like to have a few."

"So you think Leonie will be a good mother?"

"I think she will look good on my arm, and the very loving couple who raised me will raise my children."

"Ah, I see, and look how well you turned out."

Her barb made him chuckle. "So let me guess, you're holding out for a man who loves you to death and gives you three perfect kids. And you also want to have a career, not a job, but a real career, one that fulfills you."

She refused to answer him, but her silence said it all.

"So who do you think is the dreamer, you or me? I try for what I can get; you try for the dream that everyone wants but no one gets."

Perhaps his words should have bothered her, but they didn't. "Without hope you die," she said, smiling at him, and he smiled back.

"Like you have hope that you're going to be able to make a dead man live?"

"Ruth seems to think that I can, and I'm certainly going to try."

Standing, he stretched, looking like a dark animal in the firelight. Taking a burning twig, he lit a lantern and set it near her. "Want to tell me exactly what it is you plan to do?"

If Kady had been honest, she would have told him that she had no idea, that she had no plan. But she doubted that a businessman would understand such a strategy. It was like not knowing what you are going to cook until you see what food is fresh in the market that day. "I think I'll keep my plans to myself for a while," she said, trying to sound mysterious, but from the way he smiled, she had an idea he knew what was in her head—or, more precisely, what was not in her head.

Standing, she looked at the tent in apprehension, and another laugh made her turn back to him. "Don't look so frightened. You can keep your virginity for another night."

"I'm not—" she began, then halted because she could see that he was teasing her. "What in the world did you do for amusement before you met me?" she demanded.

"Worked eighteen hours a day. You can have the tent, I'll sleep in the Jeep."

"Sure you wouldn't rather bunk with your horse?"

"Is that what Cole would have done?" he asked, suddenly serious.

"What do you know of him?"

"If you can have secrets, so can I. Good night, Miss Long," he said, then slipped into the darkness, where she couldn't see him.

Picking up the lantern, Kady went inside the tent to the sleeping bag. At first she thought she might slide between the layers of down fully dressed, but she knew that was ridiculous. He'd reassured her that he wasn't intent on harming her, and whatever else she thought of him, she knew that she was safe with him. So safe that if she was in danger, no matter where she was, he would appear and protect her. Hadn't he appeared in her dreams throughout her life? And hadn't he shown up in Colorado when she'd thought he was thousands of miles away?

As she drifted asleep, she thought she heard the words, "Good night, Kady," but she wasn't sure. Whether it was the wind or not, she went to sleep smiling.

Chapter 24

"WHAT? YOU WANT ME TO WHAT?" KADY ASKED, A MUG OF hot coffee in her hands as she stared up at Tarik Jordan. It was early morning, and they were alone in the beautiful wilderness.

"Play hooky," he said, smiling. "Ditch school. Take the day off."

"I couldn't do that," Kady said, aghast. "You have no idea what's at stake here. People are depending on me. Their whole lives are waiting for me, and I have to—"

"They've waited over a hundred years, so what does one more day matter?" He paused. "Miss Long, don't you ever have *fun?*"

At the very thought of such a thing, it seemed that a thousand scenes went through Kady's head at once: coming home from school to help Jane's mother with the housework, cooking for people all weekend, then school during the day and more courses during the night, while catering parties to help pay her way through school. Then there was Onions and Gregory. His idea of "fun" was to have Kady cook dinner for twenty-five people who he said might someday help further his future political career.

Then there was Legend, and sometimes what she remembered most from those days was feeling frantic that she'd never get back home. After that was the worry about a job, and now—

She stopped thinking when she heard Tarik laugh, and squinting, she looked up at him.

"Going over your life in your head?" he asked, and when Kady's eyes widened at his words, he smiled. "Miss Long, if it seems that I can read your mind, it's because I think I can. My father believed that childhood was a preparation for the stress of being an adult, and because I was someday going to be in charge of millions, he made sure that I spent my life in school. And after that I had all the responsibility of the Jordan Company dropped onto my lap. I think my life has been about as much fun as yours has. What do you say we take the day off?"

"What are you trying to get from me?" she asked suspiciously.

"All your worldly goods," he said with a smile, and Kady had to laugh.

"You could hold everything I own in one hand," she said. "I'm thirty years old and I own nothing, have nothing. At the moment I don't even have a job."

He made a sound of disbelief. "Are you going to try to make me believe that a chef of your reputation doesn't have hundreds of offers of employment?"

"A few," Kady said modestly, looking down at her coffee cup. He had hand-ground the beans and hadn't allowed her to touch a thing as he'd made buckwheat pancakes.

"Come on," he said, holding out his hand to her. "Let's both take the day off."

As Kady looked up at him, a chill went down her spine, as it was the gesture she had seen a thousand times in her dreams. Right now shade darkened the lower half of his face, but a shaft of sunlight came through the leaves and highlighted his eyes.

"Come, *habibbi*," he whispered, and she knew it was an

endearment from another language. *"This* time you can reach me."

Kady's heart and her common sense warred with each other, but she remembered all the times in her dreams that she had tried to take his hand and had been unable to reach it. Now she extended her hand, tentatively at first; then as she neared his fingertips, she smiled up at him and slipped her hand into his.

Tarik gave a great laugh, then on impulse picked Kady up and twirled her about, and for a moment they both laughed together, Kady's hair swirling about them as he turned her round and round.

It was Kady who came to her senses first and began to push away from him. "Mr. Jordan," she said, "I think we should—"

Still smiling, he set her down, but he kept his hands on her shoulders. "I think that for today we can dispense with thinking," he said, smiling warmly at her.

Kady wanted to retain her animosity toward this man, but he was making it difficult. *Remember that he is a cold fish,* she told herself. *Remember that he is about to marry someone else. Remember that he is rich and famous and you are a means for him to get his money back, and that's all.*

"I think I should go to Legend," she said. "I have to do things there, and I have business to attend to. And, besides, I do need a job and potential employers won't wait forever." She was backing away from him.

"Damn the employers! I'll buy you a restaurant, and you can—"

"Is that what you think I'm after? That I want you to buy something for me? Do you—"

"I want to spend the day with a pretty girl," he said softly. "I want a day away from business and family tragedies and all the other worries. I'd like to show you a place I found when I was a kid. I've never shown it to another living soul, but I'd like to show it to you."

"Why?" she asked suspiciously.

"Because I've never met anyone like you, that's why," he said with a look of exasperation. "And maybe I'd like to give you a better impression of me. I'm not what or who you seem to think I am, and I'd like you to know that before we . . . before we part." Again he held out his hand to her. "Will you go with me?"

Kady started to protest, started to say no, but then she thought, What the heck? Why not? Could anything stranger or worse happen to her than what already had? "Okay," she said with a grin, then took his hand in hers. "But on one condition."

"Which is?"

"We don't talk of money and you don't try to make me tell you what happened in Legend. I would like a day off from the past."

"Done! We'll just talk about ourselves."

"Great. And later I'll sell the story of the rich, elusive C. T. Jordan to the tabloids and make enough to open my restaurant."

He didn't hesitate as he lifted her hand and kissed the back of it. "Any woman who would return a fortune as you did isn't going to do something so low-down rotten and slimy as that."

Maybe it was his confidence in her or maybe it was his big hand holding hers as she looked up at him, but she was beginning to feel the heaviness of the last weeks lift from her heart. Stressful did not begin to describe the last weeks of her life. "Are you saying that I'm boring? That I'm too good to do something treacherous?"

"No, of course not. What was it that Alice Toklas said about the eggs?"

Kady laughed. "That she'd scramble the man's eggs rather than make him an omelet because it took less butter and he'd know the insult. Yes, I might do that."

"Ah, but have you?"

He dropped her hand as he efficiently and quickly began

to remove items from the campsite while Kady stood there and watched. He certainly was self-sufficient, she thought.

"Have you?" he asked again.

"Have I what?"

He was bent over, putting out the fire as he turned to look at her. "Have you done anything truly rotten to another human being?"

"I screamed at Mrs. Norman," she said with guilt in her voice. "She's—"

"Gregory's interfering mother. From what I was told about her, it's a wonder you didn't take a meat cleaver to her."

"You know, it's odd, but she never bothered me until after I met Cole. Something seemed to happen inside me after I met him."

He was stuffing things into an aluminum-framed backpack. "Maybe you began to get an idea of how much you were worth."

"I thought we weren't going to talk about money."

As he took water bottles from inside the Jeep, he grinned. "I'm not talking about money. Doesn't the Bible say that a virtuous woman is worth her weight in pearls? Or something like that."

"I'm *not* virtuous," Kady said with a grimace. "In my lifetime three men have told me they love me, Cole, Gregory, and a boy at college, and I went to bed with two of them. I seem to go to bed with most of the men who tell me they love me."

At that he leaned toward her until his nose was nearly touching hers. "In that case, Kady, I love you, love you, love you."

"Get out of here!" she said, laughing as she pushed at his chest.

He stepped away, but he still looked at her with such teasing eyes that she blushed. "If you don't stop it, I won't go with you," she said, but even she could hear the lie in her voice. It would be wonderful to have a day off from worry and anxiety. To have a day without ghosts directing her life.

"Are you sure you don't want to try to go to Legend alone?" he asked, a mock look of horror on his dark, handsome face. "You could try to get past Uncle Hannibal by yourself." At that he gave such an exaggerated shiver of fear that she smiled. "You haven't seen him. Frightening man. When I was a kid, I thought he was Blackbeard."

"He's a thief!" Kady said. "He destroyed the lovely Range Rover Mr. Fowler bought for me."

"Ahem," Tarik said as he hoisted the pack onto his back and hooked the straps over his chest.

"Oh. I guess you bought it for me. Was it insured?"

"No money talk, remember? You ready to go? How are your feet? This is a bit of a walk."

"My feet are fine," she said, looking down at the trainers she wore. She spent most of every day on her feet and got restless if she had to sit down too long.

"Then, come, *habibbi,* and follow me."

"What does that mean?" she asked as she followed him through the brush. Within minutes they reached a narrow trail leading upward. "What language is it?"

"Arabic, the language of Ruth's lover. You don't know why she jumped into bed with him, do you? Other than lust, that is? Didn't she spend even a minute grieving over her dead husband?"

"It wasn't like that at all!" Kady said vehemently. "It was because Ruth was in such pain and grieving so much that she turned to Gamal, and—" She halted. "Oh, very clever. But it's not going to work. You said this was a day off, and that's what it's going to be. *No more Jordans!"*

"Too late," he said, looking at her over his shoulder and around the big pack, and Kady giggled because for a moment she'd completely forgotten that *he* was a Jordan.

She was still laughing as he turned back toward the trail, and they started the long, slow climb upward. And Kady soon found that walking back and forth between counters in a restaurant kitchen was not the same as climbing a mountain at about nine thousand feet altitude. Her ankles often twisted to the side and she could feel the beginning of a blister on her little toe.

But she didn't complain. As a child, she'd learned not to complain about anything, to accept her lot and get on with life as best she could. So when Tarik turned and asked how she was doing, Kady always replied that she was doing great.

And except for her feet, she was. The air was cool and crisp, and she found that she actually could forget about the past and her uncertain future. For this one day she wanted to think about nothing but the sunlight and the herbs she was gathering and putting into her small backpack.

The hardest part of walking behind Tarik was trying not to think about *him*. It was difficult not to look at him and smile when he'd turn and say something to her. He seemed to know this forest as well as he knew how to handle those swords of his.

"When did you start being interested in knives?" she asked, then could have kicked herself because this was an oblique reference to Cole.

With a knowing look, he glanced back at her. "Did I inherit my hobby from someone?"

"Do magnets stick to you?"

"Sometimes," he said, laughing. "You know, Miss Long, I've spent my life wondering what you were like."

"And I never knew you or your family existed," she said with exaggerated nonchalance. She'd give up her skillets before she told him about her dreams of him. Suddenly she thought of what Jane's reaction would be if she were to call and say that she'd found her veiled man. Jane would no doubt say that Kady should marry him instantly because under Jane's bossy little calculator of a heart she was a true romantic.

"I certainly knew about you. My father had a private detective on retainer, and twice a year he'd give my father a report, complete with photographs of you. By accident I found the combination to my father's home safe, and I used to open it and read the reports."

Kady was sure she should have been horrified at this, but instead she was fascinated. "What could the reports say about me? I have led a very boring, uninteresting life."

He took so long to answer that Kady thought he wasn't going to, but then he halted under a big shade tree and removed a water bottle from a hook on the side of his pack while Kady sat down on a rock and looked up at him. He handed her the bottle first, and it seemed perfectly natural when he drank after her.

"Your life was never uninteresting to me," he said softly, looking out over the trees, as though he couldn't bear to look at her. "I have no doubt Fowler told you all he could about me. He's not liked me since I took away most of my business from him."

"No, he didn't tell me much," Kady said. Tree branches hung down low over them and the forest was very quiet.

"I wasn't allowed much in the way of companionship when I was a child, and there was always the threat of kidnaping, so I had to make do with what I could find in the form of companionship." After a pause, he looked down at her. "It made me feel better about my lot in life that I knew of someone else on this planet who had to work for a living."

Smiling, Kady tried to lighten the mood, for she could see little white lines of bitterness along the side of his mouth. "I'd have thought that a rich kid like you would have been given every toy and plaything imaginable. If you wanted playmates, couldn't your father have bought you some?"

Tarik snorted in derision. "My father felt he had to get his money's worth for every penny he spent. He bought me a horse, then expected me to fill the walls with prizes for riding. Martial arts was another way for him to take credit for what I achieved."

"And did you? Did you excel in everything you tried?"

For a moment Tarik's dark eyes were lost in memory; then as he looked at her, his smile returned. "Damn right I did! Didn't you? If you were going to have to cook for your mother and the family you stayed with, weren't you going to become the best damn cook in the world?"

"Yes," Kady said, her eyes wide in wonder. "I never thought of it that way. I just thought that I learned to cook out of necessity. And need. People need food."

"And people need money, too. They need jobs, so when my father created them, I knew he was doing a good thing. But sometimes I wished he could have allowed me to fail at something and still loved me."

Blinking, Kady looked up at him. What he was saying was similar to what Jane had said about her family taking advantage of Kady and how Jane felt she owed Kady.

"I made you feel less alone?" she asked softly.

"Yes," he answered, grinning at her, his dark introspection seeming to have disappeared. "I read all those reports and studied all the pictures of you until I felt that I knew you." He clipped the bottle back onto his belt. "So, Miss Long, if I sometimes am too familiar with you, please forgive me. It feels as though I've known you most of my life."

"Since you were nine years old," she whispered.

"Yes," he said brightly as he held out his hand to help her stand. "But I don't remember telling you that."

"You must have, or how else would I have known it?"

"Of course," he said, but he was looking deep into her eyes, and Kady knew that he didn't believe her.

"Don't you think you should call me Kady?" she said, then hesitated. "And . . . What should I call you?"

"Mr. Jordan, just like everyone else does," he said with sparkling eyes.

"You rat!" she said as she made a lunge to smack him,

but he sidestepped her, and when she stumbled, he caught her in his arms.

"Mmmmm, Kady," he said as he pulled her close and buried his face in her hair. "What a shock you've been to me."

Kady did her best to retain her senses, as it would have been easy to melt against him, so she pushed him away. "If you know me so well, how could I be a shock?"

"Lust is always a shock."

"Oh," she said, eyebrows raised to her hairline.

"You ready to go? It looks like it might rain, and I think we ought to get under shelter before it does."

All Kady could do was nod and pick up her own pack. Lust, she thought. Didn't life have some interesting little twists and turns?

They walked for what seemed to be hours, and with each passing moment Kady seemed to relax further. But still, she kept asking herself, Who was the real Tarik Jordan? Was he the man she'd met in New York or the man who had rescued her from bullets and was now making her laugh?

In the afternoon they paused to eat cheese and bread, and Kady asked him why he'd refused to see her when she went to his office. He took a while before he answered.

"I anticipated a long fight ahead of me to regain control of what my family had created. If I could refrain from seeing you until the day after the will expired, I wouldn't have to go through any lawsuits."

"Then why didn't you just hide out for those last weeks? Or even on that last day? You made me wait outside your office for hours, so why didn't you just disappear as soon as you heard I was there?"

"Curiosity, I guess. I wanted to see what you were like in the flesh, so to speak."

"You could have met me the day *after,"* she said in exasperation, annoyed that he was purposely missing the point.

At that he laughed and put the remaining food back into

his big pack. "I could have, but I couldn't make myself leave. Maybe I wanted to see if you'd persist. I suspected you didn't know about the will, but I also thought there was something else that was making you demand to see me. Claire said you were quite stubborn."

"If Claire is that bulldog of a receptionist, could I retain interest in your company long enough to have the power to fire her? She really was quite hateful. You'd think *she* was the owner of the company, that she——"

Kady stopped because of the look he was giving her. "Oh," she said, "she has designs on you. On becoming Mrs. Boss."

"You do have a way of stating things. Ready?"

Standing, Kady picked up her own small pack. "So how many of the women who work for you think there's a chance of marrying you?"

"One or two. Jealous?"

"About as much as you are of the men in *my* life."

"Then it is something that must plague you daily," he said so softly Kady almost didn't hear him, but she did hear, and even though she told herself she shouldn't believe him, his words made her feel good.

The rain started at about four o'clock, and Tarik paused under a tree to pull long yellow ponchos from out of his pack, first draping Kady from head to foot, then pulling the hood over her head and tying it tightly under her chin. "Okay?" he asked as he put his nose to hers, and she nodded.

By the time he got his own poncho on, he was soaked, but he didn't seem to notice as he started up the mountain again, and it was an hour later that he halted in front of a vine-covered rock. Kady stood to one side, rain coming down hard on her, as he pulled the vines away and exposed what looked to be a small cave. Holding the vines to one side, he motioned for her to enter.

The cave was a small place, and it was too dark to see much of anything, but within minutes Tarik had a fire going, as there seemed to have been dry firewood stored inside. Rubbing her arms for warmth, Kady looked around her, expecting to see caveman paintings, but there were just walls of sandstone and a sandy floor. Along one wall was a broken bench and what looked to be a few moldy paperbacks. Beside the books was a rusty knife.

"Spent a lot of time here, did you?" she asked, smiling, as she removed her wet poncho, then her backpack.

With a glance at the knife, he smiled back as he fanned the flames of the fire. "As much as I could. Back there along that wall is a little shelf with a wooden box. Look inside."

She did, and when she saw pictures of herself inside the box, somehow, she wasn't surprised. By now nothing seemed to surprise or shock her. There were grainy photos taken with a long-lens camera that showed her as a child.

"This is my favorite," Tarik said, coming up from behind her as he reached over her shoulder and took a photo from the stack. It showed Kady at about thirteen on the playground at her school, children all about her, but Kady was leaning against the building reading a book.

"Probably a cookbook," she said, smiling, then made the mistake of turning toward him and found that her face was inches from his.

For a moment Kady was sure he was going to kiss her, but instead, he turned away, leaving Kady feeling relieved but also annoyed. But then, what did she expect? He was engaged to be married to someone else.

Involuntarily, she thought, *Just like you were engaged to Gregory even though you didn't love him.*

"So tell me all about Leonie," she said as she walked back to the fire.

He didn't respond to her request. "Sit down here. I want to look at your feet."

She didn't bother asking how he knew there was something wrong with her feet; he seemed to know many things about her. Sitting on a rock that had obviously been meant to be used as a chair, she started to untie her laces, but Tarik brushed her hands away. In seconds he had her foot bare, the wet sock peeled away.

"Do you have any idea how *dangerous* a blister like this is?" he asked with anger. "Look at this! You have two blisters on this foot and how many on the other foot?" He didn't wait for an answer before he pulled her other wet shoe off, then gave her a look of reprimand at the three blisters on that foot. One of them had burst, and blood had made her sock stick to her skin. Gently, he peeled the sock away.

After retrieving medical supplies from his pack, he began to doctor her feet, putting salve on them to prevent infection.

"You take care of everyone, but no one takes care of you, do they?" he asked, her small foot held securely in his big warm hands.

Kady didn't like to admit it, but there was something about the intimacy of the tender care he was giving her feet that made her feel closer to him than she'd ever felt to any other man. She'd been to bed with Gregory, but she'd never known him. She'd spent time with Cole, but she'd never felt a part of him, at least not as she was beginning to feel a part of this man. Maybe it should have been disconcerting to find that Tarik had known about her all his life, but then she had also known about him too, hadn't she?

"What did you play when you were here? Were you alone?" she asked.

"Always," he answered as he began to wrap gauze about her foot.

"Did you play that you were a cowboy? Or did you want to be a space ranger?"

"Neither," he said as he took her other foot in his hand and began to warm it between his palms. "I played Arabian Nights." With a smile he looked back up at her. "When I was a kid, I was obsessed with all things Arabian. Al el Din,

not as we westerners call him, Aladdin, fascinated me.
There was a year of my life when I played that I was a
Berber prince and ran around in a wool cloak, half of it
drawn across my face. Like a veil, I guess, to protect me
from the desert sands."

Looking up at her, his eyes twinkled. "I had to give it up
when my face broke out in a rash from the wool."

As Kady looked at him, she was not smiling. "What did
you mean when you said, *'This* time you can reach me'?"

"I don't remember. When was that? There, is that
better?" he asked, referring to her foot. "I think you should
stay off your feet tonight. No more climbing for you.
Tomorrow I may have to carry you down the mountain."

"You'll do no such thing. And what did you mean?"

"About what?"

She narrowed her eyes at him.

"Oh. About your reaching me? I have no idea. I don't
remember saying it."

She could tell by his eyes that he was telling the truth.
No one could fake such a blank look. "Did you think of me
when you were wearing your black wool?" she blurted, her
face earnest.

"How did you know it was black?"

Kady didn't respond, just waited for his answer.

As he began to take food from the pack, he seemed to
think about her question. "I guess I always thought of
you," he said softly. "You were part of my childhood."

"Did you imagine riding a white horse across the desert
and asking me to ride away with you?" she asked softly.

"Exactly," he said with a dazzling smile. "Now what
shall we eat for dinner? I have dehydrated beef Stroganoff
and dehydrated chicken à la king and dehydrated—"

"This is a joke, isn't it? You expect *me* to eat recon-
stituted . . . " She couldn't say the words of the foods, as
though to even say them would make her ill.

"Got any other suggestions?"

"Give me that pack and let me see what's in there," she

said, and with a smile, he motioned her to have a look inside the pack.

Thirty minutes later Kady had cooked a seasoned rice casserole, covered with cheese, and for dessert she had made a bread pudding with trail mix and powdered milk.

"Not bad," Tarik said as he ate three helpings, then cleaned out the bowls. "Not bad at all."

Kady had to laugh because she suddenly saw all his remarks about her cooking as what they were, teasing.

The rain still pelted outside, but inside the little cave they were cozy and warm, and as the darkness fell, Kady looked out nervously. What happened now? Was she supposed to climb into a sleeping bag with him?

Instinctively she knew that sex with this man would be different from any other sex she'd experienced. Sex with Tarik, or making love, as she intuitively knew it would be with this man, would change her life.

But worse, it would make her want him, and he wasn't for her. He was going to marry someone like Leonie, with the sound of money and Ivy League schools in her voice. Men like Tarik Jordan didn't take home cooks from Ohio to meet Mother. Especially not a mother who dedicated herself to retaining her beauty. What would she think of Kady, who never seemed able to remember to put on lipstick, much less all the rest of it?

"And what is going on in that little mind of yours?" Tarik asked as he set a pan of rainwater down by the fire and began to wash the dishes.

"That I would never have pegged you for a man to do the washing up."

"And I would never have thought you were a liar. What were you really thinking?"

"About your mother. Does she adore your Leonie?"

"Two of a kind. Mother picked her out for me."

"You mean like a set of dishes?"

"Exactly," Tarik answered.

"And your father? Did he meet your . . . your . . . before

he died?" She was hesitant about mentioning his father because Mr. Fowler had told her that it had only been six months since Tarik's father had been killed in a plane crash. And she couldn't seem to say the word *fiancée*.

Tarik very politely pretended he hadn't noticed Kady's speech problem.

"Oh, yes. He said I was an idiot. He said I should marry the cleaning lady's daughter before I married one of Mother's friends. There was no love lost between my parents."

"So why did they stay married all those years?"

"If my father had divorced her, he would have had to give away some of his wealth, so he had one mistress after another. And my mother, as far as I can tell, hasn't had sex since I was conceived, messes up the *maquillage,* you know."

Kady laughed at that. "Is Leonie like your mother?"

"Come here," he said, sitting on a rock, his knees wide apart. "No, don't give me that look, as though I'm about to steal your virtue. I want you to sit here so I can brush your hair. It has so many twigs in it that I'm afraid a forest ranger will arrest you for stealing national property."

Smiling, Kady moved to sit on the ground between his legs, and he gently began to brush the tangles from her hair, now and then tossing a twig onto her lap. She was silent as he worked, feeling the sensuousness of his hands in her hair. It was warm now in the cave, and the firelight was lovely. She was tired, but she didn't yet want to go to sleep because she didn't want this day to end. Not ever.

"No more questions for me?" he asked softly, her hair in his hands.

"No," she said, "none," then paused. "But I could listen. I'd like to listen if you'd like to tell me anything."

"My life story, maybe?" he asked, smiling. "But that's what I've been doing, isn't it? We got off to a bad start, so I've wanted to make it up to you."

"Why? What does it matter? Are you being nice to me because of Ruth's codicil?"

For a moment it was as though her hair had feeling, because she could feel his surge of anger, but she was not going to apologize.

After a moment he grew calm and resumed brushing. "I keep myself private because I don't want to be surrounded by people who want nothing from me except my money. I do have a life, a very private one, at my home."

"Oh? At your apartment in New York? Which one of those that I saw is where you live?"

At that he chuckled. "Neither. The plastic one"—he looked at her with twinkling eyes—"the one where you walked in on my shower, is for visiting clients and the other one is Leonie's apartment."

"I see. Her apartment, your building."

"Jealous?" he said with hope in his voice.

She ignored the question. "Then where *do* you live?"

"I have a big place in Connecticut with acres of land and an enormous house."

"What's the kitchen like?"

Tarik chuckled. "Horrible. Needs to be remodeled completely. But I can't find anyone who'd like to do it. Hey! Maybe *you* know something about kitchens and—"

"Go on," she said, interrupting his sarcasm. "Tell me about your house and about you. You've always known about me, but I know nothing whatever about you."

As he began to talk, again Kady realized that she identified with him. During their childhoods, there had been great differences between them financially, of course, but the more she heard about his life, the more she thought it was like her own. Money had caused both of them to be raised by strangers.

"The house in Connecticut is where you're going to live with Leonie?" she asked quietly as he began to braid her hair.

"I'll live there with our children anyway. She can go wherever she wants, it doesn't matter to me."

"That's horrible!" Kady said, turning to glare at him. "Children need a mother. Just because your mother was always gone and so was mine, that doesn't mean that children *should* be raised that way. They should——" She broke off when she saw that he was laughing at her. Again.

"Damn you!" she half shouted. "You're as bad as Cole! He was always laughing at me and always tricking me."

"Oh? And how did Cole trick you?"

He had his eyes downcast as he cleaned out the hairbrush, and his voice was innocence personified. So innocent, in fact, that Kady didn't catch on to what he was doing.

She'd said that she wasn't going to talk about what happened in Legend, but in the next breath she was telling him all about how Cole had tricked her into marrying him.

"By the time I showed up, he was so sure I'd be dying to marry him that he even had the church decorated," she said. "Can you imagine? He *starved* me into marrying him."

"Sounds as though you asked him to marry you, not the other way around."

She had been bending over the fire to stir it, and she looked across it at him. "Are you taking his side? Are you saying that he was right to do what he did to me?"

"I'm saying that I don't blame the man for doing anything he had to to keep from losing you," he said softly.

Kady turned away at his tone because all of it—the close confines of the little cave, the glow of the firelight, and this man she did and did not know—were tearing at her senses. "I believe I'm rather tired," she said, then glanced at him nervously, again wondering what the sleeping arrangements would be.

He didn't so much as make a move toward her, but instead unfastened one sleeping bag from the bottom of the big pack, then pulled another from deep inside it, and Kady gave an audible sigh of relief.

Tarik gave her a one-sided grin. "Is that a sigh of relief or regret?"

"Relief," she answered quickly, but from the way he laughed, she didn't think he believed her, and she turned away so he couldn't read her eyes.

When she turned back, he had spread the two sleeping bags out, one on either side of the fire, and she had to look away again to keep from watching him as he removed his shirt and jeans. When he was wearing only his white briefs, he put on a flannel shirt, leaving his strong, muscular legs exposed, and it was all Kady could do to make herself look away.

As for herself, she had to force her fingers to unbutton her shirt, and for a moment she considered going to bed with all her clothes on. But when she glanced at Tarik, he was already inside his sleeping bag, the one nearest the door, and he was staring up at the ceiling, not so much as looking in her direction.

Pretending that she didn't have a concern in the world, Kady undressed down to her body-hugging underwear, then slipped into her bag across from him.

For all that there was space and a fire separating them, Kady felt very close to him. And that feeling annoyed her because their relationship was so temporary. "Why do you say such things to me, about being jealous and about the men in my life?" she said without thinking. "What does my life matter to you? We're strangers to each other."

"That's not true, is it? I feel as though I've known you forever—and you feel it, too, don't you?"

"Not in the least," she said, trying to sound convincing. "You belong to Leonie."

"And who do you belong to, Kady?"

"To . . . to myself, that's who," she said, and even to her own ears that seemed a very lonely statement.

He didn't say anything for a while, and when he did, he changed the subject completely. "The kitchen in my house in Connecticut is in the oldest part of the house, and next to it is a pretty little study that looks out over a walled vegetable and herb garden. Along the south wall are grapes and espaliered apricot trees. No one has cared for the garden for years, but with work, it could be brought back to life. The study has two walls of old pine shelves that could hold probably a thousand or more books, cookbooks maybe. And as I said before, the kitchen hasn't been remodeled, so there's a storage pantry, a butler's pantry, and a third room with thick brick walls. We don't know what the third room was used for but—"

"A larder."

"A what?"

"It's a larder, used to keep meat cold. Is there a drain in the floor?"

"Why yes, there is and an underground—"

"A well," she said with longing in her voice. "A spring runs under the room, and the water keeps the room cold."

"Leonie wants to tear the auxiliary rooms out and make them all into one big, modern kitchen with black glass cabinets and—"

"No!" Kady said vehemently. "You can't do that. Those small rooms have a purpose and—" She drew a breath. "It's none of my business, of course." She took another calming breath. "What does she want to do with the walled garden?"

"Put in a private Jacuzzi. She wants to bring in boulders and make it a natural landscape."

"Apricot trees are natural."

"The trees will have to go, of course. Leonie says the leaves will clog the tub's filtering system."

Kady lay on her back looking at the firelight flickering on the cave's ceiling, thinking of the horror of destroying such beauty.

"What is hyssop?" Tarik asked.

"An herb. It's used to flavor oily fish, and it's what Chartreuse is made from. Why?"

"Oh, nothing. That's what someone said was growing in the garden, but it made Leonie sneeze, so we took it out. What about you?"

She was so involved in thinking of the desecration of the old garden that she didn't understand him. "Me?" she asked blankly.

"Yes. Does anything make you sneeze?"

"Certainly not any herbs," Kady said with her jaw clenched. "I'd like to go to sleep now," she said, as she couldn't bear to hear another word about Leonie's planned destruction of what seemed to be a beautiful old place.

"Oh, sure," Tarik said, and she could hear him turning over in his sleeping bag, his back to her, but a minute later she heard, "Bricks."

When she didn't ask what he was referring to, because she thought she already knew, he said, "The walls of the garden are made of old bricks, but Leonie hates them because they're covered with lichens and green moss. She wants to tear them down and put up something modern and tidy. Leonie likes modern things."

"Like you!" she said with feeling.

"You think I'm modern?"

"You live in New York and you—"

"I work in New York. I live in a two-hundred-year-old house in Connecticut."

"And you . . ." She broke off because she really couldn't think of much else wrong with him. Except that he made her crazy, that is. One minute he was laughing at her, the next he was rescuing her, the next he was washing the dishes. "I'd like to go to sleep now," she said again, letting him know that she wanted to stop talking. Even when he was talking about such innocent subjects as his house, he seemed able to annoy her. What did it matter to her what his *wife* did to *their* house and garden? It wasn't any of her concern, was it?

"Yes, of course, *habibbi*," he said softly. "And may you have the most beautiful of dreams."

"And the same to you," she said, pushing at the down-filled sleeping bag, trying to make it more comfortable. "Is that what you call Leonie?" she asked and then wished with all her might that she could recall the words.

To her surprise, Tarik did not laugh at her. Instead, he said softly, "No, I have never used that endearment to anyone else. It's just for you."

In spite of her good intentions, his words made her feel good, and she went to sleep smiling.

But the next morning the sunlight burned off the rain, and Kady felt that she could see life more clearly. Tarik Jordan was paying attention to her only because of Ruth's codicil.

When she awoke, he was gone from the cave, and by the time he returned, a load of damp firewood in his arms, she was sure that she had her emotions under control. She'd made a vow that no matter how provocatively he talked to her, she wasn't going to be seduced by him. Had he chuckled with his friends that Kady was merely an unemployed cook and he could seduce her into doing whatever he wanted her to?

"And what have I done to earn such a look of animosity?" he asked without hostility as he put the wood down, making a pile that could be used on the next visit to the cave.

"Nothing. Are you ready to leave? If we leave early, we might make Legend before nightfall."

"Dying to meet Uncle Hannibal, are you?"

"I just want to . . . to get out of here," she said more fiercely than she meant to.

Quietly, Tarik doused the fire, making sure that every coal was out, and when he looked back at her, his face was cold and hard, the face she had seen that first day but hadn't seen since. "You want to tell me what it is I've done that has offended you?"

Kady wished she had a list of complaints against him, but she didn't. Except that he'd been too kind and too helpful and too nice and too funny and—

"You don't have to struggle," he said coldly. "I don't go where I'm not wanted. Are you ready?"

Kady opened her mouth to explain but decided it was better to say nothing. It was better that they go to Legend, do whatever it was that she could to help Ruth, then get away from this man forever.

They didn't speak much on the way down the mountain, and as she followed Tarik, they moved fast. Twice he turned and asked her how her feet were, but other than that, they didn't speak.

When they got to the bottom, the camp was just the way they'd left it, Tarik's jeep parked under the trees, his horse grazing happily in a fenced-in pen that Kady was sure had been built especially for Jordan horses.

As they packed up the camp together, working side by side as though they had been together for years, Tarik suddenly threw down a couple of tent pegs with such force that they stuck upright in the ground. "What is wrong with you?" he half shouted. "What have I done?"

"You haven't done anything," she yelled back. "You belong to someone else. You belong to another world."

For a moment several emotions skittered across Tarik's dark face, then he grinned, showing strong white teeth, "Ah, I see, the class system. Well, you're right. Men in my station in life use little girls like you; then we discard them. We *marry* horsey women like Leonie. Is that about it?"

When he said it out loud, her complaints sounded Victorian. "Your mother . . ." she said softly, but didn't finish her sentence. What could she say, that his mother wouldn't want her son to marry a cook?

"Ah, yes, the queen," he said, and she knew he was laughing at her. "Her son the prince must marry a titled princess, right?"

"I don't like you very much right now," she said through clenched teeth.

"I think, Kady, my love, that only *you* see me as a prince. I can assure you that my mother does not." With that, he turned away toward his horse, but Kady could hear him chuckling.

Whatever he said, she thought, it was better to stay away from him. He was even better looking than Gregory, and she knew from experience that good-looking men only led to trouble.

"Ready to go meet my uncle?" he asked moments later as he returned to camp, leading his horse behind him.

Kady drew herself up to her full height and was still only staring at the middle of his chest. "I think we should keep all of this on business terms. I don't think we should get involved with one another. No more holidays, no more overnight camping trips, no more—" She broke off because Tarik leaned down and kissed her sweetly on the mouth.

"Whatever you say, *habibbi*," he said, then motioned to help her onto his horse.

Blinking, Kady got on the horse.

Chapter 25

"SHE'S MY WIFE," TARIK JORDAN SAID AS HE SLIPPED HIS ARM
tightly around Kady's shoulders.

"Your—" she began, but he tightened his grip on her so
sharply that her "Ow!" stopped her words.

"She's a bit miffed at me now, Uncle Hannibal, so pay
no attention to anything she says."

"I am *not* his wife," Kady said to the tall, thin man in
front of her. After she and Tarik had broken camp, he'd led
his horse, not down the road, but up a winding trail that
had to be a back road into Legend. It hadn't taken her long
to figure out that he was trying to sneak into the derelict
town before anyone saw him. "I thought your uncle
considered you family," she said, sitting on back of the
horse, holding on to him.

"There's family and there's family," he said cryptically.

"I see. And what did you do to him that makes you
worry that he may take a shot at you as well as a stranger
like me?"

Twisting around, he grinned at her. "You've got a brain
inside that pretty head of yours, don't you?"

"Only for remembering ingredients and figuring out lying men."

"I'm not so sure about that. You certainly seem to allow men to dupe you. Gilford sure pulled one over on you."

"Gregory," she corrected, then felt goose bumps rise on her arms as she remembered the way Cole had always pretended to not be able to remember Gregory's name. "At least *I* got away from a man who wanted something other than love from me," she said snidely.

He didn't miss her reference. "With legs like Leonie's, who cares whether she loves me or not?"

"You're disgusting."

At that he chuckled and, with his free hand, held hers that were clasped about his flat belly. "You know, Kady, I never knew riding a horse could be so very, *ah,* pleasurable." As he said this, he leaned back a bit so her ample breasts were buried even deeper against him, and when Kady, not mistaking his meaning, tried to pull away, the horse sidestepped and nearly threw her off. To keep from falling, she had to grab Tarik even tighter, which made him laugh. "Extra oats for you tonight, my good friend," he said to the horse.

Had the circumstances been different, Kady might have laughed, too, but she didn't allow herself that luxury. She was not going to become closer to this man than she already was.

But now, standing before his uncle Hannibal, who, with his burning eyes and long, scraggling beard, looked like a prophet from the Old Testament, she was ready to give up the whole idea of trying to help people who were dead.

"Driver's license says she's named Long," the forbidding old man said, looking down his long nose at Kady, as though she were a liar and a sinner and should be eradicated from the earth. Of course the only reason he'd seen her driver's license was he'd stolen her handbag from her car. So, was stealing and shooting at innocent people okay in his book?

As Kady opened her mouth to ask this, Tarik said, "We're married and I have the license to prove it."

"Would you please release me," Kady hissed, trying to pull away from him, but his grip was like steel.

With amazement, she watched Tarik pull a piece of paper from under his sweater and hand it to the old man.

"It's a copy, of course," Tarik said as Hannibal Jordan scrutinized it. "But it says that Miss Kady Long was married to Cole Jordan and, as you know, that's my name. You can see that it's all duly signed and witnessed."

"Let me see that," Kady said, snatching the paper from the man's hands. It was indeed a copy of her marriage certificate to Cole. She looked up at Tarik. "This is dated 1873."

"So it is," Tarik said, as though he'd just seen the date; then he grinned at his uncle. "No doubt it's a computer error. You know how those machines are."

"Don't know, don't wanta know," Hannibal decreed. "Machines are destroying this once great nation of ours."

With a fierce twist, Kady freed herself from Tarik's grasp. "That certificate was handwritten, and it was written long before computers were invented. I am *not* married to *this* Cole Jordan."

"Tetched," Tarik said to his uncle in conspiracy, tapping the side of his head. "But she's my wife, so what can I do? You ready to come along, dear? Uncle Hannibal is going to let us stay in the old Jordan homestead with him and the rest of his family." He glared at Kady pointedly. "And we can't stay there unless we're married because Uncle Hannibal doesn't believe in sin."

It didn't take a degree in espionage to figure out what he was saying, but Kady hesitated, then fluttered her eyes at Tarik. "But, dear, we're on our honeymoon. Couldn't we stay in a separate house of our own?" Lowering her eyes, she tried to look demure. In a house of their own she could have a room of her own. Preferably with a door that she could lock.

"The wages of sin—" the old man said as, to Kady's horror, he began to advance on her. But Tarik stepped between them.

"Forgive her, uncle, she has no idea what she's talking about." He slipped his arm back around Kady's shoulders and held on tightly. "We'll love staying with you and your children. It will be our greatest delight. All I ask is that I might take my bride exploring. We'll help you look."

For a moment Kady thought the old man was going to raise his arm and tell her she had to leave the mountain or maybe that she was to die in some biblical way, but instead, he just turned his back on them and walked away, mumbling to himself.

The moment he was out of earshot, Kady turned to glare up at Tarik. "Why didn't you tell me your uncle was crazy?"

"You thought a sane man shot at you? Or even that a sane man would choose to live up here in this forsaken place? What's your idea of *in*sanity?"

"So why didn't you warn me that you were going to tell him we were married? Obviously you planned it, or you wouldn't have a copy of my marriage certificate to Cole so handy. And where did you get that, anyway?"

Without answering her, Tarik turned and looked at the town. "I haven't been here for years, and it's difficult to believe, but it's worse than it was when I was here before. Uncle Hannibal isn't into maintenance. So, tell me, Kady, my wife, which side of the bed do you sleep on?"

"You touch me and you'll die regretting it."

Turning, he gave her a look of shock. "You seem to go to bed with other men, so why not me?"

"Has anyone ever told you that you're despicable?"

"Not any women, no, can't say that they have."

At that she swept past him and started walking up the road to where she knew the old Jordan homestead was.

As she walked, she looked around her. She had seen Legend in two different guises. First she had come to know and love Cole's dream town, with pretty houses, a school with a big playground, and no signs of the wickedness of life.

Later she had seen the town with Ruth. Then it had been abandoned for years and the buildings were already beginning to fall down. But now the town was a sad sight indeed. Very few buildings had roofs on them, and many had fallen into a heap of boards on the ground.

As she walked, she could feel sadness creeping into her as she thought how the place could have been and what had happened to keep it from being great.

"How was it when you were here?" Tarik asked from beside her, and for once he didn't seem to be teasing her. At first Kady thought she wouldn't answer him; she didn't want to hear his snide remarks about time travel, but the melancholy of her memories was overwhelming her.

"Down that road was the school with a huge sports field. I guess Cole dreamed that one up because a playground would be very important to a nine-year-old. This was the freight depot, and down there was the biggest ice cream parlor you ever saw."

She began to walk faster as she pointed out each building. Like Cole, she ignored that most of the buildings seemed to have been saloons, choosing to remember what they had been when she'd been with Cole.

"This was the Jordan Line, but when I was here, it was just a pretty hedge," she said, looking at the remains of a stone wall that had once separated the "good" and "bad" parts of town from each other. "This was named Paradise Lane, and the church there was large and pretty, and this was a huge library."

Turning right, she stopped before the little road that she knew led to the Jordan homestead. "Down there Cole built a mosque." Turning, she looked up at Tarik. "It was in memory of his best friend, who was killed with him." Her voice lowered. "He was named Tarik, like you."

While she stood there, the heaviness of the place

beginning to weigh on her, he took her hand in his and raised it to his lips.

When she saw that his eyes were full of pity, Kady jerked away from him. "You don't believe me, so don't pretend that you do."

He scowled at her. "I don't know why you have the opinion that I am a monster without feeling, but whether or not I believe you met people who lived a hundred years ago is of no consequence. I can see that this place upsets you. Would you like to leave and go back to Denver? Or New York?"

"And what about Ruth's codicil? Are you willing to forfeit the money for three years?"

"You could return to New York with me, and for the next three years, I could make all the decisions and you could sign all the papers."

She blinked up at him. "Work with you? Every day? For three years?"

He gave her a one-sided grin. "Sounds good to me."

Kady began walking again. "And how would your lovely Leonie like that?"

"She's not the jealous type, and besides, what would there be for her to be jealous of? It's not as though you and I—"

"Right," she said over her shoulder. "It's not as though there is anything between us. In fact . . ." Halting, she turned back to him. "Why don't you leave here? You've told your uncle that I'm family, so he won't be shooting at me anymore, so I don't need you any longer." In spite of her words, Kady's heart nearly stopped. Part of her wanted to throw her arms around him and beg him not to leave her with this frightening old man. But another part wanted him to go away so she'd never see him again.

Tarik didn't bother answering. "The Hanging Tree is down this way. Want to see it?"

"I have, thank you," she said, letting out her pent-up breath and starting to walk again.

But what Kady had forgotten was that the cemetery was also that way. When she'd been with Ruth, she'd refused to enter it, but now, in the bright sunlight, she stopped before the falling-down fence and stared in hypnotic fascination at the weathered stones.

"Come on," Tarik said gently, pulling her by the hand.

"No," she whispered. "I don't want to see."

But he was insistent. "Come on, you have to."

"No!" she said more fiercely, trying to pull back from him.

But he wouldn't release her hand, and when she tugged harder, he pulled her into his arms. "Kady, please," he said, holding her and stroking her hair. "I want you to trust me. Haven't I always been here for you?"

With her face buried against his chest, she nodded. The warmth of him felt so good, and the roughness of his wool sweater made her very aware of his maleness. No other man who had ever touched her made her feel as he did. He seemed safe and dangerous at the same time. She felt that he was her friend and her enemy; her protector and her predator.

"Look about you," he said softly, pulling her face away from his chest. "It's a cemetery, and all the people in here have been dead a very long time."

When she managed to open her eyes, the first stone she saw said Juan Barela, and she put her face back against Tarik's chest. "No," she whispered and tried to leave, but he pulled her back.

"Why are you doing this to me?" she asked, looking up at him.

"I want you to recognize the difference between the living and the dead. You were never married to Cole Jordan because he died many years ago."

At that she did pull away from him and ran to the gateway; then she turned back to glare at him. "You don't know anything about anything. You think that if it can't be put in a computer, then it doesn't exist. You think—Oh, who cares what you think? I don't need you or want you, and I want you to leave me alone."

Turning, she began to run toward the Hanging Tree, the place where she first met Cole, but Tarik caught her in his arms. When she fought against him, he held her tighter, until she at last stopped and began to sob against him.

"Kady, I know you say you don't like me," he said softly, "and maybe you have reason not to, but I'm not going to leave you here alone. I think maybe too many people in your life have left you alone. And whether I believe your story or not doesn't matter. I'm going to do what I can to help you."

He pulled her away from him, and when she wouldn't look up, he put his hand under her chin and lifted her face to his. "We're partners, remember?" he said.

As she looked into his dark eyes, she saw the man she'd seen in her dreams for most of her life. She remembered being a child and drawing veils on every photo she saw as she searched for the eyes that were now looking at her. And she knew that if he continued being nice to her, she'd fall in love with him, fall deeply in love with him.

And that could not be. They were from two different worlds, and all he wanted from her was help in getting his family's business back. If Ruth hadn't written that codicil he would never have seen her again. And once this project was done, he'd ride out of Kady's life with the ease he had ridden into it.

She moved away from his grasp and wiped at her eyes. "Right," she said. "We're business partners, and I'd like to keep it that way. So please keep your hands off of me." She put her chin up. "And no more of your psychobabble of trying to make me look at tombstones. What I do or do not do is none of your business. Now, if you don't mind, I'd like to be by myself."

His face changed with her speech, going from one of great concern to a mask of arrogant amusement. "Of course," he said. "I apologize for forcing myself on you. I'm sure you know your way back to the house, and as you have made abundantly clear, you don't need me." One side of his mouth curved into a little smile. "If you happen to stumble into the past, say hello to my relatives for me."

With that, he turned on his heel and headed back toward Legend.

Feeling very alone, Kady walked toward the mountains. She was fairly sure that she could find the petroglyphs by herself, and when she did, she knew that she would find the doorway. And when she went through it, what would she find? Maybe there'd be a time error and she'd arrive in Legend in 1917. Or maybe the rock would close around her as she walked through it and she'd be trapped.

Suddenly, she wished Tarik were with her, then told herself that was a stupid thought. Why was she so attracted to a man like him? Why wasn't she remembering every minute she'd spent with Cole and longing to go back to him? Why had this dark man blocked out her memories of any other man?

"He means absolutely nothing whatever to me," she said as she put her chin in the air and kept walking, not noticing that "he" meant Tarik.

In the hundred years since she'd been there last, the trail up the mountain had changed. Some of the rocks had eroded, and the trees had changed. A big old cottonwood was gone, and in its place were several seedlings. But the ancient piñon trees didn't seem to have grown an inch.

When she finally reached the sheer rock face, she had to pull aside scraggly vines to see the petroglyphs, now not as clear as they had been many years before, but she could still see them.

Stepping back, Kady looked at the rock and waited for it to open. When nothing happened, she went to it and ran her hands over the surface as though she were looking for a latch.

"Try, 'Open sesame,'" came a voice from behind her.

Turning, Kady saw Tarik standing there, the now-familiar smirk on his handsome face, but when he saw her, his expression changed. Leaping down from the rock he was standing on, he put his arms around her and drew her to him.

"Kady, honey, you're shaking like a leaf. Come on, sit down." With his arms still around her, he led her to a low rock and gently seated her, then gave her a drink of water from a bottle he had hooked to his belt.

"Better?" he asked, sitting beside her, his arms still around her.

"I'm not your honey, and what are you doing here?"

"Taking care of my wife. You like *habibbi* better?"

"I don't like any endearments from you, and I'm not your wife." Her words would have had more impact if she hadn't remained in the circle of his arms and hadn't put her head down on his shoulder and hadn't allowed him to brush her hair from her eyes with his fingertips.

"How do you know so much?" she asked softly as she leaned against him.

"I know surprisingly little, but I'm a good listener. Want to tell me everything?"

She did want to share what had happened to her with someone—no, not just anyone, with him—but at the same time she was afraid to allow herself to indulge her feelings since they could lead nowhere.

"No," she said as she pulled away from him and made herself sit upright.

"Damn it! What is it about me you don't like?"

"Lawsuits!" she said. "And . . . And . . ."

"That suit was prepared years before I met you. Fowler was instructed to call another law firm if you showed up, and the lawsuit was sent automatically."

"Is that supposed to make me forgive you?"

When she tried to move away, he caught her shoulders, turning her to look at him. "Yes," he said softly, "I want you to forgive me. I want—Oh, Kady, I want *you.*"

Before Kady could form a protest, he pulled her into his

arms and kissed her, and she knew that never in her life had she been kissed before. Not like this man kissed her. Gregory had kissed her with reservations and caution. Cole's kisses had been filled with humor and the excitement of a young boy. But this man kissed her in a way that made her want to become a part of him.

Turning her head in his big hand, he moved her mouth so he could better reach parts of it that no other man had. His tongue touched hers, and Kady felt so weakened that she seemed to melt her body into his, hers so soft, his so hard.

His hands moved down her back, entangled in her hair that came loose from its thick braid. His mouth seemed to cover hers; his hands caressed her, his fingertips easily finding her breasts and covering them.

"Kady, I . . ." he said as he moved his mouth away and pulled her close to him. His grip was almost crushing her, and she could barely breathe, but that didn't seem to matter right now.

"Yes," she whispered, encouraging him to speak. But what would he say? That he too had never felt this way? That no woman had ever made him feel this way? Not likely!

As Tarik held her, knowing that he was not going to be able to prevent himself from making love to her here and now, and thinking, *So this is what it feels like to be in love,* he glanced up at the rock and what he saw made his thoughts freeze.

It was as though the solid rock face had turned into a life-size movie screen, and through the opening he could see what was undoubtedly Legend of long ago. There was a saloon with four garishly dressed women sitting on the balcony. Horses, tied to rails, flicked flies with their tails while two men who looked as though they'd never had a bath in their lives walked through muddy streets.

The sight was so shocking that for a moment Tarik forgot all about having finally achieved his goal of holding Kady in his arms. Instinctively, his arms tightened about her, not in passion but in protection. Up until now he had not believed a word of what he'd been able to piece together of her story of what had happened to connect her with the Jordan family.

Years ago, he had researched all he could find about his family history, trying to figure out why his ancestor Ruth Jordan had left all their family's money in trust to a stranger who had yet to be born. He'd found out a great deal of family history but no explanation.

Now, as Tarik stared at the living, breathing scene in front of him, he knew that whatever Kady said had happened to her was true.

The doors to the saloon opened, and he could hear the sounds of a badly tuned piano coming from inside. And he could smell the mud and horse manure and the unwashed bodies.

"What was that?" Kady asked, but when she tried to turn her head, he held her fast.

"Nothing, sweetheart," he whispered, pushing her head back to his shoulder and holding it there. He'd never felt this way about a woman before, as though he wanted to wrap her in silk and protect her from all harm.

"No!" Kady suddenly cried as she pushed against him sharply, then looked at the rock.

To Tarik's astonishment, the second she turned her head, the rock closed, and for several moments both of them stared in silence at nothing but the ordinary rock face.

"It was open, wasn't it?"

"Open?" Tarik asked, doing his best to feign ignorance. But what he had seen had shocked him, and he was having difficulty hiding that shock. "What was open?" He gave her a hot look. "Just you, open to me." He knew he was acting like a dirty old man, but he wanted to make her angry, so angry that she'd turn and run down the mountain, as far away from this place as she could possibly get. If that vile rock "opened" again, would she jump up and run through it?

"Get away from me," she said, pushing at him. "And in the future I'd appreciate it if you kept your hands off of me."

"How can I do that when there is so much of you that I want to touch?"

Tarik had wanted to anger her, but he got more than he bargained for.

Jumping up, Kady put her hands on her hips and glared down at him. "So you think I'm fat, do you?"

"Fat?" Tarik said and was so bewildered by this statement that he forgot about the rock. What in the world had he said that made her think he thought she was *fat*? He knew she wasn't as thin as was the fashion now, but Kady was the most luscious woman he'd ever seen in his life. Every second that he'd had to force himself not to touch her had caused him real pain.

"I want you to stay away from me," she said in a hiss, then turned and started down the mountain, while Tarik sat in stunned silence on the rock.

But as soon she rounded the bend, the rock opened again, and he saw Legend in all its muddy splendor. As though hypnotized, he moved to stand just outside the opening. All he had to do was step through, and he'd be in another time and place.

But as Tarik looked at the opening, he stepped back. He knew that his ancestors lived in that town, but if he went through, he might never be able to return to this day and time. And if he didn't return, he'd lose Kady. He'd lose the woman he'd been waiting for all his life.

Turning, he began to run down the mountain toward her, but she was moving so quickly that she was nearly at the Hanging Tree before he caught up with her. She was so angry with him that she wouldn't acknowledge his presence.

After several attempts to get her to listen to him, he

grabbed her into his arms and held her tightly despite struggles.

"I am *not* Gregory," he said into her face, "and I'm damned if I'm going to allow you to think that I am."

"Let me go," she said, struggling against him. "I don't want you near me."

"I don't think that's true," he said, still holding her. "What you're saying is not what I see in your eyes. Kady, my love, look at me."

"No," she said, no longer struggling but keeping her arms close to her body and her hands balled into fists.

"I think you are beautiful," he said, then kissed her cheek. "Really truly beautiful." He kissed the other cheek. "I think you are the most luscious, desirable woman I have ever seen in my life." He kissed her forehead. "And I would like nothing better in the world than to take you to bed and"—he kissed her nose—"and make love to you all day long." He kissed her chin. "Just the sight of you inflames me to lust, and I would like to put my hands on—"

The rest of his sentence was drowned out by the very loud sound of a motorcycle coming from behind her. As Tarik's arms tightened on Kady protectively, she tried to turn to see who was coming. Somehow she couldn't imagine Uncle Hannibal riding a motorcycle.

"Damnation!" Tarik said under his breath, then looked at Kady. "I'm sorry for what is about to happen," he said, and there was great sadness in his eyes.

"Sorry for—" she began, but he pushed her away and told her to go stand under the safety of the Hanging Tree.

Kady didn't think of hesitating as she scurried to obey him. Once she was under the shelter of the tree, she turned and saw a huge motorcycle approaching with a rider dressed all in black leather, a helmet hiding the face.

As the big machine roared toward Tarik, Kady instinctively stepped closer to the tree, but Tarik, standing in the open, didn't so much as move as the bike headed straight toward him.

"Watch out!" she shouted, and could barely hear herself over the machine, but Tarik raised his hand to tell her to stay where she was. There was a look of profound disgust on his face.

As Kady watched, the motorcycle turned in a sharp circle around Tarik, gravel flying, but he didn't flinch. Finally, it halted in front of him in the midst of a whirlwind of dust, but Tarik, hands at his side, still didn't move.

Kady, several feet away, was coughing up dust as she watched the rider slowly remove black leather gloves, and she saw the hands of a woman. The next minute the rider removed her helmet, and out cascaded a yard of red hair. With a swing of an impossibly long leg, she dismounted the motorcycle and stood in front of Tarik, so close her breasts were almost touching his chest.

Of course, she could be standing a foot away and that would still be the situation, Kady thought as she looked at the woman. She was six feet, if she was an inch, and she was statuesque, powerfully and strongly built. Eye level with Tarik, she put her hand behind his head and kissed him while he stood immobile, not touching her.

But he was not pulling away, Kady thought, her hands clenched at her sides. Not that it was any of her business, she reminded herself, and knew she should go back to the house. Or maybe to . . . Well, to anywhere but here. But in spite of her sensible thoughts, she stayed glued to the spot and stared at that woman kissing *her* husband.

In the next moment, Kady reminded herself that Mr. C. T. Jordan had no official relationship with her. They weren't even friends.

"Darling, I knew you'd come for me," the woman said in a throaty voice that Kady was sure would turn on any man who heard it. "I knew that as soon as I sent you that fax you'd come and rescue me."

Tarik didn't answer, but did take a step back from her grasp.

As though the woman had a second sense, she turned

impossibly emerald green eyes to Kady. Contact lenses? Kady thought.

"And who is your little friend?" the woman asked.

When Tarik turned to look at Kady, he wore the look of a man who knew there was going to be trouble and there was nothing he could do to prevent it. "*Ah,* Wendell, this is Kady Long, and, Kady, this is my cousin, Wendell Jordan."

Wendell looked Kady up and down. "Tarik, darling, she doesn't look your type at all. Or are your standards slipping?" Possessively, she put her arm around Tarik's shoulders. He wasn't more than a couple of inches taller than she was.

The Kady of a few months ago would have been intimidated by someone like the magnificent Wendell Jordan, but after what Kady had been through, not much seemed to frighten her. "How do you do?" she asked, moving forward and smiling sweetly at the woman, then she gave an amused little chuckle. "I think my husband is a bit confused. I'm Kady *Jordan,* not Long, and we're here on our honeymoon. For a wedding gift he gave me the town of Legend. Wasn't that sweet of him?"

Kady was happy to see that this announcement startled the woman into silence, and when Kady reached Tarik, she stood on tiptoe and kissed him in a wifely way on the cheek. "After you finish catching up on old times with your *cousin,* do come along, dear, I want you to help me wash my hair. I know how much you love to brush it."

With that, Kady turned and walked away.

Behind her she heard Wendell say, "You didn't *really* marry her, did you, darling?" She heard Tarik's answering chuckle, and she knew that she had surprised and, possibly, pleased him.

Humming to herself, feeling that she had just slain a dragon, Kady went back to the house. "I wonder who does the cooking around here?" she said aloud as she stepped onto the porch.

"Whoever is hungry first," came a voice that nearly made Kady jump out of her skin.

Swinging down from the porch roof was a beautiful young man. Not of the caliber of Tarik, but he was like something out of Li'l Abner. He was wearing a pair of farmer's overalls with no shirt underneath, and his young muscles bulged, while his blue eyes twinkled under a thatch of dark blond hair. She would have recognized him as a relative of Cole's anywhere.

"Share the joke?" he asked, smiling in an infectious way.

"Ever see the movie *Li'l Abner*?"

"I think so. Do I remind you of anyone?" His pride in himself was evident.

"Li'l Abner, of course. And that woman on the motorcycle is Moonbeam McSwine." She laughed, then looked startled. "Oh! She must be your . . ."

"Sister. Much, much older sister, and I've never heard her described more aptly. I'm Luke Jordan, and who exactly are you?" He was advancing on her.

"My wife," came from the patch of grass in front of the house, and they both turned to see Tarik standing there, his eyes hot coals of anger. "And if you look at her like that again, I'll make you regret it." There wasn't a touch of humor in his voice or manner.

Instantly, the blond man leaped over the porch rail, obviously aiming to land directly on Tarik, but the older man sidestepped him, and the younger one went skidding into the dirt.

"Think you can take me, little boy?" Tarik said, his hands in the traditional pose of a person who has studied martial arts.

"I want your woman. You, I care nothing about."

To Kady's horror, the men then started to fight as she'd never seen anyone outside of a ring fight. The young man went slamming to the ground as Tarik easily twisted his lean body to one side as the other man tried to overtake him with brute strength.

For a few moments Kady stood on the porch and watched in horrified fascination. She had never seen anyone fight with the ease and grace that Tarik did, and he never lost his smug smile while doing it. He was so much better than the young man that there was no contest. Within minutes, the younger man's nose was bleeding and there was a bloody scrape on his side where he had landed on gravel.

"Stop it!" Kady yelled, but neither man paid any attention to her as the younger blond man kept lunging and the older one kept dodging, then tripping his opponent.

"Stop it!" she yelled again and ran down the stairs, and without thought for her own safety, she jumped between the two men. Unfortunately, her leap was so ill timed that she stopped just under the young man as he was in midair. He'd been aiming to come down on top of Tarik and thereby cushion his landing, but Tarik grabbed Kady and twisted sideways, so the young man landed facedown in the thinly grassed area, his mouth full of dirt.

Jerking out of Tarik's hold, Kady went to the young man. "Look what you've done. You've hurt him."

"Yeah, cousin, you've hurt me," the man said, sitting up and wiping blood from his nose.

Until now Kady had thought the fight was real, but now, looking from one to the other, she realized it was just one of those boy things that is incomprehensible to women. Sorry that she'd wasted a moment of concern over either of them, she stood up.

"You can bandage your own wounds," she said, glaring at Tarik, who had blood running from the corner of his mouth.

As she walked back up the stairs and into the house, she could hear the laughter of the two men, and when the door slammed behind her, Kady grimaced. Men! she thought and started looking for the kitchen.

Chapter 26

THE KITCHEN OF THE OLD HOUSE LOOKED VERY MUCH LIKE the one in Cole's fantasy house, with a huge cast-iron stove and a big oak worktable sitting in the middle of the room. Next to the kitchen was a pantry that was stocked to the ceiling with every conceivable canned good and great bags of flour and rice. Outside the window was a patch of herbs that were struggling to stay alive in spite of years of neglect.

Grabbing canned tomatoes and a bag of apples from the pantry floor, Kady carried them back to the kitchen. "Tarik, darling," she mocked aloud as she grabbed an apple and a dull paring knife. "Aren't I just too, too divine for words."

Tarik chuckled from the doorway. "Don't let Wendell get to you. She's been that way since she was a kid."

"And what way is that? Tall, beautiful, and a bitch?"

"Let's just say that she doesn't have many women friends. What are you doing?"

She looked up at him as though he were terminally stupid. She was so angry with him, what with not believing her about the opening in the rock, then that horrid woman, then frightening her with his mock battle with Luke, that she could hardly speak. "What does it look like I'm doing?"

"If you're planning to cook dinner, and I hope you are, I think I had better warn you that Uncle Hannibal isn't a gourmet. He won't like squid ink pasta or anything dribbled with balsamic vinegar; besides, all you've got to cook on is *that,*" he said as he nodded toward the cast-iron stove. "Ever seen one of those before?"

Kady gave him a look that should have warned him but didn't. "I've seen a few in history books."

Tarik took one of the apples she'd just peeled. "Maybe you should get Uncle Hannibal to show you how to work that stove."

"Or maybe Luke would show me," she said sweetly.

"Trying to make me jealous?"

"Trying to improve my sex life," she said without thinking.

"Oh?" he said with interest as he took a step toward her. "I could—"

"You take one step closer and you'll be missing some body parts."

Smiling, he stepped away. "I'll leave you to it then, and I shall look forward to dinner. But, remember, nothing outlandish. Just something simple, like, like . . ."

"How about spaghetti and apple pie? Or is spaghetti too foreign for your very conventional family?" she asked innocently. Hannibal and his two "children" were anything but conventional.

"No, no, that's fine," he said, smiling, seeming to enjoy that he was making her angry. "If you need me, I'll be outside. I want to see that Harley Wendell was on. Good-looking machine, isn't it?"

"I'm afraid I've never been butch enough to learn much about motorcycles. Tell me, does she also chew tobacco and play football with the men?"

As he bit into his apple, he gave her a look that nearly

singed her hair. "Wendell does whatever she wants whenever she wants with whomever she wants."

"Yes, and I can see that it has made her into a very nice
person."

As Tarik left, chuckling, closing the door behind him,
Kady threw a handful of apple peels at him.

After Tarik left, she was thinking about that dreadful red-
haired—

"May I help?" Luke said meekly from the doorway.
"And can you really cook?"

There was a sweetness about him that reminded her of
Cole. She smiled and gestured for him to join her. "Come
in and talk to me while I cook. Tell me everything about
your family."

Luke helped himself to a slice of apple. "About the
Jordans or about my cousin Tarik in particular?"

"I have no interest in him whatever. None. He is free to
do whatever he wants. He can—" She stopped because
Luke was grinning at her.

"Right. And the way the two of you look at each other
could set the barn on fire. So where do you want me to
start? With his mother, his father, or his girlfriends?"

Kady kept her eyes down on the apples she was peeling
and didn't look up at him.

Luke lowered his voice. "Or would you rather that I tell
you about his dreams?"

"What dreams?" she said sharply.

"Of a little girl on a pony. A little girl with lots of dark
hair in a fat braid down her back. Actually, she had a braid
very much like yours. Interested?"

"Maybe," she said as though she didn't want to hear
every word.

"Oh, well, then, I guess I better go outside and help my
sister tune her carburetor."

"Sit!" Kady ordered, pointing with the knife.

"And what do I get if I rat on my own flesh and blood?"

"A meal better than any you've ever eaten in your life," she said seriously.

With eyes wide, Luke stared at her. "Alexandria, Virginia! Onions! Kady with a *d*. That's who you are."

Kady couldn't help giving a smile of pleasure. "Exactly. So sit down here and talk to me while I prepare dinner."

"Yes, ma'am," Luke said as he took a seat across the table, where she put him to work peeling the rest of the apples.

Luke talked while Kady worked quickly and efficiently. He repeated what Kady had already heard about the neglect of Tarik's parents, but she had to keep her eyes lowered when Luke said he'd never seen his cousin so relaxed and smiling. "You've done something to him," Luke said. "It didn't take me two minutes to see that he's not his usual quiet, mysterious self. When I was a kid, he used to visit Legend, but he'd disappear for days at a time. No one knew where he went. Both Wendell and I used to try to follow him, but he easily lost us. But today . . . With you . . ."

Kady refused to give any weight to Luke's words. "I'm sure that if he brought a girlfriend up here, he would have—"

"He did once. When Wendell wasn't here, of course. His girlfriend was so frightened of the coyotes' howling that Tarik took her back to town the next day."

"Tarik," Kady said softly. "Did you know that in New York people don't know his name?"

Luke gave a one-sided grin so like Tarik's that Kady had to look away. "Private man. Very private. So tell me about *you*, Kady. Why did you marry my taciturn cousin?"

Kady didn't want to talk about herself, she wanted to listen. "Come outside to gather herbs with me and tell me about his dream."

Smiling, Luke followed her outside as Kady gathered herbs, explaining that, all his life, Tarik had had a dream of a little girl on a pony. When he was a child, he used to say that she was his best friend and that she was going to come live with him. His fantasies about the little girl were a family joke.

After they returned to the house, Kady listened intently as she wielded a rolling pin. She was making *fazzolétto,* handkerchief pasta: whole leaves of herbs were rolled between transparently fine layers of pasta, then cut into sheets to show the beauty of the pattern. There was no time to make her usual three-hour tomato sauce, so she used canned tomatoes, onions, and herbs.

For dessert, she made a *tarte tatin,* one of the most divine dishes ever created: caramelized butter and sugar covered with a dozen apples sliced paper thin, cooked on top of the stove, then a round of flaky pastry put on top, baked until golden brown, and at last the whole thing was turned upside down onto a plate. It was almost as beautiful as it was delicious.

At about seven o'clock in the evening, everyone began showing up, enticed by the smells coming from the open windows of the house. Hannibal looked as though he'd been working in the mines, as his clothes were flecked with rock dust. Wendell still wore her black leather, but she'd put on even more makeup, making Kady wonder how she could lift her eyelids when they were so weighted down with mascara.

As for Tarik, he came in last and from the rolled-eyed looks of reproof that Wendell gave him, Kady didn't think they had spent the afternoon together after all. Not that it mattered to her, of course, but as she turned away, she smiled. Then she began to wonder where he had been, for Tarik was very dirty, with mud on his shoes and another streak of mud on one cheek.

Kady was pleased to see that her meal was a great hit with each of Tarik's relatives. Even Wendell managed to look impressed. With her breath held, Kady waited for

Uncle Hannibal's opinion. Maybe something as pretty as *fazzolétto* wouldn't suit him. But he ate without any comment.

After the meal everyone retired to the porch to sit on chairs and enjoy the cool night air. When Tarik sat on the rail, Wendell immediately moved her chair so she was sitting nearly at his feet. As for Kady, she took a chair at the far side of the porch.

Uncle Hannibal leaned back in his rocking chair, picking his teeth with a toothpick. "Kady, girl, if you weren't already married, after that meal, I'd ask for your hand myself."

It took Kady a moment to realize that he was teasing her—or was he?—then she smiled and told him that she would seriously consider his proposal.

After that Luke told her that he had a law degree and a beautiful apartment in Denver and he'd also like to marry her.

At this Wendell pointed out that Kady already had a husband and she also owned the town. "Isn't that enough for one woman?"

"Nothing's ever been enough for *you,* big sister," Luke said, and this would have started an argument, but Tarik halted it by telling them all that yes, Kady already had a husband and they had better not forget it.

"Luke, if you're a lawyer," Kady said, "do you think that a marriage certificate that is dated a hundred and twenty years ago is valid today?"

Luke looked from Tarik to Kady. "No, I don't think so. Why? Was such an error made on your marriage certificate?"

"Computer error," Hannibal said as though he was a programmer and knew about these things.

"It was handwritten," Kady said.

"Computer fonts today are amazing, aren't they?" Tarik said, smiling.

"Now that you mention it," Luke said, looking toward Tarik, "I was wondering how you two managed to get married in secret. I would have thought your mother would have put on a wedding the size of Alaska."

"Yes, boy, now that I think of it, why weren't we invited to the wedding?" Hannibal asked, his prophet-face back in place.

All eyes were on Tarik, especially Kady's. If Uncle Hannibal found out they weren't married, would he toss them out of Legend? If he did that, would she ever have a chance to help Ruth?

As though the conversation didn't interest him in the least, Tarik stood and stretched. "Neither of you are going to get her so you can stop looking for loopholes. She's married to me no matter what that piece of paper says." Smiling, he looked down at Kady. "Besides, if we weren't married, I'd see no reason for us to stay here and try to go through any doorways, do you? Shall we take the blue bedroom, Uncle Hannibal?"

"It's always yours," Hannibal answered, smiling benefi-cently at Kady.

"What doorway?" Luke asked with interest.

Tarik put his arm around Kady. "A doorway that doesn't concern little boys like you."

Luke laughed confidently. "I may be a boy to you, Cousin Tarik, but not to the ladies."

"Tarik, honey," Wendell purred, "you can't be going to bed now. It's the shank of the evening. I'm sure your little . . . friend must be tired after all that chopping and peeling, but you and I . . . Well, as you remember, at this time of day we're usually just getting started."

When Wendell fluttered her heavy lashes, Kady feared the breeze was going to blow the chairs off the porch. "Yes, *darling*," Kady said sarcastically, "why don't you stay here and help Wendell with a . . . a fan belt or something? I'm sure you two can find lots of boy things to do together. As for me, I have knitting and crocheting that will keep me busy in my rocker. Good night everyone." Opening the door, she went inside the house.

Tarik followed her, but he halted at the bottom of the stairs, looking up at her, and for a moment there was pain on his face. "I . . . I think I'll stay downstairs for a while."

Kady put her nose into the air. It didn't matter to her what he did, but as she glanced toward the open door she saw that Wendell was listening avidly. Over Wendell's painted mouth, her eyes held an expression of such knowing smugness that Kady's heart tightened into a little knot.

"Whatever," Kady said and mounted the stairs, but Tarik caught her hand on the rail.

"Look, it's not what you think," he said softly so the others couldn't hear. "I have to take care of something. I'll be up when I can."

"Are you under the impression that I *want* you to share the same bedroom with me?" she hissed, looking down at him.

It was as though he hadn't heard her. "I want nothing more than to spend the night with you, but I have to—"

"You are too vain for words! Go on and stay with your cousin. Or is Leonie flying in to visit you? There is nothing between us except—"

She didn't say any more because he vaulted over the stair rail, took her into his arms, and kissed her until she was limp.

"Don't you think it's time that we stopped playing games? You know as well as I do that we were meant to be with each other. Destined, if you like. Ever since that first day when I looked into your eyes, I . . ." He trailed off as he smoothed the hair back from her face, tucking a curl behind her ear.

"You what?" she asked, looking up at him. When he touched her, she had trouble thinking clearly.

"Since that first day I've known that I love you."

"That's not true!" she said, trying to push away from him. Two men had told her they loved her, and they had both turned out to be false. Gregory had wanted to use her to make money, and Cole was—

"It *is* true," he said, holding her, not allowing her to move from his arms. "We have loved each other for a long time. I think maybe we loved each other before we even met."

"How absurd. That's ridiculous." Again she tried to push away, but he wouldn't release her.

"You don't have to tell me now that you love me," he said. "First I want to earn your trust."

"In which woman's bed?" she spat at him. "And what about your engagement to the skinny Leonie?"

"I broke it the day you threw the papers on my floor. She's out of my life."

"I don't believe you," she said, trying not to look at him, for she couldn't bear to look into his eyes. "We hardly know each other, and you only came here because of Ruth's codicil and—"

"There is no codicil," he said softly.

"And you live in a different world than I do, and you— What do you mean, 'There is no codicil'?"

"There, that's better," he said, smiling because she'd stopped struggling to get away and was now looking up at him in disbelief. "I made up all of it. I'm a good actor."

"You aren't an actor, you're a liar!"

"Whatever you want to call it. *Mmmm,* you taste good." He was nuzzling her neck. "That was very funny that you said you were going to cook spaghetti and an apple pie. That's like comparing a Ferrari to a bus. How do you remember all those ingredients? Do you carry a cookbook with you?"

"I have an ability to remember recipe ingredients. I can't think when you're doing that."

"That's the idea."

Kady did her best to move her neck away from his

mouth. She *must* keep her wits about her. With surprising strength, she managed to push away somewhat, but his hands were still clasped behind her back.

"What do you mean that there is no codicil? What did Ruth's letter to you say? In fact, why are you here?"

With a sigh, Tarik dropped his hands from her body. He was never going to be able to answer questions if he kept touching her. "My ancestress, Ruth Jordan, left me a letter saying something about her having commissioned you with the task of trying to make her grandson Cole live past nine years of age. She asked that I help you accomplish this task."

"But you don't believe that I can do it."

"I don't want you to try."

"Why not?" she asked suspiciously.

"Because my ancestor was killed with bullets. If you stop him from being shot, maybe *you* will be shot instead."

"Oh. I hadn't thought of that."

"Seems to me that you two women didn't think out a great many things. Such as a will like hers not holding up in court. And besides, my family has known about that will for many years. We took precautions."

Kady blinked at him, trying to understand what he was saying. "Are you telling me that all this was a setup?"

"More or less."

"Mr. Fowler—"

"He knows nothing. He thought you would be the owner of everything, and he thought he was returning it all back to me at your request." When he saw her face, he knew he'd told her too much too soon. "Look, sweetheart, let's talk about this later. Now, standing on the stairs, is not the place to talk about—"

"Talk about how you've laughed at me, lied to me, and generally manipulated me?"

"Well, yes, I did, but it was all for a good cause."

"And what would that be?" she said through clenched teeth.

"The first moment I saw you I knew that I loved you, but I wanted to know if you loved me too."

"I *don't* love you," she said angrily. "I can't stand you! You have ridiculed me, laughed at me, made fun of my cooking, and— And I never want to see you again," she said as she started to move around him to go up the stairs.

"Kady, honey, darling, sweetheart, you don't mean that. I had to do all this. After what that bastard Gregory did to you, you wouldn't have believed me if I'd said I loved you that first day in my office."

"I don't believe you *now*, so what's the difference?"

"Yes you do," he said with absolute confidence. "Your eyes say it, the way you move says it."

"You should take a course in reading, then, because I *don't* love you and never will. I don't even *like* you."

"Yes you do, and if I had time now I'd take you upstairs and show you how very much you like me. But I don't have time. Luke and I—"

Kady had once thought that Gregory was vain, but this man won all prizes. "You aren't listening to me, are you? I don't want anything to do with you. Go spend the night with Luke or your macho Wendell or your anorexic Leonie for all I care. It doesn't concern me in the least."

"Kady, honey, you really don't mean that, and if I had time— *Ow!* Why'd you kick me?"

"Because I don't have a knife handy."

"You don't mean that," Tarik said, but from his tone she could tell that he was shocked.

"I mean every word of it. Go sleep in one of the brothels, that should suit you." With that she pushed past him and went up the stairs in search of the blue bedroom.

"Looks like she doesn't want to have anything to do with you," Luke said, chuckling, to his cousin when they were alone on the porch. He'd seen too many women make fools of themselves over his extraordinarily handsome and extraordinarily rich cousin.

"Who? Oh, you mean Kady. No, she's crazy about me."

"So we all heard. Seems to me she wants to stick an apple in your mouth and shove you in an oven."

"Naw, no problem. She's just upset because her last boyfriend was a real bastard. Has nothing to do with me."

"I thought I heard you sued her and you told some great, whopping lies."

Tarik waved his hand in dismissal. "You shouldn't listen at keyholes. Listen, I need your help with something. Is there anything you can do to get rid of Wendell for the night?"

"You mean like drug her beer, that sort of thing?"

"Can you do that?"

Luke shook his head in disbelief. "What's wrong with you? Most men adore Wendell."

"I don't, which is exactly why she wants me. And, no offense to your sister, but I don't have the stamina for her. So, tell me, how can I get rid of her, and are you willing to spend the night helping me?"

"Me? A boy like me?" Luke said with heavy sarcasm.

Tarik gave him a crooked grin. "You touch Kady again and I may make you prove your manhood."

Luke laughed. "Don't tell me you were telling Kady the *truth!* Hard-hearted Jordan couldn't have fallen in love with a pretty little *woman* like Kady? I thought you went in for piranhas like Leonie and my dear, cycle-straddling sister."

"Someday, when you grow up, I'm going to tell you the facts of life, but not yet. You want to help me or not?"

"Would it be too much to ask what you want me to do? Will it be interesting enough to lose a night's sleep over?"

"What if I told you I'd found a hole through time and if we go through it we can walk into the past?"

For a few moments Luke stared at him in speculation. The story was preposterous, but he had faith in his cousin. "Right now you could be upstairs conning your way into Kady's bed—I don't believe that story of your being married for a minute—yet you want to spend the night ghost hunting?" he asked softly.

Tarik just looked at him.

"If it's that important, then I have suddenly developed a case of insomnia."

"So what do we do with your sister?"

"Leave her to me. I learned a few things while I was in law school."

"I knew all that money I spent on your education would pay off."

"Actually, I learned this in a bar way downtown, and I can assure you that it had nothing whatever to do with law school."

"So what are you waiting for? Make sure Wendell doesn't follow us; then meet me by the Hanging Tree in one hour."

"Shouldn't you spend ten minutes or so with Kady?" Luke asked smugly, implying that was all the time his ancient cousin would need with a woman.

Tarik didn't smile but looked up at the window of the blue bedroom. "If I went back to that room, I'd never leave, not for days," he said with tears of regret in his voice.

"This must really be important," Luke said softly.

"It is. I'm preventing Kady from risking her life. Now, go on, do whatever you need to so you can meet me in one hour."

"Aye, aye, Captain."

Chapter 27

SO MUCH FOR LOVE, KADY SAID TO HERSELF AS SHE WANDERED along the old path winding up the mountain. What did it matter to her that Tarik, this man who said he loved her, hadn't come home all night? It wasn't as though they were actually married, not any more than she was actually married to Cole. After all, a person can't marry a ghost, can she?

As she strode up the path, she stopped now and then to pick herbs and wildflowers and put them into the basket she carried.

This morning, just as the sun was rising, Tarik had stumbled into "their" room and flopped onto the bed beside her. He was dirty, caked with mud, and there was the faint smell of manure about him, but he didn't remove his filthy clothes, just fell onto the bed. When Kady had awakened and looked at him, he'd said, "Hi, darlin'," then instantly fell asleep.

Getting out of bed, Kady glared at him. She should have left him where he was, as he was, but instead, she'd pulled off his shoes, then struggled to pull his denim jacket off. He'd wakened just enough to tell her she smelled good and he was very glad to see her, but then he'd fallen asleep again. So Kady covered him, then went downstairs to make breakfast.

Afterward she'd packed some lunches, and taking one herself, she'd headed up into the mountains, wanting time to get away and think about her life. Which, as far as she could tell, was a mess.

Tarik had told her that he loved her, but of course that was a lie. How could a person love another after they'd known each other only a few days? Even if all the books were full of such stories, it couldn't really happen, could it?

And what did she feel for him?

"Nothing," she said aloud as she looked up at the sky and saw the darkening clouds. She felt as much for him as he felt for her, which was exactly nothing.

After she'd solved the problem of Legend, and she had no idea when that was going to happen because this morning the rock still wouldn't open, she was going to get a job cooking somewhere and never see Tarik Jordan again. He'd go back to his Leonies and his Wendells, and she'd never see him again.

Now, as Kady looked around her, she thought how she was going to miss Legend. If Tarik was telling the truth—the truth about his lie, that is—then she didn't own Legend because she'd never owned his assets and therefore couldn't give the town to herself. After she left this time, she'd never see the place again.

The first cold drops of rain hit her in the face, and she knew she had to run for shelter. She'd come out without rain gear, and in the mountains, hypothermia was a danger.

Within minutes the rain started coming down harder, and she started running. Maybe she could find a rock overhang or—

She stopped her thoughts as she stood in the middle of the trail and looked ahead of her. Blinking, trying to clear her eyes, she couldn't believe what she was seeing. There seemed to be a cabin just ahead of her.

"Cole's cabin," she said in disbelief. The cabin she had stayed in with him, where he'd growled at her and teased her and made her laugh.

Ignoring the mud and puddles, she started running, and within minutes she had reached the cabin and the dryness of the porch. With her breath held, she put her hand on the door, hoping it wouldn't be locked, for the cabin was in excellent repair. Obviously, someone took good care of it.

The well-oiled hinges moved easily as the door opened, and Kady held her breath as she looked inside. It was quite beautiful, with curtains of red, green, and gold, Berber throw rugs, a couch of dark green corduroy, and a bed with a spread that matched the curtains. To find a cabin in the middle of nowhere that looked as though it had been done by a professional decorator was like entering a fantasy.

The huge stone fireplace looked just as it had when this was Cole's cabin, and it was laid for a fire. Shivering in her wet clothes, Kady put a match to the paper and kindling, and within minutes the big room glowed with warmth.

By the bed was a carved wooden chest, and she was reminded of the lidded box that Cole had and the clothes she'd found inside. When she opened this finely carved chest, she wasn't surprised to again find clothes and minutes later she had removed her wet garments and was in warm, dry sweatpants, a thick sweater, and big wool socks.

Smiling, feeling much better, she went to the corner of the room to look in the kitchen cabinets and found, hidden from view, a microwave and a food processor, which meant that someone had added electricity to the cabin.

"Luke," she said, thinking of the young man with his law degree. Thinking back on it, she realized that she had asked Luke nothing about himself, about how he came to be in Legend yet still managed to go to law school.

The cabin also had running water, and there was a door

near the bed that hadn't been there before, and when she opened it, she found, to her delight, a working bathroom.

Suddenly, the door burst open and a very wet and very angry Tarik burst in. "Just what the hell do you mean disappearing like that? No one knew where you were. From now on, you're *never* to leave my presence without telling someone where you are going."

Her first elation at seeing him was killed by his words. "Your 'presence'? As in His Royal Highness's *presence?*"

His dark features were drawn into a scowl and water was dripping off his nose onto his sweater. Kady had to force herself to stay where she was or she might have gone to him and thrown her arms about his waist.

Instead, she forced herself to turn away and look at the fire. "You've seen that I'm all right, so you can go now," she said softly. Behind her, she didn't hear a sound. He didn't move away from the doorway, didn't start to remove his wet clothing.

She kept her face turned away from his as long as she could; then she turned back to him. He was staring at her with an intensity that made goose bumps rise on her body. She could feel his look. Staring into his eyes, she saw the man she had seen hundreds of times in her dreams, the man she had searched for and daydreamed of. He was the man she had compared all other men to and found them wanting.

Now, just as in her dream, he held out his hand to her. He wasn't riding a horse, but he'd done that when he'd ridden out of the forest and rescued her from gunfire. The bottom half of his face wasn't veiled, but he had been that way the first time she had seen him. There wasn't an endless expanse of desert behind him, just a cabin door with rain pelting down outside.

But even though this was different from her dream, it was the same. He was the same man, with the same dark, intense eyes, and the same look that said he would take care of her forever, the look that he wore in her dream. And she knew she could trust him. Whatever petty arguments they had between them, in the end, she knew that he would guard her with his life.

She hesitated only a minute. In her dreams she had tried to get to him, tried to reach his outstretched hand, but had been unable to. Something had always held her back. But now there was nothing between them except her own stubborn temper.

She didn't take his hand. Instead, she ran to him, her arms wide, and fell against his chest as he held her tightly.

"Oh, Kady," he said, his mouth against her hair. "I love you so very much. You don't know how happy I am to see that you're not angry at me anymore. I'm sorry about the lawsuit, but my father set it up. I didn't even remember it. I'm sorry I lied to you about Ruth's codicil, but I was afraid you would send me packing if you didn't have a reason to stay with me."

"I would have," she said, her head against his wet clothes.

"And the marriage . . . That was just my dream. I wanted to live with a girl with a long dark braid. You don't have a spotted pony, do you?"

It was the same dream that Cole had, the one he had told her about in this very cabin.

Pulling away from her a bit, he lifted her chin so her eyes met his. "Do you forgive me for telling a few fibs? I just wanted to be near you and to make you love me."

At that last she turned away from him. Did she love him? She wasn't sure, but then she didn't seem to be sure about her feelings for any man. All the time she was with Cole she had told him and herself that she was in love with Gregory. Then she'd found out what Gregory was truly like and she'd begun to remember Cole as though he were a saint. But she could do that, couldn't she, since he was dead and had never reached adulthood.

"I don't know—" she began but he cut off her words with a soft kiss.

"You don't know whether or not you love me," he said, his eyes showing amusement. "I'm patient and I can wait for you to find out. It's just a matter of time."

He carried her to the bed then and began to slowly remove her clothing, all the while kissing the skin that he exposed.

"Kady, I . . ." he began, as though he had something very important to say to her, but then he lifted his head and looked into her eyes, and what she saw there was fiery hot. "The hell with finesse," he said with a bit of a grin, and the next minute her clothes went flying.

And Kady found that she was ignited in a frenzy of desire such as she'd never felt before. She tore at his sopping wet clothes, wanting her hands and mouth on his skin, wanting to taste and touch him, as he was doing to her.

His hands and mouth seemed to be everywhere at once, and when he was naked, he stretched out on the bed and pulled her on top of him, his mouth on her breasts, his hands on her hips, both of them frantic, excited, kissing, tasting.

When she could stand it no more, he pushed her to her back and entered her with a driving force. Kady arched her hips to meet him and nearly screamed aloud at his first touch. This was the man she had been waiting for, the man she'd wanted all her life.

Within seconds they had both reached a peak of ecstasy, and, limp, Tarik collapsed on her, holding her close to him. For a few moments Kady lay still, trying to catch her breath, but then he began kissing her neck and his hand strayed downward and they began again.

Kady sat on the floor, her back against the bed, and she could feel her heart pounding under her naked breasts. She knew she should get up and put some clothes on but she was too worn out, too satiated to think of moving. Actually, she was too happy to care about little things like clothes.

The room was a mess. At one point during the day, Tarik had thrown her across the dining table, and in his exuberance, he'd knocked ornaments and place mats to the floor. They had stopped making love long enough for her to make them something to eat; then they'd eaten off each other's bare bodies.

Now, when the bathroom door opened, she looked up at him and started to pull the bedspread that was on the floor under her up to cover her body.

"No," he said, grinning, and she smiled back. He was naked, and she had never seen a more beautiful body. He had broad shoulders, with a great mat of black hair on his chest, and he was muscular from years of learning how to handle hand weapons. In the last hours she had learned just how flexible and strong he really was. However, there were bruises over most of his body, and when Kady asked about them, he'd given his cocky grin and said, "Training."

Now, he sat on the floor beside her, pulling her head down to his shoulder. "Like to take a bath with me?"

"Very hot with bubbles?" she murmured.

"Very hot, lots of bubbles," he said as she stood and pulled the bedspread about her shoulders. "Put some clothes on, but not many," he said, grinning lasciviously.

Kady started to ask him why she had to put on clothes to go to the bathroom, but then she knew what was in his mind: Cole's hot spring, the place where she'd washed her hair in a time long past.

Thirty minutes later they were both up to their necks in a hot natural spring, the same one Kady had used before. But there were many changes now, as a natural-looking grotto had been built, with beautiful rock ledges and ferns hanging above them.

"Did you do this?" she asked, her head back, eyes closed. "Did you restore the cabin?"

"Yes," he said softly, watching her.

"Why? If Hannibal shoots at people for trespassing,

then—" She opened her eyes to look at him. "*Does* he usually shoot at people who come to Legend?"

Tarik gave her a one-sided grin. "Not usually."

Kady's first reaction was anger that she had discovered yet another of his lies. She thought of accusing him of forcing Hannibal to participate in Tarik's . . . Losing her anger, she closed her eyes and relaxed. In his pursuit of her, she thought, Tarik had made a great deal of effort to get near her, and it felt good. Thinking back to her relationship with Gregory, yes, it felt very, very good to have a man go to such lengths to win her.

"Kady," he said softly. "I want you to tell me everything. I want to know what happened between you and Ruth."

Looking at him, she sighed. "You'd never believe me. In fact, the more time passes, I don't know if I believe what happened myself."

"I'd like to hear, whether you believe it or not."

For a moment she hesitated. Yesterday she would never have considered telling him or anyone else what she'd been through, but today he was no longer a stranger. She knew his body as she'd never known anyone else's. And, if she was honest with herself, he had never been a stranger to her.

She took a deep breath. "On impulse I bought an old flour tin. I was going to put it in my new kitchen in the house I was going to live in with Gregory. Inside the tin was a wedding dress, a watch, and a photograph."

She talked for over an hour. After a while, without interrupting her, Tarik got out of the pool, then helped her out, dried her off, and they both dressed. It was growing dark as they walked back to the cabin, yet still Kady talked. He made no comment, but she could almost feel how closely he listened to her. It was as though he were listening with his soul.

Only once did he say anything and that was to ask a question. "Did you love him?"

"Cole?" she asked, knowing that was whom Tarik meant. "I don't know. I did in a way, but I guess I knew that it would never last between us, so I held back."

"You're good at holding back," he said under his breath, then asked her to go on with her story.

By the time they returned to the cabin, Kady had told him everything about the time she'd spent in Legend with Cole.

Tarik led her to the round oak table where a few hours before they had made love. "You don't believe me," she said as she sat on the chair he pulled out for her.

"I believe every word you've said," he answered. "Now, what do you want on your omelet?"

"It's what a person wants *in* an omelet, not *on* it," she said, unconvinced that he believed her. Who could believe a story like hers? "Here, let me do that," she said as she started for the kitchen counter.

"Kady, my love," he said as he put his hands on her shoulders and ushered her back to the table. "I did not fall in love with you because I need a cook. You're my guest, and I'll take care of you. I might not be able to turn out a meal like yours, but I can certainly make an omelet."

Kady smiled up at him. No one anywhere, ever, volunteered to cook for her. Except Cole. Except Tarik. "Everything," she said. "I want everything you've got on the omelet, and in it. Drag it through the garden."

"One muddy omelet, comin' up," he said, turning back to the stove. "Now tell me about . . ." He hesitated as though the word were difficult for him. "About Gregory."

Kady laughed. "Not until I hear about Leonie and Wendell and all the others."

Turning, he gave her a grin that almost took her breath away. "There are so many women in my past that it's going to take the rest of my life to tell you about all of them. I think that for now we better stick to your men. There are fewer of them."

"Ha ha. There happen to be many men in my life."

"Give me their names so I may slay them."

She laughed as she looked at the back of him, and it suddenly occurred to her that at this moment, for the first time in her life, she was happy. All her life she seemed to have been searching for something, but she'd never known what it was. She'd never been content with what she was doing. When she'd been chef at Onions she had dreamed of being married to Gregory and having children. When she was in old Legend, she had wanted to be elsewhere. Then when she'd returned to her real life, everything she'd found there had made her want to get away from it.

But now she was where she should be and doing what she should be doing with the man she was supposed to be with.

"Want to share that with me?" Tarik asked softly as he watched her.

"Did you ever want to crystallize a moment? Did you ever say to yourself, 'I want right now to last forever'?"

He put down his chopping knife and knelt before her, taking her hands in his. "Ever since I first saw you in my office I've felt that way."

"Ha! You were with another woman when I went to your apartment. And before that you were rude and nasty and—"

"I didn't say I *liked* the feeling," he said, eyes twinkling. "I knew from the first moment I looked into your eyes that I was seeing the end of my freedom. No more wild parties. No more supermodels. No more—"

"All I hear is what a private man you are. In fact, people don't even know your *name*. You can't have privacy and still have parties and zillions of women."

Smiling, he went back to his chopping board. "Did anyone ever tell you that women with brains are annoying?"

"Gregory did."

"I bet he did. I imagine that at one time he thought he'd found his dream woman, someone who would cook and keep her mouth shut. I bet you shocked him when you told him you were never coming back, didn't you?"

Standing behind him, she smiled, for she knew that he was asking her a question. He wanted assurance that she had indeed left Gregory. "You're right. He couldn't believe it." She paused for a moment. "I guess Leonie was a bit angry when you dumped her."

Turning, he gave her a look of puzzlement. "I didn't know ladies knew such words. She used some I'd never heard before."

Kady was laughing as he set an enormous steaming omelet in front of her; then he put his chair near hers and they ate from the same plate, sipping white wine from the same glass.

"I want to know about you," she said softly, peering at him over the wineglass. "I've told you all there is to know about me, but I know nothing about you. What exactly does that company of yours do?"

"Makes money. We Jordans are good at making money. We're bad at personal relationships, but then maybe that's the curse that was put on us by the people of Legend for what they believed Ruth did to them. Or maybe it's my great-great-grandfather, Ruth's youngest son, who cursed all of us. Or, possibly, it's my own fault, but I think that's highly unlikely."

For just a moment Kady saw beneath the laughing, self-confident, cocky grin and saw the loneliness in his eyes. She also saw pain. Mr. Fowler had told her that C. T. Jordan was thirty-four years old but had never been married and now she wondered why.

"Were you really going to marry that Leonie? Just to have children?"

"Yes. I really was, because, you see, I had given up hope of finding you."

She started to ask him what he meant by that, but, actually, she knew. Putting her hand over his, she looked into his eyes. "I have to return, you know that, don't you? As soon as the rock opens again, I have to go back to Legend."

Instantly, his eyes blazed anger. "And what can you do there? Can you change what has already happened? Do you want to bring your saintly Cole back to life so you can go back to him?"

"No, of course not. I just want to do whatever I can to . . . to . . ."

Standing, he glared down at her. "You have no idea what you want to do, or even what you'll be able to. The only way to prevent the tragedy of Legend is for you to prevent Cole from getting shot. And how are you going to do that? By placing your body in front of his?"

She hadn't really thought that far ahead. "I don't know what I can do. Maybe I can find Ruth before the bank robbery happens and warn her."

"And how are you going to get past the Jordan Line?"

She looked up at him blankly, not understanding him. There was an open road between the wall that was the Jordan Line. All she had to do was walk down the road.

Tarik went on his knees in front of her and held her hands; his eyes were pleading. "The Jordan Line is a stone wall that separates the town, the clean, pure, untouchable Jordans on one side, the riffraff on the other. Did Ruth tell you that the wall is patrolled by armed guards twenty-four hours a day? Did she tell you that any outsiders who try to get near the ivory-towered Jordans are shot at? Strangers can't just go up to the royal Jordans and talk to them."

"Why do you say 'is' and 'are'? Don't you mean 'was'?"

Standing, Tarik moved away from her to go to the fireplace. "Of course I do," he said softly. "You said that you were afraid to tell anyone your story because no one would believe it, but I do, and I can see the danger of it. You cannot go back, Kady. Even if the door in the rock opens, you cannot go back."

"I must," she said simply.

"No!" he shouted, his fist coming down on the mantelpiece. "I cannot allow it."

Perhaps she should have taken offense at his words, but she didn't, for she saw the concern for her in his eyes, and she wanted to calm him. "I don't think I'll be given a choice, since every time I look, the door is closed."

At that he smiled at her, a warm, friendly smile, and he moved to put his arms around her. "Good, I hope it stays closed forever." Pulling away, he looked into her eyes. "Will you marry me, Kady?" he asked softly.

She hesitated. This was what she wanted, wasn't it? But something held her back. Maybe it was that there had been three men in her life in the last few months and she was a bit confused about them.

When she opened her mouth to speak, he stopped it with a kiss. "The offer will always be open," he said, "so take your time. Take all the time you need."

At that she hugged him about the waist and held him tightly to her.

"Come on," he said companionably, "let's go to bed and get some sleep."

"Oh?" she said, eyebrows raised.

"If you can sleep while in the same bed with me, so can I," he said as though it were a challenge.

And two hours later, after more lovemaking, Kady did fall asleep in his arms.

But when she awoke the next morning, Tarik was gone. Thinking that he had gone outside, she dressed and went out, but search as she might, she could not find him. By the early afternoon she gave up hoping that he was going to appear on his horse with some reasonable excuse as to why he had left her alone, so she started down the mountain.

By the time she reached Legend she had decided that she hated all men everywhere, especially men named Jordan, who constantly disappeared without a word of explanation.

Had it been a game with him, just to see if he could get her into bed, then after he did, he left her? For all she knew a helicopter had picked him up and he'd returned to New York. After all, there was nothing to hold him in Legend, since Kady owned nothing and never had.

There was no one around when she entered the town, and she was glad of that because she had decided to pack her bags and leave. Tarik had been right, she thought, as she stormed up the stairs of the Jordan house and grabbed her suitcase. What could she do if she did return to Legend? And, besides that, why did she want to? What did the Jordans mean to her? A few months ago she had never heard of them, and—

She paused in her packing, a garment in her hand, as Luke staggered into her room—the room she was going to share with a man she now never wanted to see again. Kady was so angry that it took her a moment to actually see Luke; then disbelief kept her from moving as she stared at him.

His shirt was dirty and torn, and there was blood on his side. There was another bloody place on his head, a raw, red mark around his neck, and he was panting for breath.

Kady ran the few feet to get to him, then put her arms around his chest to help him to sit down on the side of the bed. When he seemed beyond being able to sit up, she gently pushed him back onto the bed.

"What's happened?" she asked in fear. "Did a mine collapse? Is Hannibal trapped? What about . . ." Her eyes widened in fear. "Tarik?" she whispered, all animosity forgotten. When she saw Luke's look, she knew that that's what he'd come to tell her. Standing, she looked down at him. "There's been an accident, hasn't there? Is there a telephone here? Can I call for help? How do I—?"

"No," Luke managed to rasp out. "There wasn't an accident. Tarik and I—" Pausing, he put his hand to his throat, then motioned to a carafe of water on a bureau.

With trembling hands, Kady poured a glass of water and handed it to him. She tried to concentrate on how to care for Luke's wounds because she could not bear to think that the look on his face might mean that Tarik was not alive.

It seemed an eternity before Luke finished drinking and handed her the glass. "We went through the door," he rasped out, then put his hand to his throat. "Forgive me, but hanging plays hell with a man's throat."

At that Kady sat down on the bed and looked at him. "Did they hang him?" she managed to get out.

"They hadn't yet when I left, but I don't know how much time he has left." He looked at her. "They may have shot him."

At that Kady thought she was going to faint, and she must have looked like it, for Luke grabbed her shoulders to keep her from falling. "Why? How? How much time?" she whispered.

"Tomorrow at dawn, but who knows how much time that is in that place?"

Suddenly, Kady's head cleared, and she started for the door. But Luke caught her before she reached the stairs. "Where—?" he managed to rasp out.

"I'm going to go get him, of course."

"He said no, that you weren't to go after him." There were tears of pain in Luke's eyes as these words hurt his throat so much, and Kady saw that his energy was draining fast.

Before she went back to Legend—if she could get through the doorway, that is—she ought to know what had happened and what she would be walking into.

Gently, she led Luke back into the bedroom, then went to the bathroom to get a pan of hot water and a clean cloth. While she cleaned the wound on his head, she managed to get most of the story out of him.

It seemed that on the day he and Kady had arrived in Legend, Tarik had seen that the door opened for him but not for Kady, so that night he had asked Luke to go with him. When the two men got there, they discovered that it was the day before the shooting of Cole and his family was to happen.

Kady listened while Luke haltingly told her how he and Tarik had tried their best to warn the Jordan family that they must stay away from the bank the next day.

"But they wouldn't listen to us," Luke said. "We tried everything. Tarik got into a bloody fight with some men at the Jordan Line."

At this she halted in washing Luke. "With a knife?"

"A knife and an army sword that was hanging on a wall, and with his fists."

No wonder he fell into bed beside her the next morning and went to sleep immediately, she thought. He should have been taken to a hospital and X-rayed.

"So what happened last night?" she asked as she began to wash the cut on Luke's side. His shirt was hanging in rags, so she easily tore it away.

"Tarik said that since he couldn't stop the Jordans, he could stop the bank robbers, so we waited in the bank all day."

Kady could almost imagine what Luke was going to say next.

"We were strangers in town, and they . . ." He put his hand to his throat, his eyes shut in pain.

"They thought you were in cahoots with the robbers," she finished for him.

Luke's eyes widened. "Yes. They thought we were scouts for the thieves. They laughed at me when I said we had saved the whole Jordan family from death and that, actually, we'd saved the whole damned town. They said—"

"Ssssh," she said. "You don't have to talk anymore. Just rest."

"No," he said, "I have to go back. They were going to

lynch us, but Tarik fought them all, and he held them off long enough for me to get back through the door. But they were shooting."

Kady would not allow herself to actually comprehend what he was saying. Right now she needed to keep her wits about her. "So you don't know if he is alive or not?"

"No," Luke said as he fell back on the bed. "I have to go to him."

"Yes, of course you do. But right now I want you to rest while I pack some food for you to take back with you. And I want you to take a couple of aspirin. Will you do that for me?"

His eyes closed, he smiled and Kady could tell what he was thinking, that she was a silly female who only thought of food even in times of crisis.

But Kady had her own plans. Fifteen minutes later she had given Luke a couple of sleeping pills she had found in a kitchen cupboard, and now that he was sleeping soundly, she was ready to return to the old Legend. Wearing the clothes she'd returned in from her time with Cole, she left the room.

But even as she was going down the stairs, she felt helpless. How was she going to rescue Tarik from a hanging? None of the people of Legend would know her, so she'd have no influence over them. She couldn't very well ride a horse up to the jail, pull out a gun, and make them hand Tarik over to her. Could she?

Standing outside was Wendell, rigged out in black leather that fit as though it had been painted on her, and the words "fast transportation" rang through Kady's head.

"Can that thing climb mountains?" Kady asked, heading toward Wendell.

Wendell looked as though something distasteful had just been put under her nose. "Depends on who's driving it," she said smugly. "I guess you'd understand it as a stove being able to cook all by itself."

Kady resisted a sarcastic remark. "Then why do you

think Tarik said you just thought you could ride a motorcycle, but actually you didn't even know how to shift gears
properly?"

It took a moment for the tall redhead to recover herself
enough to speak. "Where is he?"

Kady smiled sweetly. "I was just going to see him."

"Get on," Wendell said, throwing a leg over the bike and
kick-starting it. She roared off toward the Hanging Tree
before Kady got her feet onto the rests.

Chapter 28

IT WASN'T UNTIL LATER THAT KADY REALIZED THAT WENDELL
was on a different motorcycle than the big Harley-
Davidson. This one had tires with two-inch deep rubber
teeth that clawed their way up the mountain as soon as
Kady said, "Petroglyphs," and it was all she could do to
hang on to the back of the bike as they went up.

In the turmoil of flying gravel she didn't have much time
to think, but when she did, all that went through her head
was, *What if the door isn't open?*

But when they reached the huge sheer wall of rock, there
it was, open before them, and through it she could see the
cemetery, with much fewer stones than the one in Ruth's
time had. And she could see that it was already past sunset.
Luke had said that Tarik was to be hanged at dawn. Was
that dawn tomorrow or the dawn of this day? Was he
already dead?

"Thanks a lot," she said to Wendell as she got off the
bike. "I appreciate it. I'll, *ah,* cook something nice for you
when I get back." She practically ran through the opening
and was instantly in Legend.

Then, to her horror, she realized that Wendell was

behind her, walking that big motorbike of hers and following Kady as she hurried toward the town. Stopping, she put her hands on her hips. "You cannot go with me! You must return to Legend."

"Looks to me like this is Legend," Wendell said, looking around her. "A little bit changed, but that's the graveyard. I've seen it all my life."

"I don't need this now," Kady said with her fists clenched at her sides as Wendell moved ahead of her. "I have something very important to do, and I don't need any interference."

With a raised eyebrow, Wendell looked back at Kady. "So what's going on with you, my brother, and my sexy cousin? And if you tell me that lie about you two being married, I'll do whatever I can to cause trouble. And trust me on this, I can cause a lot of trouble."

"Look, I really don't have time for this. You and I can have a cat fight later. I have to see that Tarik is alive and—" From the look of interest on Wendell's face she knew that was the wrong tack. "You *must* return. Just go back up that path and—"

"The only way I'm leaving is if someone carries me. Think you're big enough?"

"Not with two pack elephants," Kady said with her sweetest smile, then turned away and started walking quickly toward town while Wendell rolled her bike along beside her.

"Why wouldn't my cousin be alive?" Wendell asked.

Kady thought she might as well tell the truth, since she didn't have time to try to concoct some plausible lie. "He may have been hanged for bank robbery."

"I see."

Kady's lips tightened. "You can stop patronizing me, as I know very well that you see nothing."

"I see that you have no weapon and no backup army. Hell, you don't even have information, so how can you save anyone from anything?"

Kady began to walk faster.

"So what are you going to do? Cook something so wonderful that the bad guys hand Tarik over to you as a thank-you gift?"

"No, I'm going to trade you for him," she said with all the spite she could muster and could have kicked herself for ever asking this woman for a ride on her bike.

"That's not a bad idea," Wendell said softly.

Kady almost paused in walking as she looked at Wendell, who was staring straight ahead, her eyes wide. "You would certainly cause a distraction," she said, and Wendell smiled.

"Look, cookie, we ought to make a plan."

"All right, Spike, I am going to make one."

Wendell snorted in laughter and kept following Kady, the huge black motorcycle at her side, masses of red hair blowing about her. "Not that I have much use for women, but I could half like you."

"If that's a compliment, thanks. So here's the plan." Kady didn't bother with the preliminaries of asking Wendell her thoughts, nor did she bother informing her of what had led up to today. "I want you to hide. I want you to keep out of sight while I go into town and—"

"Like hell I will! I'll—"

"You'll have everyone looking at you!" Kady half yelled. "Which is what I want nearly as much as you do, but you're going to do it when I say you can."

At this Wendell almost smiled, and Kady took a deep breath. "I'm going into town alone and find out where Tarik is and what's going on. No one will pay any attention to *me.* You'll wait here, and I'll come back for you."

"Stay out of sight, huh?" Wendell asked with a little smirk as though to say that was an impossibility.

Looking at her in her skin-tight leathers, Kady shook her head. "In the real world, what do you do for a living?"

"Nothing. I married a rich old man, and he died three days after the wedding. Left everything to me." Wendell said this with a look of defiance, as though daring Kady to make a judgment.

"You must be a very lonely woman," Kady said, surprising Wendell so much the smirk left her handsome face.

But Wendell recovered herself quickly, then snorted. "Go on. I'll take a nap. I had a busy night."

Kady paused only long enough to watch Wendell roll her motorcycle under the shade of some cottonwood trees before she took off at a half run. As she knew from having seen the town with Ruth, this was Damnation Avenue, and to her left was the Jordan Line, which meant that she was illegally on the Jordan side. Would armed guards shoot her for trespassing?

To her right she passed the dirt road that led to the Jordan house, the place that she was staying in the twentieth century with Hannibal. For a moment she hesitated as she got her bearings. The town was so different each time she saw it that it was difficult to find her way around, and now the fading light was making it nearly impossible. Past the road to the Jordan house was what Cole had called the library. In his dreamworld it had been big and beautiful, but in truth it was just a small, simple board building that needed a coat of paint. Further ahead she could see the church that was half the size it had been in Cole's town.

Between the library and the church, the road turned left and there was a huge circle that could be used to turn the largest wagons, so there would be no excuse for anyone coming onto Jordan land. Beyond the stone wall that kept out the riffraff was the town of Legend, and even at this distance Kady could see the reason for the wall. Was there anything in Legend besides saloons? As far as she could see there were nothing but garish signs advertising gambling and girls: French girls, pretty girls, wild women. On and on the signs went.

"No wonder Ruth hated the place," Kady whispered before she turned and started down the street, thinking that maybe she should have strapped on a pair of six-shooters and—

She halted as she heard the unmistakable sound of steel against steel, like the sound she'd heard in a hundred swashbuckler movies. "Tarik!" she said under her breath, then stayed still and listened. When she heard the sound again, she didn't hesitate but picked up her skirts and began running through the grass and weeds toward the back of the library.

When she reached the sound, she paused in horror for a few seconds before leaping. Tarik was being held by a man who had his arm around Tarik's throat, a huge curved-blade sword ready to remove his head. As Wendell had pointed out, Kady had no weapon, so she grabbed a rock from the ground and jumped onto the back of the man, bringing the rock down on his head, and he crumpled instantly.

"What the——?" Tarik said when the man suddenly released him.

"Are you all right?" Kady asked as she threw her arms around Tarik's waist. "Did he hurt you? Are they going to hang you? Luke got away, and he wanted to come back for you, but——"

She broke off because she could feel Tarik chuckling. *Chuckling.* As in *laughter.*

Slowly, she pulled away from him and looked up at his face, which was full of mirth. "I do beg your pardon," she said stiffly, then turned to walk away, but he caught her arm and held her.

"Kady, honey, *habibbi,*" he said, but he could hardly contain his amusement. "I'll explain everything in a minute, but first I think I better look after my grandfather."

As intriguing as this was, Kady still refused to look at him. For the last several hours she had been frantic about him, as had Luke, but here he was laughing as though he hadn't a care in the world. Truthfully, she never wanted to see him again, so when he released her arm to look at the man on the ground, Kady kept walking. She'd go back to Hannibal's Legend and forget all about the whole incident. Better yet, she'd forget that the Jordans even existed.

"No you don't," Tarik said as he firmly put his arm around her shoulders and led her back to the man on the ground, who was beginning to rouse himself. "Are you all right?" Tarik asked, looking down at the man.

Kady didn't want to look at either man, as she was now sure that holding swords at each other's throats was one of those things that boys and men loved to do. But when the man looked up at her, she almost gasped, for he was an older version of Tarik, the same dark eyes, the same lips, the same look of sensuality that had always made Kady's knees weak.

Her first reaction was to go to the man and apologize for hitting him, but she held her ground. Instead of looking at him, she stared off into space, refusing to speak to either man.

"This is Kady?" the man asked in an accent she didn't recognize. "She has even more beauty than you told me of."

Tarik tightened his grip on Kady's shoulders. "And she is brave and honest and honorable and—"

"I am *not* going to forgive you," she hissed as she hit him in the ribs with her elbow, trying to make him release her. "Why didn't you let Luke know you were all right?"

While still holding her next to him, he smoothed her hair back from her forehead, then kissed it. "Sweetheart, Luke left here three days ago. If I had been hanged, it would have happened long before you came back to save me."

For the first time she looked up at him, and when she did, her anger left her. What did anger matter, as long as he was alive and unhurt? But still . . .

Reading the expression in her eyes, Tarik hugged her closer. "How about something to eat?"

"I'm not hungry, but I'm sure the people back in Legend are. I should go home and feed them."

The older man was on his feet now, and Kady could see a lump forming on the side of his forehead, and she felt guilty for it. Why hadn't she at least paused long enough to see the man's face before clobbering him?

"It is nothing," the man said as he bent to take her hand and kiss the air above it. "Such as I am not worthy to kiss one as beautiful as you."

Kady looked up at Tarik as though to ask, *Is this man for real?* but Tarik was scowling in a way that made her think he was jealous—which pleased Kady to no end. With a quick twist, she moved out of Tarik's grasp and linked her arm with the older man's. "You must be Gamal."

"I have that honor," he said as he slipped his hand over hers, and they started to walk away.

But Tarik caught her, and when he pulled her to the other side of him, Gamal politely excused himself with an amused expression. He knew when to leave lovers alone.

"You want to tell me why they didn't hang you?" Kady said as soon as they were alone. "And did you save Cole?" It was full dark now, and the night sounds surrounded them. Kady could barely see where she was going, but Tarik seemed to have the eyes of a cat, as he never faltered.

"Yes," he said, smiling. "I was able to prevent the robbery taking place, but it seems that the good citizens of Legend thought I was in on the attempt. They're a *greedy* lot. No wonder Ruth closed the whole town down."

"So how did you escape them?" She really shouldn't be talking to him, of course. If he'd had any concern for the feelings of others, he would have come back to tell them that he was all right.

"Gamal," Tarik said softly. "After Luke got away, the citizens were a tad angry. You know, in our time we have movies and TV showing hangings and murders, but here they have the real thing. People were packing picnic lunches to take with them to watch Luke and me hanged."

At the thought of how real it had been and how close he had come to losing his life, Kady tightened her hand on his arm, and at that, Tarik turned and pulled her into his arms, kissing her with a tenderness that made her forgive him everything. "So what did he do to save you? Hold them at sword point?"

"Told them I was a relative of his and I had been hired by the Jordans to protect the bank. All they had to do was look at the two of us and see that he was telling the truth about our kinship."

Hugging her, he put his cheek on top of her head. "I'm sorry that I caused you even a moment of worry. But when Luke didn't return right away with an army behind him, I figured there was some sort of time mix-up. I wanted to return to you immediately, but since I seem to have saved the lives of my ungrateful ancestors, I figure the rock will never be open again, and I wanted to take this opportunity to . . . well, to look around. And to get to know my great-great-great-grandfather."

With her arms around him, she snuggled her head on his chest, hearing his heart beat, feeling the warmth of him. Feeling the *life* of him. "Does he know where you come from?"

"No. So far I haven't told him anything, but he's quite clever, so I think he's figured out some of it. But he doesn't pry."

"What about the rest of your family? Have you seen them?"

"Only in passing. They keep to themselves. As far as I can tell, they don't bother with events as insignificant as hangings." He said this last with bitterness in his voice.

With his hands on her shoulders, he held her away from him. "Kady, my love, are you hungry? My father—that's what I call him—is cooking something over a campfire."

"Oh?" she said in a way that made him laugh.

"Maybe you could learn something," he said, egging her on. "*He* doesn't have copper pans and a gas-fired stove. All he has is a few sticks and a couple of cast-iron pots and—"

"Are you saying that *I* couldn't cook over a campfire?"

she said, glaring up at him, then realized that he was teasing her. "I'll get you for that," she said under her breath as they approached the campfire, and when she saw a whole lamb skewered on a wrought-iron spit, she forgot all about Tarik's teasing.

"Roast lamb," she said, then looked at an enameled plate by the fire. "And kebabs and . . . is that baba ghanouj?" When Gamal handed her a piece of meat pulled from the lamb, she said, *"Ooooh,* what did you marinate this meat in? No, don't tell me. It's—"

Tarik laughed. "I thought you came here to rescue me, not exchange recipes."

"I should have let them hang you."

"You would have missed me. Who would brighten up your life if I weren't around?" He looked at Gamal. "She's beautiful, isn't she?"

"Yes, very. And she can cook?"

"Divinely."

"So how many children have you given her?"

"None. Yet."

"Ah, that is what happens when you dilute Arabian blood. You get men who are not men."

At that both Kady and Tarik laughed. It was such an old-fashioned attitude to judge a man by how many children he could make.

For a moment Gamal was silent as he watched them; then he turned to Tarik. "You say you are my son, but I have been wondering who your mother is."

Before Tarik could answer, Kady, with her eyes wide, said, "It's true then. There are lots of women who could possibly be the mother of your children."

Gamal was heaping plates with food for them. When he smiled, his eyes crinkled at the corners.

"Ruth Jordan," Tarik said after a moment.

"But I have never—" Gamal said, then smiled. "But I have wanted to. She is a beautiful woman, but if you are her son, then you are not my son."

Tarik took the plate held out to him. "Actually, I'm not your son, I'm your great-great-great-grandson, and if you don't do anything with Ruth, I may cease to exist."

"I see," Gamal said, amused. "You are a storyteller. A weaver of dreams."

"Oh, yes," Kady said. "He's a regular Scheherazade. You should hear the whopper he told me about a codicil to Ruth's will." Her lightheartedness was to cover how Tarik's words were upsetting her, as it was something she'd never thought of before. If Tarik had prevented the tragedy of the Jordan family, how was that going to change the twentieth-century Jordans? If Ruth wasn't widowed and if she didn't go to bed with Gamal and give birth to a child when she was in her forties, how would that affect Tarik in the twentieth century?

Tarik was looking at her as though reading her mind. "I think someone who lives in Legend now should know all the story because some things need to happen *this year*," she said pointedly.

Tarik looked at Gamal over his plate. "Do you think I could persuade you to seduce Ruth Jordan?"

"That depends."

"On what?"

"On how much I must pay you. I am a poor man."

While the two men laughed together in conspiracy, Kady looked up at Tarik and said, "He's your grandfather all right."

As they ate, Tarik started to tell the whole story, from the beginning, and Kady marveled that he remembered every word she had told him. And, to give him credit, he didn't leave anything out about her relationship with Cole. Gamal ground coffee beans and brewed coffee with the grounds in it. Very strong. Very delicious.

As Gamal's capacity for listening seemed to be limitless, Tarik's story continued after the coffee was finished. When Kady yawned, Tarik pulled her down so her head was on his lap, Gamal spread an old blanket over her and she slept.

As she dozed by firelight, hearing two deep voices of men, so alike, made her feel good. At one point Tarik was asking Gamal all about his relatives and his ancestors, as they were also Tarik's relatives. Smiling, she turned over, her face away from the fire, fitting snugly against Tarik's hard warm belly while he stroked her hair behind her ear and ran his hands over her back.

Once again she had that feeling of being where she should be, and she realized with a smile that the date and the place didn't matter. If you were with the right person, you were in the right place.

"I love you," she whispered, so softly she almost couldn't hear herself. But Tarik heard, because he paused for just a second in caressing her hair, and under her cheek she could feel the muscles of his stomach tense then release. But he gave no sign that Gamal could have seen, and she smiled at that. Discipline, she thought and closed her eyes. Over the years he had disciplined himself to keep his true feelings hidden. Smiling, she let herself drift into sleep.

Chapter 29

WHILE KADY SLEPT, TARIK AND GAMAL TALKED ALL NIGHT, and only when it was dawn did Kady awaken, sit up and stretch. And when she finished yawning, she turned to see Tarik looking at her with eyes so hot that her clothes suddenly felt too tight.

Perhaps Gamal saw it, too, for he quietly excused himself, and the minute they were alone, Tarik pulled Kady into his arms and kissed her.

When he pulled away, he looked into her eyes with such love that Kady wondered at it. No man had ever looked at her like this before, but then, maybe his eyes were a reflection of her own.

"You risked your life to protect me," she whispered.

"Of course. What else could I have done?"

"Gone back to work and left me on my own."

"And lose a woman like you? One who'd give up millions because she didn't believe it was rightfully hers?"

"Speaking of all that money of yours, let's get married in a community property state."

He laughed. "Oh? So you do want to marry me?"

She just kissed his neck in answer.

But he pulled her away to look at her, his face serious. "Kady, are you sure? What about your Cole? What about Gregory?"

"I'm sure," she said. "I don't think I ever loved Gregory. I was just afraid I'd never get anyone else. As for Cole . . ."

His hands tightened on her shoulders. "What about him?"

She started to make a smart remark, but his eyes were too intense. "Cole could have loved any of a hundred women and they would have loved him in return. But you make me feel as though I'm the only person you could love. I think you might share things with me that you share with no other person on earth."

Slowly, he began to smile. "Yes, you make me feel like that, as though I have known you forever and that you are part of me." Still smiling, he pulled back to look at her. "I'm not the easiest person in the world to live with."

"Really? And here I thought you were. You're so even-tempered, so easy to get to know, so—"

"Okay, so I have a few rough edges."

"I'll whittle them down, sort of like carving something beautiful out of an onion."

Laughing, he kissed her again, then broke off with a great yawn. "I think I *must* go to bed. You wouldn't like to join me, would you?"

"*Mmmm,*" she said as though she were considering the matter "I might—"

"What the hell is that?" he asked, lifting his head and listening.

"I don't hear anything."

"It sounds like a motor. A two-cylinder motor actually."

Kady glanced around them at the Jordan house in the distance, the outbuildings and barn. They were new, since they were in 1873. "We haven't been transported again, have we?" she asked, half in jest; then suddenly, her eyes grew wide. "Wendell," she whispered.

Instantly, Tarik was alert. "What about her?"

"I, ah, I forgot about her."

Tarik grabbed her shoulders. "What do you mean you forgot about her? You don't mean that Wendell is *here*, do you? Please tell me that you don't mean that."

"Welllllll," she said, taking a step backward.

"With her motorcycle?" Tarik asked, eyes ablaze.

Kady put her hands on her hips. "I was in a hurry, and she gave me a ride up the mountain, and she rode through the doorway behind me. Was I supposed to stop all six feet of her? Maybe *you* can deal with women like her but the only thing *I* could do short of roasting her is to tell her to wait for me. Which she did, but I forgot about her, and have you ever slept with her, your own *cousin*?"

For a moment Tarik blinked at Kady in consternation, doing his best to understand her logic but gave up after about three seconds. "Stay here," he ordered. "Do not leave this place. Do you understand me?"

When he turned back toward the stables, Kady followed him, having to run to keep up with him. "What are you going to do? Maybe you shouldn't call attention to yourself, because they might reconsider hanging you. Maybe I should go instead and—"

At that Tarik halted and turned toward her. "Are you about to say that maybe I should stay here and wait while *you* go into a place where men wear guns strapped to their hips? Maybe I should allow *you* to try to calm down my large, enraged cousin?" He seemed to think this was a rhetorical question, because he started walking before she could reply.

"How do you know she's enraged?" Kady asked, running beside him. She was really feeling quite guilty for having forgotten Wendell.

"My cousin is always enraged. She was born that way." As he reached the stables, he glanced at her. "How could you have forgotten Wendell? That's like a general forgetting that he brought an army with him."

"Or a circus owner forgetting his wild animals," she

muttered as Tarik began throwing a saddle on a huge, eye-rolling black horse. Wisely, she didn't enter the stall with him.

"How long have you been riding horses?" she asked.

"Don't change the subject. I want you to wait here, and don't get into any trouble while I'm gone. When I return with Wendell, we'll all go back to Legend." He paused in saddling. "You didn't bring Luke and Uncle Hannibal, too, did you?"

"No," she said with a sweet smile. "I drugged Luke and left Uncle Hannibal meals in the refrigerator. I doubt if he'll know we're gone."

"Good," Tarik said as he swung onto the horse; then he looked down at her, his face stern. "I've been riding all my life. Kady," he said, "don't leave here, please. I'll be back as soon as I can, but Wendell is not easy to handle." The horse danced around a bit, and it took him a few moments to get it under control. "Oh, and I've never slept with Wendell," he said, then was off, heading toward Legend, where even Kady could now hear the roar of Wendell's motorcycle.

The instant he rode past the Jordan Line, Kady turned to look at the horses in the stables.

"Looking for something to ride?"

She was startled as a voice came from behind her. Turning, she saw Gamal standing in the shadows, his strong arms folded over his chest. Kady's first thought was that he'd heard Tarik's orders and he'd report on her to him.

"I don't know how to ride," she said innocently, "and I was just looking at the animals anyway."

Gamal smiled at her, and she knew she was seeing what Tarik would look like at his age. Not bad, she thought. "Then I am to believe that you are the only woman in the world who does what she is told?"

Kady grinned at him. "So which horse should I take? I

can't let him go alone. Heaven only knows what will happen to him in that town."

"Is this Wendell very beautiful?"

"A knockout."

Gamal may never have heard the term before, but he understood its meaning. "Then may I suggest that we ride together? My horse is saddled and ready."

Moments later she was mounted behind Gamal. "If you hold me very tight, I think it will make young Tarik very jealous."

"Oh?" she said, laughing. "Like this?" She tightened her arms about him, which made her breasts press into his back.

"Yes, exactly like that," he said, smiling, and the next minute they were heading down the road.

Chapter 30

BUT KADY NEVER MADE IT TO THE CENTER OF TOWN, WHERE, judging by the sound of it, Wendell was giving a demonstration on what a twentieth-century motorcycle could do. Instead, she asked Gamal to let her off his horse when she saw two little boys walking toward the cemetery, fishing poles over their shoulders.

"Here!" Kady said rather fiercely. "I want down here."

Instantly, Gamal halted his horse; then, turning, a smile on his handsome face, he held his arm rigid as Kady used it to swing herself down. The boys had paused in the road, staring up at the two people on the horse. Gamal said something in Arabic to the dark boy, who was unmistakably his son; then, after a polite nod and smile to Kady, he rode away.

For a moment Kady stood on the opposite side of the road from the boys, and the three of them just looked at each other. Young Tarik looked from his friend, a nine-year-old Cole, then to Kady and back again, for Cole and Kady were staring at each other with great intensity.

A man on a horse rode between them, looking at Kady with a grin of invitation, but when she ignored him, he shrugged and rode away. And when he was gone, Kady crossed the street, her eyes on the blond boy, who stood in frozen silence next to his dark-haired friend.

At nine years old, Cole was a tall boy, showing signs of the man he would grow into, and his big blue eyes and sun-streaked blond hair already told how devastatingly handsome he was going to be.

For a moment, Kady just stared down at the boy, although he was nearly as tall as she was. He was going to live, she thought. Thanks to what Tarik had done, Cole and all his family were going to live. And Cole was going to be able to build his fine house and do what he could to help the town of Legend.

"Hello," she said at last, her eyes on Cole, but he just stared at her as though he'd never seen a woman before. "Going fishing?" she asked.

Cole kept staring at her in silence, so Tarik answered. "Why were you riding with my father?"

Kady turned to look at him and saw that he was very much like his father. Her Tarik was lighter skinned and maybe his features weren't as round as this boy's, but it was easy to see that they were related. "I'm here with a relative of yours. His name is Tarik, too."

The boy narrowed his eyes suspiciously. "We have no relatives in this country. My father and I are alone."

"You're the most beautiful woman I have ever seen," Cole said, at last breaking his silence, and Kady turned to him with a smile.

"Who are you? Who do you work for?" Cole asked.

"Work for?" she asked, then paused. "Oh, I see," she said, knowing he was referring to the houses of prostitution that were so numerous below the Jordan Line. How awful that he would assume that any strange woman worked in one of the houses. "I don't work for anyone. I'm a cook." It was silly to think that he would remember something that had never really happened, but part of her hoped that—

"You didn't cook for me," Cole said, his lower lip jutting out in a way that she had seen him do as an adult.

"I did too," she said, laughing. "I cooked you a rat."

At that Cole went into paroxysms of laughter, and Kady laughed with him, while Tarik stood by in silence, staring at them as though they were crazy.

On impulse, Kady hugged Cole to her, and at that moment all indecision left her. Until then she'd wondered if maybe her love for Cole would interfere with her love for Tarik. If she had a chance, would she have gone back to Cole? But the knowledge that he was just a boy had always been with her. Even when she'd been part of his dream and he'd been an adult, there had been something not-quite-adult about him.

Kady pulled away from Cole and held him at arm's length. In the distance, the motorcycle noise had abruptly stopped, and she knew that soon Tarik would be coming for her. "Listen to me," she said, looking into Cole's eyes. "I don't have much time, and I need to tell you some things. You have a responsibility to take care of this town. Do you understand me?"

Serious, his eyes wide, Cole nodded.

"You own Legend, and you must take care of it, no matter what. These people look up to you, their very lives depend on you. Never allow anything or anyone to stop you from taking care of these people. Do you promise me? Word of honor?"

Again Cole nodded.

"What else?" Kady said aloud, searching her mind. Why hadn't she prepared for this meeting? To her left she could hear the thundering of horses' hooves, and she knew without a doubt that it was Tarik coming to take her back to her own time.

"Be happy," she said quickly. "You deserve it, and take care of your family, and say hello to your grandmother Ruth for me, and . . ." Turning, she looked down the road and blinked at what she saw. Tarik was riding toward her, and thrown across the front of his saddle was the unmistakable body of Wendell. And from the way she was hanging there, she was unconscious—if not dead.

"I have to go," Kady said, moving toward Tarik. Even at this distance she could see that he was furious.

"Cole, marry a woman who can cook and . . . and put on a feast. The biggest feast Colorado has ever known. And build Tarik and his father a mosque and—"

She broke off as she ran back and hugged Cole again, and she could feel him clinging to her. "I hope I have a son just like you," she whispered, then kissed his cheek, and when she looked into his eyes, she remembered Mr. Fowler telling her that the mines were nearly played out. "If you need money," she said with her eyes boring into his, "search for the old man's face."

When he nodded as though he understood, she released him, then, and on impulse, she hugged Tarik, too. "Be nice to Ruth," she whispered to him. "She'd make your father a wonderful wife." Then she kissed him, too, released him, and began to run toward the horse that was rapidly approaching.

When Tarik reached her, he hardly slowed the horse, but leaned far down, his hand extended toward her. Kady caught it, put her foot into the stirrup, and swung herself upward behind him.

"Your grandfather's son," she said into Tarik's ear as she put her arms around his waist and nodded toward the two boys standing beside the road, both of them staring in open-mouthed wonder. Tarik only glanced at the boys as he kicked the horse forward.

As they rode away, Kady twisted about so she could see the boys, and raising one hand, she kissed her fingertips and sent the kiss to them. "I love you," she shouted back but wasn't sure they heard her, but she continued waving until the road bent and she could no longer see them

Tightening her arms about Tarik's waist, she pressed her head against his back and held on as he led the horse past the cemetery down the road that led to the Hanging Tree. She wanted to ask him about Wendell, sprawled across the front of the horse, still apparently unconscious, but they were traveling too fast to talk.

By the time they reached the foot of the mountain, the horse was straining from the weight of three people on its back, and halfway up, Tarik dismounted and began leading the animal, traveling as fast as he could.

"Is she all right?" Kady asked, a bit concerned because Wendell still hadn't stirred. The big woman was now belly down in the saddle, which had to be an improvement over having the pommel in her stomach, and Kady was straddling the horse's rump.

"Fine," Tarik said tersely as he pulled the reins to make the horse go over some loose rock.

"Did she have an accident?"

"Yeah, she met the end of my fist," Tarik said, his jaw rigid.

"Oh," Kady said, then looked at him with a grimace. "Are you going to make me tear every word out of you? What happened?!"

"Wendell wanted to stay, that's what. She likes a time period when men wear six-shooters on their hips. She said that they were real men as opposed to stockbrokers and bankers, who weren't real at all."

"So you hit her," Kady said softly.

"Don't you give me a look like that!" Tarik snapped. "Knocking her out was the only way I knew to get her to return. As I know from past experience, she never listens to reason, so it was no use trying to talk to her, so I did what I had to."

Kady wouldn't have thought that anything could make her have sympathy for Wendell, but now she did. She knew too well what it was like to want to be somewhere you couldn't be.

When they reached the rocks with the petroglyphs, there was the opening back into the Legend of the twentieth century. Without pausing, Tarik led them, horse and all, through the opening, and they came out in exactly the place where they entered, except that it was a hundred years later.

Tarik helped Kady dismount, then pulled Wendell down from the saddle. She was waking up, and when she saw Tarik, she started struggling.

"Damn you!" she shouted. "I liked it there. I fit in with those people. I—"

"You don't belong there," Tarik said calmly, holding her firmly about the waist and moving his head to one side when she tried to claw his face. "You don't know what kind of damage you could do to history if you stayed. And there are diseases but no hospitals and—"

"Shut up," she screamed. "Just shut up." With that the energy seemed to leave Wendell's body, and she bent forward and began to cry.

Tarik released her, then went to the horse. Kady had been watching Wendell so intently that she hadn't noticed that the doorway into the past was still open, but Tarik had as he smacked the horse's rump and sent the animal back to its owner. "Are you two ready to go?"

Later, Kady didn't know why she did what she did, but she'd learned that that doorway had a mind of its own. When she was the one supposed to go through, it opened for her. But later, when Tarik was to go through, it only opened for him. Now they had returned, the horse had gone back to its own time period, and by all rights, the door should have closed. But instead it stood wide open, gaping, as though it wanted something else—or someone else, Kady thought.

Tarik had planted himself between the desolate Wendell and the doorway, and he was obviously waiting for both women to start down the mountain so he could follow. Kady could see that he wasn't going to so much as blink until Wendell was away from that open doorway.

Turning, Kady started down the path, but as she did so she passed Wendell and surreptitiously gave her hair a hearty tug. Kady had to give it to Wendell, because she didn't yelp and let Tarik know what Kady had done. Instead, Wendell looked up at Kady in question, and in the next second Kady took a tumble that sent her rolling down the path. As expected, Tarik came running after her, and when he caught her, they both looked up to see Wendell diving through the doorway. And the instant she was through, the doorway closed with a solid thunk.

Instantly, Tarik knew that Kady had helped Wendell escape, and he turned to her with a face ready to bawl her out. But when he saw Kady's look of defiance, he lost his anger and, instead, shook his head in exasperation. "Are you going to defy me at every opportunity?"

"Of course."

"Good," he said, then put his arms around her and kissed her. "Was it true?" he whispered. "Or did I imagine all of it?"

"I don't know. I think we should go see what Legend is like now to see if anything has changed."

"No, I don't mean that," he said softly. "I meant about us. Still want to marry me?"

"Yes, with all my heart."

"No second thoughts? Not even about . . . about . . ."

He didn't seem able to say the words, but she knew whom he meant. "About Cole?"

After kissing her, he nodded.

"I'm glad I saw him as a boy, as now that's the way I'll always remember him." With her arms about his neck, she put her head down on his shoulder. "I'm sure now. I'm sure that you're the man I want, the man I have loved for many years."

He didn't ask her what she meant by that, for he knew that he'd find out, because from now on they had a lifetime together. "Come, *habibbi*," he said. "Let's go home."

"Yes," she answered, then took his hand, and they started down the mountain together.

Epilogue

NEITHER SHE NOR TARIK WERE PREPARED FOR WHAT GREETED them in Legend as they walked through the trees. The falling down old houses had been repaired, and in place of the derelict town they had left the day before was a pretty little tourist town with restaurants and gift shops. Each of the buildings had been renovated in a style that was very like what it would have been in 1873. And, as far as they could tell, an attempt had been made to re-create Cole's dream town.

Hand in hand, she and Tarik walked into the town in silence, their eyes wide as they looked at all the things that had changed. The sign over what had once been a battered old building that only Cole could think of as a library said that it was now the Historical Society. The church had beautiful stained-glass windows in it, and the Jordan homestead was a museum. At the crossroads they could see three hotels that had been fabricated out of several buildings.

And everywhere there were tourists, mostly families with children, all of them shouting, "Come and see this. Look at this. Dad! You're not going to believe this!"

"It's a museum town," Kady said in wonder, looking at a reproduction general store, and next to was it a gambling saloon with a man outside who was wearing a satin vest.

"A fantasy museum," Tarik said in amusement, for this town was as much a fantasy as Cole's town had been. There were no streets lined with brothels, no drunken miners staggering about, no streets that were deep in mud and horse manure.

"I wonder if they would know in there what happened to Cole's family," Kady said, looking toward the Historical Society building.

"And I wonder what my financial situation is," Tarik said with such a frown that Kady laughed.

"If the history of the Jordans has changed so much, you may no longer be wealthy. Maybe you'll have to get a job like the rest of us."

Tarik did not laugh. "I think I'll make a few calls. I'll meet you back here in an hour." With that he gave her a quick kiss and headed toward the first hotel.

Kady immediately went to the old library building, but when she saw a sign that said there was a tour of the Jordan homestead every fifteen minutes, she went up the road toward the house.

When she met Tarik an hour later, she had much to tell him, that Cole had married a Miss Kathryn de Long, one of the greatest chefs of the nineteenth century, and she had put on a feast that was still talked about over a hundred years later.

As Kady sat down across from Tarik, at a table with a red and white checked cloth, she spread out the half a dozen booklets she had purchased about the Legend of today. "But these can wait," she said. "So tell me, are you still rich?"

He gave her a crooked grin. "*We* are doing quite well, thank you. What did you find out?"

"I'd rather hear what *you* found out. What happened to Wendell?"

"Uncle Hannibal still lives here. Seems he owns half the attractions and he's well liked by the people who work here. He has a son, Luke, who is an attorney in Denver and handles all the legal work for Legend." Tarik leaned toward her. "But he has no daughter, and never had one." He leaned back. "Your turn."

She told him of Kathryn de Long and her brilliant cooking. "And . . ." she said, drawing out her words to prolong the drama, "wait until I tell you about the rest of your Jordan family." She pushed a booklet toward him that bore the title of "Jordan" on the front cover. "There's a family tree in the back."

After a moment of reading, Tarik looked up at her. "Interesting."

"Yes, very. But—" Pausing, she turned to the family sitting at the next table. "Could you tell me if the Lost Maiden Mine has been found?"

"Not that I ever heard of," the man said, then looked at his wife. "What about you, hon?"

After the question had been asked of half the people in the little restaurant and all the staff, and everyone said that no it had not been found, Kady turned back to Tarik. "I think Cole found it," she whispered to him.

"What do you know about the Lost Maiden Mine that you haven't told me?"

"Before I went to Legend the first time, it was found by a rock formation that looked like an old man's face and—"

"What?!" Tarik nearly shouted, then calmed himself. "Why didn't you tell me this?"

"Don't you have enough money?" she asked in disgust.

Tarik ignored her question. "What do you think Uncle Hannibal was up here trying to find?"

"I have no idea. Was he looking for—"

She broke off, as Tarik was furiously flipping through the guidebooks, and he stopped at a page in one about the mines. Turning the booklet upside down, he shoved it toward her. There in the background of a photo of the

Amaryllis Mine (obviously renamed by Cole) was a rock formation that was shaped like an old man's face.

Tarik leaned back in his chair and drank deeply from the glass of water that had been set before him. "I assume you told Cole where to find the mine," he said, and Kady nodded.

"I told him that if he had trouble, he should look near that rock." She was waiting to see what Tarik would say to this. For all that she knew she loved him, she didn't know all the facets of his personality. Would he be angry that she'd had such a big secret and had given it to someone else?

But Tarik reached across the table and took Kady's hand. "I don't think all this would be here if it weren't for you. I don't mean just what you did to keep Ruth from shutting the place down, but the money also. Your Cole must have needed that money, and from what my people in New York told me and from what I see here, he used it wisely."

"Yes, I think he did. And I think he was happy. One of the books says that the name Legend comes from it being a place of legendary beauty. Better than the truth, don't you think?"

"Perhaps. But I like the truth better. Shall we get married in this town? It seems that I still own most of it."

She laughed. "Yes. Let's get married here."

"And what do you want for a wedding gift?" he asked with teasing eyes.

"A free hand with that kitchen and garden of yours in Connecticut and a couple of kids and a honeymoon in Paris with a trip to Dehillerin to buy copper pots and—"

Tarik was laughing. "Your wish is my command, *habibbi*. Now, what do you want for lunch?"

Obediently, she looked down at the menu, but she didn't see it. *Thank you, Ruth,* she thought. *Thank you and Cole and all the people of Legend. I wouldn't be where I am today if it weren't for you. Thank you.*

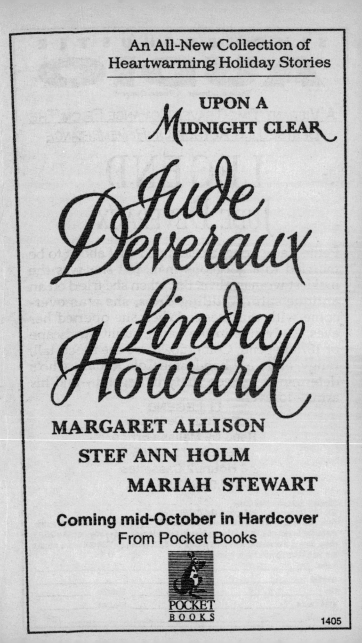

An All-New Collection of
Heartwarming Holiday Stories

UPON A
MIDNIGHT CLEAR

*Jude
Deveraux*

*Linda
Howard*

MARGARET ALLISON

STEF ANN HOLM

MARIAH STEWART

Coming mid-October in Hardcover
From Pocket Books

POCKET
BOOKS

1405

JUDE DEVERAUX

America's favorite historical romance author!

"Jude Deveraux always spins a gripping tale...
Plenty of passion —and the plot never slackens."
— ALA *Booklist*

⚜ The Falcon Saga ⚜

- [ ] THE TAMING.........................74383-X/$6.99
- [ ] THE CONQUEST....................64447-5/$6.99

◆◆◆◆◆◆◆◆◆

- [ ] WISHES...............................74385-6/$6.99
- [ ] A KNIGHT IN SHINING ARMOR...70509-1/$6.99
- [ ] SWEETBRIAR........................74382-1/$6.99
- [ ] ETERNITY............................74457-7/$6.99
- [ ] THE DUCHESS......................68972-X/$6.99
- [ ] SWEET LIAR.........................68974-6/$6.99
- [ ] A HOLIDAY OF LOVE.............50252-2/$6.99
- [ ] REMEMBRANCE...................74460-7/$6.99
- [ ] THE HEIRESS.......................74462-3/$6.99
- [ ] LEGEND..............................00170-1/$6.99
- [ ] A GIFT OF LOVE (A collection of romances from Jude Deveraux, Judith McNaught, Andrea Kane, Kimberly Cates, and Judith O'Brien)....................53661-3/$6.99
- [ ] A HOLIDAY OF LOVE (A collection of romances from Jude Deveraux, Judith McNaught, Arnette Lamb, and Jill Barnett)...................................50252-2/$6.99

All Available from Pocket Books

Simon & Schuster Mail Order
200 Old Tappan Rd., Old Tappan, N.J. 07675
Please send me the books I have checked above. I am enclosing $_____ (please add $0.75 to cover the postage and handling for each order. Please add appropriate sales tax). Send check or money order—no cash or C.O.D.'s please. Allow up to six weeks for delivery. For purchase over $10.00 you may use VISA: card number, expiration date and customer signature must be included.

POCKET BOOKS

Name _____

Address _____

City _____ State/Zip _____

VISA Card # _____ Exp.Date _____

Signature _____ 746-08 (2 of 2)